Kate Harrison was born in Wigan and, before turning to novels, worked in television as a programme developer. She has also been a director and journalist on *Panorama*, *Newsround* and *Midlands Today*. She lives in West London. Her previous novel, *The Starter Marriage*, is also available in Orion paperback. Visit her website at www.kate-harrison.com.

By Kate Harrison

Brown Owl's Guide to Life
The Starter Marriage
Old School Ties

Brown Owl's Guide to Life

KATE HARRISON

An Orion paperback
First published in Great Britain in 2006
by Orion
This paperback edition published in 2006
by Orion Books Ltd,
Orion House, 5 Upper St Martin's Lane,
London WC2H 9EA

1 3 5 7 9 10 8 6 4 2

A CIP catalogue record for this book is
available from the British Library.

ISBN-13 978-0-7528-8097-6

Printed and bound in Great Britain by
Clays Ltd, St Ives plc

The Orion Publishing Group's policy is to use papers
that are natural, renewable and recyclable products and
made from wood grown in sustainable forests. The logging
and manufacturing processes are expected to conform to
the environmental regulations of the country of origin.

www.orionbooks.co.uk

Acknowledgements

I rely on so many people to Lend A Hand when the writing gets tough, so I have pleasure in awarding the following badges:

Artist and Needlecraft: to Emma Wallace for designing the gorgeous cover.

Brownie Friendship: to the 11th Chiswick Brownies and Rosemary Fincham for welcoming me and showing me what it's like to be a Pixie in the 21st century. And to the Guide Association for allowing me to use such wonderful material from the handbooks.

Computer: to James Williams for continued web brilliance.

Friend to Animals: to Stuart Emery for looking after Ozzie the cat.

Media Studies (OK I made that one up): to my colleagues in Development, especially Emma, Jon, Lillie, Lucy, Richard and Samia, and to Victoria and Linda at Eve.

Musician: to Fiona Williams, for advice on opera and all things vocal.

Money Expert (made that one up too): to Paul O'Keeffe for explaining hostile takeovers.

Pathfinder: to Barbara, and to Araminta, for showing me the way ...

Stargazer: to everyone at Orion for launching the books into orbit, with special thanks to Juliet Ewers, Susan Lamb, Lisa Milton, Emma Noble and Jon Wood. The **Out and About** badge to the indefatigable sales reps: plus the **Agility** badge to

Kate Mills and Genevieve Pegg for incisive editing, wisdom and all-round loveliness.

Writer: for reassurance, generosity and expert advice, thank you to everyone on The Board, to Deborah and Meg, to members of the Romantic Novelists' Association and, of course, to the Girly Writers (Linda Buckley-Archer, Jacqui Hazell, Jacqui Lofthouse, Louise Voss and Stephanie Zia)

And a combined **First Aid** and **Survival Badge** to friends and family for being there: Alison, Andrea, Carrie, Lisa, Liz, Lynne, Mary, Sarah, Trudi and especially Jenny and Geri. Plus, as ever, love to Pat and Pete, Toni, Mum, Dad and Rich . . .

Finally, I'd like to award the **Booklover Badge** to everyone who picks up this novel – thank you so much for reading. I'd love to hear from you – you can get in touch via my website, www.kate-harrison.com

The Girl Guides is an organisation for character training which has been started much on the lines of the Boy Scouts movement in principle but differing in detail. Already this training has been found attractive to all classes, but more especially to those by whom it is so vitally needed – the girls of the factories and of the alleys of our great cities who, after they leave school, get no kind of restraining influence and who nevertheless may be the mothers and should be the character trainers of the future men of our nation.

How Girls Can Help to Build up the Empire: The Handbook for Girl Guides
by Miss Baden-Powell and Sir R. Baden-Powell 1912

Pixies work and Pixies play, Pixies never stop all day.
If you want a friend for keeps, Pixies love each other heaps!

Pixie motto, written by the Pixies of the 2nd Troughton Brownies:

Bethany Kendal (Sixer),
Teresa Rowbotham (Seconder),
Lucy Gill,
Christine Love,
Paula Tucker
and Simonetta Castigliano

May 1979

Chapter One

Brownies do their best. One time when you can try to do your best is when things go wrong. Try to swallow the grumble and to put on a smile.

It's not until they carry my mother's coffin into the church that it finally sinks in. All those bargains I've made since I was little – with myself, with God or any other force that might be out there – have been in vain: saying the Lord's Prayer, crossing my fingers after every bad thought, and carrying out a daily routine of superstitious rituals, from humming hymns when I brush my teeth, to always stirring tea anti-clockwise. But none of it has stopped my recurring nightmare becoming a reality.

I'm an orphan.

The fact that I'm thirty-five with a daughter of my own ought to help, but it doesn't. I feel abandoned. The organist is thumping out 'You'll Never Walk Alone' – a surprisingly low-brow choice by my mother, and I suspect she only picked it to annoy the vicar – and I grip the pew like someone shipwrecked, trying to keep my head above water.

'Mum, don't cry,' Sasha whispers. I'm not sure whether it's an expression of sympathy or a command. I've a habit of embarrassing my daughter with excessive displays of emotion.

Right now, she looks like Wednesday from the Addams family. You don't often see a seven-year-old dressed all in black, but she insisted on full mourning regalia, just as she insisted on coming to the funeral. Sasha's definitely inherited the stubbornness gene, the one that skipped a generation with me. When I took her shopping for today, she picked a serious raven-coloured velvet dress with a lace collar: she knows what's appropriate, just like her father and grandmother. It's only me who doesn't know how to behave.

Sasha's expression is grave, her big brown eyes screwed up as she concentrates on looking sombre. She's a stoical child. She didn't cry when we buried Norman the gerbil in a shoebox under the bamboo (there are no proper trees in our Zen back garden, and no lawn, just designer white shingle that the local cats use as a litter tray). She was far too curious about how long it'd take the maggots to eat the body. So it was me who worked my way through a whole packet of UltraBalsam tissues in the rodent's memory.

Mum, don't cry. I grit my teeth together so hard that I wonder if my fillings will implode. Today of all days I need to be brave, to prove to my own mother that I can get something right for once in my life.

I've always been a cry-baby. Once I start, I can't stop until I've shed some predestined quantity of tears, like a vending machine programmed to dispense an exact cupful of coffee. I missed my father's funeral – I was only five – but at my grandmother Dorothy's I was inconsolable, howling from the organist's first chord until the final sandwich was consumed at the wake in the Old Surgery. Dorothy was eighty-four. Mum was fifty-eight.

Oh God. I can taste salt and try to gulp the tears away, but more are ready to take their place. There are always more tears.

Andrew reaches out to take my hand and I grip it, more firmly than I did when I was giving birth to Sasha. Before we left the house this afternoon, he huffed and puffed because his trousers were creased and he was worried someone would notice. But the moment we arrived at St Peter's, he became the model of a supportive husband and dignified son-in-law.

It's the perfect day for a wedding, not a funeral: a honeysuckle-scented breeze wafted our way as we came in through the lych-gate. Now all I can smell are the cloying freesias on top of the coffin.

'Uhhh.' I try to swallow the first sob but fail. Now I'm lost, detaching my hand from Andrew's as the dammed tears pour down my face and with them the make-up I applied so carefully just an hour ago. I told myself that the mascara and lipstick and foundation would give me a reason not to cry. *Silly Lucy ...*

'There, there,' says Andrew, reaching out for my hand again. Before I give it to him, I wipe it on my jacket, leaving a slug-trail of snotty liquid on the fabric. When I reach out again, he registers only the tiniest wince at my damp fingers. I try hard to concentrate on something else, the way men think of their bosses or their pensions or their mothers when they want to delay ejaculation.

Andrew, of course, has no trouble with premature ejaculation, or unacceptable behaviour of any kind. He has been drilled from infancy in what to do, how to look the part. I focus on him, in the hope that some of his resolve will rub off on me. Everything about my husband is just right. His black suit emphasizes his height and his breadth and his slightly craggy face. Even as the mourners approached us outside the church earlier, with gruff regrets and awkward pats on the shoulder, I saw the women flush in appreciation. Even the vicar's wife.

It's not working, it's not working. *Try harder.* I look up at Andrew: his periwinkle eyes are crinkled at the edges, and though strangers would see only concern in those crinkles, I wonder if there's irritation there too: his mother wouldn't have dreamed of crying in public when she lost her husband.

My forehead aches as more tears build behind my eyelids. Don't start again. Focus on anything but the reason why we're here, in this chilly church, when Sasha should be on a school trip to a formerly dark satanic mill, and I should be selling shoes, and Andrew should be evaluating transport policy while his assistants swoon over his grasp of strategic infrastructure. At least, that's what he honestly thinks they're swooning over: whatever faults my husband has, I could never accuse him of vanity.

Compared to him, I know I'm only average-looking. Border-line pretty at best, with the kind of slightly plumped-up face that doesn't yet reflect my age. The downside is the slightly plumped-up body that goes with it. My hair is dirty blonde, cut in the same forgiving bob I've worn all my life. My eyes are my only distinguishing feature: deep brown with flashes of yellow around the pupils, like reflections of lightning. They're Quentin eyes, passed down the generations, though the surname's been lost. There's a sepia photograph of Great Grandma Agnes as a child at the turn of the century, and I can see the same fire in *her* eyes. But unlike the rest of the dynasty, I don't have the fire in the belly to match.

People often look from Andrew to me and then back again, wondering why he chose me. The truth is that our marriage is as appropriate as everything else he does or owns. His looks could have won him a dolly bird, but he knew what he really wanted: a traditional marriage, a copy of his parents' *Janet and John* double-act. And I wanted a family. A light, bright, modern detached home. Security. A life as far removed from my mother's lonely widowhood as possible.

We've kept our bargain: he treats me exactly as his father treated his mother, and I am sweet and easy: being a good girl hasn't saved my mother but it will save my marriage. The compromises are tiny: it's not *that* hard to remember to avoid humming operatic arias if he's in earshot. In return for my sweetness, he looks after me, even when I don't necessarily want to be looked after. There's always a catch.

'Judith's courage in the face of her illness was an example to all of us,' the vicar says, wiping his brow with a crumpled hand-kerchief. The church windows allow a pool of sunshine to fall onto the pulpit, like a celestial spotlight. I can see his dandruff and his discomfort. 'She maintained her sense of humour until the very end.'

My mother's idea of what was funny grew darker as the days grew lighter, from the diagnosis of her illness three days before Christmas, to her death on the twenty-fifth of March. It took three weary months for the cancer to complete its conquest of her body. The progress of the disease was like one of her beloved cricket series between an unconquered touring side and a small, former outpost of Empire. As each match was fought in a different location – ovaries, stomach, lymph nodes – overall defeat was inevitable, but she only stopped fighting the week before she died.

4

'I've had a reasonable innings,' she told me as we drove her to Troughton Cottage Hospital for the last time. 'Now I think I'm entitled to a rest in the pavilion, don't you?' The joke was an attempt to cover her disappointment: she'd hoped to die at home, in the Old Surgery where she'd been born.

I laughed it off. 'Oh, there's plenty of life in you yet!' We both knew I was lying. Her elbows were three times as wide as her withered arms, while her belly was pregnant with poison. She'd nursed enough cancer patients in her time: she knew what was coming.

Yet until that moment, I'd believed Mum was coping: she always did. It was only when I went back to the house at midnight that I realized the illness had reduced my super-powered mother to a mortal being. The bin was crammed with rotting madeira cakes and egg-and-cress sandwiches, delivered by friends trying to tempt her appetite. It must have been torment to throw it all away, because, as she'd never tired of telling me over the years, 'there's barely a greater sin in my book than wasting good food'.

'Now let us all sing one of Judith's favourite hymns, "Abide with Me".'

The congregation shuffles to its feet. I'm determined to stop crying long enough to sing. It's the only thing I'm any good at and I owe her this at least. I remove my hand from Andrew's and bunch it into a fist so my nails dig into my palm. Then I bite my lip until I can taste metal. The organist pounds a heavy-handed introduction and there's a moment's pause as the other mourners take a breath before singing.

But when I do the same, a strange sound emerges from somewhere deep inside me, more of a howl than anything human. And then my world stops.

Chapter Two

If you do lose your head, be sure that you put it on again the right way.

I open my eyes in the graveyard, then shut them again, dazzled by the sunlight. My left knee stings and when I reach down with my fingers, I can feel sticky blood and frayed tights.

'You've been in the wars, haven't you?'

For just a moment, it sounds like my mother's voice: low-pitched and bossy. Then I remember why it can't be and I shield my eyes with my hand before looking around. I'm sitting on a Victorian gravestone, the inscription smudged by lichen. Staring down on me are three stone angels, my husband, my daughter and my best friend Terri. It was Terri who spoke with my mother's voice: she's more like Judith Gill than I'll ever be.

'Oh, God. I fainted, didn't I? I couldn't even make it all the way through my own mother's funeral.'

'Hey,' Terri says, more softly now. 'They're nearly finished in there anyway. Then there's only the crematorium to get through and it'll all be over.'

Andrew nods. 'Terri's right, Lulu. Your mum would have understood.'

I shake my head. 'No, she wouldn't. She'd have been cross. Even Sasha's more under control than I am.' My daughter looks embarrassed. I imagine the pallbearers carrying me unconscious out of the church, my arms and legs drooping and flailing. So much for dignity.

Terri finds a fresh tissue in her handbag. 'Come on, blow

6

your nose.' She turns to Andrew. 'If you two want to go back into the service, I'll stay with her.'

Andrew hesitates. 'Well, I suppose someone from the family should be there in the service, but I don't like to leave Lucy ...'

I nod at him. 'Please, Andrew, I'll be fine.' I hate it when he sees me letting the side down. 'Sasha, Mummy's feeling a bit faint, that's all.'

He kisses me on the cheek and squeezes my shoulder before taking Sasha's hand and marching back into the church, both of them ramrod straight like Dickensian characters.

Terri sits down beside me, a small gap between us. 'It's all right, Luce. Don't make yourself feel worse. Plenty of people find funerals difficult.'

'You don't, though.'

Terri shakes her head. 'No, but I'm professionally immune. And it helps that number one, she wasn't my mother. And number two, I happen to believe she's already in a better place.'

'Do you *really* think that?'

'Come on. Do you think they'd have let me train as a vicar if I didn't believe in heaven?' She smiles her lopsided smile, the one that makes her look nine years old again. Mum always described her as Big Bird – 'with big feet, big hair and freckles to match', but there was no disguising the affection there. I've always known that Terri, with her black and white worldview and 'muck-in' attitude, was more like the daughter my mother had expected.

'Mum really wanted to hang on so you'd be whatever it is ... qualified.'

'Ordained.'

'Yes, that's it. So you could lead the service rather than *him*.'

'She *was* pretty scathing about the poor guy. Too happy clappy for her. I'd have been honoured to do the service, of course. You know how special Judith was to me.'

Was. I feel the tears pooling in my eyes again, but I'm not going to give in this time. 'I don't understand why it had to be *her*. If anyone played by the rules, it was Mum. Why couldn't

7

she have a miracle, just a tiny one, after all she did? All she'd been through?'

Terri coils a strand of red hair around her finger, a nervous habit she's had since childhood. 'I know it's hard to see the justice of it, Luce. But however unfair life seems to us, she believed there was something better, a place where she'd be rewarded for the way she was.'

'But …' I stop myself. What I want to say sounds selfish, even to me. *What about me? Why have I been punished for being good?* I try to think of something else. 'What about Sasha? You don't think she's bottling it up?'

'Children are resilient. And she's a cracking kid. Are you sure you won't rethink about her coming to Brownies?'

'You know how I feel about that.' Brownies is the only thing I ever stood up to my mother about. The last time we argued about it was in October, at Sasha's seventh birthday party; Mum was desperate for me to sign up Sasha, but I had no intention of doing it. I had no choice when I was a child: not only was my mother Brown Owl, but the Quentin women had six decades of Girl Guiding behind them. So although I preferred being tucked up on the settee with an Enid Blyton or a Noel Streatfield, I suffered three years of orienteering and badge-winning and compulsory good deeds. The only plus was meeting Terri, though she loved every second of it. She still doesn't understand why I loathed it so much.

Maybe if I'd known in October that Mum was ill I would have given in. Now it seems so petty to have refused.

'It wasn't your cup of tea, Luce, but I think Sasha would be in her element. A natural leader, I'd say.'

'Well, we both know she doesn't get that from me,' I say, forcing a smile.

Terri frowns, suddenly serious. 'It's obvious who she gets that from.' We both look back towards the church, where the congregation sings 'The Lord's My Shepherd'. She reaches out awkwardly to pat my arm. For all her do-gooding bluster, Terri's never felt comfortable with physical affection, while I've always had the instinct to soothe or cuddle anyone who needed it. But despite our differences, our friendship is indestructible. 'Think

8

about it, though, Luce. I know it didn't, you know, end all that well, but we did have some good times before that. Once a Pixie, always a Pixie, eh?'

'If you say so,' I reply, though in truth it's been decades since I've thought of myself as a Pixie.

Chapter Three

Who has been your best friend in the world? There is no one who has done so much for you as Mother.

In the car to the crematorium, I'm sandwiched between Andrew and Sasha. Both are stiff-backed and silent, as though they've read a book on how to be a mourner.

How do they manage to stay calm? They were close to my mother. From the moment Sasha's eyes met her grandmother's in the maternity hospital it was love. Each recognized a kindred spirit, a chip off the block of forthright Quentin women. On the rare occasions baby Sasha cried, the one person guaranteed to soothe her was my mother. She'd pick her up and place a hand or a gentle kiss on Sasha's scarlet forehead to make her open her furious eyes – the Quentin orange flashes appearing by three months, mirroring her grandmother's. Then she'd say, 'Now, now, youngster, whatever it is, it's not worth all this fuss and bother, is it?' The same words I recognized from my own childhood, except she sounded so tender when she spoke to my baby. I could only ever remember hearing disappointment and frustration in my mother's voice.

The limo turns the corner carefully, as though any sudden movement would be disrespectful. 'What happens next?' Sasha asks.

Andrew looks nervously at me. 'Well, the crematorium is where we have another little service, and then ... um, Granny ...'

I know exactly what happens next. Another sob escapes before I can swallow it.

'I'll explain later,' Andrew says, winking conspiratorially at Sasha. 'Won't be long now.' I've only seen him cry once: brief, awkward tears, just after Mum died. That afternoon, she alternated between moments of confusion and total lucidity, so while she was napping, we risked a snatched sandwich before the WRVS stall closed. We were on our way back to her bedside when we were intercepted by a sweating junior doctor.

He told us that she'd 'slipped away' in the five minutes we'd left her alone. It was typical Mum to spare us a deathbed scene but – and I'd never admit this to Andrew – I felt cheated of a final exchange of hand-squeezes, or breathless goodbyes. In fact, Mum's last words to me had been, 'Make sure *The Times* crossword's on the bed when you leave, would you, Lucy? I might feel up to finishing it later.'

Perhaps this is why I've managed not to cry until today. Because I hadn't seen her die, it didn't seem real. The funeral arrangements have kept me busy, but it felt like I was doing it for someone else's mother.

The car slows down and through the windscreen I see the hearse ahead, the shape of the coffin and the flowers silhouetted against bright sunlight. There is no doubt now. This is final. I'm alone.

Of course, there's Andrew, but he's not a Quentin. All that remains of the dynasty is me, and Sasha, and the Old Surgery. And if Andrew has anything to do with it, that'll be sold off now it's spring: only sunshine makes it look less like a mausoleum. He's been speculating on how much it might fetch, what we'll do with the money. When he brought it up for the twentieth time last weekend, I snapped at him. And I *never* snap. 'You keep saying when *we* sell the house, Andrew, but it's *my* house now, isn't it? I do have some say in it. What if I wanted to … I don't know, buy a one-way ticket to Hawaii or Vienna or Sydney?'

That shut him up for a split second, until that well-rehearsed charming smile appeared and he chuckled. 'What, and sing solo at the Opera House? You're the last person in the world who'd buy a one-way ticket anywhere, Lulu. Which is what makes you so lovable.'

Good old lovable Lulu. Andrew wouldn't let me give *him* a nickname, of course.

The procession seems to glide along the street at a different pace from the good people of Troughton, busy doing Wednesday morning things. Then they spot the hearse and freeze. Some break the spell by looking away, refusing to let their day be blighted by the reminder of death. But others seem hypnotized. A tall man in his seventies stares at the coffin and then back at the funeral car, looking so hard at me that for a moment I stop crying.

Why couldn't the cancer have chosen *him*, that stranger? Mum had so much more to do. After years of looking after everyone else – nursing her patients, bringing me up, and then nursing her grandparents and her mother to the ends of their lives – at last she could look after number one. She'd planned a sponsored cycle ride along the Great Wall of China in August to raise money for the church. She'd finally given in to the endless requests for her to train as a magistrate. Though woe betide the career burglar or pimply joyrider appearing in front of my mum, with her clear definitions of right and wrong. Oh, she believed in forgiveness and in helping the poor and the underprivileged. 'But when you get down to brass tacks, Lucy, we'll all be judged in the end. And it won't matter one bit what other people did to us: it'll be about what *we* did to other people.'

I wonder if the sound of my mother's voice will fade from my memory, if I'll always remember her face. I can't remember my father properly. The memories are fuzzy and washed-out, based on a handful of photos of a daddy with long hair and sandals playing the guitar, like Dylan the rabbit from *The Magic Roundabout.* I can never remember what he sang, but his voice was sweet, unlike everyone else's in my family. Even my great-grandfather, Grampa Quentin, who used to play me opera on his sideboard-sized gramophone, sang like someone gargling to cure a sore throat. So I must have inherited my voice from my father's side, though I'll never know for sure. Mum and I never talked about the Gills, though we bore their name. 'Least said, soonest mended,' she used to say. I still don't understand what she meant.

The car turns right into Main Street, and I keep my head down. The last thing I want is for the girls from the shoe shop to see me in this state. I've got little enough command over the staff of Fancy Footwork as it is. They're all strapping, stroppy teens, constantly ringing in sick or disappearing for fake dental appointments. When I was their age, that job was all I could get, and even then on a Youth Training Scheme, because unemployment was so high after all the textile factories closed. We used to call Troughton 'Toytown' but for the last decade it's been 'Boomtown': posh Manchester commuters moving in, and with them delis and boutiques and beauty parlours, all offering more glamorous workplaces than an old-fashioned shoe shop. As my colleagues left, one by one, for better jobs, I've risen to the lofty heights of store manager. Sometimes I wonder why the owner's kept me on, but it's obvious: no one else would take so much responsibility for so little money. But loyalty, and yes, fear, have kept me there.

'Right, Sasha, nearly there.' Andrew points out of the window at the squat building in the distance. The crematorium is such a nondescript place, designed so there's nothing about it that could offend anyone. As a result, it manages to be offensive by omission, pretending that death is all clean white lines and AstroTurf lawns. I wanted Mum to be buried in the churchyard so I'd have a grave to tend, but she was having none of it. 'You won't want to be bothering with upkeep and fresh flowers. At least if they cremate me, I'll stay nice and warm on my way to the pearly gates.'

The limousine comes to a gradual halt on the 'admissions' side of the crem: I can see clusters of black-clad mourners in the memorial garden, from the previous service. I try to think ahead: in fifteen minutes' time, the worst will be over. Half an hour of handshakes and regrets at the Old Surgery, then I can go home and cry into my pillow without feeling ashamed of myself.

The driver, a plump man with whisky-drinker's cheeks, opens the door and I shuffle out after Andrew. My legs feel wobbly, my eyes smart and my head thumps: the result of an hour of sustained crying. The door labelled Chapel of Rest is open and

I can see red-tinged lights inside. It looks more like a brothel than somewhere to say goodbye.

I touch Andrew's arm to stop him striding ahead. 'I can't do it.'

'What?' He sounds irritated and pats Sasha on the head. 'Give Mummy and me a moment, Sash.' She does as she's told for her daddy: she never does for me.

'I can't go in, Andrew. I can't watch when that little curtain comes across and ...'

'Are you sure, Lulu?' He faces me, holding both my hands, as though I'm a little girl who might bolt any moment into the path of oncoming traffic. 'I don't want you to regret not saying goodbye.'

'I can't go in there.'

'All right,' he says. He seems to have considered the evidence and given me permission. 'We'll come and find you.'

I don't feel much relief as I walk away from the building, the skin on my knee tight and sore where I grazed it earlier in church. I wait until the cars have collected the stragglers from the previous service before heading for the memorial garden.

The lilac trees in the centre are budding with explosive confetti clusters of pink. I sit on a bench and allow my raw eyes to be soothed by tears again, blurring the colours of the garden. At last there's no one to tut or tell me off: not my husband, not my daughter. Not my mum.

How strange that I'll never hear that disapproving voice again. Oh, Andrew and Sasha and even Buster the cat know exactly how to get their own way, but none has the knack of simultaneously making me feel small *and* a disappointment *and* a regrettable departure from Quentin family values. Mum never did it on purpose, I know that, but her face and her tone of voice conveyed what her words didn't.

Without thirty-five years' worth of my mother's dashed expectations, I suppose I could do whatever I want, follow my heart, be the person I was always meant to be.

I smile to myself: go to Hawaii or Vienna or Sydney Opera House.

The thought makes me feel giddy, then guilty. It's not my

mother's fault I'm a failure. And even if I could change, right now I don't have a clue what I want. Or who the hell I'm meant to be, if I'm no longer Brown Owl's daughter.

Chapter Four

Thousands of people every day need the help
of an extra hand, so that is why the Brownie
motto is 'Lend a hand'.

The instant the crematorium service was over, Terri excused
herself, ran to her car and drove like a banshee across town
so she'd have time to buy ten Silk Cut and still be the first to
arrive at the Old Surgery for the wake.

She made it in eight minutes – a personal best – and calcu-
lated that she had ten more in hand to do a spot-check of the
preparations and get the nicotine boost she'd been craving.

She let herself in with the key Judith had given her. Terri
liked to think of herself as an honorary daughter, and she'd
always known it would be her, not Lucy, who would organize
the wake. This morning she'd taken charge within seconds of
stepping into the Old Surgery. The scene had been dismal: half
a dozen sixtysomething women, clucking around like chicks
abandoned by the mother hen. Which was, Terri thought,
pretty much what had happened.

'Oh, Terri,' one of the chicks had cried from the kitchen. 'It's
awful. I never thought she'd go. And so young. She seemed indestructible.' The woman's face had reminded Terri of a leather
handbag, tanned and worn. Like the other biddies, she was
sweltering in respectfully thick tights and a synthetic black suit
on the first warm day of spring. Her bottom lip was trembling
ominously.

'I know,' Terri had said, instantly brisk and Brown Owl-like, 'but what would Judith want us to do? She'd want everything to be shipshape for after the funeral. Which is what we're all here for.'

'Mmm.' Handbag Woman looked uncertain. The chicks had probably congregated more to revel in mass hysteria than tackle mass catering arrangements. But concerted sandwich-making would distract them from the evidence of their own mortality.

'So I need two volunteers for the salad.' Handbag Woman had nodded and, after a commotion, another old dear joined her. 'It's all in the carrier bag. Cucumber – that needs slicing, as do the tomatoes. There are three lettuces that need shredding, and the potato salad just needs dishing out. OK?'

The chicks had obeyed her without question, as did the taskforce of three ordered to set up a ham sandwich production line, and the woman charged with stocking the cloakrooms with loo roll and soap.

Now, Terri walked through the Old Surgery, closing doors on the messiest rooms so no one would see how poor Judith had let the house go. Terri savoured the last few minutes of silence before the funeral party arrived back. She walked past the long hall mirror, and flinched at the woman reflected back at her. Big Bird. Yep, same big body and gingery curls and enormous feet, today forced into funeral heels. She'd never really minded the nickname, which Judith had given her in Brownies. The label she hated was the one the Pixies used between themselves. Bossy Boots. She resented it even now. All she was doing was responding to the inherent desire people had to be led.

Which was why ordination was perfect: a licence to boss, with the Almighty offering a little extra help to save lost souls and lost causes. It had been Judith's suggestion: she presented Terri with a cutting from the *Daily Telegraph* about women priests and told her, 'That's what you've been waiting for.'

Judith had understood her so much better than Terri's own feckless parents: Lorna, a vegetarian hippie who'd somehow missed the fact that the sixties had been and gone; and red-haired boozer Dave, who could barely stand up, never mind stand up for himself. No wonder Terri was the only one of the Pixies to graduate to the Guides, craving the order and purpose so lacking in her own home. Even once she'd started nursing in Manchester at the same hospital where Judith had trained, Terri visited Brown Owl every off-duty weekend. The Old Surgery was the only place she felt normal: nursing college made her feel like a fish out of water, hanging on to her virginity without really knowing why or for whom, while other student nurses put it about as though sex was only available while stocks lasted.

Then when she qualified – still a virgin, but with a few frustrated boyfriends behind her – Terri moved back to Troughton to work at the cottage hospital. Nursing frustrated her. She'd have made a perfect strict starched matron, running a tight ship, but the modern NHS was too hands-off for her and, as she told Judith, she felt like she'd been born three decades too late. Only once a week did she feel a sense of purpose, as Tawny Owl, Judith's deputy in the Brownie pack. Shaping the next generation.

It was Judith who'd coached her before the interview for theological college in Manchester, and Judith who'd rushed out for champagne when Terri was offered a place. Terri's parents had kept it quiet, mortified to have somehow produced a vicar-to-be. She'd lost count of the times she'd wished she'd been born a Quentin. And she suspected Judith secretly wished Terri had too.

Terri checked her watch. Just time for a cigarette – the habit she'd cultivated during nurse training, to prove she wasn't as square as she looked. These days, she usually contented herself with second-hand fumes from theology students who liked to discuss the meaning of life over a Marlborough Light, but today ... well, however much of a front she put on for Lucy, today was tough.

She walked out of the house, onto the driveway and unwrapped the packet. This ritual was her favourite part of smoking – the rewarding crackle of cellophane, followed by the first brief waft of nicotine, the anticipation involved in selecting the cigarette that would upset the symmetry of the two rows.

In defiance of death, Terri took her first lungful of smoke and sighed it out. She stepped back to look at the house. Soon estate agents would spot Judith's demise in the 'births, marriages and deaths' column in the *Troughton Tribune*, and would be salivating at the prospect of handling the sale. Of course, the Old Surgery would be Lucy's now, but she'd already said she couldn't face moving there. Too dark, too gloomy, too full of the ghosts of past Quentin tragedies.

But prospective purchasers would feel differently. Terri pictured the house through estate agents' eyes. *A substantial ...* she took another drag. No, *an imposing and elegant Victorian detached double-fronted villa in the heart of Troughton old town. Bursting with period features, from the imposing oak-panelled former waiting room, to the fantastic kitchen with range ...*

Terri remembered countless hours sitting in that waiting room as a child: with swollen adenoids, tonsillitis, odd rashes, stomach pains, growing pains, sprained ankles and more than her share of verrucas. Lucy's great-grandfather Dr Quentin – stubbornly staying on ten years past retirement age – knew the bodies of Troughton's poorly people inside out, from their nit-infested tops to their ingrown toenails. Dorothy, his daughter and Lucy's granny, had offered tea and sympathy, along with an invitation to the Brownies or Guides for girls of the right age. Helping the community was more or less compulsory if you'd been born a Quentin and it dulled the pain that also seemed to run in the family.

There were two generations of lost husbands, grieving wives and orphaned only daughters. Dorothy's husband was missing in action within weeks of her wartime wedding, before he knew she'd conceived their daughter, Judith, on their two-day honeymoon in a B&B near the South Prom at Lytham St Annes. Judith had escaped the confines of Troughton to train as a nurse in Manchester, but returned as a widow herself only ten years later, her husband's sudden death making Lucy the second successive Quentin child to grow up fatherless in the Old Surgery.

In her last days, Judith told Terri how hard it had been coming back, and how she'd looked forward to her freedom when Lucy left home. But by then, old Dr Quentin was dying, and after that her own mother, who made it just into the new millennium before Judith was free at last to please herself. The cancer came four years later.

'I don't resent them. It was a privilege to be able to give something back after they looked after me for so long,' Judith had explained to Terri one freezing day in late February.

'But now …' Terri couldn't say out loud what they both knew, that Judith had only weeks left. 'It seems so … unjust. You deserved time to live a little.'

'Oh, Teresa, I've never been much good at leisure. Or mothering.' She'd looked at Terri, defying her to disagree.

'Lucy hasn't turned out too badly.'

'No, but … I think I've been a most unsuitable mother for Lucy.'

'She could have done much worse,' Terri had said, thinking of her own chaotic, permanently inebriated parents.

'I only ever wanted the best for her. To stop her having to live like me.'

'It couldn't have been easy bringing up a child without a father,' Terri replied, then watched in astonishment as Judith's yellow eyes seemed to fill with tears. In all the years she'd known Brown Owl, Terri had never seen her cry.

But the moment passed and Terri decided the tears must have been a trick of the light, because her mentor's face was angry, not sorrowful. 'All women are single parents, more or less. Even before Jim died … well, let's just say that the rose-tinted image Lucy has of her father isn't entirely realistic.'

'I didn't realize.'

'I've never wanted to shatter her illusions. What's the point? But you must never rely on a man, Terri. They're the weaker sex, whatever they'd have you believe.' Then she'd smiled. 'They're an amusing distraction from the main business of life and death, mind you.'

The sun reappeared from behind a cloud, transforming the Old Surgery from foreboding Gothic into splendid Victorian. Lucy might hate this house, but it would also make her rich. Buyers would fall over themselves to snap it up. Terri shuddered, imagining its new occupants adding decking and whirlpools and wetrooms.

She just hoped the ghosts of the Quentins wouldn't be too upset.

A gust of warm wind sent a fragrant snowstorm of blossom across the cobbled driveway.

'Is that you, Judith?' Terri said, hiding her cigarette behind her back. 'We're going to miss you. Things won't be the same without you to keep an eye on us.'

Chapter Five

The whole object of our scheme is to seize the girl's character in its red hot stage of enthusiasm and weld it into the right state.

'Mummy, *please*,' Sasha calls from the top of the narrow cellar steps. She only ever says 'Mummy' when she wants something. The rest of the time it's a terse 'Mum,' accompanied by a raised eyebrow. She's growing up far too fast. 'I'm bored with my jigsaw. And I won't be in the way.'

'It's not very safe down here, sweet-pea,' I shout back, hoping my voice doesn't give away my weakness. Almost three weeks after Mum's funeral, and here in the cellar of the Old Surgery, Lucy the Human Sprinkler System is in action yet again.

'If it's dangerous, you should have me there to call for help if something bad happens.' Sasha has her father's ruthless logic.

'We-ell,' I dither, and as soon as she catches the wavering in my voice, Sasha begins to climb down the stairs. I tuck my disintegrating tissue up my sleeve and thank God for inadequate lighting. 'OK then. But be careful on the steps.'

Sasha squeezes her way through the tiny door. 'It's very smelly. Yuk. Has something died?'

I can't help smiling. My daughter was born without any tact. 'You'll get used to it. Watch your head on the ceiling.'

As Sasha's eyes adjust to the dim light cast by the dusty central bulb, she looks around. 'This is like a dungeon. Or *Indiana Jones and the Temple of Doom*. Is all this stuff Granny's?'

I glance at the old suitcases and the overflowing tea chests and the carrier bags stuffed with newspapers and magazines. I could do with Indiana Jones to help me shift a century's worth of Quentin junk and memories. Mum had apologized to me before she died, for leaving so much rubbish. Before she got ill, she'd planned to spend a few weeks sorting it, selling everything in a giant car boot sale, in aid of the Brownies. And then the diagnosis robbed her of time. 'Well, Granny's and then my granny's and some of my things, from when I was your age.'

'Oooh, really old things then. Perhaps we'll find antiques, like on telly. If I find something, can I keep the money?'

'Sasha! Don't be so greedy.' But I doubt there's anything valuable here. Andrew would have spotted it instantly. He did a quick tour of the house after the funeral to suss out what was worth keeping. The rest he wanted to put in a skip: 'I know you, Lulu, you could spend years going through all that stuff, bawling your eyes out every time, and you still won't throw anything away.'

He was right, of course; husbands of ten years always are. But I still resent this pressure to get the house on the market in time for the spring rush. I'll never want to live here again, but I don't want it sold until … what? I don't know, but for once in my life, I'm trying to stand my ground against Andrew.

'Are you still sad, Mummy?'

I look at her, surprised at her question. My daughter does this occasionally, proves she has my sensitivity as well as her father's pragmatism. 'Yes, Sasha. Sometimes I am.'

'Because it must be horrible for you. I'd miss you lots, if you died.' In the low light, Sasha's face contorts. For a moment she looks as though she might cry herself and I'm poised to reach out and hold her. But before I can, she raises her head, straightens her shoulders and smiles. 'It's silly to think like that, though, isn't it Mummy? Can I look in here?' She points at a big mauve hatbox that I vaguely recognize.

'That would be lots of help, Sasha, thank you.' Perhaps she'll force me to be more ruthless.

Sasha blows the dust off the top of the hatbox, giggling and sniffing as some of it rebounds up her nose. She turns the round lid of the box until it pulls off with a slight sigh, as decades-old air is released. 'Oh,' she says, sounding disappointed, 'it's newspapers.'

'Let me have a look.' I uncurl my legs from under me, feeling pins and needles in my feet, then reach across for the box and take out the newspaper, a copy of the *Troughton Tribune* from September 1944. 'I think I know what this is.' I open it up slowly, because it's printed on thin wartime newspaper. I separate the pages until I reach Births, Marriages and Deaths. 'Here you go. It's your great-grandma Dorothy's wedding announcement. *Dorothy Agnes Quentin, daughter of Dr and Mrs Harold Quentin of the Old Surgery, Briar Lane, Troughton, married Captain Thomas Kingston, son of Mr and Mrs Roger Kingston of Carr Terrace, Selly Oak, Birmingham, at St Peter's church on the 15th September 1944.*'

'Is there a picture?'

'No, but ...' I rummage around in the rest of the hatbox. 'Look, here are her shoes. Her wedding shoes.' They're wrapped in a layer of tissue that disintegrates between my fingers: a pair of fawn-coloured size three courts, each adorned with fancy white stitching. The leather is still smooth and unwrinkled: touching the unscuffed soles, I wonder whether Nana Dorothy wore them only once.

'Brown?' Sasha pulls a face. 'For a wedding?'

'There was a shortage of everything in the war, I suppose.' Including time. Thomas Kingston's death notice appeared on the same announcements page three months after his wedding. And one announcing the birth of his daughter, Judith, six months after that. My mother was always matter of fact about never knowing her father. 'No one ever said life was fair, Lucy. You play the cards you've been dealt.'

So why did it feel harder for me, knowing Dad, and then having him snatched away? It's another reason – apart from the dark wood and the musty smell – that I hate this house: it's inseparable from my first ever encounter with death, from those endlessly black winter days after my daddy wasn't there any more and we had to move from Manchester back 'home' to Troughton, a place that couldn't have felt less like home.

'Couldn't they have waited till white shoes came into the shops?'

'I don't think people cared what they wore, so long as they could be together,' I say, realizing that the shoes and newspaper are yet more things I'll never throw away.

Sasha's bored with the hatbox. She runs her fingers along the studs on a row of burgundy leather trunks in the corner, trying to decide which to open next. Eventually she settles on a square black one that reaches as high as her waist, and takes hold of the clasp. 'Ugh, it's all rusty,' she says, wiping her fingers on her jeans. But she keeps fiddling until the lid opens. 'More clothes,' she groans. 'More brown ones. Brown was very popular in the olden days, wasn't it?'

I look over at the trunk, trying to work out what's inside. 'I suppose it didn't show the dirt.'

Sasha pulls out the first piece of clothing. 'It's a girl's cardigan. Would this have been Granny's, do you think? It's yucky.' She casts it aside impatiently, and sticks her head back in the trunk. 'This is worse. It's like a dress—'

I recognize it immediately. 'It's my old Brownie uniform. I had no idea she'd kept it.' Knowing my mother, I'd have expected her to donate it to an underprivileged Brownie. Sentimentality was never her thing, so this surprises me. I push myself up from the floor and walk across to the trunk, stooping to avoid hitting the low ceiling. 'I can't believe I was ever that small. Look, those are the badges on the sleeve.'

Sasha holds it at arms' length. 'You didn't get very many, did you? What's this one with a cup of tea on it?'

'Ah, that's my Hostess badge. Impossible to fail, that one.' I smile, despite myself. 'I had to make fairy cakes but I burned my arm really badly getting them out of the oven; I've still got the scar!'

Sasha scowls. 'Bo-*ring*. I thought Granny said the Brownies was all about adventures. What's this one?' She points at a badge with a broom on it.

'I can't remember. A housewife or housekeeper, I think. I do remember having to wash my socks to get it.'

'That doesn't sound like much fun either.' Sasha drops the

uniform and begins rummaging around again.

'It had its moments,' I say unconvincingly, torn between my own memories and my mum's life's work. I pick the dress up. I was so small. And the dress was so horribly unflattering, the cut emphasizing my round shoulders and chubby legs. There are a few more badges sewn onto the arm: a pair of scissors, for the Needleworker badge. After I got that one, I remember that our Sixer, Bethany, made me sew on all her badges for her, so she wouldn't break her nails. She always was good at getting other people to do her dirty work. There should have been a badge for that. The Manipulator.

Next to the scissors is a globe, for Brownie Friendship, gained by finding a penpal called Sheree who lived in the Australian Outback: we exchanged two letters: in hers she told me she could shear a sheep in forty seconds, did her lessons by shortwave radio and had her baby brother delivered by a flying doctor. I didn't write back after that: I couldn't think of anything interesting enough to merit the cost of Airmail.

Finally there's the embroidered treble clef. The Musician. That was the easiest badge of all. I remember standing in front of the tester – cranky old Mrs Patterson from the ironmonger's shop – and feeling sick with nerves as the pianist set her metronome going, and I stared at the brass needle floating from side to side until she played the first bar of *God Save the Queen*. And that was it. I opened my mouth and the notes came out as they always did, effortless and as instinctive to me as bossing people around was to Terri. But at home, no one wanted to hear me sing.

The strangest thing that day was the shocked expression on Mrs Patterson's face. And the way it was only when I'd reached the last chorus that I noticed the pianist had stopped playing and was also staring at me.

I was sweating through the cotton cuffs of my uniform. 'I'm sorry, Mrs Patterson,' I mumbled. I reached the obvious conclusion: that I must have made the most awful racket to get a reaction like that. 'Was I horribly out of tune?'

The pianist seemed to be wiping tears from the corner of her eye. Mrs Patterson smiled. 'No, no, don't be such a silly billy,

Lucy. We must look a little dumbfounded. But only because that is the best singing I have ever heard from a child of seven. Quite amazing. I think we'll have to be having words with your mummy about getting you some lessons.'

'Mum, look, it's YOU!' I'm jolted back to reality by my daughter's laughter. Sasha's holding up a colour photograph of six girls in Brownie uniform, and pointing to the slightly plump girl on the end.

'Whatever makes you think that, Sasha?' I say, reaching out to take the picture. The Pixies in glorious Polaroid colour, all ochres and sands and caramels.

'Don't pretend, Mum. You look exactly the same. Except you're old.'

It's true. Same moon face, same hair, same rounded tummy – and the same shyness in front of the camera: the girl in the picture is peering down so you can't see her outsized brown eyes. She's probably just been crying. Her arms are tucked firmly behind her back, the bitten nails hidden in shame. The difference between me then, and my confident daughter now, couldn't be any greater.

'Who are the others?' Sasha has moved alongside me and linked her arm in mine, as she always does when she wants a story. 'She's pretty.'

Bethany Kendal. Cover girl of the 1978 Brownie annual and the richest, most glamorous, most manipulative member of the 2nd Troughton Pack. Not that I saw it at the time, of course. Bethany had most people wound right around that carefully manicured little finger.

'Yes, she is, isn't she? Actually, you might recognize her. Do you remember when we were watching *Coronation Street* and that blonde woman came into the Rovers with Mike Baldwin? And I said I used to go to school with her?'

'Mmm,' Sasha says, but as she rarely listens to me, believing like her father that I have little of worth to say, she's probably only pretending to remember.

'Well, that's Bethany. She became an actress. I suppose she always was, really. She was the Sixer, so she was in charge of us all. And then this one, with all the badges, is your godmother

Terri. She was the Seconder, which meant she did all the dirty work.'

'Big Bird! She looks the same as well.'

'Yes, she does, doesn't she? And then this is Paula. She was the Cookie Monster. Always eating, but always running around so she burned it all off.' I point at a springy-looking girl with cropped mousy hair. 'She was great, so naughty. Climbing trees and getting into trouble.'

'Like me!'

'Yes, sort of like you. Except she was a bit of a tomboy, you know. Always trying to outdo her brothers.'

'And what about her? What's she done?'

The last time I saw Paula was in Fancy Footwork, searching for trainers for her surly children. Paula was prematurely grey, overweight and overwrought – and hugely embarrassed to see me. She didn't speak while she paid for the shoes, the cheapest in the shop, and left as quickly as she could afterwards. Which wasn't very fast, carrying all that weight. It was a horrible contrast to the girl whom my mum nearly banned from the Brownies for fidgeting during weekly prayers. But a lot changed in the summer of '79 and none of it for the better. 'Oh, she's just a mum, like me.'

Sasha groans. 'Boring!' She's losing interest. 'What about this one?'

The Brownie on the end of the group looks less like a little girl and more like a woman. She's the only one who isn't smiling. 'Well, I've no idea about Simonetta. She was half-Italian. She was only a Pixie for about three months. I remember now, this photo must have been taken while we were on the Pack holiday. Just before Simonetta left.' Leaving us to pick up the pieces ...

'And the dreamy-looking one with the frizzy hair?'

I can't help smiling. 'That's Chris. Always in a world of her own. You never knew what she was thinking.'

'I suppose she's a mum as well.'

'No, I don't think she is. The last I heard, she was doing very well for herself. Running her own business, making lots of money. She's probably richer than Bethany.' I'm not about to tell my daughter what line of business Chris is in. Sasha's an advanced child in many ways, but there are things about men and women that she doesn't need to know for a few years yet.

'When I grow up, that's what I'd like to be, then.'

'What ... a businesswoman?'

'No, Mummy!' Sasha raises her eyebrows impatiently. 'Just rich. I'm bored in here; can we go home now?'

I look at the piles of rubbish that surround us and I feel utterly exhausted. Another wasted Sunday. I shrug. 'Yes, OK then. Let's get back to Daddy before he starts wondering where tea is.'

Chapter Six

Nowadays we expect our men to take the lead; and girls stay behind to 'accomplish the divine and exalted purpose of their existence as home-makers'.

Chris Love held the Stars and Stripes vibrator high above her head, trying not to let it wobble.

What a way to spend a Monday morning.

'Terrific smile, Chris. Now would you do me a sultry look, like … I dunno, maybe like you've just told your boyfriend you're not wearing any knickers?' The photographer gestured to his assistant. 'Move her toga, so we get more cleavage, will you? If she's got it, we might as well flaunt it.' And then he winked.

Chris stayed as still as the Statue of Liberty while the white drape was adjusted downwards. It wasn't hard to do sultry, as it was only a whisker from surly, which was what she was beginning to feel. Her scalp itched from the half-can of Elnett they'd used to attach the spiky crown to her badly behaved chestnut hair, and the studio was freezing. She was sure they'd turned down the thermostat to make her nipples stand on end.

The photographer was twenty years older and ten stone heavier than Chris. But, like everyone else, he assumed she was 'up for it'. Call it an occupational hazard.

'You've done this before, haven't you?' he said, flashing away.

'Yes, you could say that,' Chris replied. Though her image had evolved since that first article in the *Manchester Evening News*, where she'd played the unthreatening 'girl next door', dressed down in jeans and jumper, to neutralize the protests from local residents at her plan to open her first sex shop. Five years later, for the *Financial Times*, she'd worn her tightest, sassiest designer suit, tailored to flatter her fantastic curves, along with plain-glass spectacles, designed to suggest to potential investors that mixing business with pleasure was a smart fiscal move.

Today's shoot was for her first major profile in a lads' mag, *It's All Balls*, so she'd agreed to the picture editor's idea of an 'ironic reinvention' of Liberty, to launch Love Bites' innovative All-American range. 'The vibrator will be the torch and then you can hold, I dunno, one of your smutty books under your arm. It'll be tasteful but sexy. And dead appropriate, you know, because liberty's what you're all about.'

Chris had weighed up the possible damage the picture might cause to her long-term plan to expand into the States, but decided that the controversy might not do any harm. And it could have been worse. *It's All Balls* could have asked her to pose in the new Cheeky Cheerleader pom-pom costume that left nothing to the imagination.

'Right, just a few more,' the photographer said. 'Try to look a bit more ecstatic for this one. Like you're just about to get into bed with a bloke with the biggest knob you've ever seen.' He couldn't stop himself adding a little thrust of his hips.

It was a thrust too far for Chris. 'OK. But I'm not sure how much longer I can keep it up.' She smiled sweetly. 'I'm *sure* you know how that feels.'

He muttered something under his breath, but when he checked the camera viewfinder, he had to admit that the mocking look in her eyes made for the best shot of the morning. As Chris had known it would.

In the café afterwards, the *It's All Balls* reporter asked the usual questions. What's a nice girl like you doing in a job like this? (Usual answer: who are you calling a nice girl?) What do your parents think? (Usual answer: they know better than to interfere.) And do you try all the products out yourself?

'Not all of them,' Chris laughed, as if it was the first time anyone had suggested it. 'And not all at once, either. I'd never get any work done! But I've always been fascinated by how stuff works. When I was a kid, I'd be taking things to pieces. Toys, gadgets, watches. And then I was at the end of my first year at poly studying product design when the temp agency offered me this holiday job at a sex shop. No one else would take it.' She took a sip of cappuccino, then licked the froth from her top lip. 'Imagine how different things would have turned out if I'd taken a summer job in Marks and Spencer instead.'

She'd said the same thing a hundred times, but still made it sound off-the-cuff. The reporter, Mike, grinned as he wrote something in his notebook in capital letters.

Chris was good copy and she knew it. Her PR skills had been crucial in building the Love Bites brand: six shops now, plus a thriving website. She'd had to learn fast. Early on there'd been a bruising encounter with a Sunday tabloid which had revealed the 'secret shame of former convent schoolgirl selling sex' and though her family hadn't dared mention it, Chris had hated losing control. So she decided to play the press at their own game, by creating an alter ego to stand in for the real Chris on occasions like these.

She'd taken the basic ingredients of her life – there was no point in lying, exactly – but anything Chris did, her public persona did better, or bigger, or both. Chris was single: Super-Chris was playing the field. Chris liked sex as much as the next girl: Super-Chris couldn't get enough of it. Chris was broad-minded: Super-Chris was out to shock.

As she'd explained to her friends, it was her way of keeping part of herself back.

'I think that's it,' said Mike. 'Except ... well, I wondered if you'd like to ... meet up some other time.'

He was nice enough looking in a bland way, a boyish smile on a middle-aged body, but there were two things in the way. One, she never slept with anyone she met through work. Two, the wedding ring on his podgy finger.

She pointed at it. 'I don't go out with married men.'

He frowned. 'I wasn't really talking about a *date*, exactly.'

'Well, that's all right then.' She gave him a hungry look, a variation on the one she'd given the photographer earlier on. She paused to allow Mike a moment of thinking his luck was in, before she added, 'Because the only blow jobs I do with married men are when I blow them out. Though I can offer you a discount voucher for the shop if your sex life needs a bit of spicing up. Even if you don't think you need it, I bet your wife does.'

She left him with his mouth goldfishing as he tried and failed to think of a witty reply. If sex was a weapon, Chris had a licence to kill.

But right now, she needed a shower, and not just to get the hairspray out of her hair.

Paula Tucker was trying hard to persuade her body to move from the bed, but so far she was fighting a losing battle. It was hard work. Raising eighteen stone of bulk to vertical was the kind of challenge that would phase the testosterone-bound musclemen on the *World's Strongest Man* TV show.

She tried to motivate herself, using the seductive image of a mountain of toast dripping with butter and honey (or Marmite, on the days she was in a savoury frame of mind) to ease the journey from bed to kitchen. It was a recognized technique, called visualization. She'd seen it on *Richard and Judy*. Or was it *This Morning*?

This Italian psychologist woman had explained that the trick was to imagine your goal in every sensory detail so that it felt real. The colours (golden stripes, where the element had caressed the bread into toastiness). The sound (a satisfying pop as the toast is launched into the world with the upward thrust of a space shuttle). The texture (crunchy outside, soft and giving inside). And the smell (heaven) ...

The other trick was to practise every day, to increase the chances of achieving your goal. OK, so the woman on telly was talking about big stuff, like running the London Marathon or setting up your own business. But Paula would like to see that skinny shrink trying to lift eighteen stone in the morning. She took a deep breath in preparation.

Her letterbox squeaked open and then: 'PAUUUUUUL-AAAAAAAA ... get up, you lazy cow. I got summat for you.'

Lorraine from next door, the thorn in Paula's sidewall. Yet sometimes it was only the thought of the crowing look on that scrawny bitch's face if she didn't make an appearance on the estate, that persuaded Paula to get up at all. Who needed a life coach when there was Lorraine?

'All right. I'm coming.' The manoeuvre began with her shifting her whole body diagonally across the bed. The next step – before she ran out of puff – was to twist her hips so her legs dangled briefly in the air and then touched the spot of threadbare carpet on the bedroom floor. Gradually, she pushed herself up into a sitting position.

'Phew.' The dizziness lasted a few seconds before Paula got her breath back. Finally she gripped the edge of the bed to lever herself off.

She fumbled on the wall for the light switch and, as she turned, winced at her reflection in the mirror. It was still a shock that this bloated figure, a series of lumps and bumps from doughy face to swollen ankles, was really her. Bed was forgiving, though it hadn't always been. When she was ten and started putting on weight, she'd learned to sleep on her side because her growing belly made lying on her front first uncomfortable, and then impossible. Her mother had to buy a larger size of pyjamas because the once-loose elasticated waist created raw red welts on Paula's stomach. But soon, night-time became a refuge where she could hide from the taunts life threw at her during daylight hours.

Hard to believe that this lump had won the egg-and-spoon race three years running in primary school. Or used to beat her brothers at football. But then that was all in the period her family only ever referred to as BBB: Before that Bastard Bruno.

She forced her feet – the only parts of her body that still resembled a slim person's – into a pair of red tartan slippers and went to the door.

'You look like shit,' Lorraine said, as Paula tried to adjust to the brightness outside. There was no respite from the weather on the Primrose estate: rain washed everything the same shade of grey as the sky; sun hit the concrete and turned the landscape

34

bleach-white, like the aftermath of a nuclear holocaust.

If only, Paula thought. There were few places more deserving of Armageddon.

'Cheers, Lorraine. Did you just get me up to insult me?'

'No, like I said, got summat for ya.' She held up a letter but when Paula reached for it, Lorraine moved it out of range. 'Hang on. What do you say?'

Paula sighed. 'What about "Stop pissing about or I'll report you for thieving my stuff"?' Not that she particularly wanted whatever it was. The post never brought anything good.

'Charming. I had to persuade the postman to let me sign for it, otherwise you'd never have got it. It's from a solicitor's in town.'

Fear gripped her, like a hand reaching into her stomach and squeezing hard. As a child, nothing scared Paula, who was untroubled by a vivid imagination to conjure up ghouls lurking in the dark. But as an adult, there was plenty to be afraid of, and recorded delivery letters from lawyers came high up the list.

'You bitch! You've opened it.' Paula lunged forward, a risky move when her centre of gravity could be so easily upset.

'Don't be so bloody daft; the address is on the back.' Lorraine pointed at the return label then handed the package over. 'Never good news, though, is it, when solicitors are involved?'

'No,' Paula agreed, before slamming the door in her neighbour's face.

She set the kettle boiling and sat at the kitchen table, wondering if she dared open the envelope. It might *not* be from the Housing Association. They were meant to give at least three months' grace on the rent and it couldn't have been that long? And as a single mother with two children, they couldn't turf her out on the street just like that, could they?

Looking on the bright side, perhaps it was about the divorce. Paula had been expecting Neil to leave for years – well, if she was honest she'd been surprised when he didn't jilt her at the altar, but then as he worked for her dad's painting and decorating business, Neil probably only married her because he was told to. It would be a relief when it was all over. She was impossible to live with, she knew that, and when the kids moved out, she planned to stay alone for good. Better for everyone that way.

The computer in the corner was blinking at her and her fingers itched to liberate it from standby mode to see what had changed in *Lawless*, her current online escape route. In *Lawless* she was a lithe freedom fighter, working alongside other gamers thousands of miles away to protect their virtual homeland from the factions who wanted to run it for their own evil ends.

But for once, there was something in the real world that held more mystery. She found a packet of ginger snaps (a breakfasting habit that had begun as an anti-nausea remedy during her first pregnancy fifteen years ago and was a useful standby when even toast seemed too much like hard work), tucked her overgrown fringe behind her ears, and tore open the letter.

> *Dear Mrs Tucker,*
> *I am the executor of the Will of the late Mrs Judith Gill and I am writing to you because you are a beneficiary.*

Judith Gill? Paula had to think hard. Then she remembered. Brown Owl. And almost immediately after that, an image of That Bastard Bruno appeared and stayed there when she closed her eyes.

> *The bequest is the sum of £1,000 …*

Bloody hell. Paula had to reread the sentence a few times before it sank in. £1,000? It was hardly untold wealth but it would come in handy to keep the wolves from the door. It all went on the kids, of course. Paula wasn't one for fancy clothes (they didn't make them in her size) or fancy food: toast was fine. Neil had controlled her spending binges, explaining that the kids loved her anyway, but now he'd gone, there was nothing to stop her. Though it never seemed to make things better: the more she spent, the less respect the kids showed. She'd even had to ask her mother for a loan and her parents weren't exactly rolling in it either.

But why had Brown Owl done this, after all these years?

What happened wasn't Judith's fault, it was Paula's. Of course, her parents had tried to tell her that wasn't true, but the more they said so, the more certain she became that they were lying. If it hadn't been for her friendship with Simonetta ... well, life for her family could have been very different.

Tucked into the solicitor's letter was another envelope. Paula tore it open.

Dear Paula,

The handwriting was a faultless Royal Blue copperplate, thick, confident strokes from a fountain pen.

I do hope this letter won't come as too much of a shock. I had plans to contact you directly, but though the spirit is willing, the flesh is increasingly weak.

Anyway, to the point. The bequest may surprise you. I know it's not a life-changing amount, but I wanted to do something. I bumped into your mother, and heard that things aren't easy for you. We each make our own choices, Paula, but I do wonder if things might have been different if it hadn't been for the Brownies.

Too bloody right, thought Paula, looking down at her bloated body and then around her dismal living room.

Please think of spending it on something for you, a treat. I know what you're like, Paula. It is possible to be too generous, you know. Buy something that might remind you of the good times, of the things you learned when you were a Brownie.

Paula sighed. The things she'd learned: what, like never trust a man with an Italian accent? Beware of little girls bearing tropical fish? And it was all very well saying have fun with the money, but the people whose billet-doux were stacked on the breakfast bar – Mr B. Gas, Mr T. Council-Tax, Mr B. Telecom – had other plans for her windfall.

There is one more thing, Lucy. I wondered whether, perhaps, you might like to get in touch. She needs friends at a time like this. But of course it is up to you. I'm not making this a condition of my will; people must make their own decisions.

Look after yourself, Paula. Life is too precious to squander.

Your Brown Owl,

Judith

PS: I hope the enclosed bring back a few fond memories of Brownies.

Poor Lucy. Having Brown Owl as her mum had done her no favours: in the three years they'd been together in the Brownies, Paula had seen Lucy shrink under the weight of her mother's disappointment, at a time when everyone else was growing. But Paula didn't think getting in touch with Lucy after twenty-five years would cheer either of them up.

She rummaged around in the bottom of the envelope and pulled out three pieces of stiffened fabric.

Brownie badges.

The first was square, twice as big as a postage stamp, and when she turned it over, she couldn't help smiling. A Pixie. The little green creature seemed to be dancing, its face in profile with round cheeks swollen in a big smile.

The other two were triangular. Interest badges. The first was embroidered with a rabbit. She tried to remember what it was for, something to do with wildlife and all those sunny evenings spent playing hide-and-seek in the woods at the back of the Drill Hall.

No one would have any trouble finding her in hide-and-seek these days, Paula thought.

The other depicted a little girl standing in a gym skirt and T-shirt, arms outstretched and one leg pointed to the side, balancing. With another giggle, Paula remembered. The Agility badge. She'd have to show it to the kids later; they'd never believe she could have won *this* one.

Terri was under pressure. Not only was she late for lectures, but the cause of her lateness was the same old row with Colin.

The one that had no obvious solution. After two years together he felt he'd waited long enough for sex and he was trying to convince her that God would turn a blind eye.

'It doesn't work like that,' Terri said, though she was only saying what she'd said a hundred times before. Colin always threatened to leave, but she knew he wouldn't. He'd never made a dramatic gesture in all the time she'd known him, unless you counted throwing up over the restaurant table on his fortieth birthday. And that was only because the booze interfered with his hayfever medication.

One of the problems with trying to save non-Christian souls – especially your boyfriend's – was that your own came under relentless attack. Perhaps Colin had been sent by Satan, though he was the least devilish man she knew. Judith had called him 'a typical Teresa Rowbotham lame duck' which Terri thought was unfair. If she happened to have a fairy godmother effect on her boyfriends, then where was the harm? After all, Judith had warned her not to rely on men ... and Terri made sure her men could not rely on her either. Her desire to be with a man seemed to diminish as their confidence grew, and her break-ups were always civilized, as she waved off her exes like a mother packing a reluctant son off to university.

There'd been Rob, the farmer's son who hated animals. He'd set up his own business thanks to her. And then there'd been Noel, who longed to see the world but was terrified of planes. She'd packed him off to hypnotherapy and the last she'd heard he was island-hopping by helicopter in the South Pacific.

She'd met Colin in a pub, in her first year doing theology. You couldn't miss him: a short man with curly, almost angelic blond hair, belting out a karaoke version of 'My Way'. She'd only talked to him as a favour to another male in distress, the landlord of the Anchor, who'd confided as she bought a round that he was worried Colin's howl would empty the pub if it continued. So she'd stepped in to stop him doing a second number and had been surprised that this slightly hangdog specimen had a dry wit and a dream: to write a blockbuster movie script. Through the smoky fug, she could see that he needed *her* to help him realize his vision and she felt that tell-tale urge: not a lust to get into his pants, but an itch to get into his life.

Two summers later, he still lived in the same tiny one-bed flat round the corner from the Anchor. He still did shift work in the same factory (making road signs, though he failed to see the ones that said 'U-turn your life before you run out of time'). And he was still on page six of his screenplay. Judith had once suggested that Colin outlasted all Terri's previous beaux because he'd spectacularly failed to live up to expectations. But Terri had bristled, unable to abandon the cherubic Colin. So what if he was a work-in-progress? Terri wasn't about to dump him for that.

He was outstanding at one thing, though: pushing her emotional buttons. Making her feel wanted. Trouble was, his insistence on pushing her sexual buttons as well was growing – and her progress towards ordination only seemed to have made him hornier. God help her once she got her dog collar. He'd be unstoppable: she could already imagine his single-entendres about trying it 'doggie-collar' style.

There was a simple solution, of course. Marriage. With a bit of training, Colin could make the perfect vicar's consort and Terri had to admit she'd feel a lot more confident lecturing future parishioners about the place of sex in relationships, if she'd ever had it. She was probably the oldest virgin in Manchester.

Marriage had one drawback. She wasn't sure she was in love with Colin. Then again, Terri wasn't sure she'd ever loved anyone properly, except God and, by default more than anything else, her hopeless parents. And then, of course, there was Judith.

She tried not to think about Judith these days, unless she was on her own, because it made her feel so empty, as though someone had snatched away everything that was comforting or reliable and left nothing but blackness behind.

'You're scared,' Colin said, as they walked back towards the college after another frustrating session in his flat. When she stayed at his place, they slept in the same bed and she liked the novelty of waking up with someone else. But he saw every morning as a new challenge to her virginity. 'You've avoided it so long that you're scared.'

He was right *and* wrong, she thought. Right that she was

scared but wrong about why. She was nervous about sex, as she'd be nervous about ballroom dancing or synchronized swimming or any other physical activity she'd not done before. But it wouldn't take her long to grasp the basics; she was a fast learner.

No, what Terri was scared of was being needy, of depending on someone the way her parents had depended on each other. At least she knew this about herself. Most people didn't realize and went through life being hurt, or worse, hurting anyone who tried to get close. As she'd explained to the Church selection board, being ordained would allow her to care for all her future parishioners. What was the song in Brownies? *Love is something if you give it away ... you end up having more.*

Which still left Colin, of course.

'Colin, it's not about me being frigid. It's about me not being sure.' They were outside the college now, at the porter's lodge. And she was late for Pastoral Theology.

'But *I'm* sure,' he said, and she recognized the signs of him working himself up to a tantrum. Not now. Especially not with that nosy bloody porter staring out of the window. 'I don't understand why you're not—'

The porter waved an envelope at her. It was the first time *ever* she'd been pleased to see him. 'Oh, Colin ... later. We can talk about it later. I think the guy there has something for me.' She kissed Colin quickly on the cheek.

'That's it. Walk away. As usual.' He stomped off towards the bus stop.

The porter gave her a meaningful look as she stepped into his lair, which smelled faintly of Brylcreem and Shippam's Meat Paste. 'Man trouble?' He knew she hadn't spent the night in college. But then she knew about his porn stash in the cleaning cupboard. It was stalemate.

'Nothing I can't handle. Is that envelope for me?'

'Mmm. From the college authorities.'

Terri took the envelope and left the lodge, 'without a word of thanks', as the porter would tell his wife over tea. As she ripped the envelope open, she already knew what was inside. A formal warning. She'd really let things slip over the last month, finding it harder and harder to get out of bed, to see the point of lectures. It was so unlike her.

She looked at her watch. She'd be ten minutes late for Pastoral Theology now even if she ran, so instead she changed direction, walking out of the college gates towards the cathedral.

She wanted to think of Judith, call on her wisdom somehow. One of the tutors had a sticker in the rear windscreen of his Mini that read *What would Jesus do?* Which was all very well, but Terri was pretty sure Jesus had never been late handing in his 'Christian Doctrine in the Middle Ages' essay.

So she preferred to ask another question: what would Judith do? If she could find the answer to that, Terri was sure her life would be so much easier.

Only after Paula had killed four renegades down a dimly lit alley and earned some extra ammo by jumping the gap between two skyscrapers did she start to feel better.

Judith's letter had made her feel so unsettled that she'd raided the bread bin, which was now empty. And she'd snapped at her mother when she'd phoned to ask whether Paula needed anything from Homebase.

'Are you saying my flat's falling down round my ears?'

'No, Paula. It's just, without a man about the house, well ...' Patsy hesitated, her girly voice becoming shriller, as it always did when she was nervous. 'Your dad's under my feet here without any work, and he'd bite your hand off for any odd jobs that might need doing now that Neil isn't around.'

They'd been trying very hard since Paula officially became a single parent. Though, according to Neil, her folks were partly to blame because they'd encouraged her to buy that bloody computer in the first place.

It was meant to be an investment in the kids, Charlie and Sadie, who were doing as badly at school as Paula had. The deal was that they'd all club together to buy the computer on HP and then Paula's mum Patsy would donate some of her pension to pay for internet access. They couldn't afford it, really, but then the kids had always been her weakness, and at least the laptop might have a more long-lasting effect than the endless designer trainers and trinkets from Claire's Accessories. Computers certainly seemed to offer a more comfortable career option than the grimy, cold existence both Paula's dad and Neil were locked into as jobbing builders and decorators. Not that they ever seemed to get jobs any more. The wave of taciturn, exotic-looking Poles who'd arrived in Troughton over the last few years did it cheaper and, Neil had once admitted when drunk, better.

But the kids were typically ungrateful for the sacrifices the computer had required. Charlie surfed for porn and Sadie was far more interested in chatting up boys online than researching her French homework. In a rare burst of discipline, Paula had banned them from surfing the internet: it was only when she stopped coming to bed that Neil had worked out why. One click-through from an advert on a sci-fi site – Paula had always been partial to a spot of *Star Trek* – and she'd been hooked.

The ad hotlinked her to *Lawless*, a dreamworld where you could be anything you wanted to be, could choose to be on the side of good or evil. An online game with around seventeen thousand worldwide addicts and it took a single mouse click for Paula to become addict number 17,001.

In the end, it was *Lawless* that put the nail in the coffin (or, in *Lawless* style, the laser-charged flame-thrower through the heart) of their sixteen-year-old marriage. When he gave her an ultimatum: 'It's me or that sodding game,' she didn't pretend to think about it. He'd be better off without her, anyhow.

At least now Neil was living back with his parents, Paula could play unhindered. But tonight, for the first time in the eight months since she'd discovered the wonderful online world of the Lawless Kingdom, the game didn't seem enough to distract her from the realities of her life. And she wasn't on form: she'd let at least two virtual vagabonds get away.

She pressed the pause button on the screen, leaving her gorgeous alter ego hovering in mid-sprint, and clicked instead into the *Lawless* chatroom. It was busy, as usual: Europeans taking a break from some early evening crimefighting to talk tactics, Americans getting their fix during working hours, plus the odd Antipodean who was still online at three a.m. Sydney time.

She scanned the list of occupants for people she knew, though really she was looking for one name in particular. And there it was. She felt a tingle of excitement as she invited SheriffJack to engage in private conversation.

> CUTEYCRIMEFIGHTER: Hey Jack. How's crimefighting tonight on your side of the globe?
> SHERIFFJACK: You know how it goes. Easy come. Easy go. You?

The thing Paula loved when she first 'met' Sheriff was that he rejected the smileys and impenetrable shortcuts of cyber-chat in favour of something resembling full sentences. It was the online equivalent of a well-brought-up man holding a door open for a woman. And it had been a long time since any man had deemed her worthy of good manners.

> CUTEYCRIMEFIGHTER: Bit of a shock today. Have been left some money by someone haven't seen for years. Lots of years.

The thing about talking online was that you got straight to the point. No wittering about the weather or other trivia. So much better than the real world. Paula couldn't bear the thought of small talk and thanked her lucky stars that she'd never have to date again. No one could possibly fancy her and anyway, where would she meet them when she only left the house for a few minutes at a time, scurrying to the corner shop and back?

> SHERIFFJACK: Yeah? You upset?

Jack knew Paula better than anyone now. He'd introduced himself in a chatroom not long after Neil left and she didn't know what she would have done without his pithy sentences and correctly-spelled wisdom. He was thirty-eight, ran a computer company in Seattle, divorced, no kids. Five ten, medium build, into swimming and baseball.

Or so he said. Paula had no way of knowing if he was

stringing her along, or if any of this was accurate. Sometimes she worried about it. Imagined how it would feel if he was a short, fat balding turnip farmer from East Anglia.

Then again, she had no right to complain. As far as her comrades on *Lawless* were concerned, CUTEYCRIMEFIGHTER was five five, an American size zero (how could anyone genuinely be a zero? If you lost weight, would you end up being minus-sized?) with blonde hair and a successful PR job in Manchester.

Well, the hair wasn't far off: she was on the mousy side of blonde, when she could face washing it.

> CUTEYCRIMEFIGHTER: Hardly knew her anyway. No idea why she's named me in her will.

This bit wasn't quite true, of course, but the thought of trying to explain why Judith might feel guilty after twenty-five years made Paula want to crawl back under the duvet.

> SHERIFFJACK: Bit of a result, then? No pain, all gain.
> CUTEYCRIMEFIGHTER: I dunno. Brings back bad memories.
> SHERIFFJACK: ?
> CUTEYCRIMEFIGHTER: Long story.
> SHERIFFJACK: They always are. Am good listener ...
> CUTEYCRIMEFIGHTER: I know you are! This woman used to be a kind of youth leader. You have Brownies in America?
> SHERIFFJACK: Yeah, I love them. We invented them! My mom makes the best.

Paula laughed despite herself as she typed.

> CUTEYCRIMEFIGHTER: Not that kind. Brownies are a sort of Scout. For younger girls.
> SHERIFFJACK: OK I got you. Girl Scouts. How come they're Brownies?
> CUTEYCRIMEFIGHTER: Well, the uniform's brown. And the leader is known as Brown Owl. We earned badges and did

good turns, like doing shopping for old ladies. Camping was the best bit – we used to go on Brownie Pack holidays where we'd sing songs and eat bananas from the camp-fire.
SHERIFFJACK: Songs?

Paula smiled. Life had all seemed so simple when she was seven.

CUTEYCRIMEFIGHTER: We had one, *Oh you'll never go to heaven ...on the QE2 ... cos the QE2 ...ain't got no loo!*
SHERIFFJACK: Loo?
CUTEYCRIMEFIGHTER: Short for lavatory. Toilet.
SHERIFFJACK: You mean there's no bathroom on a luxury liner?
CUTEYCRIMEFIGHTER: It's a joke.

There was a pause.

SHERIFFJACK: Oh I get it. That famous English sense of humor.

She tried to remember the other ones. What was the song about the angels? *Three little angels all dressed in white ... tried to get to heaven on the end of a kite. But the kite tail was broken, down they all fell. They couldn't get to heaven so they all went to ...*
Hell. Which, she thought, peering out of the window, was probably a lot like the Primrose Estate.

CUTEYCRIMEFIGHTER: Brownies had its moments. Anyhow, last time I saw our leader – Brown Owl, the woman who died – I was nine. Something happened. Something bad.
SHERIFFJACK: ?
CUTEYCRIMEFIGHTER: I don't want to talk about it really.
SHERIFFJACK: That's cool, Cutes. So how much has she left you?
CUTEYCRIMEFIGHTER: Hmm, in dollars ... just under two thousand.

46

SHERIFFJACK: That's nice. What are you gonna spend it on?

CUTEYCRIMEFIGHTER: She said I should spend it on something for me. But I don't have much money right now.

As soon as she hit return, Paula realized she'd given away far more than she meant to. She held her breath.

SHERIFFJACK: Hey, you been spending too much on a new sexy wardrobe for summer?

Paula breathed again.

CUTEYCRIMEFIGHTER: Yeah, you bet.

SHERIFFJACK: I bet you look terrific, Cutes. So you ready to get shooting up renegades again?

CUTEYCRIMEFIGHTER: Yep. I'll race you to Mean Street.

SHERIFFJACK: You're on.

Paula clicked out of the chatroom and back onto the map showing the parts of the city that were under attack. Cutey sprang into action. Thank God Jack would never see the reality.

The train from Euston to Manchester had taken twice as long as timetabled and Chris's 'just the one' vodka Red Bull had turned into four. Or was it five? By the time the driver pulled into the station, she was snoring gently in her first class seat. The ticket collector nudged her awake. 'Ugh, what?' Chris opened her eyes: they hurt, as they always did when she slept in her contact lenses. When she rubbed at them, the last flakes of mascara from the *It's All Balls* photoshoot stuck to her hands like squashed ants. 'Shit, are we here at last?'

She picked up her overnight bag and crossed the concourse to buy a double-strength coffee. Napping on trains was an efficient way to claw back the sleep she lacked. With her coffee in one hand, she dialled Matt with the other, before tucking her mobile under her left ear and heading for the taxi rank.

'Hiya, you old sod,' she said when he answered. 'Yeah, I've

finally got here. It'd take less time to fly to Ibiza. Listen, I need to get home to sort myself out ... I know, I know. Sorry ...' She climbed into the back of the black cab. 'Carpenter's Wharf flats, please, mate. You know where that is? Cool ... So, Matt, why don't you come round and pick me up in your new pussy magnet, eh? Forty-five minutes? Perfect.'

Matt was an ex from college, newly single after a two-year relationship, so he'd be looking for a shag, which she'd probably agree to. If anything he was a bit too fond of her, but he knew the score. He was her favourite of a portfolio of exes she kept for the days when one of her sex toys wasn't enough. Though the pace of her life did tend to mean that contrary to her image, Chris's libido was lower on her list of priorities than sleep. For someone whose livelihood was so dependent on bed, she spent virtually no time there.

Chris tipped the driver well enough to get a big smile in return. She took her post from the concierge, and began sifting it as she travelled up to her penthouse in the space-age lift. She was fond of her little studio in Covent Garden, but the Manchester warehouse conversion was something special. Younger *Coronation Street* actors and Man U players were among her neighbours, enjoying *droit de seigneur* over the city's star-struck groupies, before the lads about town settled for *Hello!* weddings, Portland clinic babies and neo-Georgian piles in Alderley Edge.

She found the remote and used it to close her blinds, dim the lights and switch on some soulful music. One of those teen female jazz singers with smoky voices – she couldn't remember which one. She found another Red Bull in the fridge and began to throw off her clothes in preparation for a quick blitz in her multi-massage-jet shower.

As she downed the drink – without it, she didn't have the energy to go out again – Chris flicked through the folder of paperwork from Kian, her PA. Huge cheques to be signed, the odd charity begging letter or conference invite that had passed the Kian filter. Chris was still amused at having a male PA to screen out her weirder correspondence. She'd had one stalker, a fiftysomething clerk from the Isle of Man who used to send her flowers. He stopped after a brisk letter threatening legal action, but sometimes she missed his declarations of love. Maybe she'd overlooked the man of her dreams? As if there was any such thing …

The note from Kian detailed tomorrow's diary – a breakfast sales meeting at the Lowry Hotel, a staffing problem to fix at the flagship Deansgate shop, plus a dozen or so decisions needed on trade fairs and the new catalogue and a viral marketing campaign for the All-American range. Maybe she'd kick Matt out afterwards, instead of letting him stay the night.

PS, it said at the bottom of the note, *I opened a letter marked personal. Sorry. It's a solicitor's letter from Troughton together with another envelope I didn't open. Looks like someone has died. Hope you're not too upset.*

Chris stiffened and found the envelope, marked with a purple Post-it on which Kian had written 'sorry sweetie' and drawn a tearful face. As she fumbled with the letter, she realized she was drunker than she'd thought. She scanned the formal sentences and understood, with some relief, that it was Judith Gill who'd died. Which was sad and all that – she must have been quite young, and it'd be tough on her poor daughter – but it wasn't something Chris would lose sleep over.

What *was* odd was Judith bothering to write. Naked but for her Sloggis – Chris couldn't bear thongs, though they were one of Love Bites' top sellers – she ripped open the second envelope. Out fell a letter and three Brownie badges. The Pixie emblem, the Book Lover and another one with a boat on it; she couldn't remember what it signified.

My dear Christine,

She giggled. No one called her Christine. Not even her parents; they wouldn't dare.

Teresa passed on the newspaper cuttings about you. I always knew you'd go far, but I never expected you to become what the newspapers call a porn baron! Not exactly what we were aiming for in the Brownies, now, is it? Though I do seem to remember you excelled yourself earning your Toymaker badge.

That's what it was! The boat was Noah's Ark. She giggled again: Judith seemed so strait-laced, yet maybe sending the badge was her idea of a joke. After all, Chris had made her fortune selling toys for grown-ups.

I've prevaricated about whether to write, but I've contacted the other Pixies. I have left a little money to Paula, because she needs it, though from what I've read, that's less of a concern to you. However, I didn't want to leave you out entirely.

Being left out had never worried Chris. As a child, she preferred daydreams to reality and constantly resented being jolted out of her many fantasies by someone demanding she play rounders or wash the car or go to the corner shop for milk.

I know that the last days of the Brownies probably don't hold very positive memories for you, but I hope you'll take a moment to think about the better times, the fun we all had.
When you know you're dying – of course, we all know, but when a doctor spells it out in months – it makes you think. Awkward business, thinking. I've always been more of a doer. But thinking is, it seems to me, a mental tidy-up before we move into a Better Place. The Pixies have filled my thoughts, for reasons I know you'll understand.

Chris felt sick. She'd worked so hard to escape bloody Troughton with its bad haircuts and bad memories. Most of the time she managed to fool herself. The flat was a prime example. It couldn't be more different from the cosy semis of her childhood in the place she mockingly called Toytown. No one there had halogen-lit abstract paintings, 42-inch plasma-screen TVs, Gaggia espresso machines. Not that they mattered to her: what she valued most was the space. And *real* silence, so unlike the sinister stillness at home, punctuated by her father's vicious whispers.

It was different all right. But all it took was one meddling woman, and the notion that she could ever be free of her past seemed to crumble around her.

You've done terribly well for yourself. The others, I fear, less so. But the Pixie I worry about most is my Lucy. She's isolated and I worry she won't manage once I'm gone. I wouldn't want her to know I'm writing to you. I don't believe in interfering in people's lives, as you'll recall—

Chris suppressed a sneer.

However, perhaps you'd consider whether you might like to get in touch. Small gestures can make all the difference.

Chris sat on her Conran leather sofa, knowing she didn't want to. There was nothing to be gained going backwards.

Of course, it's your decision. I just hope you make the right one.
  With very fondest memories,
  Judith.

Chris sighed. She felt stitched up. If she did contact Lucy, she knew it probably wouldn't help either of them. Yet if she didn't, she'd feel guilty about disregarding a dying woman's wish.

Suddenly she wasn't in the mood for going out. And by the time Matt arrived, she wasn't in the mood for sex either.

'But why ask me?' she said, after she'd read him the letter. He'd listened carefully, those calm, kind olive eyes magnified behind his chunky framed glasses.

'Sounds like she thinks you're a soft touch. Doesn't understand that you've turned into a hardened businesswoman who uses people, then tosses them aside. Or if they're really lucky, tosses them off.' Matt grinned, pleased with his joke.

Chris ignored him. 'I suppose we were all quite close, for a while, but I never have been that good at keeping in touch with people, have I?' She sipped her vodka – this time without Red Bull, as a small concession to cutting down on caffeine.

'Well, you've always got so much on your plate.' Matt moved from the armchair to the sofa to sit next to Chris. He was tall and broad and the few grey strands in the thick black hair at his temples suited him. One of those bastards who'd look better with age. 'Maybe you should slow down a bit. Enjoy life.'

'Yeah, maybe. Listen, Matt, I know you're single and randy and everything, but this death stuff has really put me off the idea. And I'm knackered as well.'

'Oh.'

'I'm sorry.'

He pulled a face. 'Bloody Brown Owl. I thought death was meant to make people horny. Make you want to grab life by the bollocks. Or grab someone by the bollocks, anyway.'

Chris shook her head sadly. 'Not me, sorry. We could have a snog if you like. See if that gets me in the mood? If you're really desperate.'

'God, Chris. What do you take me for? I'd rather DIY than have you do something when your heart's not in it.'

She grinned at him. 'Matthew King, I swear you're turning into a grown-up after all these years.'

'Yeah, yeah,' he said, draining his bottle of beer. 'I'd better go before I spoil my new caring, sharing reputation.'

'I owe you one,' Chris said, kissing him on the cheek as they waited for the lift.

'Just one?' Matt hugged her. 'Call me if you want to talk.'

'You're a mate.'

After he'd gone, she wondered why he was single again. He was a serious catch: funny, laid-back, and with a partnership at his law firm within his reach. A wife would secure the deal.

Maybe in another life they might have settled down. They'd both been too young at college, had split up amicably, proud that they were mature enough to stay friends. But now he'd reached that random point men hit in their thirties, when they decide to look properly for Ms Right, and another gulf had opened up between them. One drunken night, he'd confessed that no girl he dated came up to the Chris Love benchmark.

Now she felt awkward. She knew she didn't want a life as a wife, with the danger of turning from Ms Right into Mrs Wrong overnight. She'd led a debate against marriage at university, her arguments so passionate and compelling that she'd had her pick of men to take to bed that night. The rather earnest guy she'd chosen – God knows what his name was – had just launched into a rant about the trauma parents caused their children by divorcing, when she'd interrupted him.

'My parents are still together.'

'But I thought … I assumed from the way you spoke that you're from a broken home too?' he'd said, pouting.

'Believe me, it's not always happy ever after if they stay together,' she'd told him, before reaching over to undo his jeans.

So life as Mrs King held no appeal. She didn't have room for a boyfriend, either. Instead, she had her freedom. If her parents' marriage told her anything, it was that a longing for freedom didn't disappear just through the act of making wedding vows.

And if occasionally she wondered whether freedom didn't involve too high a price, she dismissed it. That middle-of-the-night moment when a gap opened up in your life, a gap so big you felt dizzy looking into it: that happened to everyone, now and then, surely? At least she'd earned the money to fill it.

From nowhere, an image of Brown Owl came into her mind: short, stout, smiling as she pinned on the tiny tin badge that marked Chris's graduation to fully fledged Pixie. And then another of Brown Owl two years later, white-faced, at that final Pack holiday.

Half-cut on vodka, Chris bunched her fists in a child's rage at the way Judith and her 'do your duty at all times' morality had muscled their way back in, conspiring to remind her of events she'd managed to forget. Only Brown Owl could manage that from beyond the grave.

Chapter Seven

A Guide's duty is to be useful and
to help others. She is to do her duty before
anything else.

'I bet I am the coolest there,' Sasha says, but her voice sounds less convincing than her words. She's unusually pale and a tiny muscle just below her left eye keeps twitching.

The last time I saw my daughter look nervous was the day she started infants' school, three years ago. 'You're bound to be brilliant, sweet-pea.' I draw up alongside the Drill Hall and pull the handbrake on with a little more force than I intended. She gives me an alarmed look.

Oh, very grown-up Lucy. Taking it out on the car and on Sasha. It's not their fault I'm a pushover.

Tuesday night has been my choir night for over ten years. It's just about the only thing I've hung on to from my premarriage life, and although Andrew couldn't be less interested in my singing, he's never actively objected to babysitting for a couple of hours a week. He occasionally adopts a martyred look if I stop off at the pub for a Diet Coke after rehearsals, but then I suppose even one night of full parental responsibility is more than his father ever took. And given that Andrew holds up his parents as the definition of Happy Families, it's a big step to deviate from that in any way.

But when, after that afternoon in the cellar, Sasha suddenly expressed a stubborn desire to join the Brownies – 'it's what Granny would have wanted me to do' – and the Pack meeting turned out to be on a Tuesday as it was in the old days, he seized his chance.

'I know it's something you enjoy doing, Lulu, but it's only a hobby and I'm under such a lot of pressure at work at the moment; I can't guarantee to be back in time to fetch Sasha and then ferry her to Brownies. You can always rejoin the choir, I don't know, near Christmas or something?'

But which bloody Christmas? Christmas 2015 when Sasha's at university? In the meantime, I'm destined to be chauffeur-in-chief. Maybe it's a fuss about nothing, but my singing has always been the only thing that distinguishes me from the rest of the harassed housewives of Troughton. Now it's in my past.

I slam the car door. Sasha looks at me but says nothing. These days, I get a lot of looks from my daughter and my husband, but they don't push it, knowing I'm still not quite myself. They don't realize that I'm losing sight of what the hell 'myself' might be.

The Drill Hall is lit up against the dusky trees and May sky, like a tumbledown fairytale cottage. I feel waves of emotion – nostalgia, perhaps, but apprehension too – as I walk towards the entrance. The last time I came here was for one of the agonizing teen discos Mum used to host. She frisked everyone for illicit booze and had security lights installed all round the hall to catch any snoggers. Once she caught Chris with some boy's hands down her well-filled bra and marched her straight home to her parents: I was more embarrassed than Chris was. No wonder I reached the ripe old age of seventeen before I had my first kiss.

'Hey, Luce!' Terri comes out of the hall as Sasha and I walk up the path, an ever-reliable security light flicking on to illuminate our way. 'And Sasha! It's smashing to see you here. Why don't you go and take your coat off and I'll introduce you to the others?'

Terri is wearing brown tracksuit bottoms and a Brownie T-shirt that hugs her solid figure in all the wrong places, and her red hair is held back by a crocodile clip, the kind you use to hold office documents together. I raise my eyebrows and Terri shrugs. 'I couldn't find anything else and I was in a rush tonight.'

There are already half a dozen Brownies in the hall, sporting trendy yellow sweatshirts in place of the drab uniform I was coerced into wearing for three long years. I feel anxious on Sasha's behalf, though she's already striding forward, introducing herself to the other girls. Where does that self-assurance come from? Not for the first time, I'm envious of her fearlessness.

'She's going to be a natural, isn't she?'

'Mmm.' I know I'm being graceless, but I can't shake off my irritation.

'If you don't mind me saying so, Lucy, you seem a bit out of sorts.'

I grin, despite my annoyance. Terri's language hasn't evolved since Brownies. If she had her wish, she'd be the Peter Pan of the Girl Guide Movement, collecting interest badges till retirement, and spending her life Lending a Hand. 'Yes, that's one way of putting it. Totally bloody pissed off is another. Andrew's refusing to give Sasha a lift here which means I can't go to choir any more.'

We look over at Sasha, who is showing off her ability to walk on her hands. 'Oh no. What a pain. Can't you make him do it? Threaten not to cut off the crusts in his packed lunches or something.'

Terri's always thought I'm too soft, but it's hard to change after thirty-five years. Where would I begin? Concentrate on the big stuff, like what we're doing with Mum's house? Or start small, tackling choir night, on the grounds that it's less important if I lose.

Though right now, it all feels important. I sigh. 'I know I ought to, but it takes energy. And at the moment I don't feel I have any to spare.'

A small girl is tugging at Terri's arm. 'Carly's having a nosebleed.'

'Sorry, Lucy, I'll have to get this sorted. But, listen, we could meet up afterwards. I could stay over if you like, don't need to be back in Manchester till midday.'

'Maybe ...' Somehow I doubt that a 'pull your socks up' talking-to is what I need.

Terri gives me an encouraging smile, then walks towards

bleeding Carly, pinching the girl's nose with her left hand, and clicking her fingers with her right. 'Settle down, Brownies, and get yourselves into your pow-wow ring. Tonight is a very special night, because we're welcoming a brand new recruit.'

Within seconds, the girls form a circle and, still leading Carly by the nose, Terri continues: 'And though we always give a warm welcome to newcomers, there's an extra-special reason why we should be thrilled about this addition to our Pack.'

Sasha blushes a little, but grins back at the Brownies sitting either side of her, the ones she was dazzling a moment ago with her handstands and back-flips.

'It was Sasha's great-great grandmother who set up the first ever Guide troop in Troughton nearly a century ago – and her great-grandmother formed the Brownies. So let's give Sasha a grand hello as only we know how.'

Terri winks across at me as the girls stand up and perform the Brownie welcome – accompanied by three loud claps. I try to catch Sasha's eye, but she's oblivious, accepting the welcome as gracefully as a minor European princess. I turn to leave.

Perhaps I should be grateful for my essential role as housekeeper and driver. Otherwise I have a horrible suspicion that my daughter and my husband would get along just fine without me.

Chapter Eight

Girls will do no good by imitating boys. One
loves a girl who is sweet and tender, and who
can gently soothe when wearied with pain.

Twenty minutes later, I'm trying hard not to take out my
irritation on Andrew's soles. When I arrived back from the
Drill Hall, I found him on the sofa, watching football, with a
pizza on his lap.

'Working late again?' I said, but he ignored the sarcasm. I
don't suppose he was even listening.

'I ordered you one as well,' he said. I retrieved the takeaway
box from the kitchen and joined him in the living room. The
Fiorentina pizza – he forgot I loathe spinach – was lukewarm
and soggy, with a film of cold oil across the top. I pushed it
along the coffee table in disgust, knocking over Andrew's
Corona bottle.

'Good job that was empty,' he grinned, before swivelling his
body around so that his feet landed in my lap. In the early days I
enjoyed administering the daily massage, but now it's just another
chore. It wouldn't be so bad if he asked nicely, or thanked me
afterwards. Instead he generally thrusts his feet without warning
into my space and even expects me to remove his smelly socks.
I've tutted a bit, but to say anything outright just sounds petty.
I can almost hear his answer. *It's not much to ask, is it, Lulu? My
mother always said it was her favourite time of the day* ...

I suppose everyone's marriage ends up like this in the end. A
compromise.

'So did she settle in OK?' he asks me now, eyelids fluttering as I knead away on the right foot, digging my thumb into the arch the way he likes it.

'Yes. You know Sasha.'

'Chip off the old block, isn't she? She'll end up Brown Owl, like your mum, I bet you ...YES! What a save!' He thrusts his hands into the air as some Italian goalkeeper blocks a penalty delivered by a Spanish striker. He doesn't even like football. But his father did.

I stop kneading. 'I don't want to give up the choir, Andrew. It's the only time I get for me.' I bite my lip. Confrontation makes me feel sick, but this matters. And now I've said it, I feel this new sense of purpose, along with the nausea.

He opens his eyes. 'Don't stop, I was just getting into it.'

'I'm serious.' Who did that come from? Me?

Andrew sighs. 'You know I can't guarantee to be back in time every Tuesday. It's just not how it works at my level. It makes sense for you to take her. You could find another choir.'

'But I like *my* choir. And I take Sasha everywhere else: to swimming and judo and all those parties.'

He closes his eyes again and his forehead loses the lines that criss-cross his brow whenever he's tense. For a moment, he looks so much like Sasha that I almost forgive him. He can't help it. Work is non-stop stress – Andrew is the North-west Big Cheese in Transport and spends his life weighing global warming against the latest road proposals and the desire of commuters to be home before midnight – so I know he doesn't need hassle at home. I swap feet and begin firm sweeping movements from his toes to his bony ankle.

'I know you do, darling.' He mutes the TV, to show he's giving the problem his full attention. 'Mmm, that's good. What if ... you could find someone else to take her? I don't mind paying if it means you can carry on with the choir.'

Now the anger resurfaces, and my fingers itch with aggression. 'This is also about you taking responsibility. She's your daughter, too, you know.' Strange. The words come as almost as much of a surprise to me as they do to him.

'I don't need reminding of that, Lulu, but if you're going to get silly—'

'Silly?' The word comes out far louder than I'd intended and Buster cowers by the door. Something unfamiliar is happening to me. I feel a surge of something – adrenalin, perhaps – and when I turn to Andrew, he looks nervous. 'Silly? For wanting to do something on my own for once, something that doesn't revolve around keeping you happy or keeping Sasha busy? I'm fed up, Andrew. You never listen. And you always assume you're right. About the Brownies, about choir, about Mum's house.'

He stares back at me, shocked. 'Not that again,' he says, quietly.

'Yes, that again. You've just assumed that Mum's house is a ticket for you to buy some cottage in France or a motorboat or an extension. None of which interest me, which you'd know if you ever bothered to ask.' I pause, knowing what I want to say, but fearing the consequences. Then I say it anyway. 'Mum's house is mine. And if you don't sort out your priorities, it might just be *my* ticket out of here! One way!'

And with that I push his feet out of my way, storm out of the living room and grab Andrew's car keys. My Fiesta just doesn't have the power for the kind of driving I need right now.

Ten minutes later and I'm already regretting leaving in a hurry. Andrew's in-car CD collection consists mainly of croaky Bruce Springsteen soundalikes. All the air-conditioning and electric windows and GPS in the world can't compensate for the lack of opera to sing along to, as I thrash his Audi Quattro out of Troughton towards the prettiest part of Cheshire.

I learned to drive on these country lanes in Mum's baby-blue Vauxhall Chevette, cautiously navigating the twists and turns, avoiding tractors and rabbits that appeared like animated obstacles in a computer game. Terri's dad, Dave, took over after my only lesson with my mother ended with me in tears and Mum grabbing the steering wheel. But though Dave was great – so laid-back he dozed off once as I tried to reverse round a corner – I spent every lesson wishing my own father was teaching me. It's what every teenage girl needs, isn't it? A man who adores her, believes she's beautiful despite the acne and the brace, and talks about protecting her honour from boys, even when no boys are interested.

It should have been my father who kissed me and tore up my L-plates when I passed my driving test. It should have been my father giving me away at my wedding to Andrew (though right now, as I hit the gas, I wonder if my father would have refused to give away his little girl to an arrogant, lazy, bad-tempered, bossy bastard).

It should have been my father going misty-eyed when presented with his first granddaughter.

I feel the telltale pricking in my eyes and reach onto the passenger seat for the tissues in my handbag. But it's not there. The unfamiliar rage propelled me out of the door without looking back and now I'm without my personal life support system. No tissues for mopping up, no lipstick for tarting up, no unopened junk mail for distraction in traffic jams.

I try not to panic as the anger begins to subside. What was I thinking? This is not what Lucy does. I switch on the radio, pushing the seek button until it finds *Classic FM*.

At last, something's going right. The car fills with Maria Callas as Violetta in *La Traviata*.

The sound quality is so stunning that it feels as though each note is travelling through my bloodstream, straight to my heart. I have to pull over. I love *La Traviata* – it was one of Grampa Quentin's favourites, and we'd sit next to each other on the sofa, following the words together on the libretto that came with the LP boxed set, flicking between the Italian, and the clumsy English translation.

I used to dream of playing Violetta. It was nothing but a dream, of course; I knew that. OK, if I'm honest there were a few months when I didn't – when I was thirteen and had a music teacher who lied to me and said that anything was possible, that my voice might be my future. Silly Lucy. Teenagers are so naïve. I worked out the truth soon enough.

I remember the words and join in with Maria:

Ah, fors'è lui che l'anima
Solinga ne' tumulti
Godea sovente pingere
De' suoi colori occulti.

I try to remember the English: Is he the one who in my dreams brought peace so often to my heart … painting it with magic colours?

It doesn't quite make sense, but in Italian, a language I don't speak, somehow it does. People can't agree what La Traviata means: a fallen woman? I prefer the most literal translation: a woman who has gone astray.

In the car, my voice sounds rounded and rich. If I'd been at choir tonight, we'd have been rehearsing some turgid Victorian hymn. I can only sing the music I love in my car. The sound quality on the Fiesta's stereo is not as spectacular as the Audi's but the journey to and from school and my Little Job is precious singing time. If I ever so much as hum when Andrew and Sasha are around, they immediately clasp their hands over their ears. *Embarrassing* Mummy …

I can't blame Sasha: children learn by example. But then I can't blame Andrew either. He's always been like this: he'd never understand why being the Little Woman no longer seems enough.

After all, it's only since Mum died that I've started to wonder that myself. Everything in my life these days is wife-sized, shrunk to fit my role. There's the Little Job at Fancy Footwork, without a chance of promotion. The Little Hobby in the choir is gone, another minor sacrifice on the altar of motherhood.

And finally there's the Little Car: the metallic ocean-coloured, double-airbagged Fiesta Andrew had delivered to our driveway (complete with a bow) when I announced I was pregnant with Sasha. 'You'll be too big for that soon,' he said, nodding at my old orange MGB. He always hated that car. It was so fundamentally un-Lucy, flamboyant and fast, hinting at the person I could have become when I left home at eighteen. I fought for that car, lived on baked beans for a year to keep up the loan repayments, so as not to give my mother the satisfaction of seeing me having to sell it on.

But that was before Andrew. He promised me I'd never go without if I married him, and he's been true to his word. It's never occurred to me before now that it might not be in his power to give me everything I need.

Sempre libera degg'io
Folleggiare di gioia in gioia,
Vo' che scorra il viver mio
Pei sentieri del piacer.

This time I remember the translation: Free and aimless I must flutter, from pleasure to pleasure, skimming the surface of life's primrose path.

And I don't think Violetta's talking about the Primrose Estate.

There has to be more than this. Could there still be? I close my eyes and imagine the heat of a spotlight, soft rose petals on my feet as the audience throw bouquets onto the stage ...

I open my eyes with a start and look at my watch. Shit. Ten to eight. I'm a good nine miles from Troughton and have to make it back to the Drill Hall by the dot of eight.

Thank God I'm in the Audi.

Chapter Nine

Let each Guide remember that her title is
LITTLE FRIEND OF ALL THE WORLD.

The wine glasses ring like bells, clinking together as I carry the tray outside. It's not really warm enough for *al fresco* drinking, but Andrew's showing no inclination to vacate the sofa to offer me and Terri any privacy. So once Sasha's in bed, we retreat to the giant litter tray, a.k.a. the back garden.

'I envy you so much, not living with someone,' I say, fiddling around trying to light the patio heater.

Terri grins. 'What, apart from the two dozen other students in my halls?'

'Yes, but you've still got a bedroom to yourself, out of bounds to everyone else. There's nowhere here that's just *mine*. Andrew's got his study and even Sasha's got her room and woe betide me if I go in without knocking.' I kick the patio heater. 'Bloody thing. Never works for me. Let me know if you want a sweater.'

'I suppose you're right about the privacy thing. But then I don't have all this, do I? The executive home and the executive husband. And I've never come within a whisker of having a garden like this, never mind a patio heater to put in it.'

'The grass is always greener. Well, any grass would be greener than this shingly stuff.' I peer out at the garden. In the dim glow of the solar lights, it resembles the surface of the moon. 'I knew I'd hate it; I told Andrew it'd look dated before they'd shipped in the tree ferns from Australia. But he ignored me. As usual.' I pour out two generous slugs of Shiraz. 'Cheers.'

Terri takes a sip before speaking. 'Every marriage goes through its ups and downs. So I'm told, anyway. Not that my parents ever got angry about anything, but then they were usually too drunk to care. I never once saw them have a full-blown row.'

'We don't row either.'

'Well, that's because you never shout at anyone, Luce. Which is all very sweet but does you no favours with Andrew. You'd have to put a banner up on the railway bridge with six-foot letters reading I AM PISSED OFF before he got the hint.'

I grin at her. 'Yes. Well, I think I told him tonight.'

'Yes, nicking his car is the other way to get your message across. Probably better than the banner, actually.'

'Yeah. Maybe. Anyway, I'm bored talking about me. Tell me how Sasha got on.'

'Luce, she was brilliant. A natural. She's already been invited to the birthday slumber party of the coolest, oldest girl in the Pack. I'm really chuffed you changed your mind – though I'm sorry about the choir and everything.'

'Well, I'm a mum after all. My life takes second place.' I look at Terri. 'Shit, that sounded bitter, didn't it? Funny though. I spent all those years not letting Mum recruit Sasha and now there she is. I wish I'd never let her in the cellar!'

'Yeah, have you got that stuff you mentioned? I'd love it to show the Brownies, if you don't want it. Or maybe the Guide Association could have it for their archives.'

I fetch the bag from the hall cupboard and hand it over. 'You're welcome to it. There's all sorts in there, not just from Mum's time as Brown Owl, but from Nana Dorothy and from Great Grandmother Agnes before her.'

Terri empties the contents onto the table. 'What are these?' she says.

'They seem to be logbooks, records of what we all did at our sessions. Who had paid their subs and who hadn't. What happened at camp.'

She frowns. 'Was there anything about ... that last camp?'

I shake my head. 'I don't see the point in looking. We all know what happened.'

Terri sighs. 'That's true.' She pulls out my old Brownie handbook, with a cheerful-looking girl in brown and yellow on the front cover. 'Bless! I always thought she looked just like you, Luce. Oh … I recognize this.' Now she's holding a navy-blue book, stained and dog-eared and held together with discoloured Sellotape. 'What?'

'It's the Little Blue Muddly,' she says, as if this explains everything.

I take it from her and read out the title in full. '*How Girls Can Help Build Up the Empire: The Handbook for Girl Guides.*'

'I can't believe Judith never showed you this,' she says. 'I mean, how could a girl possibly cope without …' she opens a page at random, 'knowing how to deal with a runaway horse or a rabid dog,' she flicks the pages again, 'or hearing the riveting story of The Coachman whose Wife Never Gave Him Kidneys for Breakfast.'

I reach over to snatch it from her. 'You're having me on.' I look through it myself. 'God, you're not, are you? Look at this.' I point at a tiny line drawing of a bowl with two frogs in it, one dead at the bottom and the other crouching at the top of what looks like an iceberg. I read out loud: 'Two frogs fall into a bowl of cream – as you do, of course – and one "sank to the bottom and was drowned through having no pluck. But the other was a more manly frog and struggled to swim using his arms and legs as hard as he could to keep himself afloat."'

'Oh how I long for a manly frog,' Terri says.

I read on. '"Just as he was getting so tired that he thought he must give up, a curious thing happened. By his hard work he had churned up the cream so much that he suddenly found himself standing all safe on a pat of butter." Bloody hell, Terri, you couldn't make it up!'

'See, I told you there'd be some good stuff.'

I keep leafing through. 'I might keep this, if that's all right. I need a good laugh at the moment.'

'Sure,' she says. 'And there's nothing else you want?'

I rummage in the carrier bag. 'Only this.'

'Ooooh,' she says, clapping her hands together as I hold up the photograph. 'Oh, look at us. Take away the wrinkles and we haven't changed a bit.'

'That's what Sasha said when I showed it to her. She was asking about the others, and I told her about Paula being a tomboy. And she asked me what Paula did now and I remembered the last time I saw her, in the shop. She was fat and ... kind of defeated. When I told Sasha she was a mum, all she said was "boring". And she's right. It is.'

'You're not just a mum.'

'Oh yes. There's my executive job in Fancy Footwork, too. How could I forget?'

Terri frowns at me. 'You know you're capable of more than that. What about that job at the Mermaid?'

I wince. It was only Terri's persistent nagging that persuaded me to apply for Assistant Manager at the Mermaid, Troughton's theatre and arts centre. And when they offered me the job, two years ago this summer, I knew it was too good to be true, working with actors and musicians and creative types. As Andrew said, it was all very well, but how was I planning to juggle looking after Sasha and working so many evenings? It wasn't a job for a mum. 'That was a pipe dream, Terri.'

'The people at the Mermaid didn't think so, did they? You're being very hard on yourself, Luce.'

'Don't get me wrong, I know I'm lucky. Look at Mum, a widow by the time she was my age, and never finding anyone else. Same with Nana Dorothy. But looking at the photo, I just wondered if things should have turned out different ... better, I suppose. Weren't we meant to be out there smashing the glass ceiling?'

Terri raises her eyebrows. 'I don't really believe in destiny. We make our own choices. At least we had some, unlike our mothers.'

'I know, but we've wasted them. I've been blaming Mum for indoctrinating me via the Brownies into being a little housewife, but then I thought about it properly, and it wasn't like that at all, was it? Look at the badges – Discoverer. Athletics. Music. I mean, I could have done something with that, couldn't I? Instead I moan about being trapped. I admit, this house isn't a bad place to be trapped. But—' I stop short. 'Bloody hell, I haven't even drunk that much. I'm in the weirdest mood these days. Sorry.'

Terri smiles at me. 'You know, you're not trapped if you don't want to be. If you're *really* unhappy, you don't have to stay here.'

'I thought you were meant to believe in marriage?'

'I do. But I also believe in the people I lo— I care about being happy.'

I shake my head. 'I'd never leave Andrew,' I say, automatically. 'I don't want Sasha to grow up without a dad. I wouldn't wish that on anyone. She has to do better than we did. That's the point of having kids, isn't it? To give them what you couldn't have.'

'Don't worry,' she says soothingly. 'Sasha's a survivor. We all are, aren't we?'

I laugh. 'Is there any choice? But you're more than that. You've got your vocation and everything.'

'Took me long enough. And without your mum, I don't know if I'd ever have found it.'

I frown, then take a breath and ask the question I can only ask Terri, because she's too honest to lie. 'I was a big disappointment to her. Wasn't I?'

'No ...' Terri tries to sound convincing. 'I loved your mum, Luce, but she wasn't perfect. Sometimes ... well, sometimes I think she was too tough on you. It works with bossy types like me. But not you. In the last few months, she told me she felt guilty.'

'Guilty? Mum?'

'I know. What did she always say? "Looking back's for idiots; you have to look forward to see where you're going." But the cancer made her more reflective. She wondered what the point had been of her life. Whether the Brownies was any help. Whether she'd done anything useful. I mean, how daft. Your mum!'

I pick up the photograph again. 'I bet Paula wishes she'd never got involved, though. Do you remember, this was taken the last night at camp over at Bethany's?'

She winces. 'I remember. Do you think Simonetta knew already?'

I study her face. 'Hard to tell. She never gave anything away, did she? I wonder where the hell she is now.'

Terri twists a curl from her fringe round her finger, tightening it so her skin is as red as her hair. 'Your mum ... she asked me to try to find out. Not Simonetta specifically, but all the Pixies.'

I stare at her. 'Bloody hell. Why did she do that?'

'I suppose it's partly about what I said: trying to work out if she'd made a difference. And I suspect it was also about Simonetta. For all of her "don't look back" philosophy, perhaps your mum felt somehow that if she'd never let Netta join the Brownies, then maybe her father wouldn't have been able to create such havoc.'

'Maybe she was right about that.'

'Come on, Bruno Castigliano would have found a way to infiltrate Buckingham Palace. Troughton high society was a doddle.'

I mull it over. 'Hmm. But maybe he wouldn't have caught so many people up in the mess. Did you manage to find Netta?'

'No. I'm no private detective. Bruno spent his life on the move, so who knows where she ended up. The others were easy. Paula was in the phone book, and I found some newspaper cuttings about Chris and her sex empire.'

I giggle. 'Sasha was most impressed when I told her Chris was loaded, but I didn't explain how she got it. What about Bethany?'

'I couldn't find her home address, but I gave Judith her agent's details.'

I try to puzzle it out. 'I wonder what Mum was going to do with it.'

Terri tries to cover up a yawn, then looks at her watch. 'I think she wanted to write to them all. Maybe she wanted to remind them of the good times. Also—' She stops speaking.

'What? You were going to say something.'

'She was worried about you, how you'd manage, I think. There's me and Andrew, but I think she hoped if she wrote to the Pixies, they might get in touch, you know. You need your friends at a time like this, don't you? Old friends.'

I peer into the darkness. 'God. Talk about Be Prepared. That's so typical of her, planning ahead for after she's ... shit, I am *not* going to cry again.'

'She did love you, Lucy.'

'I know.' But I feel a slight twinge of irritation: Mum didn't trust me to manage once she'd gone. Maybe she was right.

At the far end of the garden, Buster begins to miaow insistently. Then, suddenly, he shoots back into the house, kicking up the white shingle with such force that a haze of chalky powder hovers in the air for a moment after he's disappeared.

'What's got into him?' Terri says.

'Terri ... you're going to think I'm mad, but you don't ever get the feeling that she's still, I don't know, *here* somehow?'

'What, that was Judith? Putting the fear of God into Buster?' She smiles. 'Oh Luce, I don't think you're mad. I've had a few strange moments, too. Maybe it's just that we miss her and we're not quite ready to accept she's gone yet. It's not easy. No one expects you to get over it in a few weeks or anything.'

'Andrew does.'

Terri drains her wine. 'I know I'm not his biggest fan, but perhaps he feels clueless. You know how men like to feel useful. Women are so much better at times like these, which is why ...' She hesitates. 'I've been thinking of getting everyone back together. The Pixies, I mean, like your mum wanted. I'd like to do it and could try to organize it, if you like.'

I think it over. A few weeks ago, I'd have laughed at the idea: get back together with the bloody Brownies? But I do feel lonely: decades of married life ahead of me, punctuated only by short journeys in my Fiesta, and disparaging comments from my closest living relatives. 'I'll think about it,' I say eventually.

She beams. 'Terrific. I'll start making some plans.'

'I didn't say yes! I said I'll think about it,' I protest, but something tells me the battle's already lost.

'You know I wouldn't do anything you didn't want,' she says. Then she reaches out awkwardly to touch my hand. Hers is hot and I realize I must be freezing. 'Time to go in, I think, Lucy. But we will have you on the mend before long. Leave it to me ...'

April 1979: A new Brownie joins the Pixies

Bethany Kendal stared at the new girl, then looked back at Brown Owl.

'We're perfectly happy as a five. Why can't the Sprites have her?'

Judith Gill gave her a stern Brown Owl stare. 'Because it's your turn. And that's not much of a welcome, Bethany. You're a Sixer now. You have responsibilities.'

'I just think that the Sprites already have Heather so they're more used to dealing with foreigners—'

'Heather is Scottish, Bethany. That's hardly foreign. And hardly the point. We Brownies are an international movement; we make friends across the oceans.'

'But we can't speak Italian.' Bethany pouted and tossed her head, sending her plaits up into the air with a huffy 'whoosh' before they landed loudly on her back.

She'd been a right little madam even before she was picked as cover girl for the Official Brownie Annual last Christmas but now Bethany was insufferable. Judith would never have put the girl's name forward, but thanks to some misguided experiment in democracy, every Pack in the country had been asked to nominate their candidate to be the face of the movement this year. And once Bethany had secured the votes of the 2nd Troughton Brownies, using a combination of flattery, threats, Sherbet Dib-Dabs, and offers to ride her piebald pony, Dobbin, the result was inevitable. The competition judges in London had fallen for her enormous blue eyes, her long blonde curls, her damson cheeks and lips, her creamy complexion, and her armful of badges, from Artist to Water Rescuer.

If ever there was evidence that beauty was only skin deep, surely it was Bethany. The face of an angel, the morals and cunning of Richard Nixon.

And Judith knew that the real reason Bethany was objecting to this particular new recruit had nothing to do with language difficulties. It was because the new recruit was too pretty.

'Well, it's a good job Simonetta's half English, isn't it?' Brown Owl turned to the others. 'Come on, girls. Give her a proper Brownie greeting.'

Paula opened her mouth to do just that, but Terri nudged her under the table. They were all waiting for Bethany's permission. Finally, she nodded, without smiling. Lucy took her cue and shyly held out her hand to the shocked Simonetta. Judith felt a rare sense of pride at her daughter's good manners.

'Welcome to the Pixies, Simon—'

'It's See-monetta,' said Simonetta firmly. She was tall for a nine-year-old, with pale English skin, eyes as dark as black olives, and uncontrollable Italian hair. The latter gathered in wiry ringlets on her shoulders. Perhaps pretty was the wrong word. Simonetta was a striking child and it was clear that she would soon become a more striking young woman.

'Seemon ... See ... mon ... etta.' Lucy tried it out slowly. She'd have looked nice on the cover of the annual, but Judith couldn't have voted for her own daughter. Lucy had her share of Brownie qualities: kindness, cheerfulness, obedience, patience, modesty, loyalty. Oh, and her voice. So sweet that often Judith couldn't bear to hear it, wanted to hold her hands to her ears to block out the memories it triggered.

Though they'd all heard less of the voice recently. Lucy had started mouthing the words during the weekly singsong. Judith suspected it was because of bullying by Bethany, whose own voice reflected her personality: strident and as sour as month-old milk. The girl's rendition of 'Matchstick Men and Matchstick Cats and Dogs' at the Christmas Gang Show last year was three minutes of out-of-tune torture, but no one dared say so. Hell would freeze over before Lucy stood up to her Sixer.

That was the trouble with Lucy: too many 'nice qualities' and a complete absence of the qualities she really needed to survive: guts, determination, the 'frontier spirit' that the first Girl Guide leaders had tried so hard to engender. Because, after all, there was no point in having a British Empire if its daughters didn't have the stamina to live in its outposts. For a movement with a reputation for turning girls into little women, the Brownies had a surprisingly subversive side. That's why Judith had pushed Lucy so hard to join up, where a more laid-back mother would have let her sit reading or making daisy chains in the huge garden at the Old Surgery. Judith's own attempts to escape Troughton had ended in disaster: she didn't want the same to happen to her daughter.

It would have done Lucy the world of good to have been chosen for the front of the annual, built up her confidence. But it was unlikely she'd have been picked by HQ, because her mother had to admit she was only, at best, averagely pretty and a little chubby. She had the Quentin build, stout and powerful, but without the gumption. In that respect, Judith thought, she took after her father.

Terri held out her freckly hand. 'Pleased to meet you. Simonetta. That's a ... pretty name,' she said uncertainly. Good old Big Bird. Terri could be clumsy with people but there was no girl in the Pack who tried harder.

Bethany mulled it over, like a judge considering an important point of constitutional law. 'I think it's silly. Like a boy's name.'

So Bethany wasn't going to give up. Judith wondered for a moment whether she'd done the right thing, whether Simonetta might have been better off in the Sprites, rather than being used as a pawn in this power struggle. But the new girl didn't flinch. Was it defiance, or was she just used to keeping her emotions in check? There was something behind Simonetta's self-contained expression that was unfathomable.

'And your name? Bethan-eee?' A gain, Simonetta spoke quietly and neutrally. 'To me, it sounds like an illness.'

Bethany stepped back as if she'd been slapped, while the other Brownies stared at the new girl: Terri and Lucy with concern, Chris with her usual head-so-far-in-the-clouds-she-was-virtually-airborne confusion, and Paula with a hint of admiration. She smiled. 'Do you play football, Simonetta?'

'I've never tried. But the Italians are the best footballers in the world.'

'Don't be silly,' Paula said, but she was grinning. 'Everyone knows the best footballers in the world come from Manchester.'

'Do we have to discuss football?' said Bethany, trying to regain control. 'We've wasted enough time on Simonetta –' she was still pronouncing it 'S-eye-monetta', challenging the new girl to correct her '– never mind rubbish like football. We should be practising putting arms in slings. Come on, girls.' And she turned her back to head towards the Pixie home corner.

As the others followed, Paula winked at Simonetta and she winked back.

Judith tried not to smile. Bethany was still Queen of the 2nd Troughton Brownies, but at last, it seemed, her reign was under threat.

It was about bloody time.

It was raining hard when the girls came back into the Brownie circle for vespers, and the gaggle of mums gathered in the Drill Hall porch, sweating in their pac-a-macs and listening to the water swishing down the guttering. Judith could hear the women chuntering, without being able to distinguish the words. She had nothing in common with them. It would have been easy, when she'd first come back to Troughton from Manchester five years ago, to make friends. She'd agreed to her mother Dorothy's suggestion of taking over as Brown Owl, to keep her busy, and soon she was surrounded by inquisitive mothers, as enrolments in the Pack saw a sudden increase. They knew the official story, how she'd headed for home after the mysterious and tragic death of her young doctor husband (it was like a storyline from *General Hospital*), and they were sympathetic in a ghoulish way, hoping to be rewarded for their compassion with the full details.

But she'd knocked them back, ever so politely. A second opportunity had come a couple of years ago, when Lucy had joined the Pixies. Parents of girls in the same Six tended to form a loose bond, as they tracked the twists and turns of friendship which could see a child in tears of despair at lost kinship one meeting, and glowing with happiness the next after a reconciliation brokered over a packet of Wagon Wheels.

But again, Judith had chosen to stay on the outside. What did she have in common with Paula's tarty mum Patsy, whose clumsy attempts at social climbing made her cringe? Or with Dina, Chris's mother, a dour woman in her early forties who rarely smiled and clearly felt she was a cut above the rest because she worked at the bank? Bethany's parents were separated – the rumour was that her mum had run off with her Open University lecturer and gone to live in a squat in Notting Hill – so Bethany lived with her businessman father in a vulgar Southfork-style mansion a couple of miles outside Troughton: her dad had his chauffeur deliver her to and from the Drill Hall.

Perhaps the most natural ally might have been Terri's mother, Lorna. But in contrast to the tenacious little girl Judith was so fond of, Lorna was the definition of lethargic. Judith wasn't sure if it was due to vodka, Valium, or a combination of the two, but in any case Lorna hardly ever turned up to the Drill Hall, expecting her daughter to walk the mile home on her own. Once Judith realized, she always gave Terri a lift and longed to ask her if there was anything she could do. But knowing how much she herself resented intrusion, Judith kept quiet.

The truth was, she found the company of these women utterly depressing. Their suburban preoccupations only reminded her of how hard she'd fought to get away and how much she missed Jim and their friends and a life that had revolved around parties and music, and, yes, drugs. Together, the young medics and student nurses formed this large, but somehow still tight-knit group who were constantly faced with the reality of suffering and death during their working hours, and who consequently lived their off-duty lives as if tomorrow was the only thing to be afraid of. It was the sixties after all.

But they'd been wrong. When tomorrow came, when the seventies arrived and Jim died, there was so much more to be afraid of. Of days and months and years that stretched ahead, of the fact that she wanted to die, but couldn't because Lucy was meant to be her reason for living. Of the ultimate unfairness, that Jim, who'd spent so long trying to heal people, couldn't heal himself and died alone with no one to help him.

What the hell did these Troughton women know? They'd never been anywhere, never tried to escape. That was why Judith preferred the company of children. At least girls still had a chance, and at least she might be able to make a difference.

'Also, we pray oh Lord, for the poor children in foreign countries where people don't have enough to eat or even enough to feed their ponies.' Bethany had volunteered to read out a prayer she'd composed. She wasn't a pious child, but she'd managed to write something that would keep her the centre of attention for a good four minutes. 'We pray for them, although they are not as civilized, in places like Africa and Mexico and ... Italy.'

She sneaked a look up at Judith and Judith frowned back. What a nasty piece of work. But the girls kept their eyes closed and their heads bowed. They always looked at their most innocent during final prayers.

Suddenly there was a commotion in the porch. Judith looked up to see a dark head of hair towering above the transparent rain hats of the mums. The hair was curly and was attached to a large man who emerged through the women like Jesus parting the Red Sea. Except on closer examination, he looked more like John Travolta than Jesus. He wore a broad smile and a beige suit with huge lapels, like the one Travolta had in *Saturday Night Fever*, the only film in history that the *Troughton Tribune* had tried to ban, due to excessive innuendo and swearing.

He seemed oblivious to the prayers, turning to each woman and grasping her hand and repeating, 'Hello, I am Bruno. I am delighted to make your acquaintance.' The accent was trattoria Italian, the voice opera-strong. He must be Simonetta's father. Not what she'd expected, having met her mousy mother.

The girls were opening their eyes, the shyer ones peering through the gaps between their fingers and even Bethany paused in the prayer, relinquishing her position in the limelight to look at the man.

Judith clapped her hands. 'Right, girls.' Her voice was loud, determined. She'd teach this interloper who was boss. 'Nearly home time, but first let's sing Brownie Bells. "Oh Lord our God ..."'

The girls joined in and Lucy had clearly forgotten to mime, because her voice rose above the others, giving Judith goose-bumps.

'Thy children call. Grant us thy peace. And bless us all ...'

'Goodnight, goodnight.'

'Great work tonight, Brownies. Same time next week and don't forget your subs; you know who I'm talking to.'

There was a scramble as the girls leapt up and to the sides of the hall to retrieve coats and umbrellas. Judith turned to begin packing away the practice bandages, then felt a light tap on her shoulder. Before turning around, she knew it was the Italian.

'Hello. I am—'

'Don't tell me, let me guess! You're Bruno and you're de-lighted to make my acquaintance?' Judith knew she was being rude, but she didn't care.

But he just smiled back and held out his hand. Reluctantly she held out hers and for a moment she thought he was going to raise it to his lips to kiss it. She could smell lemons and something else ... garlic? 'I am so sorry I interrupted your prayers. It was a lovely thing to listen to, those children, they sounded so ... sincere.' The accent was less showy now.

Judith felt flustered. 'Yes, well. That's because they are.' She didn't know what else to say.

'To me, nothing should be said unless it is sincere. Children have that; they won't say what they do not mean, but we adults ... we lose this.' He looked into her eyes. 'So I hope you will know I speak the truth when I say I *am* delighted to meet you.'

Despite the implausible accent, the extravagant lapels and the gigolo eyes – she'd just noticed how dark they were, nearly black under the dim hall lights – Judith thought she did believe him. 'I'm Judith. Judith Gill. Otherwise known as Brown Owl.'

'And which of those should I call you?' His eyes flicked towards her ring finger, then back to her face. 'No, no, don't answer, let me decide. I should like to call you Brown Owl. In Italian, *allocco* ... It sounds nice, yes?'

It had been so long since it had happened that Judith couldn't be sure, but she thought he was flirting with her. She felt hot and awkward. 'Well, it is what your daughter's going to call me, so why not? *Simonetta!*' She called the girl away from chatting to Paula.

Bruno opened his arms wide in an exaggerated gesture, and his daughter raised her eyebrows at him before granting him a cursory kiss on the cheek. 'My Netta has always wanted to join Brownies, but we have never been able to stay in a single place for long enough before. Now, it is different. Troughton is going to be *home*.'

He said it with such passion that for a moment, Judith saw her town through a stranger's eyes: the nosiness that could be mistaken for community spirit, the tumbledown mill-workers' cottages that might seem picturesque, the carnivals and the festivals and the other parochial gatherings on the claustrophobic calendar of events that you might crave had you not been brought up here and tried so hard to get away.

'Well, Mr Cast ... Castog ...' She stumbled over the name.

'Bruno.' It was a fait accompli.

'Well, Bruno, and Simonetta. Welcome to Troughton.' And Judith had to stop herself adding, *I only hope you'll be happier here than I am.*

Chapter Ten

'Tenderfoots' have always been looked down upon by the natives as being unable to march far or to endure long, incapable of suffering trials and ignorant of all the arts of living in uncivilized lands.

It's Thursday lunchtime, broad daylight, but I don't think I've ever felt this vulnerable. The sign that reads *Welcome to the Primrose Estate, home to our community since 1966*, is the gateway to an unfamiliar world.

The yellow flower emblem has been transformed with black marker pen into a skull and crossbones. The graffiti scratched into the metal proclaims that Sheryl Cummins is a slapper. The Primrose is only thirteen minutes' walk along the canal from Troughton's pedestrian precinct, but it feels like Bosnia, not Cheshire.

The estate is a giant concrete figure of eight, with flats along each inside edge, in two storeys. The concrete offers the perfect canvas for more graffiti (I learn from the scribblings that, in fact, every member of the Cummins family has an active sex life and several are particularly close to their pets). The flats in the bottom row each have a patch of weeds the size of a small hatchback. This isn't a guess: there's the shell of a Mini Metro, wheel- and windscreen-less, on the front 'lawn' of the first flat I come to.

I'm trying to find number sixteen Clover House, but the feeling of being watched is playing havoc with my concentration.

There's no sign of life, but there are dozens of windows facing me. Behind each one a gang could be tracking my movements through no-man's-land, organizing an ambush. I pull the piece of paper with the address from my handbag and then curse myself for bringing a purse full of cash. The muggers of the Primrose would have rich pickings with me today.

Each side of the square seems to be named after a different flower. Honeysuckle is behind me, and a little sign shows that Poppy is on my left and Daisy on my right. Which means, hopefully, that Clover is straight ahead. I keep to the path, taking shallow breaths, ready for an attack.

Number sixteen has a battered front door, painted primer-grey: whoever started the DIY obviously lost the will to live halfway through the job. There's an electric bell, below which is written *Tucker* in faded biro. I press it once, briefly, but can't hear whether it makes any noise inside the flat. I try again. Nothing.

Bloody Terri and her bright ideas. 'Why don't you drop in on Paula? See whether she might fancy meeting up again.'

I only agreed to come because I was pretty sure she'd be less keen than I am, putting an end to Terri's stupid idea without me actually having to do the deed myself.

Oh, and there was the tiniest touch of nosiness, too, I'll admit.

Still no one at the door. I look down at my shoes – they're my current favourites, a spring-like round-toed pair in pink, with tiny bows at each ankle. Below my feet, forgotten forget-me-nots are thrusting through the cracks in the concrete paving, the only sign of life I've seen on the estate so far. Maybe Paula has moved.

'You won't get an answer from Paula before two.' A scrawny middle-aged woman in a velour tracksuit steps out from the next-door porch. 'Her kids are in school. For once. The social must have been on to her.' The woman's missing most of her teeth, but it doesn't stop her gnawing open-mouthed on a large piece of chewing gum. 'You'll know that, though. You'll be from the social yourself.'

'No, not exactly. An old friend.'

'A *friend*?' The woman sounds like she doesn't believe me. 'Right you are, then.' And she disappears into her house, as if anyone willing to admit to being a friend of Paula is clearly dangerous.

I step up to the window and try to see inside Paula's flat, but there's a stained net curtain in the way and however much I try to defocus my eyes – the way Sasha does when she's looking at one of those Magic Eye pictures – I can't work out if someone's inside. All I can see is the collection of fat, dead flies on the sill.

Finally, I try rattling the letterbox. 'Hello?' There's post on the floor and a musty smell as I call through the gap. 'Paula, hello?'

There's the sound of stirring from somewhere inside the flat. I wait ... and wait. Just as I crouch down to see if I can see anyone moving through the letterbox, the door opens. As I straighten up, I can't help myself. 'Oh!'

The creature in front of me is like a giant toddler in a grey sleep suit. Just for a moment, I feel this surge of hope and amusement, that Terri's made a mistake and her amateur sleuthing has led her to the wrong Paula Tucker, some other unfortunate sentenced to life on the Primrose Estate. No matter what the crime, no one deserves that.

'What the hell—?'

But the gruff voice is the same as it ever was. I try to restore my face to neutral. Paula's angry stare changes into a puzzled smile as she recognizes me.

'Lucy? What are you doing ...?' Then she remembers. 'Oh, God. I had a letter. I'm sorry to hear about your mother.'

'Thanks.' I'm mesmerized by the rolls of fat enclosed by the faded material. Paula's far bigger now than when she turned up in Fancy Footwork that time. And the streaks of white in her mousy, chin-length hair have also spread.

Paula looks worried. 'Oh no, I've upset you now. It must still be really hard. Would you like to come in?' She frowns. 'It's not very tidy, but ...'

I nod. It's better that Paula thinks I'm upset rather than realizes it's her blubber that's silenced me. As I step inside, the stale smell is stronger and the wallpaper is peeling in the hall.

'Come on through.' Paula leads the way and the layers of her body ripple as she walks, each movement creating a new chain reaction from legs to hips, waist and arms, like one of those executive toys with the silver balls that knock against each other.

We end up in a living room with a thin oblong window overlooking the grassless central square of the estate: the room beyond the grubby lace curtain I'd tried to peer through. It's not quite as depressing as it looked from the outside: there's a bright red rug across the brown carpet, and some fake pink flowers in a pot on the glass coffee table. Next to a plate of toast crusts. Paula grabs it. 'Oh, those kids!' she tuts.

My eyes drift towards the brick-built fireplace and the family photos on the mantelpiece. The most recent shows two surly teens sneering at the camera: a boy of maybe fifteen, wearing a black rapper T-shirt, and a younger girl whose mousy hair betrays the unsubtle streaks of experiments with Sun-In.

Paula pulls a face. 'The gruesome twosome. They were so cute when they were little.'

I nod. 'We all were!' I wonder if Sasha will turn into a monster when she hits her teens.

'Would you like some tea, duck?'

I look at my watch. 'No, thank you. I can't be late back. There'll be anarchy on the shop floor if the girls don't get away for lunch on time.'

'You still working in the shoe shop?' There's a hint of derision in Paula's voice.

'Yep. What about you?'

'Running a multinational in between my modelling assignments.'

I smile obligingly. 'Really?'

'No. Unemployed and unemployable, that's me.'

'Oh I'm sure that's not true, if you wanted to—'

'What, get on my bike and look for work? It'd have to be reinforced first. There's not many options for fat, lazy women. I mean, you wouldn't have me in your shop, would you?'

'Um ... I don't see why not,' I say, hoping my lie isn't too obvious. In truth, I can't imagine Paula'd be able to make it up and down the stairs to the stockroom. Everything about her is making me feel depressed.

Paula sighs. 'I'll believe you; thousands wouldn't. Anyway, I mustn't keep you from stiletto sales.'

'Right. Thanks.' I pick my handbag up from the floor and resist the urge to dust it off. I can't wait to get out of here.

'Aren't you forgetting something, duck?' Paula's smiling now, and I catch a glimpse of who she used to be. In the Pixies, her face was permanently set into a cheeky grin, so you could never be sure if she'd done anything naughty or not. As I look around for what I've dropped, she says, 'Like, maybe, the reason you came round here?'

'Oh! Yes, good point. Well, the thing is ...' I wonder whether I can bluff my way out of this. I've seen enough to know that spending any more time with Paula definitely won't help my recovery. But what if she's desperate enough to say yes? 'Terri and I were talking, you know, about the old days. And, um, she thought it might be nice to get together. The Pixies reunited.'

Paula shrugs. 'I don't remember those days as being so bloody amazing that I want to repeat them.'

'Exactly!' I say, relieved. 'It was such a bore. I only said I'd come to get Terri off my back.' But her eyes have gone all distant.

'Mind you, thinking about it, they were better than now,' she continues and for a moment her face is so empty of hope that I can't catch my breath.

'Oh come on, I'm sure it's not as bad as all that.' I sound like my mother, though less convincing.

She sinks down into the sofa. 'Wanna bet? A fiver says it is that bad. Go on. I could do with the cash.'

'Well, what about your family? I know the teens are going through that difficult stage, but ...' I rack my brains for something else. 'And what about your husband? At least you're not alone.'

'I'd quit while you're ahead, Lucy. Neil's gone. The kids'll be gone soon. So should you. You know when there's an accident and the police say, "Move along, there's nothing to see," well, that's like me. It's too late. All over.'

And I'm the person who came to gawp. I feel hot with shame at my reasons for visiting. 'But that's not true, Paula. We're still young women. You used to be so—'

'Used to be. We all used to be things we're not. You were going to be an opera singer. Bethany was going to live in Hollywood. My mum and dad were going to be rich. Oh and, as I remember it, the Pixies were going to be friends for keeps. Hah!'

'But that's why I'm here!' I say, having a brainwave. 'Because I know I used to moan all the time, but if you rack your brains, there were good times! You were so brilliant when we used to do the team games. And the parties and the good deeds and the—'

'You hated it even more than I did, Lucy. What are you talking about?'

I plough on, realizing suddenly that Paula needs us far more than she ever did when she was seven. 'Well, we didn't know how lucky we were, did we? The camp fires and the camp fire songs ...' I slow down slightly, grasping for good memories. 'Nature trails ... and the gang shows and the camp fire songs ...'

'That's the second time you've mentioned the camp fire songs. But you're forgetting the bitching and the way Bethany used to bully you and the fact that you were in tears half the time.' She shakes her head sadly. 'Maybe grief has affected your memory.'

The grief? Oh yes, the grief. For a moment, just a second, I was so busy trying to persuade Paula that I forgot to be sad. It gives me an idea. 'Yes. You're probably right,' I say, biting my lip. 'I have been feeling very low. I think that's why Terri wanted us all to get together, but I completely understand why you're not keen. I'd better be going.'

She blushes. 'Lucy, I'm sorry. I'm so wrapped up in my own dramas that I'm not thinking straight. I'm so selfish. Listen, if you think it'll help, then yeah, I'd be up for an evening out. It's not like I have a packed social calendar.'

I try not to smile in satisfaction. Eat your heart out, Bethany Kendal. These days, even silly Lucy knows a bit about emotional blackmail. Though at least I'm using it for Paula's own good. 'Great! Thank you, Paula.'

'It'll have to be somewhere dark, though. And cheap. I never was one to watch the pennies, was I?'

I remember my mother's frustration when Paula forgot her subs week after week. 'No. I'd better go, now, Paula. I'm sorry to hear about your husband.'

'Oh. Don't be. Husbands aren't what they're cracked up to be, are they? Lucky escape for him and me, I reckon.'

As I walk through the door, I wonder what I've just talked us both into.

Chapter Eleven

Every year numbers of lives are lost by panics, which very often are due to the smallest causes and which might be stopped if one or two persons would keep their heads.

'Oh, fuck.' Chris knew all her staff were watching, but she couldn't help swearing. She felt the newsprint smudging under her fingers as she began to sweat. *Stay calm*, she told herself, then looked up at the expectant faces of the people who needed her reassurance and relied on her for their rent.

'Well, all I can say is, we must be doing something right if we're in this much demand!' The mood changed instantly as people smiled at her joke, nodded at each other.

'Listen, guys. I promise, this is the first I've heard of any takeover plans, but I can tell you for nothing that I haven't built up the business just to let someone else come in and turn it into another anonymous chain. And I haven't put together the most talented bunch of people around, to have them replaced by a load of suits. OK?'

They mumbled their agreement and then drifted back to their desks. She stood up and hoped no one noticed how unsteady she felt on her feet. 'Geoff, can I have a word?'

Her operations manager followed Chris into her office and shut the door. 'So, tell me straight. How does it look?'

Geoff was the only person in Love Bites who was older than Chris, five years her senior, with a market-trader's fast brain, a track record in retailing, and a thirst for profit only matched by a love of Scotch. Broad as a bulldog, with the same determined jaw, he had a high opinion of himself, which most people in the business shared, although few actually liked him. Chris had recruited Geoff when she floated the company, knowing she needed someone more ruthless than she was, with the drive to put her ideas into practice. So far, he hadn't let her down.

He looked again at the *Financial Times* article, a few short paragraphs of rumour that Eros, the international sex aids company, had been courting shareholders in Love Bites, and might be planning to launch a hostile takeover bid. The piece quoted an unnamed source as saying that Eros management were interested in the 'cheeky, funky boutique approach' to roll out across half their city centre stores. It was the opposite of Chris's slow, considered expansion plans.

'Well, it's up to the shareholders. We knew it was a risk when we floated. I'd be flattered if I were you.'

His seen-it-all-before tone instantly made Chris feel better. She stared through the tinted glass window, out at the minimalist office beyond. All those people. She felt a mother's need to protect them from the big bad multinational. 'So what are our options?'

Geoff smiled his rakish smile. He knew Chris wasn't ever going to succumb to his raddled sexual charms, but he relished the moments when he could give her the benefit of his wisdom. 'We've gotta fight. You're gonna have to get on your glad rags, head for the Smoke and dazzle the major shareholders while I fight dirty behind the scenes. It means moving faster with our growth plans, though.'

'But I don't want us to lose control—'

'The shareholders aren't going to give a shit about the niceties, Chris. They want the best return and we've got to convince them they'll get that staying faithful to you and not through a quickie with Eros.' He cast a lascivious look down her body, dwelling on her breasts. 'But you might need to spice things up a bit, to keep them keen.'

She nodded. 'Right. Have you got any plans for the next month, Geoff?'

'Nothing I can't cancel for you, boss.' He always called her boss, though she knew he thought he could make or break her on a whim.

'Fantastic. Get Kian to pull in a few takeaway menus for lunch. And for dinner. I have a feeling it's going to be a late one.'

Standing outside the warehouse conversion that was Love Bites HQ, Terri was suddenly having doubts about her plans for a Pixie reunion. And on a practical level, she was terrified of entering Chris's designer sex empire.

It was all very well being a virgin at eighteen … maybe as old as twenty-one. It was cute, in a slightly saccharine *True Love Waits*, knit-your-own-yogurt kind of way. But at thirty-five, it was looking pretty terminal and the religious objections began to look like an excuse, rather than a choice. Her role models would be Ann Widdecombe and … Terri struggled. Even the Vicar of Dibley had a lusty outlook on life.

Colin's persistence wasn't paying off. His unsubtle overtures while they were in bed, accidentally on purpose rolling over onto her or spooning too enthusiastically first thing in the morning, were counterproductive. The two of them did – how would Judith have put it? – mess around below the waist. And she didn't blame him for wanting more. But she wasn't ready. Perhaps some people were simply undersexed. It was just her luck to have been born into a society obsessed with the whole business.

But a fear of seeming unworldly in front of Chris wasn't her only concern. Her own grief at Judith's death was so all-encompassing right now, that the idea of a reunion 'helping Lucy feel better' seemed trite in the extreme.

Terri's pain bubbled to the surface at unexpected times, like the last Brownie meeting. As Sasha took her rightful place in the Pack – there was a future Brown Owl if ever there was one – Terri felt that emptiness again, and an anger that Judith hadn't lived to see her granddaughter join. She'd taken refuge in the dark storecupboard, among the Brownie pennants. *2nd Troughton Brownies, Lending a Hand since 1947.* But who would lend Terri a hand? That was the trouble with being super-capable: there was no one to turn to when you had a crisis of your own.

Judith had understood. There was no question of a shoulder to cry on, because neither woman believed tears served any purpose, but they'd sit together and discuss Terri's latest feckless boyfriend or work crisis, like two academics faced with an interesting maths problem, determined to make the numbers add up.

Being understood. That was the difference between humans and animals. God, of course, was Top of the Pops when it came to understanding, but it wasn't the same as a hug or a held hand or simply hearing the words, 'I know how you feel.'

Terri wished she could be like Lucy and ask for help, but she always felt detached from people. She'd been an efficient nurse, cajoling her patients to eat or take tentative steps after surgery, but she lacked the warmth that earned her more approachable colleagues cards and chocolates. While the 'angels' were kissed goodbye when a patient left the hospital, she was left out: they didn't want to embarrass her.

Maybe the Pixies were right and she was unforgivably bossy. Who was she to tell Lucy what was wrong in her marriage? Or to set Colin a target of Christmas for finishing his movie script? It didn't work, anyway. Colin was still on page six, and Lucy would never stand up to Andrew.

Nothing was making sense. At college she was nodding off in lectures, while in bed, in her nightmares, long-forgotten classmates turned their backs on her, laughing. Terri blinked, and shook her head to try to concentrate on the matter in hand: talking Chris into the reunion. Maybe it would help. She'd run out of other things to try. She stepped up into the doorway to view the six buzzers, each sporting a logo alongside the button. *i-Candy Web Hosting ... Cool-Hunters North ...The Brainstorm Works ...*

Level Four, Love Bites.

She sighed before pressing the button. A chirpy male voice answered and then buzzed her through. By the time she reached the fourth floor, Terri was out of breath. A youth with bleached streaks and a piercing in his cheek greeted her. 'Hiya! I'm Kian. Welcome to Love Bites central!'

Terri nodded – she didn't have the oxygen to form words – and stepped into the abyss.

Instead of the dungeon-like moral vacuum she'd been expecting, the office looked ... well, rather a lot like an office. A very *trendy* office, the sleek gunmetal desks contrasting with the weathered plank floor and the whitewashed brick walls. There were huge fishermen's lamps suspended from the ceilings, supplementing the light from the big windows. Terri thought the overall effect would have been rather institutional if it wasn't for the brightly dressed kids who populated the office. As well as cheek-pierced Kian, who didn't look more than seventeen, there were three girls sitting at their desks, though they didn't seem to be doing much work. One was openly reading a magazine, and the other two were giggling over something on their computer screens. In the corner, around a strange protean-shaped table, were another two girls and a slightly older man, who was still only twenty-five at the most. They were poring over a map of the world and every now and again the man would stand up and go to write a new word on the flip chart next to them. They'd obviously got to Australia because the phrases Terri could work out included: THE LAND DOWN UNDER. BEER 'N' BARBIES, NICOLE KIDMAN, OUTBACK.

'Chris is running a bit behind; it's proving to be a well busy day. Can I get you a drink?' Kian asked. 'We've got espresso, decaff, Diet Coke, caffeine-free Diet Coke, Red Bull, orange juice, spring water?'

'Um ... tea?'

He grinned. 'You sure? The Red Bull'd put lead in your pencil.'

'Quite sure, thank you.'

As he put the kettle on in the kitchenette, Terri looked more closely for signs of depravity. Still nothing. There was a leather sofa next to a coffee table covered in magazines; there were arty black and white photographs on the wall of men and women, but they all had their clothes on and ranged in age from teens to pensioners. Then she saw it, on the draining board next to Kian: a pink plastic contraption shaped like a cone, with strange grooves all down the side and a deeper pink nodule on the end.

'You went to school with Chris, then, did you?' Kian said, ignoring the sex aid and handing the mug of steaming tea over to Terri. 'She's a great boss, always up for a laugh, despite her age. What was she like as a kid?'

'Um . . .' Terri couldn't take her eyes off the pink thing. *Where could you stick* that *without doing yourself an injury?*

'Are you OK?'

'No, I mean, yes . . . but, is it . . .' she pointed 'quite . . . hygienic to keep that near where you make your tea?'

He stared at her as if she was mad. 'Well, yes. I mean, we always wash it after we've used it.'

Terri felt sick. 'What . . . you mean you all *take turns?*'

'Not all of us. Only the ones who like cheese on their jacket potatoes; some of us prefer tuna. But the sandwich shops around here are so expensive, you know—'

Terri began to laugh so hard that hot tea splashed over the side of the mug. 'I thought . . . oh . . . I thought,' she picked up the designer cheese grater and waved it at the boy, 'that this was one of your products!'

Kian smiled uncertainly. 'Oh. Right. Yeah, I can see why. Let me go and find out whether Chris is ready.'

She felt calmer by the time Chris emerged from her office, followed by a much older man whose face had the florid tone of Terri's father's. Alcohol. No doubt about it. 'Terri! Hey, Big Bird! How are you?'

The first thing Terri noticed was the way Chris held out her hand, rather than opened her arms for a hug: the two girls had always shared a dislike of kissy-kissy behaviour. Then she took in the manicured dark-red nails, the glossy chestnut hair, the well-cut grey trouser suit, the cherry-red silk blouse revealing just too much cleavage, and the matching cherry-painted lips. This was a very different Chris from the dreamer she remembered in the Pixies.

Terri was ashamed of the state of her own rough skin as she shook hands. 'Chris, you look amazing.'

She shrugged. 'Thanks. It's hard work for me of all people to keep groomed, to be honest, but it's what's expected in business. You haven't changed a bit, though. Come on through.'

Chris led Terri into her office, which was small and stylish. A laptop computer was open on a desk made from a large piece of weathered wood, and the space was dominated by two huge canvases painted with flowers whose rich red and pink petals were distinctly erotic.

'They're lovely, aren't they?' Chris said. 'Only prints at the moment, but one day I'd love to afford an original Georgia O'Keeffe. Anyway ... I'm sure you don't want to hear about my taste in art. And I'm really sorry but I'm up against it today. So do you mind if we get down to business? You want to talk about Lucy, don't you?'

She listened while Terri told her everything: the promise she'd made to Judith to look after Lucy, and her feelings of failure as her friend became more withdrawn and depressed. 'I mean, I know she's always been quiet, but she's different now. There's almost something *angry* about her, though she'd never dream of admitting to it. I think she needs something to look forward to, a bit of fun. And the best fun I've ever had was in the Brownies, so I thought it might be nice, well, if we all got together again. For old times' sake.'

'All of us?' Chris sounded guarded.

'Well. Maybe not Simonetta.'

'*Definitely* not Simonetta.'

Terri nodded. 'To be honest, I haven't really tried to track her down. Judith only wanted to write to Paula and Bethany and you.'

'Yeah, I had a letter.' Chris smiled. 'And a couple of badges. I suppose it was fun, while it lasted. Before ...'

'I know. But it'd be a shame to let what happened poison all our memories.'

Chris thought about it for a moment, playing with a paperclip on her desk. 'What about Paula? And Bethany?'

'Lucy's getting in touch with Paula, but I'm pretty sure she'll be up for it. When I did my research, she wasn't working or anything. As for Bethany, I've only managed to leave messages with her agent so I'm not exactly holding my breath. But I think that's better anyway: just the four of us. The old gang, you know?'

Chris bent the paperclip around her fingertip to form a tiny spring, her face lost in concentration. It reminded Terri so much of the eight-year-old Chris.

'OK.' Chris looked up from the desk. 'I bet we've nothing in common now, but if you really think it'll help Lucy, then why not? It *is* a manic time at the moment and I definitely can't do next week as I'm in Amsterdam at a sex toy convention, but maybe the week after? Let my PA know the possible dates and I'll see what I can do.'

Terri stood up. 'Thanks. I appreciate it. And Troughton can't be that bad, can it?'

'Wanna bet?' Chris stood up and where her jacket slipped aside, Terri noticed a big thick smudge on her silk blouse. Chris caught her eye. 'This elegance business is bloody hard work, you know. I'm sorry we haven't had a chance to talk properly, but we'll do it when we meet up. And let me know if you want me to bring any free samples. Might give us something to talk about if we run out of camp fire stories.'

Paula ignored the door bell. She'd been having a lie-down after lunchtime, though she hadn't slept. Her stomach was too full of toast, half a loaf's worth consumed in an uncontrolled binge that succeeded momentarily in taking her mind off the red bills, but now seemed to have reformed as a lump of dough in her gullet.

The pile had been growing and this morning she'd decided to tackle it, sitting down with a calculator and a notebook to work out exactly how much she owed.

The total was worse than she had ever expected. It amounted to more than six months' worth of Child Benefit, Income Support and Neil's cheques put together. The panic was growing, but she'd tried to keep control, starting three piles on the dining room table: threatening letters, urgent and low priority. When the first pile towered over the other two, she'd torn the damning list into tiny pieces and raced to the shop in her mac to buy bread and butter.

The bell rang again and she looked at her alarm clock. Three p.m. The kids weren't due home for another hour, and then Neil was coming to take them out, something none of them seemed thrilled about. She rolled over, burying her head in the pillow. Anyone else could sod off.

The sound of the front door opening changed her mind.

'WHO THE FUCK IS THAT?' she shouted, trying to sit up as quickly as her body allowed. The world spun as she raised her head but she hung on to the mattress and eventually things righted themselves as she heard:

'Paulie, it's me.'

The best that could be said about her unexpected visitor was that he wasn't a burglar. He stood in the doorway to her bedroom, chewing on his bottom lip, slouching because he hated his height. Neil was tall and thin and in their wedding photographs they'd looked like Laurel and Hardy. Even then, she'd been convinced he only married her because her dad was Neil's boss and he always did what he was told.

'Neil.' It didn't seem enough, as a greeting for a husband you hadn't seen in months. 'I didn't know you still had a key.'

'Well, my name's still on the tenancy agreement. I do still, technically, pay the rent.'

That's what you think, she thought. The rent had gone on new trainers and DVDs for Charlie, and make-up and jewellery for Sadie. 'And I am technically still your wife? That's what you were going to say, wasn't it?' Now she was nearly upright, Paula felt surer of her ground.

'No. That's not what I mean.'

She stood up, walked around the bed and into the kitchen. In the daylight, Neil looked uncared for: thinner than ever, and what remained of his hair was greasy. But it was his face that alarmed her: he looked terrified, his skin so pale she was sure she could see the bones underneath. What kind of a monster was she, that she could have this effect on her husband?

'So what are you here for? You're way too early for the kids. Not that they want to see you anyway.' Neil didn't deserve to be treated like this, she knew that, but if she was nice, he might want to come back and he could do so much better than her.

'I wanted to talk to you, Paulie.' He held out his palms as if to say, I carry no weapons, take pity on me.

'Is it another excuse about the maintenance? Because I can't pay the bills as it is.'

'No. Listen, can we sit down?' He pulled out a chair, which squeaked on the lino, and Paula gave him a dirty look for taking liberties with her furniture in her home. Though, strictly speaking, the furniture belonged not to her or him, but to the loan company.

She lowered herself carefully onto the other chair, knowing it could barely take her weight. 'If I'd known you were coming, I'd have been out.'

He sighed. 'I miss you, Paulie. I know it was me that went, but I made a mistake. I miss you and I miss the kids and I know they miss me.'

'Ha. Miss you? Is that what you think?' She lashed out and then thought about it. Of course they missed him. He'd always been a better father to them than she was a mother. 'Well, take them. Feel bloody free.'

'Paulie, this isn't you. Please stop pushing me away. We've had a good time, haven't we? We can have it again.'

'This *is* me. I'm not the person you think you married, Neil. I'm not a jolly fat bird, like on TV. I'm bitter and twisted as well as fat and that's why I'm better off on my own. Maybe the kids should move in with you. Then everyone will leave me in peace.'

'Is that what you really want?' He didn't sound like he believed her.

Paula hesitated. Was it? All she knew was that everyone around her made her angry. That the deep sense of injustice she felt had tainted everything in her world, bleached it of colour. 'The kids are OK. They can't help being annoying; it's their age.'

'And me?' His voice was quiet.

'Look at our marriage, Neil. How we were, arguing, penny-pinching, never going out. Why would you want that back?'

'Because I love you.'

She laughed at him. 'Then you're more stupid than I thought.'

He opened his mouth to say something else, but then thought better of it. 'Tell the kids I'll wait for them in the caff on Charles Street.'

'Right.' Paula watched him walk out, his shoulders more slumped than when he came in. She felt sorry for him, and for herself. What a waste of two lives.

Chapter Twelve

To wear your heels down on the outside
means you are a person of imagination and
love of adventure; but heels worn down on
the inside signify weakness and indecision
of character.

I know I shouldn't feel sick to my stomach before what's meant
to be a night out for my benefit. But I do.

I've been pacing the house for half an hour – Sasha's at
Andrew's mum's house and Buster's sensed my edginess and is
miaowing constantly. I make myself some tea and sit down in
the kitchen. The Blue Muddly's lying on the table. I've been
dipping into it over the last couple of weeks, feeling amused,
appalled and charmed. I open it idly, wondering whether it has
any advice on going out to dinner with people you don't want
to see.

I pass the diagram showing the right way to hang a Union
Jack, and the illustration explaining how to tell if a track has
been made by a lame horse, before reaching anything remotely
relevant. Page 373, right opposite the frogs in cream, is a whole
section on Good Temper and Cheeriness.

*If we cannot strew life's path with flowers, we can at least strew
it with smiles, says Charles Dickens. Tears being out of date, even
in the nursery, it is distinctly bad form to cry, but crossness does not
seem to have gone out of fashion yet ...*

Well, that's telling me. I don't think Lord Baden-Powell
would have had much time for me.

You will find it useful in any situation to keep a supply of good humour by you. Mrs T. Seton says: "Take a large stock of it with you ready made up for use."

Bully for Mrs T. Seton. Don't suppose she'd like me much either, as I seem to be hauling round a large stock of grumpiness, with a side order of resentment.

One of the ways of feeling happy is to have achieved something, as the blacksmith said. HAVE AN OBJECT IN VIEW, and while you are trying to get that done, you are sure to have a sense of cheeriness.

The last time I had something to aim for would be … well, giving birth to a healthy baby was one, but then it was something that happened thanks to biology, with no credit to me. And before that? Driving licence. O levels? All stuff that anybody on earth could do.

Then I think of the Brownie Musician badge and realize that was probably the pinnacle of my life's achievements. And I did it, what, twenty-seven years ago …

I drain my tea. That's enough of that. I close the Muddly and head for my bedroom, shutting the door on the world – including Buster, who mews pathetically at being banished.

Time to pick the perfect shoes for tonight. My love of shoes pre-dates Jimmy Choos. Nana Dorothy used to say it was because I was too shy too look anyone in the eye, so spent my childhood divining character from people's footwear. But I have a different theory.

There's an image in my mind: maybe it's a real memory, maybe just an invented moment planted by adults retelling the story behind my favourite childhood photograph. I'm with my father, getting ready for a birthday party. The photo shows me on Daddy's knee, his face in profile as he kisses me on the cheek. I'm wearing burgundy culottes and a frilly white blouse, but what makes me think it's a real memory is that you can't see my shoes, yet it's those I remember most vividly.

Navy patent leather, with a strap across each foot. Daddy unwrapped them from their tissue-filled box and we could see our faces – my long hair and his curls – reflected in the shiny toes. He helped me put them on, his thick fingers clumsy with the tiny buckles, before closing his eyes and telling me to climb back up the stairs so he could appreciate my grand entrance.

I remember the clickety-clack of my heels on the bare wooden steps. Mummy and Daddy had spent a whole weekend ripping up the moth-eaten floral carpet and were gradually hand-sanding away one hundred years of layered paint that blurred the detailing on the banister. They were humming and joking and kissing all the time, and I felt a nasty nagging emotion that, in retrospect, I now recognize as jealousy. It sticks in my mind because, if I'm honest, I don't remember a lot of laughter from those days.

There was the resinous smell of the varnish that Daddy had opened, dipping his paintbrush into liquid the colour of the golden syrup we used to make chocolate Krispie cakes. And then the taste of sawdust and the hairspray I'd been allowed to wear.

'Are you coming down now, Looby-Lou? Tell me when to open my eyes.'

I'd shrieked in excitement as I tap-danced down the stairs and Daddy opened his eyes and shrieked with me. 'Who is my *gorgeous girl*?'

'Meee!'

He picked me up and span me round so the shoe-weighted feet flayed out like the little metal chairs on a merry-go-round.

'Who has the prettiest shoes in Manchester?'

'Meee!'

Later, my shoe habit made things easier for my mother, as while other children screamed blue murder in Clarks at the officious women wielding width-measuring contraptions, I held out my feet like Cinderella waiting for my Prince Charming. But of course, he never came back.

Years later, the novelty has palled a little: selling shoes to fat men with foot odour and spending my life traipsing up and down the stockroom stairs. But I still love opening the boxes of new stock at Fancy Footwork: glittery high-heels for Christmas parties, pastel courts for the wedding season, strappy scarlet sandals for the beach, or the stiff brown lace-ups promising full marks for the children who'll wear them.

I stare at the tower of pristine shoeboxes in the walk-in wardrobe. Black and white line drawings and French names promise a new identity. Would I be happier as a flirty *Delphine*? Or a *charmant Chloe*? Better surely than Lucy, accessorized by an arrogant husband, a bossy daughter and a clingy cat.

In the end, I choose *Sophia*. Pointy, strident, scarlet, with heels thinner than my little finger. The first pair of adult shoes I bought with my own wages – nurtured over the decades more carefully than my complexion, and showing fewer signs of age – *Sophia* always give me confidence, as well as blisters.

As I slip them on, I feel pleasure starting in my toes and travelling up my legs and spine, giving me the energy I need, as my fairy godmother shoes whisper:

Lucy Collins, you SHALL go to the ball.

My feet sting as they make contact with the pavement when I climb out of the car, but it's worth it. As I look down at my *Sophia*s, I feel like a real person again, not just somebody's wife and somebody's mother.

Andrew leans over the passenger seat to kiss me. 'And you'll be OK to call a cab to get you home? I could pick you up if you like.' Tonight he's being unusually attentive, perhaps finally sensing the level of my discontent.

'I can look after myself, believe it or not.' I'm being snappy but I've no intention of apologizing. 'Don't wait up.'

He hesitates, as if he's going to say something else, then shrugs before pulling the car door shut and coasting away.

I brush down my fawn mac with my hands and then walk into the restaurant. The Balzac is still essentially the Cozee Café at heart, with its bowed front window divided into tiny bottle-glass sections, like something from *A Christmas Carol*. The owner, Joyce, has been a fixture for fifty years, but she's a smart cookie. Spotting the gentrification of Troughton, she employed a painter from Crewe to transform the interior and a French chef from Macclesfield to transform the menu. In the daytime, crowds of kids make a cup of hot chocolate or glass of Diet Coke last all afternoon. But at night, Joyce dims the lights and doubles the prices. When Andrew and I have a rare night out, we usually head into Manchester because he won't be seen dead anywhere so suburban, but the Balzac fits Paula's requirement for dinginess. And it also seems fitting to return to a teenage haunt.

'Madame, good evening. You have a reservation?'

I'm about to give her my name when I see Paula sitting at the window table, next to a woman with shiny, slightly kinked chestnut-brown hair. 'Chris?'

'Hey! Lucy!' She stands up, we air-kiss and then I look properly. I'm stunned. Her shoes are *gorgeous* – Emma Hope embroidered blue pumps, or a very convincing copy – and the rest of her outfit looks equally expensive. Even her hair is almost under control.

'You look fantastic, Chris.' I turn to Paula, trying hard to find something positive to say about the way she's dressed. I know what a big deal it is for her to come out. 'And Paula ... what a great shade of lipstick.'

'It came free with a magazine,' Paula says. 'I probably spend less on food than Chris does on make-up. But then again, I never was one for glamour, was I?'

Chris smiles politely. 'Neither was I. I find it really boring dressing up, but apparently I've got an image to project!'

'I would have thought the image that'd work best in your business would involve fishnets and a boob tube,' Paula says.

'Anything to make the business grow, that's my motto,' Chris replies. 'And this is also my first night out in two weeks; thought I'd push the boat out. Lucy, why don't you sit down – you look in pain in those shoes. Let me pour you a glass of wine – red or white?'

I point to the red and sit next to Paula: her scalp shines with grease. Where the hell is Terri? It was all her idea and if it's going to be a long night, then the least she can do is be there for the duration. 'So ... Chris. I can't believe the baby of the Pixies has turned out so well. How does it feel to be a top businesswoman?'

'It's great not having to work for anyone else. I mean, you know how dreamy I am. Can you imagine me having to turn up for work on time? Being my own boss means I can come and go as I like, though what ends up happening is I forget to go home half the time. Especially now we've got a takeover bid going on.'

'Blimey.' I feel envious. Why didn't I have the vision to set up my own chain of shoe shops, rather than slaving away to increase someone else's profit margin?

The waitress arrives with menus in gilt-edged leather folders. 'Specials tonight are –' she takes a deep breath '– *moules mariniere, avocat avec crevettes, sole meu* ... mernie ... *merniere*. And then for dessert—'

'Let's leave dessert till later, shall we?' Chris says, and her confident manner surprises me. I feel like a child being taken out to dinner by a sophisticated favourite aunt. In the Pixies, Chris was the youngest, so in the simple hierarchy kids have, she was bottom of the pile. Yet now she's clearly top dog.

'I didn't understand a word of that, duck,' Paula says, frowning. She opens the menu. 'Oh great, the whole bloody thing's in French.'

'We do have an English version, if you *really* need it,' the waitress says, then flounces off to fetch it.

'What, so I'm some sort of retard for wanting an English menu *in England*?' Paula whispers. 'Now I remember why I don't like eating out.'

Chris puts her menu down. 'Let's wait for Terri before we order. There's so much to catch up on in the meantime ... like your kids. You've got two, haven't you, Paula?'

'Yup. They're teenagers now. I got knocked up early. Charlie wants to be a mechanic. And Sadie's not interested in anything except boys. But they're OK, considering who their mum is.'

'And do they look like you?' Chris asks.

'Do you mean, are they fat?'

'No, I—'

'They're fine. Their dad's as thin as a rake. They remind me of how I was, before I began eating like it was an Olympic sport.'

There's an awkward pause until the waitress returns with the English menu.

'And what about you, Lucy? How old's your daughter?'

'Seven. She's called Sasha. She's just started the Brownies, actually.'

Paula looks surprised. 'I can't believe you'd do that to anyone, duck. I know it's why we're here and everything, but you hated the Brownies. So did I. And Chris too.'

'I promise you, it was all Sasha's idea. You can't impose anything on kids these days, believe me.'

'That's true. Unlike us. Mum forced it on me, hoping it'd make me ladylike. And it managed to ruin our lives. Not what she had in mind.' Paula laughs, a sour sound that sends us retreating behind our menus.

'Yoo-hoo! Sorry I'm so bloody late!' Terri shouts across the restaurant, then stomps across to the table where we're all sitting in gloomy silence. 'Am I interrupting something? We haven't fallen out already, have we?'

Chris smiles back and, to give her credit, it almost looks genuine. 'No, not at all. Your timing's perfect – we're about to order. Then we can really head off down Memory Lane.'

Though we all know there are far too many cul-de-sacs that we daren't travel down.

Chapter Thirteen

Keep clear of girls who tell you nasty stories
or talk to you of indecent things.

By the time we Pixies have polished off three bottles of wine, the mood's lifted enough for Paula to order the dessert she really wants – chocolate profiteroles – without caring what people think; for me to stop worrying when the chat dries up for a few seconds; for Chris to confess that she hasn't had sex for a whole three months. And for Terri to confess she's never had sex at all.

'What, never, ever?' Chris can't believe it. I'm not surprised, but Terri and I have never discussed it. It would be like comparing notes with my mother about the best brand of spermicidal jelly.

Terri shrugs. 'I never got round to it, you know.'

'But you've had boyfriends?'

'Yes, and they've moaned and groaned a bit about it. But you know me, I've always been stubborn and the more they make a fuss, the more likely I am to stand my ground. And it's funny, but I've never been dumped. It's almost like they're so . . . *curious* that they're determined to try to be *the one.*'

Chris shakes her head. 'But haven't you ever felt the . . . urge?'

'Of course. And I have, you know, kissed and cuddled and a bit more. But I've never felt strongly enough to go all the way. I want that to be with the Big One.'

'Don't we all?' Chris laughs, then looks embarrassed. 'Sorry, don't mean to be flip.'

'Don't worry. It's tricky to explain. Think of something you've never tried. I mean, have you ever been skiing?'

Paula peers up from her profiteroles. 'Well, don't bloody look at me. I'd break the skis. And the ski lift.'

Terri grins. 'What about you, Lucy?'

'Nope. Andrew's always on about it but then he used to go when he was a kid. I'd be scared now. Don't you have to be really bendy? Or you'll break something.'

'That's exactly how I feel about sex. I missed my chance to get good at it. Kind of like ... you know how olives are an acquired taste? What's the point in acquiring it when they don't taste very nice?'

Chris frowns. 'But you'd only decide that *after* you'd tried olives, wouldn't you? Whereas you're writing off one of the top three human experiences without giving it the benefit of the doubt.'

I try to work it out. 'And the other two are?'

'Eating and sleeping, of course,' Chris says.

Paula sniggers. 'I definitely prefer those two.'

Terri is still thinking. 'I suppose ... God's part of the equation, too. I do think our bodies are precious. And in nurse training, all I saw was girls sleeping around, then being dumped, and from where I was standing, the pleasure didn't make up for the emotional pain.'

Chris says: 'But monogamy's not all it's cracked up to be, either. If you force people to behave according to some random values system, it only causes more misery in the long run.' She takes a gulp of wine.

Even now we're a little drunk, there are these man-traps in the conversation that stop us short for a moment, before someone steers us in a different direction. And then we all know instinctively that there's one Pixie who can't be mentioned. It'd be like actors naming Macbeth.

Terri rescues us this time. 'Anyway, the urge wears off, doesn't it, as you get older?'

Paula nods. 'That's true enough.'

I laugh a little too loudly, flushed from the wine and the unexpected pleasures of gossip. Usually I feel intimidated in a group, but this is different. Shared history – even the kind we can't acknowledge – makes it easier to talk about now. 'God, yes.

I mean, I still think Andrew's handsome. *Everyone* does. He's got the whole tall, dark and handsome thing sorted. And I sort of fancy him, in theory at least. But there's so much other stuff. I don't just mean the domestic stuff. I mean ...' I wave my glass around, searching for what I mean, sloshing Beaujolais onto the already stained tablecloth, 'the emotional stuff. The resentments and the hurt. The way he puts me down and then expects it all to be all right later in bed, and he doesn't know ...'

I suddenly realize I'm crying, not laughing. Get a grip on yourself, Lucy! Terri reaches out one hand to take mine, finding a hankie with the other. 'Don't be upset, Lucy. You're having a horrible time at the moment, with your mum going like that, so fast and so young. It'll all look better soon, you know that.'

I manage to stop crying and speak, though I sound rather like a Dalek. 'But I don't think Andrew even *likes* me. Never mind respects me. I'm like the cleaner, except the cleaner gets paid.'

Paula reaches out for my other hand. 'Men are just *like that*. They all leave in the end anyway.' She stops. 'Sorry, I guess that isn't much of a comfort. Come on, someone else must have a pearl of sodding wisdom?'

Chris shrugs. 'What I know about marriage could be written on the tip of a Japanese-fit condom.'

'Hey!' Terri says, her voice Brown Owl bright again. 'Look at us, holding hands. Come on, Chris, take mine and Paula's and then it'll be like a Six pow-wow. "Look out, we're the jolly Pixies, helping others when in fixes!"'

Chris looks uncertain but does as she's told.

'And then there was that rhyme we made up ourselves. Do you remember?' Terri seems less drunk than the rest of us, but her voice carries across the restaurant as she begins: 'Pixies work and pixies play, Pixies never stop all day ...'

The tears have stopped – a triumph for me – and I join in: 'If you want a friend for keeps ...'

The few remaining diners stare openly as the other two murmur along with us:

Pixies love each other heaps!

When we finish, there's a second's pause, then Paula begins

to laugh, a low growl that grows in volume until it seems to take her over. One of those laughs that defies other people not to join in. Before long, we're all fighting for breath between laughs, faces pink with wine and exertion.

I know my problems aren't going to go away, but for a few minutes, they don't matter.

'So. The Brownies weren't that bad after all, were they?' Terri says, after we've finally managed to calm down enough to order coffee.

'I suppose they had their moments,' Paula admits. 'And apart from my typing exam, those badges were about the only qualifications I ever passed. You know Judith sent me a couple, when she wrote to me?'

'Me too,' Chris says. 'The Book Lover and the Toymaker. The first ones I got. And now I make my money from toys and dirty books.'

'House Orderly was my first badge,' Terri says.

'We all got that one,' Paula says. 'The biggest con around, that one, turning little girls into skivvies.'

Terri thinks about it. 'And First Aider, of course. I was always going to be a nurse, like your mum, Lucy ... sorry. There I go again, putting my foot in it.'

'No, don't worry. I don't want people to think they can't mention her ever again. My first badges were Musician and Animal Lover. Neither have proved a lot of use, though the cat's done OK out of it, I guess. He eats better than I do and has a nicer time all round. But the singing ... well, that was never going to happen, was it?'

Terri gives me an odd look. 'It's never too late, you know, Luce.'

'Yeah, right,' I say, sounding like Sasha when she's being stroppy.

Chris plays with the sugar in the bowl on the table, circling round and round with her spoon. 'It's a shame they don't have a badge for being a grown-up, really, isn't it?'

'I'd never pass it,' Paula says. 'But maybe I'd have made a better job of it if I'd known what the hell we were meant to do.'

'So what do you reckon we really needed to know if it wasn't the Green Cross Code and reef knots?' I ask. 'There should definitely have been a section on *Men are from Mars, Women are from Venus.*'

'I know they teach kids how to put a condom on a banana these days, but a bit about how to persuade a bloke to put a condom on his penis would be more use,' Chris says.

'An entire badge about dealing with adolescence would have been good,' Terri says. 'Acne, bras, how not to care if you never get asked out. And a lesson in knowing that it doesn't matter what other people think.'

I nod. 'God, I still need to learn that one.'

The last diners walk out of the restaurant. The waitress delivers the tray of coffees, looking pointedly at her watch as she leaves our table.

'Well, she wouldn't get her Hostess badge, would she?' Chris says. 'But then I bet none of us would pass them now.'

'Well, there's no way on earth I'd get my Agility badge,' Paula says, and no one contradicts her.

'You might have a laugh trying, though,' Terri says. 'I mean, they were only aimed at seven-year-olds. We'd be in a sorry state if we couldn't do something aimed at people who're a fifth of our age.'

I sigh, thinking for the second time this evening about taking my Musician badge. 'I was so chuffed when I got my badge for singing. It was the first time I ever felt I'd done something Mum could be proud of.'

Terri's nodding. 'You know, there's definitely something in this. What did the badges give us?' No one answers. She'll answer her own question soon enough. 'A sense of purpose! And isn't that what we're all struggling with, now?'

'Well, I wouldn't say so, not exactly—' Chris begins, but Terri holds up her hand.

'OK, Chris, you might have a sense of purpose, but there doesn't seem like much fun in your life.'

'Well, I do work hard, but . . .' Then Chris tails off. There's no point in arguing with Terri in full flow.

'Look, girls. Haven't we had a good time tonight?'

We nod. It's been unexpectedly good fun. Comforting, even.

'So I think we should do it again. And to give us that purpose, I think we should try something a bit different.' She takes a sip of cappuccino before delivering her verdict, the foam moustache remaining above her top lip. 'I think we should do our Brownie badges all over again.'

Chapter Fourteen

The idea underlying the award of badges is
to offer the girl continual inducements for
further improving herself.

I tiptoe into the porch of my house like a naughty teenager,
my feet blistered and swollen in my *Sophia* shoes. But the
sound of Andrew's snoring creeps downstairs and reassures me
that I can make as much noise as I like without waking him.
That particular pitch of snore signifies middle-of-the-night,
not-a-care-in-the-world sleep, the sort Andrew rarely misses out
on, however stressed he is.

I'm envious. It's one of the unexpected things about marriage: knowing more about someone else's sleep patterns than
they know themselves, and resenting their easy relationship
with the Land of Nod. And then hating yourself for hating
your partner's good fortune. Even when I'm slightly drunk, like
now, I find sleep elusive.

'Hey, don't shut the door on me!'

I turn round. I had forgotten about Terri. 'God, sorry. I'm
a liable ... liability when I'm pissed. Come on through to the
kitchen where we can talk.'

'I'm knackered, to be honest, Luce. Do you mind if I get on
up to bed?'

'Oh, OK.'

'Don't be hurt. I thought it went really well tonight, didn't
you? And I'm really pleased at my idea about the badges. Rather
good, if I do say so myself.'

I pour a glass of Sancerre from an opened bottle in the fridge and leave it on the kitchen work-surface, without its cork. Andrew would disapprove, which is probably why I do it. 'You don't really think that's going to happen, do you, Terri?'

'Well, why not?'

'Because it's silly. I mean, we're grown women. With responsibilities. We don't have time for messing about with badges.'

Terri looks tired, her eyes bloodshot, her freckles standing out on pale cheeks. 'I never thought I'd say this to you, Luce, but you're boring. What do you do that isn't about duty?'

'I play with Sasha.' I hear the sulkiness in my voice.

'That doesn't count. You need to have some time for you.'

I slam the glass down on the kitchen table and the noise reverberates in my head. 'Like when? All my life people have been telling me what to do, and now you. It doesn't help, you know!'

'I promised ...' She stops.

'Go on. You promised what?'

'I promised your mum I'd look after you,' she says quietly.

The pressure in my head will shatter my skull if I don't let it out. 'Oh, terrific. You and Mum scheming behind my back. And for what? To try to make feeble Lucy more like good old Terri. I don't know why she didn't just have done with it and adopt you and put me in a home!'

'It's not like that—' she begins, but I haven't finished.

'Do you have any idea what it's like? No, you don't, do you? Because you're worse than her. A frigid, thick-skinned bossy-boots, just like you always were.'

Terri steps back, waits for a moment, then says: 'Is that the worst you can do?'

I lean against the fridge, exhausted and ashamed of myself. Where is this all coming from? I've gone decades without losing my temper, but in the last few months it seems a daily occurrence. 'Oh God, Terri, I'm sorry. You've done so much for me and this is how I pay you back. I didn't mean it.'

'I've heard a lot worse than that from patients, believe me, Luce. Look, it's all right. I know how it must look but I also know that just because your mum was fond of me, doesn't mean she loved you any less.'

I nod. 'I know, I know. It's just I hate the way no one thinks I'm capable of doing anything on my own. I'm not a helpless baby. I'm thirty-five years old and if I'm not grown up enough to look after myself now, I never will be.'

For a moment, I think Terri's going to tell me I'm not, but she waits before saying, 'So, does that mean you're too grown up to do the badges then?'

I laugh, despite myself. 'You don't give up, do you?'

'I'm like the frogs in cream! You're up for it, aren't you?'

I shake my head. 'It's pointless trying to argue with you, Terri. OK, I'm up for it but don't be disappointed if the others aren't. It's a big enough deal getting us all together – especially when Paula won't leave the house unless it's pitch dark. I just don't want you going to all that trouble and then being hurt.'

Terri yawns again. 'Hey, the one good thing about being thick-skinned is that I don't dent easily. And, of course, being a bossyboots means I don't take no for an answer.'

She holds out her arms and I give her a slobbery, wine-infused kiss while she pats my back awkwardly, releasing me as soon as she can.

'See you in the morning, Terri.' I watch her retreat then I swallow the last of the wine in the glass, before opening the dishwasher to put it away. But then I think, sod it. I pick up the two-thirds-full bottle and take it, my glass and myself upstairs to the study.

The study has none of the book-lined romance its name suggests. When we first moved into the house – easily the grandest of the detached executive homes on the new estate – I loved everything about it. The double garage, the spa bath, the six-ringed gas hob ... but most of all the fresh, unpolluted air that filled its evenly proportioned rooms. This was a home without history, somewhere me and Andrew and our future family would fill with our own memories.

And so it's turned out. OK, so the family's too nuclear to fill the five bedrooms, and Andrew's promise of more babies, 'once I make Grade Ten', hasn't been mentioned recently, although he was fast-tracked to Grade Twelve before Sasha was out of nappies. I craved another child straight away, but I've never been the kind of woman to throw my pills down the loo behind my husband's back, however powerful the instinct.

And now … well, the master bedroom is ours. Sasha has a big double, recently redecorated in denim blue after she prematurely outgrew the Barbie pink fantasia we'd had interior-designed as her third birthday present ('Mum, Barbie's for *little kids*. Don't you know? Bratz are where it's at now.'). There's the guest bedroom no one but Terri ever stays in, as everyone else we know lives in Troughton anyway. The fourth bedroom stays empty, a barren nursery-in-waiting, and the fifth is the study, though in reality that means Andrew's office. It's equipped with an entire Dixons' worth of technology and I've no idea what most of it does: ISDN, Broadband, ADSL (perhaps they're all the same thing) and no less than three printers. One for shopping lists and homework, one for photographs and presentations, and one that's also a fax and a scanner and could probably communicate with aliens if you had a fortnight spare to decode the manual.

I shut the door behind me. There are enough winking electronic lights to illuminate my route towards the window, and I put down the glass and bottle next to Andrew's swanky laptop. I climb into his ergonomic chair and put my swollen feet up on his desk, savouring the little victory of doing something he'd hate. Then I wonder how nice, calm, sweet Lucy has been reduced to taking pleasure in such petty acts.

Outside, Saxon Close is streetlamp yellow, with no sign of life behind any of the mullioned windows in the other four houses. Are the other wives in their master suites lying awake in the dark, feeling this trapped? Is it normal to be thirty-five and wish you'd done everything differently? And worse still, not know what you wish you'd done instead?

Suddenly I feel a yearning for the real study in the Old Surgery, with its entire back wall covered in bending shelves, each one crammed with books coated in a thin layer of cough-inducing dust. There are paperbacks by Arthur Hailey and Jean Plaidy, with broken spines and pages that smell of Ambre Solaire. There are classics, their pristine condition revealing that members of the Quentin dynasty have always preferred pulp fiction. Then there are the rows and rows of stiff-backed medical textbooks that belonged to Grampa Quentin, my great-grandfather, full of cures for palsies and blood-poisoning and other ailments of the early twentieth century. Finally a newer, shorter pile with modern typefaces and modern diseases and modern colour illustrations of people with terrible growths: my father's books. I used to sneak in there with Terri when we were children but while she was fascinated by those gory pictures, they always made me feel queasy: another example of how I failed to live up to the Quentin ideal.

I wonder how Grampa Quentin took it when Mum announced she was marrying a doctor. Was my father welcomed into the Old Surgery, treated to Scotch on ice and an offer to put a word in the ear of the right consultant? I know nothing about the days before I was born, and now I suppose I never will. All I do know is that after he died and we moved back there in 1974, all that remained of James Gill, doctor, husband, father, was a few washed-out photographs, an old chocolate-coloured suede jacket and a pile of gory textbooks. And I never questioned why Mum shut down all conversation before it began, and why we were never allowed anything to do with my paternal grandparents.

But that *can't* be all there is left of him, can it? There must be more memories, more photographs, perhaps of his school days, or of my father as a handsome young medic.

I sip the wine, my eyes drawn by the cloakroom light appearing in the house opposite. Somewhere, there have to be people who remember my father, who can tell me who he was, and who I could still become.

I am going to find them.

May 1979: Simonetta makes her Brownie Promise

'Tonight, girls, is a special night as we welcome a new recruit to the Brownie family.' Judith paused to let the significance of the moment sink in.

Sitting in their pow-wow ring, the 2nd Troughton Brownies looked solemnly at Brown Owl. She loved it when they were like this. Adults misunderstood little girls, thought their minds were stuffed with cotton wool, sugar and spice and all things nice, not a single serious thought in their heads.

But even the tiniest Brownies, just turned seven, could be reflective. Their soft brows were furrowed in concentration, their mouths parted to take shallow breaths so they made less noise in the quiet hall.

'It's a time to remember the promise we made when we too became Brownies. I remember making mine in this very hall twenty-six years ago.'

Their eyes widened, finding twenty-six years an impossible concept. Of course, it had been inevitable that Judith would become a Brownie, with such an impeccable Girl Guiding pedigree. Her grandmother Agnes set up the first ever Guide company in Cheshire in 1913, shortly after she married Dr Quentin. She'd faced opposition at first, as Troughton dignitaries feared that adventurous activities like camping and cycling would make tomboys of the town's young ladies.

But Agnes won them over in the end. Her daughter Dorothy then established the Brownie pack in 1947, like the heir to a business dynasty being given control of a subsidiary to learn the ropes. Dorothy later told Judith, her daughter, that Agnes had cajoled her into it, as a distraction from the trials of life as a young war widow. It had worked – which was why Dorothy talked Judith into taking over when she returned to Troughton as a widow herself. And she had to admit, it helped a little. She still missed Jim, still felt a rage that he'd left her for ever, when things could have been so different, but mostly she was too busy to indulge in feeling sorry for herself.

'So to begin with, I'd like to ask Simonetta's Sixer, Bethany, to bring our new member to the Wishing Pond to tell the story of the Brownies.'

Bethany stood up in a single graceful move and held out her hand to Simonetta, who looked surprised but took it. At the last moment, Bethany released her grip, allowing Simonetta to tumble onto the hard floor, her legs flailing as she tried to right herself. Her knees and elbows cracked against the chestnut-brown parquet.

'Oh dear. Are you all right?' Bethany asked.

'Yes, thank you,' Simonetta replied, but her eyes were fierce.

Judith frowned, knowing no one else would have noticed – or if they had, they wouldn't believe it was on purpose. Then she looked towards the parents and caught Bruno's eye. Simonetta's mother had been invited, too: the making of the Promise was a family occasion. But only Bruno and his daughter Carlotta, a miniaturized version of her older sister, were there.

He raised his eyebrows and Judith realized he'd noticed Bethany's sneaky trick. She felt satisfied at their complicity. Most adults failed to see past Bethany's baby-blues.

Bethany forced her hand back into the reluctant Simonetta's, and walked her towards the Wishing Pond, a sheet of green felt with an oval mirror glued in the centre. The mirror was yellowing and spotted with age.

'I'm going to read out the story of how we Brownies get our name,' Bethany told her audience. 'This story was by Mrs Ewing. But it's nothing like JR or Dallas as it's dull, so I have made it up to date.

'A long time ago there were two selfish little children called Tommy and Betty who were a complete pain in the neck.'

Whereas you are a pain in the backside, thought Judith.

'Their mother said she was at her wits' end, wherever that was.

She used to shout at them, "*Shut up, brats. I've got a headache.*"'

Judith smiled, despite herself. That line wasn't in the official handbook version of the story.

Bethany turned over the page in her notebook. It looked like this was the unabridged version. 'They'd leave their socks and pants on the floor and once spilled a whole pot of Slime with Worms on the carpet and Mum shouted, "What did your last servant die of?"'

Judith noticed that Bruno was grinning too. She suppressed the urge to giggle.

'One day Mum really lost her rag. "I wish I had a Brownie living here instead of you terrors."

'Tommy was the mouthy one so he said, "What's a Brownie when it's at home?" And Mum said, "Don't get lippy. A Brownie's useful and clears up, but best of all you never see him. Or hear him. Chance'd be a fine thing with you two."

'Now the kids thought this was a right good idea. "Think on, Tommy," said Betty. "If we had a Brownie we'd have an easy life. Where can we find one, Mum?"

Bethany paused for effect. 'Mum sighed. She did that a lot. "You could try asking the Brown Owl. But if you do go down to the wood, try not to get your clothes mucky cos it's muggins here that does the washing."'

Judith looked at the wall clock. Enough was enough. As Bethany opened her mouth to continue, Judith raised her hand. 'Very good, Bethany, but you need to hurry it up now.'

Bethany glared back. 'In the woods it was right spooky. No one had invented torches so it was dark, and the owl was making a weird noise. *Hoo-hoo.* Tommy was all set to do a runner, because he was a boy and boys are chicken. But Betty was braver. She called out "Hiya, Mrs Owl. Can we have a chat?"

'Mrs Owl answered straight away because she was a bit of a lonely old bird; she didn't have a husband no more and no one liked her. "Come up the tree if you must. But mind your heads. If you hurt yourself you'll only have yourself to blame."'

Judith wasn't sure whether to laugh or cry. No prizes for guessing who Mrs Owl was meant to be.

'So they ask Mrs Owl about Brownies and she nods and says,

"Go down to the pool and turn around three times – don't make yourself dizzy – and say this rhyme: 'Twist me and turn me and show me the elf, I looked in the water and there saw ...'" But she wouldn't finish the rhyme. Said they had to work it out for themselves. Typical grown-up.'

'That's *enough*, Bethany,' Judith said. 'Do you want me to finish the story for you? Get on with it.'

Bethany pouted. 'So, Betty went to the pool, said the rhyme, did the twisty thing three times, and then looked into the water. But there was nowt there except the moon and her reflection. Betty goes back to Mrs Owl and tells her, and Mrs Owl says, "What, no one there at all? Are you sure?"

'And Betty goes, like, "Well, yeah, except myself." And Mrs Owl looks all smug and goes, "and wouldn't *myself* fit the rhyme?"

'So Betty tries it out: "'Twist me and turn me and show me the elf, I looked in the water and there saw ... myself.' But Mrs Owl, I don't get it."

'Personally, I think Betty's a bit dim because the whole point is that there is no elf. Mrs Owl goes "Betty, you can be a Brownie. Clean up, make your mum a cup of tea or wash the dishes. Then your mum might not be so mardy."

'Betty and Tommy decide to give it a go, make an effort. And it's a good job in fact because Dad sits them down next day and says, "Actually, kids, Mum's done a runner with her fancy man, so you're going to have to do all the chores now—"'

'BETHANY!' Judith rushed into the circle and had to restrain herself from slapping the child. 'That isn't what happened and you know it.'

'It was only a joke.'

'Look around you, Bethany; is anyone laughing?' Judith hissed. One of the youngest Brownies, whose dad had left home a few weeks earlier, was already sobbing. Lucy had cuddled up to the girl and was patting her hand to comfort her, but looked close to tears herself. 'Finish the story properly or you won't be a Sixer any more.'

Bethany sighed. 'OK. Well, their mum hadn't done a runner, she'd just gone to the shops, but she was chuffed to mintballs at the tidy house, and they all lived happily ever after and that's the reason we're called Brownies, because we always think of other people.' She stopped short and then, in a quiet voice, said: 'Especially our mums.'

Oh, shit. Judith had forgotten all about Bethany's mum's departure to the legendary squat in Notting Hill. The child was a spiteful brat, but was it any wonder?

'Very good, Bethany. What a vivid imagination you have. Now it's time for Simonetta's special moment. Come on then, Simonetta, come up to the pool. Turn around three times, that's it.'

Judith peered over her shoulder in the mirror as she always did, and was struck by how adult Simonetta's face was. She was older than most girls were when they joined, nearly nine, but that didn't explain the absolute poise, no, it was more than that. Self-control.

She whispered the words in Simonetta's ear, and the girl spoke, as confidently as Bethany:

'"Twist me and turn me and show me the elf, I looked in the water and there saw myself."'

Judith nodded. 'Simonetta, do you know the Brownie Guide Law?'

'She thinks of others before herself and does a good turn every day.'

As Judith spoke the same words she'd said herself dozens of times, she imagined she could hear her mother Dorothy and grandmother Agnes joining in. 'And do you know that if you make the Promise, you must always do your best to keep it, and carry it out everywhere but especially at home.'

'I know.'

'Will you make your Promise as a Brownie Guide?'

Simonetta held up her right hand, her little finger bent over and kept in place with her thumb in the traditional salute. 'I promise that I will do my best: to do my duty to God, to serve the Queen and help other people, and to keep the Brownie Guide Law.'

Judith smiled at her, and Simonetta smiled back, but her eyes were cool. Judith reached into her pocket and pinned the metal Promise badge onto the yellow tie. Bruno had bought the whole uniform second-hand, from Pack stores: 'a bit of a cash flow issue, the Italian banks are so slow unless you are Mafiosi, you know, my *allocco*.' He'd begged Judith not to tell anyone his daughter was wearing cast-offs, which had been unnecessary as she was not a gossip, but it was nice to see a father so concerned that his child shouldn't be singled out. He could teach Bethany's dad a thing or two.

'Brownies, it's time to welcome your friend with our Pack Salute.' The girls scrabbled to their feet, amid giggling, before clapping three times, calling out *Welcome* above the sound of each clap.

'Lovely, Brownies. Now let's say our special prayer and then it's time for squash and biscuits.'

The newest Pixie stayed perfectly calm as the others thronged around her. Lucy was the first to congratulate her with a hug; Terri shook her hand, and Chris presented her with a handmade card decorated with a green and brown glittery Brownie on the front. Paula, who'd already claimed Simonetta as her new best friend, linked arms and dragged her over to meet her mother, Patsy.

'Another beautiful ceremony.'

Bruno had crept up on Judith and she jumped a little. She looked around for Carlotta, who was being babied by a couple of Sprites. 'Yes. Though I was worried I was going to spoil it all by laughing during Bethany's speech.'

'She is a naughty child. Bright, but naughty. And I think, perhaps hurt. Am I right?'

Judith was surprised. 'Yes, I think you probably are. Bethany's tough, but her mum left a while back and she probably misses her more than she'd allow herself to admit.'

'The loss of a parent is a terrible thing. So is the loss of a husband,' he said.

Judith stared at her feet. 'Who told you?'

'I am sorry; I did not mean to make you uncomfortable.'

She shook her head. 'No, don't worry. There are no secrets in a place like Troughton.'

'Really?' He smiled. 'I am so grateful to you for making my daughter's dream come true. She has always wanted this.'

Now Judith looked uncertain. 'She's quite a reserved child so far. I'm the last person to pry, but there's nothing the matter at home, is there?'

Bruno thought it over. 'I think, my Netta, she likes to hold her cards close to her stomach, you know?'

'Her chest?'

He laughed, deep lines framing his eyes and mouth. 'Her chest, yes. Sorry. We always speak Italian at home and sometimes I forget the phrases.'

Judith saw Patsy and Chris's mother, Dina, staring in their direction. 'Come on, let me introduce you to some of the other Pixie parents.'

'Do we have to? I know all I need to about them. It's your company I enjoy, Brown Owl,' he said, but she was already striding forward, wishing her cheeks weren't so hot. This wouldn't do.

'Bruno, this is Patsy, Paula's mother. Paula's already trying to get Simonetta to switch her football allegiances from Italy to Manchester United. And then Dina is Chris's mum. Chris is the brains of the Six, no doubt about it.'

Dina frowned. 'She's definitely got the brains, but she was at the back of the queue when it comes to common sense. You've never met such a daydreamer.'

Bruno turned on his full-beam smile. 'Dreaming is good. The great painters, the great writers, they all were dreamers. And the great footballers, who play in their dreams. So many of them Italian, of course.'

Dina's face softened, something Judith had never seen. She ran her fingers through her wiry red-and-grey hair, and stood up straight, so that a hint of papery cleavage appeared above her sweater. 'I love Italy. I travelled to Florence before I was married. Such a beautiful place.'

'I bet you were very popular with the men of Firenze.'

'Oh, well, I don't know ...'

'We Italians have always had an eye for a pretty girl.' He winked at her before turning to Patsy. 'And I believe I met your husband last week. He, like me, is an entrepreneur, no?'

Patsy flicked her peroxide Olivia Newton-John fringe back and lowered her eyes: the lids were heavy with kohl and pink metallic shadow. 'Well, I don't know about entrepreneur. He's ... in property, I suppose.'

Dina butted in. 'He built our garage last year.'

'Today, garages, tomorrow, who knows?' Bruno said. Judith felt a sneaky admiration for his ability to mete out his charm so evenly. 'As our new prime minister she would say, it's about ambition. '

'Oh, that's the kind of thing Nigel's always saying as well,' Patsy cooed. 'He voted Tory for the first time in his life last month. Though he can't quite believe there's a woman running the country.'

'Yes, but she is a woman like no other ... a woman who is strong.' Bruno grinned at Judith. 'You know, maybe we should all get together? The parents of the Pixies. With my wife. She's unwell tonight, but we want to be part of the community. We've had unsettled times and we like what we see here.'

Dina nodded. 'It's a good town. Some people might call it stuffy –' she looked pointedly at Judith '– but if you make the effort, it will be rewarded.'

'Mum, can Netta come round for tea tomorrow? To watch *Grange Hill*?' Paula skipped up, her arm linked with Netta's, glorying in their newly discovered camaraderie.

'You let them watch that?' Dina said. 'All that swearing!'

Patsy let loose her girlish laugh. 'I think they've all heard worse than "flipping heck", to be honest, Dina. But we'll have to check with Netta's mummy.'

Bruno shook his head. 'No need. She will be delighted. We are very keen for my Netta to make good friends.'

Judith turned and spotted Lucy, Terri and Bethany in the corner. Bethany was shooting poisonous glares towards Netta, and Lucy was chewing her nails. It drove Judith mad with frustration and worry about what would become of her daughter: why couldn't she toughen up? Life was hard on people who didn't fight back. Jim was proof of that.

Perhaps with a little encouragement, Lucy could become Netta's friend and some of that self-assurance might rub off.

Simonetta could hardly be a more malign influence than the Pixie Princess.

Chapter Fifteen

Parents are to us 'like a lamp on a dark night'
and so we take our troubles to them, to have
light thrown on them.

Sasha disappears into the Drill Hall in her brand new Brownie uniform without a backward glance, and for once, I don't feel slighted. Tonight I have plans.

The security light at the Old Surgery flicks on as I park on the driveway. When I let myself into the darkened hall, there's the usual pile of free newspapers, double-glazing leaflets and a couple of letters 'to the owner' asking if they'd consider selling, 'because the desire for prestigious properties continues to outstrip supply'.

Which will be music to Andrew's ears. He's desperate to get this place on the market, but I'm resisting. It's not as though I ever want to live here again, but seven weeks after the funeral, nothing's clear any more. I don't even know whether I'm disagreeing with him for the sake of it, or if there's more to it.

It's cold in the house – it was built facing north, to give shelter to feverish patients, while the tuberculosis cases could lie on stretchers in the south-facing garden – I keep my fingers crossed as I switch on the central heating. It splutters and the pipes moan at the unfamiliar request, but then I hear the gas surge and know it'll be warmer soon. As I pass through to the kitchen, the dust and smell of damp depress me. It took only four months of sickness for Mum to lose control of this rambling old place. And no one hated losing control more than she did.

I boil a kettle and choose one of Mum's herbal teabags, bought during the brief period when she believed that vitamins, infusions and old-fashioned Quentin willpower would overcome the cancer. The fact that it didn't submit to her iron will was probably a greater shock to her than the initial diagnosis. Strange that teabags should outlast my mother.

I shiver but, for once, I don't feel on the edge of tears. I don't have time to wallow in grief. I'm a woman on a mission.

I carry the hot tea into the cellar, gripping the mug with both hands to keep them warm. Down there it's still a terrible mess. After those few initial visits, I'd given up on sorting out the stuff, too exhausted by the task. It reminded me of a Greek myth I learned at school, where some poor bugger – was it Hercules? – had to clear out endless mounds of horse manure, only to find more appear.

But now my objectives are clear and I immediately unroll the heavy duty bin bags from my handbag. By the time I have to leave here to pick Sasha up, I want them to be full of clothes, hats and, yes, even shoes, destined for the charity shop. I have no use for them. What I need is information.

Although I have a plan, it's easy to get sidetracked. The trunks and boxes are filled as randomly as life itself; a tiny handwritten card from a long-dead bouquet buried between an old bedspread and a crochet shawl; a shopping list for a children's birthday party underneath a pile of 1970s editions of *She* and *Woman's Own*. I feel guilty about disposing of my family's domestic history, but I suppose this is what every generation has to do.

I empty a box full of old clothes – I recognize a purple paisley anorak and some bobbly Fair Isle jumpers from photographs of myself as a child – and I use the empty container to store promising letters and wallets full of negatives. There isn't time to examine the evidence now. That comes later.

Gradually the pile of bloated rubbish bags grows and I work my way through half the cellar before the alarm I've set on my mobile goes off. Fifteen minutes before I'm due back at the Drill Hall. I leave the full bags where they are, then carry the boxes of paperwork up the cellar stairs.

Finally I walk over to the kitchen dresser to find the key for the study. Since Grampa Quentin died in 1990, the study was Mum's hideaway, though I don't know what she did there, except sit by the sunny window that overlooked the garden, and breathe in the past. Now I'm about to do the same.

As I try to unlock the door, I feel as though Grampa Quentin is going to tap me on the shoulder and ask me, in that mock-stern way, what I think I'm doing, young lady?

The lock is tricky and I wonder if the key might break, but eventually it relents and the door opens. Before my eyes adjust, the smell hits me: a damp flannel sourness that I never smell in my own house. It's oddly comforting.

The mahogany shutters are closed so I switch on the light. There's no clue about where to search first; the ugly green leather-topped desk is clear of paperwork and the shelves are densely packed, clubbing together to hang on to their secrets. For now I only have time to take the pile of photographs, a few of my father's textbooks – God knows what I expect to find in those, but they were *his*, with his little scrawls in the margins, the product of night after night of study – and the old metal document file where Mum used to keep all the important stuff. I lock the door behind me.

It all only just fits in the boot of the Fiesta and when I step back, the lower half of the chassis slumps suspiciously over the wheels. As I drive to the Drill Hall, I feel like a murderer taking a body to be dumped, aware that I mustn't do anything to at-tract suspicion.

I arrive just as prayers are finishing, and wait with the other mums in the crowded entrance to the hall. Sasha is surrounded by little girls, distributing air kisses and hugs. For a moment, she reminds me of Bethany and the way she controlled the Pixies by granting or withdrawing attention at random. I shiver.

'Penny for them?' It's Terri.

'Oh, I was just thinking about the old days.'

'Not the good old days, judging from the look on your face,' Terri says.

'I was thinking of Bethany.'

Terri looks back at Sasha and her coterie. 'Hey ... Sasha's not like Bethany. She's popular, that's true, but she's not a user. And the other important difference is that unlike the Pixie Princess, Sasha has a good, stable family background.'

I feel like telling Terri that I exchanged six sentences with Andrew over the weekend – I counted – but it doesn't seem the right time. 'I'm being daft. How's she getting on?'

'Brilliantly. She should be ready to make her Promise next week. So maybe you and Andrew would both like to come and watch?' Terri smiles then reaches out to touch my arm, withdrawing her hand again quickly as though it's red hot. 'Anyway, have a think about it. You look a bit peaky.'

'Having trouble sleeping, that's all. And you? Course still going well?'

'Yeah. Well, you know. Finding it hard going, to be honest. I really miss your mum.'

I look over at my daughter, who is still at the centre of a huddle of Brownies. 'I've been to the house tonight, to look through her things. *I want to find out about Dad*.' I whisper the last words. For some reason, saying it out loud seems shameful.

Terri stares at me, horrified. 'Are you sure that's a good idea? Your mum must have had reasons why she didn't talk about him.'

'I want answers, Terri. Everything feels so, I don't know how to describe it … fractured. I feel like it wouldn't take much pressure for me to break completely.'

'Well, that's what I mean. You're not strong, Luce. You don't know what you might find out.'

'I need to find some way of moving on.'

'But there are lots of other things you could try. Take singing lessons.' She moves closer. 'Or what about talking to Andrew about having another baby? I know that's something you really want.'

It was. I'm not sure I want it now. 'Oh, yes, because a baby always improves a relationship, doesn't it?'

'It's more positive than raking over the past.'

The way she says it sounds like a warning. 'Did Mum tell you something?'

She flushes. 'I know you resent the relationship we had, but you shouldn't be so paranoid.'

But I notice she hasn't denied it. 'So you'll swear to God that Mum said nothing—' I stop. 'Hello, Sasha! Did you have a nice time?'

'Brilliant. But, Mum. I've been invited over to Catrin's on Saturday for her party. I can go, can't I?'

'Provided your dad's up to taking you. I'm working this weekend.'

'Oh, do you have to?' Sasha is pouting.

'Well, I could give up work and spend my whole life ferrying you around and tending to your every whim, I suppose.'

Sasha blinks. 'Mu-um,' she says, uncertainly.

'Let's ask your dad when he gets in.' I raise my eyebrows at Terri. 'I'd better get this one home. And hopefully we can both make it for the ceremony next week.'

Terri frowns. 'You must call me if you're thinking of doing anything ... rash. You can always talk to me.'

'Oh, I never do anything rash, Terri. You know me. Good old reliable Luce. And why would I when I have so much to look forward to?' I try and fail to keep the bitterness out of my voice.

'Well, apart from Sasha's Promise ceremony, there's getting together with the Pixies again at the weekend. I've got a little surprise up my sleeve,' Terri says.

My heart sinks. I still can't believe she's talked the others into meeting up so soon. And though she hasn't mentioned badges lately, Terri's like a dog with a bone if she believes in something.

'Hmm. I never have been that fond of surprises.'

'Trust me,' she says, and I can't be bothered to argue back.

I wake up with a brilliant idea. Today I'm going to do something I've never done before. Throw a sickie.

'Oooh,' I say and it sounds utterly unconvincing. So I try again. 'Oww.'

Andrew mumbles in his sleep. 'Wha'?'

'I don't feel well.' My voice is still too strident so I whisper this time. 'I've got the most terrible headache.' That's better.

You could almost mistake me for a Merchant Ivory heroine with an attack of the vapours.

'Headache? You don't get headaches.' He sounds more awake now, as the repercussions of a poorly wife dawn on him.

'Well, I've got one now. Owww.'

'Shit. I'll get you some Nurofen.' He clambers out of bed towards the ensuite, his black hair choppy with sleep-induced waves, and returns with water in the tooth mug and a couple of white pills. 'Sit up, take them now and you'll feel better by the time Sasha needs getting up.'

I half open my eyes. If there's genuine concern in his face, I'm not going to be able to go through with it. Fortunately, his forehead is creased in irritation so I don't have to feel guilty at all. 'I'll try, but this is the worst headache I've ever had, Andrew. I don't think I can get up.'

'Shit,' he says again, 'I've got an early meeting.'

I moan lightly.

He checks himself. 'Sorry. Look, it can't be helped. I mean, you don't think it's anything really serious do you?'

Now he does seem worried and I force a weak smile. 'Oh, no. I don't suppose it's a brain tumour or anything. I don't think they come on all of a sudden. Perhaps it was something I ate.'

'Don't worry. I'll sort Sasha out. It'll be fine.'

'Maybe you could call one of her friends and see if she could go over there after school?'

'Her friends? Like who? I mean, hopefully you'll be feeling better by teatime.' He sounds panicked.

I take my pills then burrow under the duvet again. 'Yes, hopefully. But would you call work for me, tell them I won't be in?'

'Right.'

'And Andrew ... don't forget Sasha's packed lunch.'

I lie awake, listening, as they make a meal of the morning routine. Raised voices, banging and crashing in the kitchen, and a final whine from Sasha about the poor standard of her packed lunch, followed by a slammed door and then ... silence.

I wait until I hear Andrew's car reverse away with a screech of expensive tyres, then sit up. I've concentrated so hard that I do now have a headache, which serves me right. But my feelings of guilt fade when I step into the bathroom and see the state he's left it in – damp towels on the floor, big beads of toothpaste stuck to the washbasin like cement. And my remorse disappears altogether when I go downstairs to put the kettle on and see he's left me a note: *Hope you feel better soon, Lulu. If you do perk up, would you be able to drop my suits into the dry-cleaners? They're a bit grubby. But if you're not up to going out, my shoes could do with a polish. I wouldn't ask but I know how you hate just sitting around. Love, A.*

I screw the note into a ball and throw it up into the air: Buster obligingly chases it around the kitchen and tears it to pieces with his claws. After an indulgent twenty minutes in the shower, I dress in Day Off Sick clothes, a stained old T-shirt and tracksuit bottoms, in case Andrew comes back to check up on me, then go out to my car. The cat hovers by the front door as I carry the boxes and books from the boot up to the study. Then I make myself a pot of tea and begin to read.

Buster brushes up against my hand, meowing impatiently, but I ignore him, just as I've ignored my tea and the phone. The tinny speaker on the laptop is playing my old favourite, *La Traviata*, and I hum along. So far I've made no breakthrough, but every bill and birthday card promises to take me closer. I've switched on Andrew's spare laptop and created a document called Christmas Food Shopping.doc because I know there's no way he'd ever look at that. But instead of stuffing ingredients, I'm listing all the dates and evidence I have about my father's life. I don't know what I'm going to find out, but I'm more certain than ever that his existence has to have meant something. And it has to offer me an insight into my own.

The facts look thin on the page. Date of birth, 31 January 1940. Aquarian (according to my internet search, babies born on that day would be spirited, independent, broad-minded, perhaps a little distant). Went to primary and grammar school in the Midlands, before heading for Manchester University to begin medical training in 1958.

So far, so limited. Looking at the photos will come later,

the reward for my meticulous examination of the paperwork. I've gathered, from an unsigned Valentine's card addressed to Mum in Dad's spiky handwriting, that they met some time before February 1965. He'd have been qualified by then, and Mum in her third year of nurse training. I try to remember any snippets of stories I've been told about the circumstances of their meeting. I have a feeling they were both working in paediatrics together. In my log, I've written *?December 1964? James and Judith meet.*

I feel frustrated, angry with myself and with Mum. Why did we never talk about it? Half of my history was written off in 1974, maybe for ever. I wonder again about what Terri said, whether I am digging up secrets that should be left alone. The old Lucy would have been cautious. But now . . .

The textbooks have provided no answers, though it helps me understand the world he worked in, where kids with polio were locked into iron lungs, where their best prognosis would be to leave the hospital in callipers.

It's one o'clock already. I've got my work cut out to sort all the stuff and tidy it away by the time Sasha needs picking up. I feel the need for a little light relief, so I reach for the Muddly and flick through till I reach the section on Observation:

One of the most important things that a Guide has to learn, whether she is a hunter or a peace scout, is to let nothing escape her attention; she must notice small points and signs, and then make out the meaning of them.

I sigh. I know the signs must be there, but somehow I can't put them together to 'make out the meaning'.

Buster nudges me again and this time I give in. The rumbling of my stomach is the biggest sign right now; maybe lunch will give me a new lease of life.

Bingo! I turn the photograph over in my hands again. It's a breakthrough, I'm sure of it. The class of '64 graduation photo. My father's intelligent eyes stare back at me from the second row. He was good-looking in an earthy way. I bet he cut quite a dash on the wards, his rugby-player's body straining the house-man's coat.

But it's not his presence in the line-up that excites me. I've seen photos of Dad from the sixties before, formal pictures at his wedding and my own christening, posed to make him look the same as everyone else, to fit the role: the handsome groom, the proud new father.

What's different about this photograph is the back. Because scribbled across the faint reversed shadows of the faces on the back of the photograph are *names*. Twenty-five names, in Dad's angular writing, each one given the title 'Doctor' to celebrate their newly minted status in life. At first I think they'd be lined up in alphabetical order, according to some university regulation. But then I look closely and realize it is more random than that, and perhaps the men either side of Dr James Gill might have been his friends.

My excitement grows when I notice that two of them have nicknames. Colin 'Sagger' Humphries, a thin man with curly hair, and Augustus 'Sunny' Bandele, the only black doctor, whose smile is the broadest in the photograph. Surely nicknames are only noted when you've been close to someone?

I know what I have to do next. I look up the number for the hospital in the phone book, but dread the disappointment of a dead end.

It's ten past three. I've got four minutes before I have to drive to school to pick Sasha up. I dial.

The line rings out for so long that I wonder if they've changed the number.

'Hello, hospital switchboard. Can I help you?'

'Hi, yes. Could you put me through to Dr Colin Humphries, please?'

'Hold the line please.'

I wait, trying to divine what the silence means.

'Sorry. We don't have a doctor of that name.' The operator sounds dismissive, about to end the call.

'Um, could you try Dr Augustus Bandele, then?'

A brief pause: 'We have Mr Augustus Bandele, the cardiac surgeon?'

Bingo! 'Yes, yes. That'll be him.'

'I'll put you through to his secretary.'

I hold my breath as the phone beeps, then switches to voice-mail instructing me to leave a message.

'Hello. Hi. My name is Lucy Collins, but my maiden name is Gill. I'm not a patient; this is more of a personal call for Dr, I mean, Mr Bandele. I believe he may have been a friend of my father, Dr James Gill. I know it's a long shot, but I'd be grateful if you could pass on my message. Thank you very much.'

It's only when I replace the receiver, my face hot and my hands shaking, that I realize I've forgotten to leave my number.

Agility

1. Show that you can stand, sit, walk, run, jump and land well.
2. Skip $\frac{1}{2}$ a minute without a break, turning the rope backwards. Perform three fancy steps.
3. Show that you can perform a leapfrog.
4. Balance-walk along a narrow bench or on flower pots over a distance of six metres.
5. Join two of these actions into a sequence:
    a) a forward and backward roll
    b) a shoulder stand
    c) a handstand against a support.

Chapter Sixteen

To carry out all the duties of a Scout properly
a girl has to be strong, healthy and active. A
short go of Swedish or ju-jitsu exercises every
morning and evening is a grand thing for
keeping you fit.

At eight a.m. precisely, the door bell rings. Andrew says it's
powered by a computer more powerful than the one that
put Neil Armstrong on the moon, but that doesn't stop the
chime sounding more fake than a twenty-pound Rolex. The
bell is like everything else in my life: it doesn't stand up to
scrutiny.

Terri had suggested an 'oh-eight-hundred-hours' rendezvous,
and Terri is always on time. Being late would probably cause
her physical pain. I just hope she's not going to give me another
lecture about how *vulnerable* I am.

'Morning, Lucy.' She's wearing a brown jumper with patches
on the sleeves and her hair's swept back from her face in an
unflattering ponytail. In the sunshine she looks far older than
thirty-five.

'You're ready for action,' I say. 'Still no clue for me, then?'

She's so excited about her surprise, but it's tiresome. She
reminds me of the only kid in the playground who knows the
facts of life, but won't let on, because it's the single thing that
keeps them the centre of attention. 'You'll see for yourself in
less than an hour.'

She marches off and I pick up the bag that holds my trainers
and tracksuit. I'm only going so I don't hurt her feelings. It'll be

nice to see the others again, but I'd rather spend my Sunday back at the Old Surgery, looking for more evidence about my father. Though I haven't had the nerve to call the hospital again.

'Bye,' I shout up the stairs, but no one calls back. Andrew didn't stir when I got up, and Sasha can't hear me above the hysterical kids' programme she's watching in her bedroom. At least Andrew didn't make a fuss about me leaving the two of them on their own. He's still on best behaviour, but I can tell there's a limit to his patience. I can almost see him looking at the kitchen calendar, wondering on what date my official mourning period will finish, and lovely Lucy, compliant wife and mother, will return in place of this alien that's currently inhabiting my body.

Chris is already in the back of Terri's rusty Metro, and I climb in beside her, knowing that there's no way we can expect Paula to squeeze in there. Chris raises her eyebrows at me and whispers, 'What the hell is she up to?'

Terri clicks her folding front seat back into place. 'What was that?'

'I was just saying what a good idea it is for us all to get back together,' Chris says, without a trace of guilt. I blush on her behalf.

Terri reverses out of the driveway with a grunt. The gears screech and then the tyres do the same as Saxon Close becomes a blur. I remember why I never get a lift from Terri if I can help it. Her driving's deteriorated as she's got older: now she seems to believe that her status as trainee vicar grants her immunity from death or road rage revenge attacks.

'I'm so pleased we're getting together again,' Terri shouts over the sound of the engine. 'I think this could become a regular thing!'

Chris glances at me, then takes a deep breath. 'I think it's terrific that you're up for organizing us all, Terri. But after today, I'm sure we don't want you to go to any more trouble.'

'No trouble,' Terri says, taking the right turn out of my cul-de-sac and forcing a white van to brake sharply.

Chris shrugs her shoulders in resignation. '*I tried*,' she mouths at me.

She looks knackered. Her skin is pimply, and her hair's less coiffed than it was at the restaurant and much more like the coppery birds' nest I remember from the old days. 'You OK?' I ask her.

'Yeah. Work, as usual,' she says, then looks away.

In the front, Terri's juggling audio cassettes and a can of Coke, which leaves no hand free for the steering wheel. I assume she must be manoeuvring the car with her knees. Finally she manages to get the tape into the player, and 'I Wish It Could Be Christmas Every Day' booms from the speakers.

'I wondered where my *Fab Festive Hits* had got to,' she says. 'The labels keep falling off. No one minds, do they?'

By the time we arrive at the Primrose Estate, we've put up with 'Last Christmas', 'All I Want For Christmas is You', and two Cliff Richard tracks. It's a relief when Terri turns the engine off and goes to fetch Paula.

The two of them emerge a few minutes later, Paula pouting like Shirley Temple. Her thin hair is tied into two tiny side-bunches with elastic bands. As she squeezes her way into the seat, the car suspension sighs and she turns awkwardly to Chris and me. 'This bloody magical mystery tour bollocks is freaking me right out.'

Terri smiles patiently. 'What a lot of moaning minnies we've turned into! Honestly! Where's your sense of adventure?'

'It buggered off in 1979,' Paula mumbles.

'Well, I think it's fantastic that you're going to all this trouble, Terri,' I say, feeling the need to stick up for my best friend, however crazy she is. 'Can't you give us a clue, though?'

She smiles at me in the mirror. 'All I'll say is that I've called in a bit of a favour from someone I know. An ex-boyfriend, actually. Don't look like that! I have had boyfriends, however hard you lot find it to believe.'

'A favour?' Paula still sounds stroppy as hell.

'You'll see. Are you sure you don't want to bring a change of clothes?' All Terri's told us is that we need trainers and something we 'don't mind getting a bit grubby and sweaty'.

I can't see much of Paula's outfit, but what I can see is unflattering in the extreme – a pair of black leggings made from material so stretched you can glimpse the network of thread-veins on her thighs, and a pink T-shirt with a grey woollen jumper pulled over the top. Plus a pair of black moccasins that look like relics from the Battle of the Little Bighorn.

'This is the best it's going to get, duck. You don't get a lot of designer gear in size twenty-two.'

That shuts us all up. That, and Terri's white-knuckle ride into the wilds of Cheshire. First she drives towards the motorway, then takes a left turn as though she's in the Monaco Grand Prix. We're off up Barm Hill, named after the local word for bread roll, because of its brown bracken-covered rounded top. The landscape is studded with old farmhouses, though most of them are now luxury homes for the kind of executive who prefers rural character to the modernized comforts of Saxon Close. I can't blame the farmers for selling up: on a day like today, the view is stunning, but in winter, the weather does everything it can to obstruct attempts to cultivate the land, with piercing winds, and frost that renders the ground harder than granite.

'I can't remember the last time I came this far into the country,' Chris says, gazing out of the window. 'You forget, don't you, about what's on your own doorstep?'

I think about my last journey up here, joy-riding along my own doorstep in Andrew's car.

Paula squirms. 'I hope you're not planning any bloody fell-walking. Because I can barely make it to the post box.'

'No, nothing like that,' Terri says. At least she's switched off the Christmas songs, but she's humming in satisfaction as she takes another bend at fifty miles an hour, sending me and Chris flying across the back seat. After that, we hold hands. We both have sweaty palms.

Finally at the bottom of the other side of the hill, Terri takes a narrow turning marked with a hand-painted sign: *To Lone Wolf Farm.*

'Lone Wolf?' Paula says. 'That sounds a bit ... creepy.'

'Just wait.'

We pull up in a farmyard, with a low stable block on one side and a sprawling modern bungalow on the other. A squat man in his forties steps out of the stable block. He looks very sure of himself, with bouffant combed-back hair, tiny eyes and an upturned nose. He reminds me of a hedgehog.

'Hey, Terri,' the Hedgehog says as we clamber out of the car. 'You made it, then. And these are our victims, eh?'

'Not victims. These are the girls I used to be in the Brownies with. Lucy, Chris, Paula – meet Robert.'

'Oh, blimey,' he says, staring at Paula. 'It's quite a tough course in places, Terri.'

'Course?' Paula looks accusingly at Terri. 'That wouldn't be as in … assault course, would it?'

The Hedgehog snarls. 'We don't use old-fashioned phrases like that any more, love. There's nothing military about what we do. Terri put me right there. We're *holistic*.' He doesn't smile as he says it. It makes me feel nervous.

Terri nods. 'When I first met Robert, he'd had this idea to turn his dad's farm into one of those paintballing centres; you know the kind of thing: blokes with too much testosterone trying to shoot each other to get rid of all that office tension.'

'Very 1980s,' says Chris.

'Exactly. That's what I said. So I suggested that a much better approach would be to make things a bit more *spiritual*. Yoga and chanting and self-discovery is far more now.'

'Thank God for that. Yoga's just lying around on a mat, isn't it? Even a fat cow like me can manage that,' Paula says. 'In fact, I bet I'm better at it than you lot. More practice.'

Robert shakes his head, a sarcastic expression on his face. 'Oh, the yoga comes afterwards. If you make it through to afterwards. You'd better follow me.'

The stable block has been converted into changing rooms with solid wood lockers, Molton Brown body lotion and snow-white towels. I relax as I step inside – and I see Paula's looking relieved.

Terri points at her. 'She hasn't got any kit, Rob. Do you think you've got some you can lend her?'

He frowns. 'We might have some in her size in the men's locker room.'

Paula laughs weakly as he disappears and I wish I could make it all better for her.

'Say cheese!' I press the button on my disposable camera, but the flash doesn't fire. Probably just as well. It's hard to imagine a more mismatched, ill-equipped set of Lone Wolves.

Paula, predictably, looks the worst. The threadbare leggings have been replaced by a pair of men's army fatigue trousers. They'd swamp any normal-sized person, but they strain around her monster thighs, highlighting the uneven contours of her cellulite with the mottled browns and greens. The trousers are too long, so they've been tucked into the borrowed boots, which are black and yeti-sized. Still, at least Paula's ready for anything.

Terri doesn't look much better. As well as the Brown Owl jumper and jogging bottoms, she's added sensibly brown hardcore cross-terrain shoes and a brown baseball cap, red curls escaping around her ears. She looks like Benny from *Crossroads*.

Next to them, I feel almost glamorous in my tracksuit and Reeboks. Then I spot Chris.

The daydreamer of the Pixies now seems to belong to an entirely different species, a kind of super-race. Her designer trainers are bright-white-new and her velour Juicy Couture tracksuit clings to each gym-honed curve.

'You look amazing,' I tell her.

'Thanks to my personal trainer. Such a sadist that it's less effort to do sixty sit-ups than try to argue with him.'

'I'd settle for ever seeing my toes again, duck,' Paula grunts.

The Hedgehog appears through the door of the changing room, rubbing his hands in anticipation. 'So we're all ship-shape?' He's changed into a boxer's vest and shorts, which reveal thin, almost hairless legs. He's terminally unfanciable, but he must have been one of Terri's projects. In a way, I feel like we all are.

He leads the way through double doors at the back of the stable block, down a little path, through a gap in the hedgerow.

'Oh shit,' Paula says. 'If that isn't an assault course, I don't know what is.'

In front of us, a harmless paddock has been transformed into a terrifying sight. Nets, climbing walls and ditches are packed into a field the length of half a football pitch. As I look at each obstacle in turn, working out whether I can ever get over it (no … no … maybe on a good day … not in a million years), the sun disappears behind a grey cloud and the temperature drops several degrees.

Paula turns around and scowls at Terri. 'Is this National Humiliate the Hippo Day or something? There's no way I can do this.'

'Oh, Paula, Paula, Paula,' Terri says slowly. 'It's no wonder you're stuck in a rut. Have you ever heard of positive thinking? If we think of ourselves as hopeless, we might as well just roll over and give up.'

'Yeah, well that's exactly what I'm going to do. I mean, look at that tunnel thingy. There's no way I'd ever get out in one piece.'

She's got a point. The tube is a bigger version of one you'd get for sheepdog trials: caterpillar-like, divided into sections by metal hoops, with a mouth barely wide enough for Paula's shoulders, never mind her hips.

The Hedgehog catches Paula's arm as she walks past him, back towards the changing room. 'Listen, love. You don't have to do all the obstacles but it's a bit pathetic to give up without trying, don't you think?'

'Who the hell do you think you are?' Paula pulls away from him.

'Somebody with a lot more self-control than you, love. About time you took a long hard look at yourself.'

'Oh, fuck off!' And Paula moves faster than she probably has in years, shuffling back towards the stable block. I'm not sure whether to follow her, but I wait to see what Terri's going to do, as it is her show.

She sighs. 'Well done, Rob. Nice to see your customer service skills haven't improved any.'

'What did I say?'

'Why don't you take the rest of the afternoon off? We'll be fine.'

'Whatever.' He grins at me and Chris. 'I learned early on not to argue with Terri. Saves time. She always gets her way in the end.' Then he slopes off.

'I tell you one thing,' Chris says, 'if he's an ex, then I'm starting to understand why you're still a virgin, Terri.'

'Yes, well, I've always liked a challenge. And I try to see the best in people. Luce, you've got a face like a wet weekend. Are you all right?'

'No, not really. I'm worried about Paula. Shouldn't someone go after her?'

'What, and hold things up even more? Just because she's being too childish for words?'

I feel torn. 'Paula's upset. And I think it was a bit out of order to drag her here when she's never going to be capable of getting over this course.'

'So you'd rather let her carry on eating until she's too massive to get out of bed. Paula's a mess, Lucy, and it's our duty to sort her out.'

'And she doesn't have a say in it?' I look to Chris for support.

'I . . . for what it's worth, Terri, I think it's a high-risk strategy to try to force anyone into something against their will.'

Terri's face is turning bright pink. Perhaps she should take that bloody hat off, let the steam escape. 'I don't believe in allowing people to ruin their lives if there's an alternative.'

'Because yours is such a rip-roaring success?' I say it without censoring myself. It's becoming a habit.

'No.' Terri sounds calmer now. 'But at least I'm doing something positive. The way your mother always used to. Not that you'd understand that.'

For a moment, I feel paralysed. Then my hand takes a decision for me and moves towards Terri's face, so quickly that I'm still unsure what's happening until I hear the noise of the slap and feel the sting on my fingers.

'Ow!'

'Bloody hell, Lucy.' Chris looks alarmed.

I stare at the red mark already appearing on Terri's left cheek. 'Oh, my God. Terri. I'm sorry . . .' There they go again: the tears are pooling in my eyes. 'I've never … I've never even smacked Sasha. What is happening to me?'

Terri smiles ruefully. 'I don't know for sure, Luce.' Then she opens up her arms, as awkward as ever, and pulls me forward so I bury my face in the Brown Owl jumper. 'But I've got a feeling it might be known as grief. And I've got a feeling we're in it together.'

'It's like being behind the bike sheds again,' Paula says, taking a drag of a cigarette. She looked astonished when we came after her, and more surprised when Terri offered us all a Silk Cut.

I've even taken one myself. I need to calm down after what I just did. What the hell am I going to do next? Arm myself with a machete and run rampage through Fancy Footwork singing 'Happy Feet'? I am a bloody mess. So how come no one else can see it?

'As I remember it, you were the only one of us cool enough to be allowed behind the bike sheds,' Terri says. The four of us are sitting on the step at the back of the stable block, overlooking the empty assault course.

'Nah. I wasn't cool. I was just the only one of us who was too thick not to make the A-stream. Oh, and the other girls were scared I might sit on them.'

'But you weren't that fat then—' I stop. Oh, well done, Lucy. 'Sorry. I didn't mean …'

Paula shrugs. 'What, compared to how I am now? You're dead right. If I'd known the size I'd get to now, I'd have been wearing mini skirts when I was fourteen to make the most of my slender years.'

'Have you ever tried dieting?' Terri asks her.

'Yeah, a few. The pineapple diet, obviously the cabbage soup diet, the cornflakes diet, that boiled egg one. Never for much longer than a day, mind you. Usually I end up resorting to the toast diet, which isn't that effective.' She pinches considerably more than an inch from her midriff. 'As you can see for yourselves.'

'Well, we can't all have a body like Chris,' I say. 'Hey … earth to Chris, I'm paying you a compliment.'

'What?' Chris's cigarette has almost burned itself out and as she jolts out of her daydream, the ash flies through the air. 'Sorry, I was thinking about work. As usual.'

'Daydreaming about dildos?' Paula suggests.

'No, not exactly. You know I said at dinner about this take-over bid? Well, the big boys seem to be winning.'

Paula frowns. 'But isn't that good news, duck? I mean, you'd get a shedload of cash and spend the rest of your life, I dunno, on a yacht in Cannes. Bathing in asses milk. Whatever you want.'

But Chris is shaking her head. 'I can't imagine anything worse. I haven't done this for the money. God, the thought of having nothing to do ... I mean, why would I get up in the morning?'

'That's how I feel now,' Paula says, staring at the ground.

'And me,' I say very quietly. Then I look up at Terri.

She shrugs. 'Oh, blimey. You want me to tell you it's worthwhile, don't you? That there is a point to all this. I do believe that. I do. It's just that lately, well, I haven't felt like getting up in the mornings either.'

This shocks me more than anything. If Terri's feeling like this, what hope is there for mere mortals?

The sounds of the countryside fill the gap: the sun's out again and there's birdsong twittering from every tree, the occasional car passing a mile or so away, its engine noise carrying through the clear, bright air.

Terri stubs out the butt in the turf, grinding it with her heel. 'What a bloody mess. We're not much of an ad for the Brownies, are we?' All the certainty has disappeared from her voice.

I reach out to touch her shoulder. 'Hey, I don't suppose we're doing that much worse than anyone else.'

'But that's not the point, is it? We were meant to do *better*. We had so much going for us. And look at us now. I'm a candidate for the north-west heats of Most Ancient Virgin in Britain and I don't know why any more. You might as well be the cleaner for all the notice Andrew takes.'

'I'm OK,' Chris protests.

'Really? When was the last time you had a day off?'

'I'm here today, aren't I?'

Terri isn't going to let her get away with it. 'Before that?'

'I ... I didn't go into work on Christmas Day. Or Boxing Day.' But then she smiles. 'Though I did sneak away from my parents' place to send some emails. I had this great idea about using the dinner as a theme for *this* year's festive season ... you know, stuffing— '

Terri cuts her off. 'You don't need to draw me a diagram. But don't you ever want a *life*?'

'It is my life.'

'No wonder you're worried about someone buying it off you. OK, I'll give you the benefit of the doubt. But then Paula ...' Terri raises her eyebrows.

'Yeah, I know. I'm a bloody failure. Separated. Washed up. The size of a bus. And all my mum wanted for me was a nice semi, maybe a detached house, meeting my husband at the Rotary Club where Dad would have been chairman. Ha bloody ha,' Paula says. 'What do they call them? Yummy mummies. Like Lucy.'

I nod. Yummy mummy. I suppose that's what I am. But does a yummy mummy slap her best friend, take her husband's car without permission? 'I know. Things could be a heck of a lot worse. That's what I mean, Terri. Everyone has doubts about the point of life sometimes. It's about being a human being. Or maybe a human being in your thirties.'

'I don't care,' Terri says. She sounds as petulant as Sasha on the rare occasions I refuse to let her have her way. 'It wasn't meant to be like this.'

Chris stands up. 'It doesn't have to be, though, does it? We're still young enough to do things differently. Seize the day. Like now. Why don't we do this bloody course? Might cheer us all up a bit.'

Paula shakes her head. 'Don't be daft. I can't.'

'You could if we helped you,' Chris says, which seems a bit over-optimistic to me.

'Maybe in the movies, Chris, but this isn't *Private* sodding *Benjamin*, OK?'

'What are you so afraid of?'

'Well, let me see ... falling on my arse, squashing someone, breaking a bone, having a coronary; do you want me to go on?'

I stand up too: I'm no keener than she is, but Terri needs a boost every bit as much as Paula. 'But now we're here. We could help you. You used to be so good, so fearless. There's no point pretending you're not bigger than you were, but we can skip the ... narrow bits.'

'I suppose we could.' Terri looks less downcast.

Paula sighs. 'I know when I'm defeated, but don't say I didn't warn you. You'll see soon enough what a bloody crap idea this is.'

The first obstacle — a rope net to crawl under — is easy, though my knees hurt as I reach the other side. I turn to see Paula getting het up. She looks like an elephant trapped by a party of upper-class British trophy hunters in the Raj. I imagine her head and shoulders, stuffed and mounted, on the banqueting hall wall of a dusty stately home. But then I reckon she'd be enough to put anyone off their dinner.

I blush, ashamed of myself. 'Come on, Paula: you can do it!'

She finally emerges sweating and panting, as Chris and I reach out our hands to pull her up.

'I did it!'

'Of course you did, silly,' I say. 'You always were the bravest of all of us. Come on.'

The next obstacle is a low, narrow wall, made of single bricks. It looks easy, but as I step up, I feel shaky. Paula is behind me and as I reach the end of the wall, I turn and see her holding out her arms as if she's playing aeroplanes. She blushes, realizing how silly she looks, and then she teeters. 'Shit.'

Behind her, Chris whispers: 'You've got to do it fast. That's the trick. And keep looking ahead.'

Paula takes a deep breath and launches herself along the rest of the wall, left foot, right foot, left foot, right foot ... the sun is hot and sweat's running down her face but then she reaches the end and steps down, smiling broadly. We all watch as Terri stumbles, jumping off and frowning. But Terri's determined; you have to give her that. She returns to the beginning and completes the obstacle.

The water-filled ditch that comes next would be grim on a cold day, but now the sun's out again, it's refreshing. The cool water soaks up the ankles of my tracksuit bottoms and I link arms with Paula as we wade through. She leans down with her hand to splash me, and I can see that she's beginning to enjoy herself. Somewhere under the blubber, the tomboy is still alive and kicking.

'This is a bit of a laugh,' she says and her voice is missing the edge that's tainted everything she's said since we were all reunited. Even she looks surprised at herself.

But then we peer up from the water and hit a wall. Literally. This one is as tall as the top of our heads and, to Paula, surely as insurmountable as Kilimanjaro. I know I'm going to struggle to propel myself over it and I weigh nine stone. At double that ... well, it must be a physical impossibility.

Paula's shoulders slump.

'You can walk round it,' I say. 'It's no big deal, not really. Rules are made to be broken.'

Paula looks defeated. 'Yeah. And we need to make allowances for the fat lump. After all, she's not like *normal* people.' The bitterness is back.

Chris appears. 'Hey, don't stop now.'

'Unless you've got a fork lift truck handy, there's no way I'm getting over that wall.'

'Hmmm.' Chris sounds unconvinced.

In a single, forceful movement, Chris knocks into Paula, pushing her towards the wall.

'Ooof ...'

Chris's tiny hands sink into the flesh of Paula's enormous buttocks and I blush for both of them.

'Reach up with your arms and grip the top of the wall with your wrists.' Chris's voice is encouraging but non-negotiable: Paula does as she says. 'That's it. Now if I count to three, on the three, you've got to jump up, and at the same time, I'll give you a shove and you'll be over in no time.'

'But it's hopeless.'

'Don't give me that shit, Paula. I learned all I know from you. Trust me. One ...'

Paula shoots me a helpless look and I try to smile hopefully. Chris's grip looks surprisingly strong, considering what a skinny creature she is, but Paula only has to let go of the wall and her bulk would flatten Chris.

'Two ...'

I hold my breath as Paula stares at the wall, just inches from her face now. She used to be so bloody daring – in her three years as a Brownie, she managed a broken arm, endless twisted ankles and a head wound that needed a dozen stitches. I remember her coming in the week afterwards and showing off her war wounds, the new scar spectacularly red against her shaven scalp. And she never cried.

'THREE!'

In that moment, Paula launches her feet off the ground, as Chris gives her an almighty shove. Paula winces as her hands grip the bricks and then some long-forgotten instinct makes her propel her legs sideways, scrambling and kicking in the air before ...

And there she is, straddling the wall, looking down at us. I can't quite believe it, and judging from the expression on her face, neither can she.

'Do you know what I want to do now?' she says, between breaths. Most of her hair has escaped from the bunches, and her skin is glowing.

'No,' we say together. Have a go at Everest? Run a marathon?

She opens her mouth and begins to sing. 'I'm the king of the castle, you're the dirty rascal.' And then she laughs so hard that I worry she's going to do a Humpty Dumpty and fall off.

We reach up to help her down and as she thumps back on the ground, Terri catches my eye and grins. She'd never say I told you so, but she knows that I know she was right to push us. Though I'm starting to realize that there is a limit to how far I can be pushed before I will fight back.

Chapter Seventeen

What is a Promise? Your Brownie Promise
will last the whole of your life so you will
want to be quite sure you understand it
before you make it.

Somehow I manage not to cry during Sasha's Promise ceremony. She looks what my mum would have called 'pleased as punch' when they pin on the trefoil badge that marks her graduation to the ranks of fully fledged Brownies.

I'm too angry to cry. Andrew, after all his promises, is late. The ceremony happens at the end of the meeting, just as the other parents arrive to pick the kids up, so there's no excuse. As I watch Sasha beam in response to the song her fellow Pixies are singing to welcome her to the Six, her eyes dart towards the door, and then away again, careful not to show any disappointment. I know she must be disappointed, though: Sasha is Daddy's girl and Daddy has let her down.

Right now I'm having a hard time remembering why I shouldn't hate my husband.

The doubts don't subside when he steps through the door just in time to see Sasha stooping to pass under a tunnel of little girls' raised arms. His skin is slightly moist with sweat, and the colour in his cheeks makes his eyes look bluer than ever. He gives me a rueful glance, which I blank, and then I see our daughter's face transformed when she spots him, and her body leans in his direction as if she's struggling not to break away from her new friends, to run into his arms.

I feel envious: of Andrew, for Sasha's unconditional love, and of Sasha, for having a father. I shake my head slightly, trying to banish my irritation, before sidling up to him to present a united front once the ceremony finishes.

'Bloody awful traffic jam,' he whispers from the side of his mouth, keeping his eyes fixed on Sasha. 'Lucky I made it at all.'

'Yes, lucky us,' I whisper back.

He doesn't look at me, but his mouth curls downwards. 'Oh, terrific. In one of your moods, then?'

'That's right,' I say, through a forced smile. 'Off I go again. Nothing to do with you prioritizing work over our daughter, of course.'

He turns to me now. 'I'll drop out, shall I? We can move to the Primrose Estate and live on the dole.'

'I don't mean that. I just want you to take more of an interest.'

He stares ahead, like a soldier on parade. 'If you wanted a New Man, you should have married someone else.'

In that moment, I know he's right. I should have. I've never thought of it like that, as if I'd had a choice. The boyfriends I had before weren't the marrying kind, so when I met Andrew at a party, I knew very quickly that he met the criteria for a reliable husband and that seemed the best I could hope for. Solid, pensionable career: tick. Loyalty: tick. Good relationship with his mother: double tick. Traditional values: tick. Wanted children: tick ... though maybe I should have double-checked how many.

Before I can reply, the ceremony finishes and Sasha rushes over to us, hugging Andrew first, then me for what I'm sure is only half as long. I go through the motions of nodding goodbye to some of the other parents, and thanking Terri, before we get outside.

'Are you coming home with me, or with Mummy?' Andrew asks Sasha as we stand in the car park. She doesn't hesitate before running over to his Audi.

'Later,' I mouth at him.

He frowns back.

*

150

I thought Sasha would be too excited to sleep, but after her bath, she goes as floppy as a toddler, almost needing to be carried to bed. I watch her sleep for a few minutes. I don't want to talk any more than Andrew does, but there are things we can't keep putting off.

'Calmed down yet?' he asks, handing me a glass of wine as I walk into the living room. I sit down on the chair, rather than next to him on the sofa. 'I guess not, then.'

'This isn't PMT, Andrew.'

'No, at least that's only once a month,' he says. 'So what else have I done wrong, then?'

'It's not about a list of *things*,' I begin, not knowing where I'm going to end. 'It's more about feeling supported. Or noticed, even.'

'Oh God, have you had your hair done?'

I shake my head, slowly.

'Lost weight? New jumper? New *bra*?' He tries a sheepish schoolboy grin. 'I give up. I'll never work it out.'

'No. You won't.'

'I can't stand these cryptic conversations.' His voice is raised now. I've only heard Andrew lose his self-control half a dozen times, and this is how it begins. 'Just tell me what you want me to do and I will bloody do it, but I will not play guessing games.'

'I want us to be ... I don't know, more like a team.'

'We *are* a team,' he says, more conciliatory now. 'It's just we have different roles. That's the way we always said it was going to be, didn't we, Lulu? I know it's old-fashioned but you know what they say: if it ain't broke—'

'It is broke ... broken. I don't mind being a wife and a mum but it's not enough on its own.'

'You've got your job.'

'That's not enough either. I want ...' I tail off. I can't explain it.

He nods to himself. 'I think I know what this is about. It's about having another baby, isn't it?'

I laugh, before I can stop myself.

He smiles at what he's convinced is his amazing insight. 'I

knew it. You know why it's not possible at the moment. I mean, look at our lives. We're busy enough as it is.' Then he stops, as if he's weighing it up in his mind. 'But I suppose, maybe in a year or so, once the Old Surgery's sold and things are more settled ... well, I wouldn't rule out another baby then, if it'd make you happy.' He leans back into the sofa, pleased with his generosity, wondering how long he has to leave it before he can switch the TV on.

'It's. Not. About. Babies.' The volume of my voice rises with each word, however hard I try to keep it down. 'Why would I want another bloody person who treats me like an unpaid servant?'

He recoils. 'A servant? But ... you always wanted a home. You wanted to look after people, you told me that; I distinctly remember what you said when we first got together. It was how you wanted—'

'I know,' I say, trying to think of a way to take back the words, without taking back the meaning. 'But people change. I've changed. Mum going has made me realize I need more.'

He narrows his eyes. 'Oh, I knew it'd come back to your mum, playing the sympathy card. Poor Lucy. Well, funnily enough, the world doesn't only revolve around your needs. We have a daughter, and she comes first.'

I open my mouth to speak but nothing comes out. He's confusing me, twisting my words, making me feel dizzy with anger and frustration. It's *him* that ignores Sasha's needs and yet it's him she goes to when she wants someone. 'I ... I just want to feel like someone wants to be with me for me ... not just for the dinners I can cook and the lifts I can provide.'

He stands up. 'I don't like the way you're turning selfish, Lucy. Did your mother ever complain about her life? Does mine? And they both had it a hell of a lot worse than you. I've worked so hard to get all this – ' he waves vaguely at the plasma TV and the leather sofa and the Conran Shop lighting '– but I didn't do it for me. I did it for you. Do you think I don't resent sitting in endless meetings about dual carriageways and traffic strategy and tolls? Do you think I don't want to run away and sit on a beach and never have to go to another bloody planning inquiry?'

I have never thought of Andrew as the sort to want to run away.

'But I never would, Lucy. I made a deal with you. A promise. I thought we both felt the same way about family. And promises.' He looks at me like a dog owner after Rover has made a mess on the new carpet. 'I'm not sure I know you any more.'

He closes the door behind him so quietly I can tell he's furious. I hear his footsteps on the stairs, each tread carefully moderated when I am sure what he wants to do is stomp and shout.

The house is silent. I'm only separated from my closest family by plaster, underlay and rainforest-friendly floorboards, but I feel completely alone.

Chapter Eighteen

Directly poor people in England are invalided they go into hospitals. But do they remember that then some rich person is paying for them, for their doctoring and food and all.

My hand shakes as I press the lift-call button in the hospital lobby. The antiseptic fumes and the purposeful bustle of uniformed medical staff remind me of Mum's last few days. There's a world of difference between this heaving city infirmary and the cosiness of Troughton Cottage Hospital, but they both have the same smell: of pine disinfectant and wee and suffering. Having a doctor and a nurse as parents hasn't stopped me hating hospitals.

But my discomfort is outweighed by my desperation for knowledge about Dad, and if I'm honest, my hand's shaking as much from excitement as fear. I woke up yesterday after the row with Andrew knowing I had to try again, and called Mr Bandele's office from work five times before I finally got through to his secretary. She sounded highly dubious when I gave her my garbled explanation. Then, last night, just before we cashed up, my mobile rang and a man with a deep, public-school voice asked me if he was really speaking to Jim Gill's daughter. When I said yes, he sighed deeply.

'At last ... I *knew* you'd be in touch one day. My dear, we must meet. Soon? What are you doing ...' I heard papers rustle as he consulted his diary, ' – tomorrow? No time like the present, I say. And seeing you again will be the greatest of pleasures.'

Again. One word that made me feel better than all the other things people had said to try to comfort me since Mum died. Here was someone who knew me when I was a normal little girl in a normal little family: someone else in the world who had memories I might share.

All day I've been trying to summon up those memories. I thought about it on the train, too, after I left work early (the girls in the shop thought I'd finally flipped). Was that Sunny, sitting at the dinner table when I came down in my pyjamas after having a nightmare, when Daddy let me sit with the grown-ups while they drank coffee and smoked and listened to him playing his guitar? Or perhaps he was there at my fifth birthday party, the one where I was so excited that I was sick down my daisy-print yellow dress and Daddy cleaned me up? And was it Sunny who brought a tiny brown baby for me to coo over, who let me hold it when it slept?

I take the lift to the third floor, then follow the signs to cardiology. Strange to imagine my father wandering these corridors forty years ago, joking with the nurses. He'd have been confident but not cocky, eager to learn and eager to get to know his patients, to understand what made them tick.

I push open the swing door to the heart clinic. A young woman is dragging an industrial vacuum cleaner across the bumpy lino. 'We're closed,' she says, without looking up.

'I know. I've come to see Mr Bandele on a ... personal matter.'

The woman still doesn't look up. 'Second on the right. Name's on the door.'

I hesitate before knocking. I have to think myself brave. I remember a phrase from the Muddly: being brave is 'just like taking a header into cold water' – you need to practise to become stronger. I rap my knuckles against the wood.

'Come in.' The voice is the same as the one I heard on the phone, an accent more cut-glass than the Queen's. I push open the door.

He's sitting in a battered orange swivel chair, its foam contours fitting snugly around his massive frame. I study his face – broad, slightly jowly, sympathetic – but see nothing I recognize. I just hope he can't tell how disappointed I am.

'You're just like him, you know,' he says, smiling. 'But you always were, I thought. Your mother's hair and eyes, but the rest of you ... you have Jim's bearing.'

His voice warms me from the inside out. 'When was the last time you saw me, Mr Bandele?'

He shakes his finger. 'No, no formality. I was Sunny to your father and will be Sunny to you. I last saw you in ... let me see. Jim died in the November, so it would have been Christmas 1974. Just before you moved. I brought you a present. A little library of Beatrix Potter books. I used to read you the story of Mrs Tiggywinkle.' His eyes look teary as he speaks. His forehead is almost unlined and the only signs that he must be approaching retirement age are the thick glasses and the clusters of white curls against the hazelnut skin of his temples. 'Sit down, Lucy. Can I get you a coffee? I'm having one.'

'Yes, please.' I take the plastic chair that's positioned at right angles to Sunny's, and wonder what news he's given to the occupants of this chair today. The thumbs-up, or the thumbs-down? I sense that his bedside manner would make either verdict easier to hear.

He leaves the office, so I can have a good look around. The room's a hotch-potch of NHS furnishings and personal touches: an interiors magazine might call it medical eclectic and pronounce it the latest thing. So the examination couch is screened by a curtain emblazoned with tropical pink flowers, and the plastic chairs have matching cushions. The desk is ugly and worn, but it's covered with framed photographs. They're of different people, all ages and races, each one pictured in front of a landmark. A fat man with huge underarm sweat stains, cooling off alongside Niagara Falls. A family group eating ice-creams with the Eiffel Tower in the background. Two middle-aged women 'holding up' the leaning tower of Pisa.

'Ah, my collection.' He comes back into the room carrying two mugs. 'I ask my patients to make me a promise when they leave me. To go and see the world. And then to send me back a picture of them doing it. I like to show them to the newcomers; it proves that they have a bloody good chance of making it out of the hospital alive and kicking.'

'Right.' I've only just noticed Sunny's clothes. Underneath his blazer he's wearing a patterned shirt, but looking more closely, I spot that one side is striped and the other checked. 'Trendy shirt.'

'Ah ... I like this one. I like things that challenge people's expectations, Lucy. So ... I can't believe your mum's gone too. You must be feeling terribly alone.'

His directness is disarming. 'Yes. That's exactly how I feel. Silly, really. I'm not alone, not at all. There's my husband and my daughter and—'

'I know, I know. It doesn't make any difference. When my parents died I felt bereft. Even though I see death most weeks and even though I was much older than you when it happened, I was so *unprepared*. And Judy was so indestructible, always.'

'Judy?' I test this version of my mother's name out loud. 'No one ever called her that. It sounds ... informal. And strange. But good-strange, if you know what I mean. Like a different part of her.'

'Kids can never quite believe that their parents had a life before they arrived.'

I nod. 'You're so right. My daughter, Sasha, she just laughs when I tell her about me being young. And she's stunned that I ever dated anyone before I met my husband.' Not enough people, I want to add.

'So Jim has a granddaughter.' Sunny smiles. 'And is she like you?'

'No. Nothing like me. Much more like Mum ... like Judy. Sure of herself, which is something I've never been. Mum couldn't understand my shyness. She found it frustrating that I wouldn't say boo to a goose.' I stop, surprised. 'Did you put the truth drug in my coffee or something?'

He takes a sip of his drink and pauses a moment before speaking. 'You're missing half of the picture, aren't you, Lucy? That's why you're here.'

I think it over. 'Yes. It's exactly like that. I know he's there, but he's out of focus.'

Sunny leans back in his chair and it moans. 'It's hard to know where to start, but why don't I tell you what I remember most about your father, first, and then I'll answer any questions you have. How does that sound?'

'Perfect.'

'Not that there's any hurry, of course. I hope we're going to be friends. So ... Jim Gill. Your father was the most ... tricky person to pin down. Smart – much smarter than me, that's for sure – and funny. Thoughtful. And principled. It wasn't easy for me, the only African in my year. The only African doctor in the hospital, actually. My father was a doctor back in Nigeria and he wanted me to have the best medical education, which in his eyes was in England. And it cost him so much that I couldn't tell him how bad it was, never mind ask to go home. If it wasn't the other students talking behind my back, it was the patients refusing to be treated by me. But your father was my friend, when I needed one more than anything. When he and your mum bought their house, they knew I was having trouble, yet again, finding a landlady. So they had me as their lodger. I'm sure it was the last thing they needed, as newlyweds, but that was Jim and Judy.'

His voice falters slightly. 'What else can I tell you? He was great with kids; it was no surprise that he went into paediatrics. He knew instinctively how to act around children. I remember when we first went to the kids' ward as students. You have to remember, we were big loutish men, most of us had nothing to do with children, so we were flailing around, patronizing them, more afraid of them than they were of us. But he was a natural. Not only obvious stuff like crouching down to their level, but the tone of voice, what to talk about ... how much information they'd want about how ill they were. And he used to carry a recorder in his pocket, when he specialized, teach the kids to play. The nurses called him the Pied Piper.'

I nod. The relief of hearing that my own memories – or daydreams – of Dad seem to fit the reality is immense.

'But ... Jim wasn't perfect, Lucy. The way he was with children, well, I think it's because, in a way, he was a child. More like Peter Pan than the Pied Piper. The doctor who didn't want to grow up. I don't know what you know about his childhood.'

'Nothing. We never had anything to do with his parents after ...'

'Ah. Well, Judy had her reasons. He didn't talk about his parents much, or what was wrong, but the child is the father of the man, after all. Jim had a tendency to, how can I put it? Extremes. Oh, don't worry, he wasn't violent, not at all. But we never quite knew how he'd react to certain things – the death of a child he'd become close to, money worries. Sometimes he'd retreat into himself and sometimes he'd go into almost a tantrum, like a toddler who can't accept life won't always go his way. A kind of depression, in a way.'

'He was ill?' I feel a sharp, physical pain in my stomach.

Sunny narrows his eyes, thinking. 'What is illness? Some of us are glass half-full folks, and some half-empty.' He looks at me more warily than before.

'But you said he was depressed.'

'Perhaps more of a ... malaise. We all had our stresses and strains and our ways of reacting to them, and in a hospital you can be sure that there are plenty of ways to relieve it.'

'What do you mean?'

He pauses. 'Oh ... you know, wild parties. The usual.' He looked at his watch. 'It's five already. Do you have to go home straight away, Lucy?'

I told Andrew I was going into Manchester to go shopping and then meeting Terri for a quick drink, and for once he didn't make any fuss, though he did ask if I could pick up some Falke Berlin Sensitive socks (the only ones he'll wear) from Kendals department store. 'No, not really.'

'Because I'd love it if you could come back to my house. It's not far, but I've got some photographs I can dig out and it's so much less clinical, at the end of the day. And there's someone there I'd love you to meet.'

Chapter Nineteen

The woman who has most influence
with men is the woman who is gentle and
sweet, unselfish and true.

'Here we are,' says Sunny. 'Bandele Towers.'
The journey in Sunny's ancient Saab has taken less than ten minutes in rush hour, and I'm surprised at how modest the house is. True, it is three storeys tall, but surely as a consultant surgeon he must be able to afford more than a scruffy terrace in a street full of double-parked cars and overflowing skips.

'It's very … convenient for the hospital,' I say, failing to think of anything else nice.

He laughs. 'Yes. Believe it or not, it's coming up in the world as well. Pretty much the last bit of Manchester to be gentrified. I quite liked it as it was.'

I follow him up the path. 'How long have you lived here?'

'Oh, longer than you've been alive. I bought the house while Judy was pregnant with you. She and Jim kept telling me there was no rush for me to leave their spare room, but I knew it'd be a different story once you arrived.' He pushes open the door. 'And they were only round the corner, anyway.'

'From here?' I turn to look back out at the street. The red-bricked houses do seem familiar.

'I can take you there some time if you like. Come on through.'

The hall is cluttered with coats and shoes, and has a comforting smell of wet dog and roast coffee. I can hear languorous jazz coming from upstairs. Sunny leads me into the cluttered living room, where a West Highland White terrier is sleeping in a basket. 'This is Snowy,' he says and the dog's ears prick up, the tail trembles slightly, but his eyes stay shut. 'Though not quite so snowy any more, bless him. Look at his paws: they've gone pink with age, haven't they, old boy? We're all getting past our best in this house.' Loud footsteps pound down the stairs. 'Well, all except one of us. Seb, come in here.'

The face that appears in the doorway is like Sunny's, but this man is younger and thinner, with skin that's lighter than his father's.

'Seb. Meet Lucy. Though actually, you've met before.'

As he walks into the room, I feel breathless. He's as tall as his father, with a shaven head that emphasizes his cheekbones. I wonder where I could have seen him. Unless ...

'I'd remember meeting you,' he says. He has a laid-back Manchester accent quite unlike Sunny's posh vowels and precise consonants, and a wolfish smile.

Sunny grins. 'You were in nappies at the time. Lucy called you a little chimp.'

I'm blushing. He must have been the baby I remember. But how could I have said something like that? 'Oh, God. I didn't! That's appalling.'

'As you were four years old, I suppose we can excuse you being hopelessly politically incorrect. It was quite funny at the time.'

'A chimp?' Seb frowns. 'And do I still look like a chimp?'

I look up at him properly and the blush deepens. He is *beautiful*, in a kind of Calvin Klein model, not-born-of-this-world way. His skin is like varnished wood, smooth and gleaming, and his eyes ... His eyes are so deep brown that they merge with his pupils, but I can tell he's staring at me, inquisitive. 'No,' I say, coming to my senses. 'Not like a chimp at all.'

'I'll just go and dig out those photos,' Sunny says. 'Seb's into music, like your father was,' he adds proudly and I instantly picture Seb in a smoky club, moodily strumming a bass guitar or caressing a microphone.

'Really? Do you play in a band?' I say. Even to me, my nervous voice makes me sound like the Queen on a royal visit.

Seb shrugs. 'Kind of. Play the clarinet for a band I like to call the Phil. You might have heard of us ...' He gestures, long fingers pressing imaginary keys in front of him. And the slowest of smiles spreads across his face. Is he mocking me?

'Yes,' I say. 'I've heard of the Philharmonic Orchestra. I'm a singer myself. Classical. I could have gone on; my teacher said I might have been able to make it professionally, but ... life sort of got in the way.' Why am I showing off?

'How?' he says.

'Well.' I feel flustered by the question, and by my need to defend myself. 'You know, earning a living. Marriage. My husband's more of a rock music man. Bruce Springsteen.' I laugh disloyally.

'Bad luck,' he says. 'You ever want someone to go to a concert that isn't *rock*,' he spits the word, 'get in touch, eh?' And he twists to pull a wallet from the back pocket of his low-slung jeans, giving me a glimpse of his six-pack. He takes out a business card: 'Seb Bandele, Clarinet', and hands it to me.

'Right,' I say, putting it away in my handbag. I can't tell if it's a genuine offer or if he's teasing me. He has his father's natural charm, but employs it far more dangerously than Sunny, who steps back into the room with an envelope.

'Here we are,' Sunny says, passing it over. 'I could actually only find one, though it's a good one. Your father was usually a bit camera shy.'

'Dad, I'm off out. See you later,' he winks at me. 'And maybe you too, Lucy. Might be fun to do some monkeying around, eh?' And he disappears out of the door.

'He's a bit full of himself, but lovely really,' Sunny says. 'Classic only child. My wife's always spoiled him, still does.'

'And did your wife know ... Jim and Judy?' It feels strange to speak their names.

'Oh yes, Michelle trained with your mother. We're all in the photo,' he says, as I reach into the envelope. 'She was one of the few nurses daring enough to be seen dating a black man! So I married her, of course.'

Inside the envelope is a protective clear sleeve, and inside that, the photograph. It's black and white, and instead of the informal shot I was expecting, it shows the cast of a play, a dozen or more young men and women lined up on stage. I scan the faces – Sunny's beams out at me first, but I skip onwards and there, nearer the centre, are my parents: Mum in a ball dress with tight bodice and puffy skirt and sleeves. And, holding her hand, my father, in full penguin suit: his hair shorter than I remember it and his eyes, framed by black eyeliner, more intense.

'The hospital Christmas panto. Must have been 1965, maybe '66? Your father *had* to be Prince Charming, of course. Which meant your mum was Cinders. I played a kind of post-colonial Buttons.'

'This was for kids?' I'm still mesmerized by my father. He looks so young.

'There were two versions. One for the kids. Then the adult version that we put on the same night. Definitely X-rated. There's Michelle.' He points to a thin girl at the end of the line-up. She's not smiling. 'I think she wanted to be Cinderella. You know what women are like. But I can't sing for toffee, whereas Jim could, and Prince Charming had a couple of solos.'

'What did he sound like?'

'Oh, *wonderful*. He was always good with his guitar, of course. I hope you remember. But the solos were more your light opera type. And he brought the house down.'

'I sing, too.'

'Now that doesn't surprise me in the least! I'd love to hear you someday too. And I know Michelle would feel the same. I wish you could have met her, but she's on a night shift. Though I hope I'm not being presumptuous, Lucy, in suggesting that today's the beginning of a friendship. I would love it if you'd come over for dinner one night. Perhaps with your husband, too?'

'I'd love to. Though my husband works late hours so it might not be so easy for him,' I say, knowing Andrew would see this house very differently from me, would be itching to leave and complain in the car on the way back about how they'd let a period property deteriorate. And I can't imagine him getting on with Seb, either.

'Fair enough. And I suppose you need someone to babysit your little girl, anyway. Though she'd be very welcome to stay here. We love a full house. Seb's one fault according to my wife is not providing any grandkids.'

'I'll see what I can do,' I say, then look at my watch. Andrew will be getting restless. And so will Sasha, on the night before school breaks up for half-term. I'm dreading it. 'I ought to head off home now, Sunny.' I kiss him and breathe in the scent of the house, realizing I feel far more at home than I ever do in Saxon Close.

Chapter Twenty

Guides should be like birds and flowers,
who are 'up with the sun and who sleep
with the sun'.

Terri was shattered. She hadn't slept for a whole night since the agility day out, and her body clock had settled into the worst possible regime. If she managed not to nod off in lectures, then by teatime she'd be craving sleep like a junkie craves heroin. But every time she gave in to her body, she was punished by another night of mind games, strange noises that dragged her back into consciousness every time sleep approached. And then there were the thoughts: about Judith, about Lucy, about God. Nothing she did stopped them coming.

Tonight she was going to see if it was any less lonely having insomnia with someone else beside you. Colin wasn't perfect. But he was human and he'd chosen to be with her. That counted for something.

She let herself into Colin's flat and wondered if she should have stopped to buy some Nescafé. Colin had been on a health kick since Christmas, so there'd be nothing caffeinated on the premises, not even tea, and without caffeine she didn't stand much chance of staving off her afternoon nap. It wasn't likely that Colin's account of his day at the signs factory would be enough to keep her awake.

The kitchen was spotlessly tidy, the toaster perfectly aligned with the kettle and the draining rack, as though Colin was on constant alert for an inspection by a particularly anal sergeant major. He had few possessions and everything he did own came from a budget range. His chairs were second-hand, his baked beans bought in bulk. He insisted he wasn't mean, but *cautious.*

The only time he'd thrown caution to the wind financially was to buy his laptop. It was open now, the fan whirring loudly, on the fold-out dining table. Terri had hoped that the investment might spur him on. She didn't honestly think that he would be able to break into Hollywood with his story of a misunderstood factory worker who single-handedly thwarts a terrorist attack on Manchester, but she knew that finishing the script might give him enough of a boost to look for a new job. It hadn't worked: even allowing for his terrible two-fingered typing, his work rate of two pages a year wasn't promising.

She ran her fingers over the touchpad and the screen came to life. Sure enough, the script for *Seeing the Signs* appeared. She knew the opening scene inside out. A tracking shot follows our unlikely hero on his way home, picking up litter discarded by a couple of hoodie-wearing teenagers, greeting an elderly woman by the pedestrian crossing, throwing a few coins into a beggar's cap. As he emerges from a newsagent, he spots a Middle Eastern man handing money to another, in exchange for a box. As the stranger takes the box, the bottom collapses and out falls ...

And that was where Colin was stuck. He knew that later there'd be explosions and car chases and fights to the death, but he couldn't work out what was in the box.

Terri scrolled down. The document looked longer than before and, sure enough, there was an extra page. Perhaps he'd had a breakthrough. It was in note form, rather than screenplay layout.

REASONS TO GIVE
Under the heading, there was a bullet-point list.
- Not you, it's me – midlife crisis???!
- Not the same people we used to be
- Going in different directions in life
- Sex (but don't make big deal of this)
- There's no one else

Terri sat down in front of the screen, wondering if this was what she thought it was.

NOW OR LATER?
- Strike while iron hot?
- She's upset about j but when will she feel better??
- Before birthday?

She shut the laptop lid. The little *toad*. How *dare* he? Not only was he planning to dump her, but he was planning it on the laptop she'd helped him choose. How could he consider this without consulting her? And if he thought he could do without her in his life, he was pathetically, stupidly mistaken.

She opened the cupboard where he kept his tiny selection of cheap booze, and poured herself an own-brand brandy. As the bitter warmth travelled down her throat, she felt the anger subsiding enough to let her think straight. Was this the worst thing that could happen? Was she in love with him?

If she was completely honest, it was more that she felt fond of him, the way you'd feel for a characterless pet you'd never expected to live long, like a stick insect. So why had she stuck around?

She swigged the final drop of brandy. And then she realized: Colin wasn't finished yet.

The acid alcohol burned in her throat. The only reason she'd stuck around as long as she had was that she couldn't leave a job halfway through, and Colin was certainly still a work in progress. Not that he was progressing noticeably at the moment.

But if he was a work in progress, what did that make her?

A sculptor of people? Someone who saw people as clay, to be moulded and shaped into her own vision? A manipulative Svengali?

She felt sick now, but poured herself another drink. Her hand shook slightly and the amber liquid in her glass sloshed from side to side, as if she was on the deck of a ship.

No. If she tried to help people, it was up to them to take it or leave it, surely. Just as some of the Pixies had listened to Judith, as she had, and some had ignored her. Like Paula.

Terri heard the key in the lock. She rinsed out the brandy glass and as he entered the room, she turned slowly to face him.

'Colin,' she said, her voice as calm as she could make it. 'I think there's something you're not telling me.'

Paula stuck her head out of her front door and looked both ways, like the Green Cross Code man had commanded all those years back. The coast was clear. The orgasmic moans coming from next door suggested Lorraine was otherwise engaged with her toyboy, but you could never be sure.

She moved as fast as she could, which wasn't very. The evening was sultry and even the Primrose looked almost appealing in the velvety light of sunset. Teenagers were hanging out in the quad, but they looked more mellow than usual. The appearance of a grotesquely fat woman in leggings and trainers would normally be enough to trigger catcalls, but they were too laid-back to look up from their alcopops.

Paula walked as close to the wall as possible, so she could retreat into the shadows if someone she knew appeared. She was already sweating profusely, but she was prepared, with a packet of tissues wedged between her skin and the overstretched elastic of her knickers. Why didn't leggings have pockets? It wasn't as if she could look any lumpier.

She turned down the narrow lane that would take her towards the canal, and caught sight of her reflection in the one unsmashed window of a freshly abandoned car. Despite the tinted glass, her face glowed pink, and the curve in the window made her look like a Weeble toy she'd owned in her childhood: a Humpty Dumpty egg-shaped plastic figure whose claim to fame was that 'Weebles wobble but they don't fall down'.

She looked away. It wouldn't do any good to dwell on how she looked now. She had to imagine the future. The psychologist had been back on *Richard and Judy* talking about using the power of the mind to get a bikini body for the beach. Usually she'd have flipped channels at the mere mention of swimwear, but after the experience on the assault course, she was wondering if there might just be more to Paula than this, another choice besides getting progressively gloomier and fatter until one day she'd probably be too big to fit through her front door.

The shrink's advice was to 'find your motivating vision. Imagine yourself as you've always wanted to be: powerful, slender, sexy, relaxed. Feel the sand between your toes and the sun on your toned body ... hear the waves and the compliments people pay you as you stretch out on your lounger. Who is *that* babe?' Then she'd suggested 'plotting your journey to that magical kingdom' – and she didn't mean Disneyland Florida. 'Each journey begins with a single step. Take that step. Take it now.'

At that point, Paula had switched off and stepped into the kitchen for a packet of biscuits. Then her online shopping had arrived and in the bottom of the final carrier was an extra package she hadn't ordered, a 'free gift from your favourite delivery service'. Usually the gifts were useful – a bottle of wine or a new brand of chocolate – but this wasn't edible or drinkable. At first she thought it was a travel alarm clock – as if she ever travelled or needed to get up in time for anything – but then she looked at the packaging, which read: Walk Yourself to Fitness with our Amazing Pedometer.

One coincidence, she could have ignored. But the assault course, the bikini-body woman and the pedometer seemed like a conspiracy and she wasn't sure she had the nerve to subvert whatever dark forces were at work to convince her to get off her arse.

Paula reached the canal and stopped, disturbed by the loudness of her own rapid panting. Even Lorraine was quieter in the throes of passion. She glanced down at the plastic contraption clipped to her hip: 412 steps. That couldn't be right: she must have set it up wrong. According to the leaflet that came with it, translated into English from Korean, 'a person is advised to be completing a magnificent grand total of ten thousand walking steps within a period of twenty-four hours or one day, to be ensured of a beneficent amelioration in levels of physical prowess and reduction in torpor-induced fattiness'.

Ten thousand had sounded easy enough, but now Paula felt

depressed at the task ahead. Ten thousand steps A DAY. For ever. No time off for good behaviour.

She screwed up her eyes and tried to summon up her 'motivating vision'. She'd steered away from beaches and bikinis, choosing instead to imagine herself at parents' evening, turning up in a smart size sixteen suit with her hair highlighted, her lips glossy and her confidence high, being taken seriously for the first time in her life.

But the image was fading. She saw herself sitting down and the skirt splitting with an exaggerated tearing sound that attracted the attention of everyone in the school hall. This imaginary Paula was forced to retreat with her suit jacket wrapped round her bottom half to cover up the knee-to-thigh split, her hair lank and mousy with sweat and her make-up smudged like a drunken clown's.

A child's voice drifted through the bushes and she turned to see the outline of a boy on a climbing frame in his enormous back garden.

'I'm the king of the castle ... you're the dirty rascal,' he sang to himself, triumphantly surveying his domain.

Paula smiled at him and remembered sitting on top of the wall at Lone Wolf Centre, the same song ringing in her ears. She couldn't remember feeling that good in so many years, the trivial nature of her achievement only adding to the lightness she'd felt. And, God knows, lightness was not a sensation she experienced often.

She looked at her pedometer. Turning to look at the garden had gained her another six steps. Maybe it wasn't going to be that hard after all. She set her sights on the canal bridge half a mile up the towpath and put one foot in front of the other. Every journey begins with a single step ...

'I was going to tell you,' Colin said sulkily.

'Yes, I can see that.' Terri was surprised at how close she was to tears. If she didn't love him, why did she feel so frightened? 'When, exactly?'

'Um. I'd been waiting for the right time. But it never seemed to come.'

Terri sipped her camomile tea, buying herself a moment to think. No one had ever finished with her before and it was something she was proud of. She'd *always* known the right time with her exes and she had always told them exactly why it was over: because she had waved her Fairy Godmother wand, sorted their lives out, and now they could manage on their own.

Maybe that's what the tears were about. Tears of frustration that she was being forced to abandon a project halfway through.

'Why, Colin?' she asked. 'And please don't give me the version you've typed into your computer.'

He leaned back in his chair, stretched his legs out in front of him. There were sweat patches under his arms and his chin was marked with machine oil from the factory. She was glad she hadn't slept with him now.

'Honestly? Well, a man has his needs, Terri.'

'So it is about sex, then?'

'Well ...' He smiled at her and she sensed he was *enjoying* this. The *pig*. 'Partly about sex. But also ...' and he paused again, scratching his head.

She stood up. 'Oh, look, forget it. I don't want to hear any more. I'd have done it myself a long time ago, but I kept thinking you might grow into someone with a bit of gumption.'

'I've always known that, in a way,' he said calmly. 'Maybe I'm fed up with being one of your lost causes. I might be too useless to find another girlfriend, but I'd rather take the chance of finding someone who wants me as I am, and not as I might be with remedial help.'

Terri felt stung, but she also felt ashamed. He was right. She did spend her life conducting relationships the way Victorian philanthropists conducted campaigns to rescue the poor or reform prisoners. As charity work. How very *Christian* of her.

'I'm sorry, Colin,' she said, quietly. 'I hope you do find that person ... oh, and good luck with the script.'

'The script?' He laughed. 'I haven't touched the script for a year. It was a pipe dream, Terri. I know *my* limitations,' he added pointedly.

She walked away, angrily scrubbing at the stubborn tears that refused to accept she was relieved rather than upset. *Maybe*, she thought, *it's about time I started to see my own limitations.*

As Matt's hand began to trace its familiar path from her cheek down her collarbone towards her breasts, Chris knew she should stop him. The time when she could pretend that he was after the same as her – friendly, good-quality, no-strings sex – was over.

'Oh, God, I miss you when you're not around,' he murmured, reaching under her T-shirt with one hand, and flipping off his glasses with the other. His pupils grew bigger as those determined eyes focused on her face.

There really was no excuse for leading him on. None at all. Aaah ...

'Matt,' she whispered, intending to finish the sentence with a reasoned argument why he shouldn't go any further. But then he kissed her, half a day's worth of stubble grazing her cheeks, and the arguments beat a retreat into the logical part of her brain. She knew they were still there, ready for a renewed assault later, but they knew they were temporarily outmanoeuvred by lust.

He'd come over to listen to her presentation, the one she was giving to shareholders the next day, to convince them to stay loyal and reject Eros. She'd deliberately set the scene to be as unarousing as possible. She bought Matt pizza with extra garlic, and beer with extra gas, put an *Eighties Party Hits* CD on as background music, and worn her slouching-around outfit of faded T-shirt and jogging pants. She hadn't even washed her hair, so it was as tangled as a red setter's coat after a walk in the country. And he had given her presentation his full attention, made some pertinent suggestions that transformed her concluding remarks, and then told her he couldn't live without her.

'Matt ...' she'd said. He'd placed his fingers on her lips.

'I know, I know. You don't have time for a relationship. If you did have time, I'd definitely be in the running. I know it off by heart, Chris. You learned all you know from me. But that was then ... and this,' he paused to land a tiny kiss on her neck, 'is definitely,' and another kiss, 'now. Time to stop running away.'

He wasn't the most surprising lover she'd ever had, but that in itself was unsurprising as they'd known each other for so long. But he was easily the best kisser, his lips flexible and intuitive, capable of delivering soft, feathery touches that could turn without warning into firmer bites.

No! she thought. *Don't break your rules. Sex and love are too dangerous a combination. Stop him now.*

Matt was teasing her, pinching her right nipple and then letting go, while his other hand ran up and down her spine.

'Let's go to bed,' he said and she nodded. He seemed to sense that wild sex across the Italian sofa or balancing on the Corian kitchen work surface wasn't what she wanted right now. Perhaps she was getting old.

He realized he couldn't give her time to reconsider, so he shed his clothes quickly, before removing her T-shirt and her joggers and moving down her body with his lips, crouching between her legs and finding her clitoris with his tongue.

Oh God ... she'd been all over the world evaluating the most advanced, most expensive sex toys, but nothing could compete with a man who wanted to turn you on. And knew enough about your body to make it a dead cert.

He dodged her attempts to touch him, and when she was too persistent, he looked up at her. 'Well, if you're *that* determined to bring me off ...' He reached over to open the drawer to her bedside cabinet, where he knew he'd find the condoms. 'Let's get down to business. I know how much you *love* business ...'

She came within seconds of him pushing his way inside her, and then again when he rolled over and pulled her on top of him, rocking her and reaching forward to kiss her, until his concentration lapsed and he cried out. 'Oh, fucking hell!'

It took only a couple of minutes for the warm, fuzzy feeling to fade, and the reasons why this had been a terrible idea to resurface. His arms around her shoulders felt like they were pinning her down and she could smell the beer on his breath, and on hers. She felt ashamed of herself for giving in, losing control. Letting her body overrule her brain. 'Matt,' she said, as his breathing became more regular. 'Don't fall asleep.'

'Uh?'

'I've got *stuff* I need to do before tomorrow. Would it be totally bloody rude of me to chuck you out?'

He frowned, then sat up, disentangling himself. 'Yes. It would.' He stood up and pulled his jeans on, his back to her. Then he disappeared into the bathroom.

'Matt,' Chris called from behind the door. 'I'm sorry. I've just got a lot on, you know. It's nothing personal.'

His face was expressionless when he came out again. 'I understand,' he said. 'I don't want to be in your way.'

'It's not like that,' she said, but he'd already walked into the lounge to pick up his wallet. 'I didn't mean you had to go straight away.'

'Whatever. Good luck tomorrow, Chris. I know how much it matters to you,' he said, and there was bitterness in his voice this time. 'Sweet dreams, eh?'

She watched him step into the lift and as the lift doors closed, he turned. Then the doors stuck for a moment – the warehouse conversion was only two years old, but was already deteriorating – and she caught sight of his face. He'd lost all his colour but, even more alarming, she thought she could see tears on his cheeks. The lift was on its way before she could be sure.

'Sweet dreams, Matt,' she mumbled. She needed a drink to take away the taste of guilt and garlic.

June 1979: A Brownie nature trail in the woods

'I think we should split into two groups,' Bethany said, taking off her new Mickey Mouse watch with its moving arms and legs. 'We have to beat the Sprites and we stand the best chance of doing that if we've got the whole woods covered.'

Chris wasn't jealous of the watch – she'd lost every watch she'd ever owned, forgetting where she'd left them – but she was jealous that Bethany knew all the police jargon. Bethany was the only Pixie allowed to watch *Kojak* and *Starsky and Hutch* on her own, although Chris's mum Dina said that was only because Bethany's dad couldn't care less what she was up to. 'Nothing but trouble storing up there, a girl growing up without her mother. It's unnatural.'

Terri sighed. 'But it's not a *competition*, Bethany. It's a nature trail.'

Bethany pouted. 'Is there, or is there not, a prize for the Six with the most clues answered?'

'Well, yes, but—'

'Then it's a competition.' The finality in her voice didn't allow for any challenge. 'So we should go in threes. Me ...' she looked and sighed at the limited options available. 'Plus Lucy, I suppose. You won't be able to keep up with Paula. Me, Lucy and ... Terri.'

Terri smiled, although it was obvious she'd been picked because she was the only one who owned a compass *and* actually knew how to use it.

'So that means Paula, Chris and Simonetta' – Bethany still pronounced it as Simon, not See-mon – 'will be heading anti-clockwise, while we go clockwise. Let's meet back here at quarter to eight, so we can all go back in together.'

'But isn't that cheating?' Lucy said quietly.

'Don't be silly. There are no rules, Lucy. You have to use your initiative. Look after numero uno, like the Americans say.'

'That's Italian, not American,' Simonetta said.

Bethany looked put out for a second, then recovered. 'Well, they're living in America, aren't they? They must have left Italy because the people are savages. Try not to get lost.' And she led her team into the wooded area to the left of the Drill Hall.

'I'm glad she's buzzed off,' Paula said. 'I don't want to win a stupid nature trail for *her* anyway. Do you fancy a kick-about, Netta? I can nip home and pick up my football.' Then she remembered Chris. 'You can come too, if you like.'

Chris shook her head. 'Nope. I might sit here for a bit. Keep an eye out for the Sprites.'

Paula didn't try to change Chris's mind; she sprang forward as if she'd been held back by a tightened elastic band that was suddenly released, catapulting her into the woods. Simonetta followed, her long legs allowing her to keep up with Paula effortlessly. She was too grown-up for the Brownies. Dina kept saying how sweet it was that Netta's dad had gone out of his way to help her achieve her childhood ambition of joining, but Chris wasn't fooled. Number one, Bruno was just like an oily Italian conman she'd seen last week on *Hart to Hart*, the one American show she was allowed to watch. Number two, if Netta really wanted to be here, how come she looked so sulky all the time? She never joined in and only talked to Paula, ignoring everyone else. Though that had the fringe benefit of driving Bethany mad, so Netta wasn't all bad.

Chris looked at her own watch, with its boring Roman numerals and straight, grown-up hands, and felt excited. A whole hour of freedom. At home, she was rarely allowed to spend more than ten minutes 'doing nothing' as her mum put it. There were always chores to be done, though most of them seemed to be invented with the express purpose of Preventing Christine from Thinking. Dina regarded thinking as a dangerous activity, to be suppressed at all costs. Her elder daughter Jill was a mathematician and had been born without an imagination so she'd never been nearly as much of a problem. But Chris worried Dina, so she gave her daughter endless mindless tasks like sweeping up leaves, taking books off shelves to dust them (not that Dina ever seemed to read them, Chris noticed) and putting all the socks in the drawer in the order of the colours of the rainbow. Richard of York Gave Battle in Vain. Looking for violet socks to complete the sequence, Chris knew how Richard of York felt.

Sixty whole uninterrupted minutes to herself couldn't be wasted. Chris decided to avoid the path – the chances of bumping into another Brownie were too high – and walk straight ahead into the woods. It would still be light by the time she had to return to the Drill Hall, and the wood wasn't a proper scary forest, just a strip of tall trees half the width of a football pitch, running in between two new housing estates. Chris wondered whether the whole area had once been forest, home to Stone Age people who communicated in grunts and had yet to invent the wheel. Imagine all that excitement ahead of them, all those fantastic discoveries to be made.

Chris hoped to become an inventor. Unlike Jill, who'd just gone to study *numbers* at university. All you could do with numbers was add, subtract, multiply, divide. How could anyone do that for three whole years?

As she wriggled her way between the branches of the trees, towards the denser patches of ferns and thigh-high nettles, Chris heard a rustling. Her eyes followed the direction of the sound. She could just make out the grey tips of a rabbit's ears above the undergrowth: they twitched as the animal tried to sense whether it had been spotted by prey.

Chris liked rabbits, especially since the trip with the other Brownies to see *Watership Down* (predictably, Lucy had bawled from beginning to end). But Chris wasn't allowed a pet, which was surprising. A pet represented endless time-consuming chores: feeding, watering, cleaning away pellets of rabbit poo. Her mother should have been all for it.

The rabbit moved, its furry tail appearing and disappearing with each bounce. Chris decided to track it as far as she could.

She tiptoed behind, staying as distant as possible without losing sight of it. The Brownie uniform was good camouflage as she darted behind trees and dodged round bushes.

Crack! She stepped on a twig and the noise echoed around the woods, bouncing off the foliage. Both Chris and the rabbit were paralysed.

The rabbit made a run for it first, judging quite correctly that the giant in brown cotton behind it couldn't possibly compete with animal instinct and a powerful pair of back legs. Chris tried to chase it, abandoning any attempt to move quietly, but she lost the trail when she tripped up on a tree root, grazing her right knee and staining her white socks with chlorophyll.

She sat down on the mossy carpet beneath the tree that had tripped her up, carefully pulling the lower half of her uniform up above her waist so only the dark brown fabric of her knickers made contact with the earth. There was no point getting into trouble for messing up her dress as well.

Ha-ha-ha . . .

Another noise. This was undoubtedly human, a man's laugh coming from somewhere ahead of her. It was hard to tell how far away he was: even in this tiny wood, sounds became distorted. It wasn't surprising witches and demons always lived in forests: everything about them was mysterious, from the body-like trunks of the trees that swayed and rustled in the breeze, to the dense patches where no light seemed to get through.

Uh-huh-huh-huh . . .

A different laugh, a woman's, from the same direction. It sounded strange, false yet familiar. Like hearing your own voice when you tried to sing underwater in the swimming pool.

Chris had got her breath back by now and decided to follow the sounds. This time she could move more slowly, as her targets were stationary. Trying to remember the skills she'd learned to win her Pathfinder badge, she looked down before taking each step, checking where to put her feet, favouring soft silent earth over rustling green weeds.

The noises kept coming, more muffled, though she was sure she was getting closer. Her muscles were tensed as she controlled each movement, walking in slow motion. Finally she heard the laughter again and knew she was within yards of those who were making the noise.

She stood still and turned a half-circle before she caught a glimpse of colour behind the trees. Orange and purple: the colours of clothing, not nature. Two people intertwined. Kissing.

Chris felt the blush on her cheeks as she realized they were laughing, not at a shared joke, but the way lovers on TV did (before her father, who'd clearly only had sex twice, noticed what was on screen, tutted and creaked into an upward position to change the channel). Chris felt foolish and decided to creep away again.

But just before she could, the lovers came up for air. Facing her – but not seeing her, his huge eyes unfocused – was a man she recognized.

Bruno.

She was paralysed, like the rabbit, until the woman turned too, confirming what Chris already knew somewhere deep inside her, but had been trying hard to ignore.

The woman was her mother.

Toymaker

To be a toymaker, you should make, without any help, three of the following toys. They must be well-made and finished and ready for use before you take them to the tester.

(a) A toy from materials that would otherwise be thrown away.

(b) A simple puppet using any suitable material. This could be a glove puppet, a shadow puppet, a jointed puppet, two finger puppets, or something similar. Show how you would use it.

(c) Using cardboard or other strong material or matchboxes, either a set of dolls' furniture for yourself or a Brownie scene for your Six Home, the base of which must be 30cm by 23 cm.

(d) A toy of your own choice which is different from the other things you have made.

(e) A well-arranged, clean scrapbook as a special Good Turn for a grown-up or child in hospital.

Chapter Twenty-one

Evil practices dare not face an honest person ... Keep your thoughts as clear as a crystal stream.

Squashed into the back of Chris's pastel-green Noddy car, I don't know which bit of me to cover up first. My pink top's too low; my denim skirt's too short. I seem to have lost not only the anger that's been a fixture since Mum died, but also my inhibitions, picking the most ridiculous clothes from my wardrobe. It is, I am sure, in no way connected to where I'm going later tonight.

I didn't realize quite how daft I looked until Paula greeted me with 'Hmm, that's a very *summery* outfit,' when we met at Troughton railway station. And the warning bells grew louder when I saw the expression on Chris's face when she picked us up from Manchester Piccadilly. Not quite a frown, not quite a smile, the kind of noncommittal look you'd give to a friend's new, disastrous hairstyle.

At least Andrew didn't see me. He's headed off on one of his golf days, but had at least volunteered to drop Sasha off at his mum's before he went, yet another sign that he's scared of what I might do next. And, frankly, it's what I deserve after a miserable bank holiday weekend followed by a tense half-term break: Sasha knows something's up so she's been clingier than I've ever known her.

I waited until the house was empty before I got up and got dressed, but now I wish he'd been around because then I'd never have dared wear this. I don't look *quite* certifiable, but neither do I look like a woman planning an afternoon's catch-up with some old friends.

Of course, that isn't all I'm planning. But that's my secret.

'Open sesame!' Chris activates the electronic gate alongside a converted canalside warehouse. She really is living the life. The car is very retro, with a convertible roof and endless round knobs and switches inside: apparently Eric Clapton owns one and it took a year to get it shipped from Japan. And the designer of the warehouse conversion seems to have taken her inspiration from Sunset Boulevard; it's all curly balconies and sugared-almond paintwork, out of place against these dull Manchester surroundings and even duller Manchester clouds. I think about Sunny's terrace, built from layer upon layer of rust-coloured bricks that would have been cast only a few miles away. I know which I prefer and I feel a tingle of guilty pleasure that I'll be back inside Sunny's solid walls within – I look at my watch – four hours.

I mustn't tell the girls.

Chris parks the car in a space marked out *Penthouse Only* and helps Paula climb out. 'Have you lost some weight, Paula?'

Even in the dim light of the car park, I can see she's blushing. 'Well, um, maybe. Not that it's going to make a lot of difference, though. I mean, I'm still the size of a house. Doesn't matter much whether it's a four-bed detached or a three-bed semi, does it?'

'Don't be daft,' I say. 'It'll make a big difference if you can shift a bit of weight. Are you on a diet then?'

'Well, I've started walking a bit.'

We step into the tiny lift, which has a plaque instructing MAXIMUM THREE PASSENGERS, and we all fall silent as we take this information in. Paula doesn't look any slimmer to me. I try to stop myself doing the sums. The lift weight limit must be based on three *average* people. So with or without her couple of pounds shed, Paula has to count as at least a person and a third. While I'm probably one point one of a person. Which means in order for us not to be in deep trouble, elevator-wise, gym-toned Chris has to count as much less than a whole person.

Before I've finished my calculations, the lift arrives safely at the top floor and I let out the breath I've been holding at exactly the same moment as the others.

'I know what you were thinking, duck,' Paula says. 'You were thinking that I was in danger of breaking the lift cables.'

I giggle. 'Well, I was keeping my fingers crossed. But it's great that you're getting out and about at last.' Then I step through the security door that leads straight from the lift into Chris's flat. 'Bloody hell!'

It's the space that's most surprising. My voice echoes up to the double – or is it treble – height ceiling and back again, so that I have to fight the urge to shout or sing la-la-la, just to hear how it sounds. As I look more closely, I'm not so keen on what Chris has done with the room. The furniture all looks uncomfortable, and the lighting is industrial; the overall effect is like an overly trendy hotel suite from a glossy magazine. But there's so much *air* compared to home, where I feel hemmed in by the low ceilings and perfectly square rooms, each one devoted to a single function: cooking or washing or dining or sleeping. Chris's flat seems to dare you to sleep or eat in front of the TV, or to carry on a phone conversation in the enormous bath that's just visible past a wall of backlit glass bricks.

'So what do you think?' Chris says, sounding nervous.

'I didn't think anyone *normal* lived in places like this,' Paula says. 'It's like a film set. And it's all yours?'

Chris nods. 'But do you like it? Lucy?'

'It's … smashing,' I say. 'How long have you lived here?'

'I bought it off-plan when I opened my third shop. I thought it'd be a good investment. And I managed to pay off most of it when I floated the company. You haven't seen the view yet.'

She walks across to the wall and flicks a switch. The blinds begin to rise, revealing the canal and beyond it, the city. I walk to the window, which is twice as tall as I am, and peer out. The rain's stopped but it's glistening on a million roofs, as far as I can see. Sometimes, I forget that *this* is my birthplace, not boring, suburban Troughton. Until I met Sunny, Manchester frightened me with its vastness, a network of complicated streets holding people and lives more threatening than anything

I might encounter on the Primrose Estate. But now as I look down, I know it could offer me answers and that fills me with excitement instead of fear.

'Just below me lives the head of the North West Media Agency, and next to him is the physio for Manchester United.'

Reluctantly, I turn round and tune into Chris's commentary about her neighbours as she leads us into the kitchen area. It's dominated by a massive glass-topped table covered in papers, with a large ironwork bowl of over-ripe fruit in the centre. As I step closer, the powdery-sweet smell of bananas makes me feel sick. 'You've not been getting your five fruit and veg a day, have you, Chris?'

'Oh, God.' Chris picks up the bowl and tips the fruit into her bin with a dull thud. 'I've worked late every night this week. I should be there today, really, but I couldn't let you guys down.'

I pull out a wrought-iron chair – it's shockingly heavy – and sit down. 'Are you still worried about this takeover bid?'

'Well, I'm trying not to be worried. I'd like to think I thrive on a challenge.' She pulls three tiny espresso cups from one of the stainless steel cupboards, leaving, I notice, three fingerprints on the corner of the door. 'But actually, I'm terrified. Coffee?'

Paula sits down and the metal groans slightly as she sinks into the seat. 'I'll have one. I still don't see why it's such a worry. I mean, you could stay on with the new company, couldn't you?'

Chris moves across to a gleaming black coffee machine as big as my microwave. 'If the shareholders take the offer from Eros, I might as well throw in the towel. I don't want to give away control. It's like ... both of you have got your kids. And you love them, however much you daydream about freedom. Well, I don't have a family so my work is *my* family. *My* baby. I mean, you wouldn't give away your kids for someone else to bring up, would you?'

'Wanna bet?' Paula says. 'And they'd jump at the chance. Hey, maybe we could swap lives, like they do on the telly? If you get taken over, I'll take your bank balance and you can take my flat and my kids. Shake on it?'

Chris manages a strained smile. 'Much as I hate to turn down such a tempting offer, I don't intend to give up my business to anyone. I'm going down fighting.'

She turns away to make the coffee, as Paula says, 'What about you, Lucy? Fancy a life swap? My two are lovely really, nearly ready to fly the nest as well. Plus there's the Primrose Estate Arts Festival coming up; honestly, you can't touch our area for community spirit. And under my parental guidance, your Sasha will be a teenage mum in no time.'

I force a laugh. 'Let me think it over.' I watch as Chris takes ground coffee from the fridge and fills the little drawer in the machine, then moves the lever to pump steam through the system. Would I swap Sasha and Andrew and the litter-tray garden and the bloody patio heater for another life? Paula's is a non-starter, but even Chris's money and accessories and *space* are too empty to be tempting. At least drudgery distracts me from the big questions: who am I? Why am I here? And how should I pass the rest of my time on the planet?

But the idea of moving in with the Bandeles ... now that's another matter. I don't know if they have a spare room, but if not, perhaps I could live in the garden shed and come in for lovely, lively breakfasts, chatter over the morning newspapers and the muesli, or some traditional African dish – what is it in that song? Ackee and salt fish – or is that Caribbean? God, I'm ignorant.

'Luc-eee?' Paula waves her chubby hand in front of my face. 'Is there anybody there? Chris wants to know how you take your coffee.'

'Oh. Strong, please.'

'Like your men?' Paula laughs.

'Yeah, right. Andrew's the civil service equivalent of Mr Universe.' But I'm blushing because there's an image of Seb in my mind and I can't seem to get rid of it.

The intercom buzzes and Chris finishes pouring the coffee before heading towards the lift. 'That'll be Terri.'

When Chris brings her through, at first I think Terri's shell-shocked by the flat: she seems hesitant, waiting to be told to sit down, where normally she bursts into a room full of unharnessed energy looking for an outlet.

Even odder, her blouse and skirt are creased. Like my mother, Terri believes the iron is an instrument of God. And her fire-engine-red curls are dull, as if she hasn't washed her hair for a week.

She blinks at us, as though she's only just noticed we're here. 'Hello, girls. Everything OK?'

'Well, Paula's lost weight. And I'm ... well. The same, really. Better, though. About Mum and everything,' I say, trying to sound as upbeat as possible.

Terri nods. 'That's good.' Her voice seems too small for her. She hasn't called me all week, which is unusual. I've been too preoccupied to notice until now.

'What about you?' Then I whisper, 'You seem *different*.'

'Fine. Truly.'

But the more I study her, the more convinced I am she's lying. 'And Colin?'

'Same as always.' She looks away now and I wonder what she's not telling me. Our confidences have always been one way, me pouring out my neuroses, Terri telling me everything will be OK. Mum was the only person Terri ever confided in.

'Terri ... now that Mum's not here, I want you to know that ... well, just that I know you think I'm a bit of a basket case, but I might be able to help, just listen ...' I tail off.

'Thanks, Luce,' she says, but her eyes are blank.

Paula tips the last of her espresso into her mouth – the cup is so tiny in her hand, it looks as if she's raided a dolls' house tea service. She puts it down and we stare at each other. The fat girl, the middle-aged virgin, the hotshot businesswoman, and the yummy mummy. What do we have in common? And how are we going to get through the afternoon?

Chris stands up. 'I know it's obscenely early, but does anyone else think that a bottle of wine might just get the party going?'

Another hour later, we Pixies are into our third bottle of wine and the booze has once again done wonders for Brownie Guide relations. My mother definitely wouldn't approve. But it's helped us find the common ground. Men. Sex. And getting older.

'I definitely don't feel my age,' Chris says. 'Except when the

186

kids at work say that they were born in, like, 1981, and I think, bloody hell, that's the year I started secondary school.'

'I know, it's the same with the girls in the shop. It doesn't seem possible, does it?' I pour myself more Pinot Grigio. 'We're *middle-aged*.'

'Well, I feel about a hundred, duck,' Paula says. 'All this stuff creeps up on you. I looked in the mirror the other day – something I avoid doing normally – and I noticed my teeth had gone all yellow. Like an old crone.'

We turn to Terri, waiting for her to tell us to buck up, that our best years are ahead of us, that at least we have our health. But she just stares into her wine, which she's been knocking back faster than any of us, and then sighs.

Chris fills the gap. 'But you know what's worse than the grey hair and the wrinkles and the saggy boobs?'

She has none of those, of course, but I play along. 'Um, realizing you like Radio Two?'

Even Terri smiles at that. But Chris shakes her head. 'God, I haven't gone that far yet. No, it's thinking we had it tougher! Someone'll moan because, I dunno, their phone doesn't have an MP3 player on it, and I'll have to bite my lip not to say, "Well, when I was your age, mobile phones weighed as much as a small hatchback and cost more than a mortgage." It's like when your granny used to go on about sharing a tin bath with her fifteen brothers and sisters.'

Paula is nodding. 'I get it from Sadie all the time, about needing the latest brand of trainers, and she can't believe it when I tell her I used to make do with black pumps from Woolworth's. Well, maybe she can believe it, but she doesn't care!'

'It's hard, though,' I say. 'Because in a way, they *have* got it tougher. I am scared to death of letting Sasha play outside, so instead I drag her round endless judo classes and pottery painting sessions, whereas what she'd probably prefer is messing about by the river and coming home when the sun sets, covered in mud.'

'You know that's the bit I always remember about the Brownies,' Chris says, laughing. 'When we were allowed off in little gangs. Especially you and me, Paula. The only thing we were worried about was being caught by Brown Owl. Or by you, Terri! You could be every bit as scary as Lucy's mum.'

We look at Terri, waiting for a feisty defence of her bossier moments, but all she says is, 'Yes. I don't blame you. I was pretty awful.'

Chris says, 'No, you weren't awful. Sorry, I didn't mean it like that. You were just a lot more sensible than us.'

'I was an insufferable little bossyboots. There's no point arguing.' She stops suddenly. 'You see, there I go again. I still haven't learned my lesson. I'm always right.'

'Hey …' I want to put my arm round her, but hold back. 'This isn't like you. We needed bossing around. If you hadn't been there, we'd never have done anything. I mean, you were the brains behind the Pixies. Bethany was too busy preening in the mirror to do the real work.'

'That's true, duck,' Paula says. 'Do you know I once caught her peering into that mirror we had for the Wishing Pond, and talking to herself? She was saying, "You look nice with your hair up, Bethany, but it's a shame not to wear it down when it's so shiny and glossy." Can you believe it?'

I think about Bethany. 'I suppose she couldn't help it. Must have been hard for her, not having her mum around.'

'Oh, Lucy, trust you to see the best in her,' Paula says. 'She was a manipulative little cow and you got it worse than anyone. Remember how she used to make you sew all her badges on because she might break her perfect nails? I bet she hasn't changed.'

Terri looks up from her wine. 'I did write to her agent before we met last time. To see if she wanted to come along. Never heard back. But people don't learn, do they? We're all the same. I'm bossy, Lucy's scared of her own shadow, Chris is on another planet.'

Chris shrugs. 'That's true, but then I prefer it to planet Earth.'

Terri doesn't reply, so Paula pipes up. 'I've changed, though, haven't I? Not in a good way. I used to be brave and skinny, now I'm fat and it scares me leaving my own house. So which one is the real me?'

We try to think of an answer and I feel uncomfortable. This was meant to be a cosy afternoon off, but it's turning into a group therapy session.

'This is getting a bit deep for a Saturday afternoon,' Chris says. 'So as your hostess, I think I have just the thing to lighten the mood.' She disappears into her office area, returning with a large cardboard box. 'I haven't hosted one of these for years, but when it comes to female bonding, there's nothing like it.'

She reaches into the box and rummages around, then a triumphant grin spreads across her face.

'Ladies, I'd like to introduce you to my first ever creation.'

And out of the box, she produces an enormous chestnut-coloured vibrator, complete with ears and a plastic-moulded bushy tail.

'Tufty the Secret Squirrel ... because a squirrel in the hand is worth two in the bush!'

By the time Chris has given us a full presentation on her numerous inventions – from Tufty to the eye-wateringly large Empire State of Ecstasy for her new American-themed range – I know more about sex toys than I ever wanted to. Though the look on Paula's face when she discovered the secret vibrating function on the end of an innocent-looking wooden spoon ('inspired by Nigella Lawson's orgasmic expression on her *Domestic Goddess* programme,' Chris explained) was priceless.

Terri looks less amused, but I feel too drunk to do anything to change the direction of the afternoon.

'So what age did everyone first have a bit of a fumble, then?' Paula says. 'On your own.' She doesn't seem drunk at all, but then maybe her excess fat is absorbing the alcohol more efficiently.

Chris is tidying away her props. 'Masturbation, you mean? I was quite innocent until I was twelve or thirteen, I think. And then I remember daydreaming about one of the boys from your school. Peter someone ... in the fifth year. Blondish hair, tall ...'

'Peter Clark!' I smile at the memory. 'God, I fancied him too.'

Chris puts the box under the table. 'Well, you can imagine what it was like at convent school. I used to think about him before I went to bed and then I put a pillow between my legs and sort of squeezed ... that was my first orgasm, though I didn't realize it. We were so naïve, weren't we? Not like now, eh?'

Paula groans theatrically. 'Oh here we go again – the good old days.'

Chris shakes her head. 'No, I don't mean that at all. I don't think it did us any good being so sheltered. I mean, you don't want primary kids knowing about butt plugs, but I've never thought ignorance is automatically bliss. Not at all. What about you, then? First ever wank?'

'Chris!' Terri's face is slightly slumped now, from the wine, and she slurs as she says, 'Really. Is there any need to talk like that?'

'I can't believe you used to be a nurse. You must have heard worse than that. OK then, let me rephrase. Paula, when did you first masturbate?'

'I think I was probably six or seven.'

'Oh my God,' I say. 'Before you joined the Brownies?'

'I didn't know that was what I was doing at the time, silly. I was in the school gym and you know how we used to have those monkey ropes you'd swing on?'

'Hmmm.' I think back.

'Well, let's put in this way – didn't you ever wonder why I was so bloody keen on swinging?'

'Come to think of it,' I admit, 'you did used to hog the ropes. And that was ... ? I mean, you were ...'

'Enjoying more than just the exercise. Yep. Shocking, isn't it? And you?'

'I was a really late starter compared to you two, needed a boy to show me what to do.' I blush, but the wine makes me feel braver. 'And after that, well, there's always been a boyfriend, really, and then a husband, so I've never been bothered with ... solo.'

Yet again, all eyes are on Terri. She's gone quite red in the face and I can't tell if it's wine or irritation. 'Why is everyone so obsessed with sex? It was the same last time. I know you think

I avoid the issue because I've never done it, Chris, but to be quite honest, if sex turns you into such bores, then I'm glad I've never bothered.'

She stands up, the chair legs screeching loudly on the slate-tiled floor. 'I'm going for a walk.'

'Do you want me to come with—' I begin, but the fiery expression on Terri's face tells me to let her go.

'Blimey!' Paula says, when the lift has carried Terri away. 'What do you think's up with her?'

'Maybe it's not working out with her bloke,' Chris says. 'Maybe he got tired of waiting.'

Paula takes a pizza menu from Chris's pile. 'She'll be back. In the meantime, I fancy an American Hot. Sex always used to give me an appetite. And, Chris, what makes you such an expert in the bedroom?'

Chris laughs. 'I don't know that I'd describe myself as an expert.'

'You know more than me, I bet,' I say, trying hard not to worry about Terri.

'OK, I've probably seen a few more videos or handled a few more sex aids, but it doesn't make me a Professor of Sex or anything. It's a shop, that's all. It's not that different from being, I dunno, a greengrocer. Or, maybe, a DIY superstore.' She giggles.

'How many?' Paula asks.

'How many what?' Chris dribbles out the last of the wine.

'How many lovers have you had?'

Chris takes another bottle from her ergonomically stream-lined wine rack. 'Well, the correct answer to that one, if you're a woman, is five less than you've actually had, so long as the number you end up with is well under double figures. Three to six is perfect. Whereas if you're a bloke then you can get away with a dozen. So much for equality, eh?' She opens the bottle with the built-in pressurized gadget and tops up our glasses. 'Whereas the true figure in my case is thirty-one.'

I know it's uncool to seem shocked, but I can't think of the right response. Paula isn't so shy. 'Bloody hell. You really are a slapper, aren't you!'

'Thanks,' Chris says, but she doesn't look offended. 'It works out at only just over one point something a year since I lost my virginity. Not *that* many. What about you two?'

'I suppose if I say three now, you won't believe me,' I say. 'Andrew, plus the two boyfriends before him. I am just so Mrs Average of Suburbia.'

'God, suburbia's ten times more obsessed with sex than the city, in my experience,' Chris says. 'But three is respectable. Paula?'

Paula takes a large glug of her wine. 'Well, let me think about it. I don't count Dennis in the fifth form because all I did was toss him off and it turned out afterwards we both only did it for a dare. So ... one.'

'One?' I'm more surprised than I was about Chris.

'Think about it. What Dennis taught me – apart from the fact that a penis won't break no matter how fast you tug on it – was that blokes only shag fat birds because they think it'll be less hassle than trying to shag the thin ones.'

Chris shakes her head. 'That's not true, Paula. Bigger women are way sexier for lots of men. And I've seen the videos to prove it.'

'Depends on your definition of big. Men like tits, sure, and they might put up with a size fourteen body, but if you're just averagely grotesque, all you get is blokes doing it for a bet, or blokes who are so blind drunk they won't be able to find their way in. I still don't know why Neil bothered. Though I reckon my dad might have asked him to, as a favour. Because he works for him, Neil always does what Dad says.'

'Oh, Paula, that's an awful way to think about yourself,' I say. 'Anyway, I think it's really sweet that your husband was the first.'

'And the last,' Paula mutters.

'Everyone feels like that when they break up,' Chris says. 'But you'll change your mind.'

'No I won't. Even if there was some mug out there willing to have me, I'm dangerous.'

'What?' I stare at her. 'Dangerous?'

'I fuck people up. I do. Neil was a nice bloke until I messed with his head and now he's had to leave his house and his kids because of me. You all know what happened in Brownies: I drive people away. End of story. I just think that I'm better off on my own.'

'Oh, Paula.' I stand up and immediately feel shaky, but make my way towards my friend and thrust my arms around her. Well, as far around her as I can get them.

Chris looks uncomfortable. 'I'm beginning to think that the wine wasn't such a good idea after all. Paula, have you thought about ... *seeing* someone?'

'What, like a counsellor?' Paula spits the word out.

'Well, yes. Why not? Isn't a marriage worth saving?'

'Mine's dead and buried. What good does talking do, anyway?'

Chris takes a deep breath. 'To help you find out what went wrong. How you could still fix it.'

'I know full well what was wrong with our marriage. Me.'

Chris bites her nail and I remember her doing the same twenty-five years ago. Judging from the perfect manicure, it's a childhood habit she's largely outgrown. 'What about your kids?' Chris says, more softly.

'They'd be better off with Neil. I might move home, then he could move back in and look after them.'

'Are you sure?'

Paula frowns. 'This isn't just about me, is it, Chris? I mean, great, your parents stayed together. Bully for them. But was life really that hunky-dory in the Love household? And however fantastic all this is ...' she waves around the kitchen, 'I don't see you making a storming success of your private life, either. So me and Neil going to marriage guidance isn't necessarily going to hold the secrets of happiness for Sadie or Charlie.'

'But that's exactly the point. My parents *didn't* ask for help. In fact, they haven't asked each other anything more revealing than ... I dunno, to pass the remote control, for two decades.'

I feel dizzy and it's not just the wine. The afternoon is slipping out of control. I can't bear to hear about so much unhappiness, yet the others seem determined to bring us down. 'Do we have to ... I mean, I know it's awful and everything but ...' I sigh, defeated by my inability to explain. A fragment of memory, of my mother settling a squabble between Bethany and Simonetta in her usual no-nonsense manner, taunts me. I'm entirely useless. The tears that I've staved off for weeks now are beginning their short journey from my heart or brain or whichever bit triggers my cry-baby tendencies, to my eyes. I pinch myself, hard.

Chris and Paula turn to look at me and as they too realize the tears are looming, the anger in both their faces changes to concern. Chris speaks first. 'Don't get upset, Lucy. I'm sorry.' She looks at Paula. 'I don't mean to be so bloody one-track. You'd think after all these years I could leave it alone. Move on. I thought I had, but after today ...'

As she tails off, Paula picks up. 'And I'm sorry too, duck. The wine, you know. I don't really feel as bad as all that. It's life, isn't it?'

I wait. Paula's protests aren't convincing, but Chris doesn't seem to have the energy to challenge her either because all she says is, 'Do you think Terri's actually coming back?'

'God knows,' Paula says. 'Why?'

'Because I reckon we're in need of phase three of Operation Pixie.' She stands up and goes back to the takeaway drawer. From the back, she produces a little plastic bag and a tiny oblong parcel of Rizla wrappers. 'This is the best way I know to calm down after a hard day at the sex toy empire.'

Chapter Twenty-two

If you want a cool head in difficulties
and strong nerves for emergencies, do
not take any wines. Spirits never did a
woman any good.

Two hours later, smelling of weed and carrying a scrapbook and a gift-wrapped free sample of what Chris has assured me is the most discreet and low-noise vibrator sold at Love Bites, I'm in a taxi to Sunny's house.

Somehow, despite the booze and the drugs, I managed not to tell the girls my destination. Earlier on, the alcohol loosened my tongue, but my first experience of cannabis seems to have tightened it back up again, sending me into a pleasant world of my own where every random thought is the funniest line in history.

'Have you got a bit on the side?' Paula asks me when the taxi pulls up outside the station to drop her off. She's a bit pissed off about having to travel back on her own, though she seems sober enough to make it back in one piece.

'No, don't be daft. Just catching up with an old friend,' I say, relieved that Paula knows so little about my life. If it was Terri – who called my mobile when we were halfway through the joint and said she'd gone back to her halls and didn't want to talk about it – then I'd be in trouble. She knows I don't have any friends here except her.

I fumble with my change as I pay the driver, and my ankles feel rubbery when my feet hit the pavement, like a cartoon character's. I will them to keep me upright and somehow they pull it off, though each step up Sunny's front path seems to involve extensive negotiations between brain and muscle. *Left foot next, that's right, no, not right, left. Slowly now.*

I reach out to push the door bell and it seems to sound before I touch the metal, reverberating so loudly that I'm surprised the cars on the street don't brake in shock.

It occurs to me that this might be a side effect of Chris's wacky-backy, but in every other way – that's apart from the rubber ankles and the strange sounds and the hysterical one-woman comedy show on stage in my brain – I feel normal. Well, more than normal. Ultra-alert.

The front door opens; it's such a big door, so swingy in its movement. I'm like Alice in Wonderland, because everything's bigger or smaller or stranger or plain funny.

Like Sunny's nose.

'Hello,' I say, trying to suppress a giggle at the astounding size of it. I really don't remember it being that big when I first met him. Perhaps it's grown. That's what happens when you're old, your nose and your ears grow and your eyes and your lips shrink until you're a caricature version of the person you used to be and that must be what's happened to poor funny Sunny.

Oh, that rhymes! Funny Sunny. Hee hee ...

'Lucy, are you all right? You seem to be a little unsteady.'

'I'm fine.' I skip past him into the house and the lovely doggy smell hits me again, followed moments later by the lovely doggy himself, who rushes at me with such enthusiasm that my bendy ankles threaten to give way again. 'Lovely doggy,' I say to the dog, but his yellowy eyes turn to black and he runs away, whimpering.

Sunny puts his hand on my shoulder. 'It's great to see you again, Lucy.'

'You too,' I say and I feel tears of happiness gathering in my eyes so when he turns his back to lead the way, I scrub away at them with the backs of my hands. As I walk through to the kitchen, I hear chamber music: each note buzzes, like a swarm of pitch-perfect bees.

'Lucy, I'd like you to meet Michelle, my wife,' he says and as he steps out of the way, a tall woman with cropped red hair is holding out her hand. I recognize her from the photo Sunny gave me last time: she was slim then, but looks scrawny now. I reach out to shake and realize too late that my hand is still greasy and tomato-stained from the pizza I ate at Chris's. She notices, but is too polite to mention it.

Instead she says, 'You look exactly the same as you did when I last saw you.'

The way she says it, this is not a good thing. 'Everyone says I haven't changed since I was tiny.' Though as I say it, I remember that Sunny and Michelle may be the only people in the world who can say that from memory, not photographs. 'Even my daughter said that when she saw an old picture.'

'Yes, Sunny mentioned that you have a little girl. I can't see Seb ever settling down long enough to give us a grandchild.'

I look around for him, blushing already. Sunny appears with a glass of red wine. The off-fruit smell makes me feel queasy. 'Michelle and your mum always used to joke that perhaps you and Seb might have ended up together.'

Michelle frowns at him. 'Like I said, he's not the marrying kind.' And it sounds like a warning. 'He was supposed to be joining us, but you know how men are: if he's not here by now, then I guess he's not going to bother. Probably off with another of his girls. They find him irresistible.'

I spot the clock on the wall of the dining room but it's decided not to cooperate in telling me the time – the second hand has speeded up to blur the outline of the others. 'Am I very late?' I say, dreading her answer. This woman doesn't like me. I dread to think what I did as a child to cause a grudge that's lasted three decades.

Sunny speaks before she can. 'We weren't ready until now, anyway, Lucy. You have perfect timing.'

Michelle turns back into the kitchen as Sunny and I sit down. As she switches on the light, I can see the worktop is covered in little glass dishes of ingredients, as if Delia Smith is about to demonstrate a fiddly recipe. There's only one stray mug and the moment Michelle spots it, it's upended into the dishwasher. It's like she has a radar system behind her eyes, *beep, beep, beep*, constantly scanning the world for anything irregular.

Mugs, dust, unwelcome blasts from the past like me ... all need to be put in their place.

She turns to catch me staring at her.

Beep ... Beep ...

The dining room must be Sunny's territory because it's a mess. Radar Woman probably hates it, but I find it soothing. There are eight mismatched chairs: only four of them are free to sit on; the others are piled high with journals and papers and large spiral-bound notebooks. On the floor there are more stacks of magazines and files. 'Do you work in here, then?' I say, feeling bizarrely proud of myself for asking such a sensible, observant question.

'Yep. Writing articles and whatnot; you'd be amazed how much there is to write about the heart. Only when Michelle's working nights, though, we get little enough time together as it is. Don't we, my love?'

Beep ... Beep ... She's coming in with a huge platter of appetizers, strange bite-sized combinations of colours, which she then proceeds to describe so seriously that it feels like she's announcing the guests at a diplomatic function. The Count of Cherry Tomato topped by Lady Guacamole. Earl Sardine with his loyal companion, Monsignor Horse Radish. The Ambassador of Blini with Mrs Creamed-Beetroot.

I daren't meet her eye – that radar might be capable of reading thoughts – so I murmur with what I hope is an appropriate level of enthusiasm after she introduces each guest, I mean, dish. I reach out for my wine but someone seems to have emptied it for me, so I wait for the lovely Sunny to top it up again. Then I take one of each appetizer and arrange them on my plate. I try to work out the most pleasing pattern: a long line, then a funny triangular shape. Finally I decide on a smiley face, with the tomato as a nose, the beetroot blini as lips – and I take a second sardine to make a pair of eyes.

I look up to see concerned looks on the faces of my hosts. I have no idea how long I've been rearranging my starter, but I suspect it might have been several minutes.

'If you don't like them, you don't have to eat them,' Michelle says, with the forced tolerance of a mother having to be nice to someone else's child, when she clearly believes a good slap would be the best course of action.

'Oh, no, they're lovely,' I say, popping the tomato into my mouth and swallowing it whole. For a moment, I'm convinced I am going to choke. But instead the ball forces its way down my gullet and seems to find a natural home somewhere in the middle of my neck. I'm pretty sure that if I looked in the mirror, it would be protruding, like a goitre.

'Michelle's always been a great cook,' Sunny says proudly. 'And a baker. She baked everyone's birthday cakes when you were small. Even yours.'

'Well, your mother was never into baking,' Michelle says.

I nod, still uncertain whether I can get enough air past the tomato to speak. Perhaps that's it. Perhaps I once refused to eat one of Michelle's cake creations and she can't forgive me.

The sardines seem to be winking at me on my plate, daring me to get them down. I pick up the smaller of the two and put it on my tongue, knowing I am going to have to employ the tactics of a desperate dieter, chewing the fish a hundred times until it's mashed up enough to swallow. The horseradish brings new tears to my eyes and as I try not to splutter, the pressure in my head is almost unbearable.

'I was sorry to hear about Judy,' Michelle says. But her voice is cold.

I nod, unable to say anything until I can stop chewing, and I am only on Chew Number Thirty. It's probably just as well. Now I'm with the Bandeles – perfect wife and mother Michelle and the relentlessly positive Sunny – I can't understand why these people, Mum's friends, let her disappear to Troughton after dad died, why they were never in touch. Some friends ...

Sunny seems to read my mind. 'I wish we'd been able to see her, Lucy. We wanted so much to stay in touch with Judy, after your father died. But she cut all ties. She didn't feel it was *helpful*.'

That sounds like the kind of word my mother would use. I look again at Michelle, who is reaching out for her husband's hand. How would I feel if Terri moved away, refused to talk to me or see me? Perhaps I'd be wary if her long-lost daughter turned up out of the blue, too.

But she's still scaring me. *Beep.*

The final blob of chewed sardine squeezes its way down my gullet and I take a gulp of wine. Strangely, the more I drink, the more sober I'm becoming. 'I never really understood *why* she had nothing to do with anyone from before. Did she ever say anything to you?'

'Not exactly, but I suppose we can guess,' Sunny says.

Michelle glares at him. 'Can't it wait until after dinner?'

'I think that as Lucy's brought it up now, we ought—' He stops mid-sentence as we hear a key in the lock.

'Hope you've saved some for me.' Seb's voice singsongs from the hall, before he appears: wrapped in grubby motorbike leathers and huge boots, he's as stunning as I remembered. There are thousands of tiny beads of sweat on his face, drawing attention to his unblemished skin, and making me want to touch it, to see if it can be real. I notice that he has his mother's slightly haughty eyes, but his smile, directed at me, has the same effect as last time, turning me quite wobbly. 'What? Have I interrupted something?'

Michelle stands up and begins to gather the plates. 'Not at all. I was just about to get stuck into making the main course, so by the time you've changed, dinner will be on the table, your lordship.'

'Fantastic,' he calls as he runs up the stairs.

Sunny waits until Michelle's stacking the dishwasher, then whispers, 'Later, Lucy, I promise. I will tell you everything you ought to know.'

I feel disappointed yet excited at his arrival. I'm torn between finding out about my past and finding out about Seb. In a way, the two are intertwined: if we'd stayed in Manchester, would my life have been more like his? Perhaps that's why I want to get to know him.

Then again, perhaps it's just a monster, old-fashioned teenage crush. Peter Clark of the fifth form, eat your heart out.

He reappears wearing a pale blue T-shirt that clings to his six-pack. But I'm distracted from his physique by his mother, who is bringing out a huge casserole dish. At last. Something heavy and stewy might ground me, stop these disturbing ideas about people reading my mind, and hor d'oeuvres being guests at black-tie dinners. The effects of Chris's 'little treat' are fading, but I still don't feel fully in control of my brain or my body.

'So, Lucy, has there been any improvement in your husband's musical tastes?' Seb says, squeezing into the chair next to me, his legs brushing against mine. Now I feel even less in control and my skin is covered in goosebumps.

'Not that I've noticed.' I struggle to find something witty to say but I've never been any good at flirting, whereas I suspect Sebastian Bandele is the Greater Manchester Flirt Champion. And if I had what he has – stunning good looks, musical ability, and an entire football team's worth of charm – then I probably wouldn't hesitate to use it either. What I don't understand is why he's directing that charm at me, a dowdy and stoned shoe shop manager from the suburbs. Perhaps he's playing a game with me. I just wish I didn't feel so childishly eager to play it too.

Michelle takes the lid off the casserole dish and we wait for the steam to escape before peering inside. Uh-oh. So much for a hearty stew. Inside are four tiny chickens – I'm sure there's a posh French name, but to me they simply look like the runts of the litter. As Michelle positions one on my plate, I can smell oranges and brandy. And I can also see that dissecting the poor undernourished bird for its frugal portion of meat is going to be a frustrating experience. One I'm not convinced I have the stomach for.

'This looks *delicious*,' I lie.

'Mum's under the mistaken impression that she's Gordon Ramsay,' Seb teases his mother and she blushes. Even Radar Woman isn't immune from his charms.

'So what are you performing at the moment?' I ask him.

'Rehearsing for our Summer in the City season,' he replies, looking at me while his knife and fork effortlessly strip the flesh from his chicken. 'Come along; bring your husband. Or not. It might be a bit highbrow for him.'

'I haven't been to a classical concert for years.' As I say it, I feel angry with myself, the incredible shrinking woman.

Sunny claps his hands together. 'Oh, then you definitely must come. We always go and have a big party when Seb's on.'

'Yes, we always have a *family* outing on the first night,' Michelle says, forcing a smile. I wonder if this is how it'll always be. Me craving admission to the Bandele household, her as gatekeeper turning me away because I don't know the password.

'What about you? You mentioned you were a singer when we met last time,' Seb says, his eyes fixed on mine. 'You singing at the moment?'

I consider making something up but I feel too muddled to come up with a convincing lie. 'The singing's on hold for now. Bit of a luxury when I'm running a home and working full time.'

He shakes his head. 'I hate it when people give up on their dreams.'

'I haven't given up, exactly, I just . . .' I decide I don't need to justify myself to this stranger. 'It's easier said than done, that's all.' I reach for the wine but my glass is empty again.

But he's not letting go. 'If something's really important to you, you'll make time.'

'Do you think? When exactly would you suggest, then? Before getting up at six thirty to feed the cat and make packed lunches? I suppose I could rehearse at lunchtime in the staffroom, but it might be grounds for dismissal. And in the evening, I could slip in a few arias between helping with homework and cooking tea and washing and ironing and shopping and ferrying my daughter around. I'm just not dedicated enough!'

Suddenly I see myself as they must be seeing me, a ranting drunk, pointing with her knife to drum home her point. All the energy leaves me and I slump, putting the knife back on my plate next to the uneaten chicken.

'I think,' Seb says, far more gently this time, 'that no one's life should leave no time at all for a bit of selfish fun.'

Sunny holds up his hand. 'That's enough, Seb. Lucy, forgive my son for going over the top as usual. He has a somewhat childish view of the world and when he grows up he'll realize that things aren't quite that simple.'

'No,' I say, 'I know you're being polite, but actually he's right. I am a mug, spending my whole life looking after other people and never looking after myself. It's about time I started, isn't it?'

'I'll drink to that,' Seb says, and clinks his glass against mine. 'I propose a toast.' Sunny and Michelle follow his lead and raise their own glasses as Seb says, 'Here's to Lucy reclaiming a bit of her life.'

'To Lucy,' Michelle murmurs.

'To Lucy,' Sunny says, blowing me a kiss.

'To me,' I say, trying to work out just how many glasses of wine I've drunk today. And then wondering what the hell Andrew is going to say when I finally make it home.

Chapter Twenty-three

Ten Good Qualities: The poet Robert Burns
was of the opinion that the perfect wife was
made up of ten parts. Four parts good temper,
two parts common sense, one to a keen
intellect, one to beauty of person, and two
parts were apportioned to family or education.

Andrew didn't say anything. And while that seemed like the best result possible last night as I crept into bed alongside him, knowing from the forced regularity of his breathing that he was awake, this morning it's chilling.

Sunday mornings in our house are when we play at being *The Partridge Family*. Andrew will bring me breakfast in bed – well, toast and coffee, with the low-fat cholesterol-reducing margarine we've been buying since the GP told him his score was too high. And the newspaper, the front page torn because the letterbox is too small for all the Sunday supplements. When Andrew first brought me breakfast in bed after we moved in together, I found it charming and funny. But now I realize it's just a copy of what his parents did because every aspect of the way he behaves at home is based on that blueprint of marital perfection. Down to expecting me to change the sheets by Sunday night so the toast crumbs don't irritate his skin.

After breakfast, Sasha will climb in beside me to read the *Funday Times*, and look at the pictures in the Homes section, asking me if this house or that house is worth more than ours. She's a property developer in the making. I suppose if the

Brownies were really coming up to date, there'd be a badge for House Doctors.

It's not perfect – Andrew rarely joins us and when he does, the feeling that we're play-acting becomes stronger – but like all routines, it has a kind of comforting familiarity. Or it did. Lately it's harder to remember my lines.

This Sunday I know it'll be different from the moment I open my eyes. My hangover is astonishingly mild, just a slight over-sensitivity to light and a tightness across my forehead as I raise my head tentatively from the pillow. When I shift over to face Andrew, his eyes are wide open and expressionless. I attempt a smile, and wait for it to be reciprocated.

'Are you having an affair?'

His voice sounds the same as it does when he is dealing with out-of-hours gridlock crises on his mobile: artificially calm and controlled.

'What on earth makes you think that?' I sit bolt upright, then it occurs to me that the correct response ought to be an immediate denial. 'No. Of course not.'

He stays horizontal and this irritates me. 'I don't like what's happened to you, Lucy. I know your mother's death was highly upsetting – even ten years later, I still think about my father every day, but I also knew when to move on. I've been patient and supportive but I think it's time to try to put it behind you.'

'You're giving me a timetable for grieving?'

Now he does sit up. 'That's not what I'm saying.'

'It sounds to me as though that's exactly what you're saying. And if I don't want to follow that timetable, what then?' I'm curious, more than scared. Something changed last night. Time is suddenly my most precious commodity and I have lost too much of it to Andrew. I have to stand up for my future seconds and minutes and hours.

'No one could accuse me of being unreasonable, Lucy. I've been very tolerant. But when you arrive home after midnight, stinking of booze and God knows what else, and I have no idea how you got home or even where you were—'

'You knew I was with the girls from the Brownies.' Sunny

insisted on driving me home, and dropped me off at the end of the road, so Andrew wouldn't see his car and wonder who he was.

'Till midnight?'

I turn away before he can read my face. 'I don't have to put up with interrogation, Andrew.'

'No?' He grabs my shoulder and turns me round. 'Well, I don't know that I have to put up with the way that you're behaving.'

I shrug him off. 'My first late night out of safe old Troughton since ... well, if I think about it, since before Sasha was born, and suddenly I'm the world's worst wife, the world's worst mother.'

He nods smugly. 'That's another thing. The effect on Sasha. OK, if for some unknown reason you want to make my life a misery, that's one thing. I can take it. But it's not fair on her. She's noticed that you're not at all your normal self. And she kept asking me last night what time you'd be home.'

'Oh, and I bet you made sure she knew I was being *naughty* in not giving you my detailed itinerary for the day, didn't you, Andrew? The two of you are always ganging up on me.'

Now he does something really unforgivable. He laughs at me. 'Ganging up on you? She's your daughter. You're not in the playground now, Lucy. You're a *grown-up*, remember?'

I look at him for a long time. His face has the same perfect proportions, yet I don't recognize him. What was it I loved about him? I honestly can't remember a single thing. 'If I'm doing such a shocking job of being a grown-up ...'

I count to ten in my head, to be certain that this isn't just anger talking, that I won't regret it. In those few seconds I plot my next steps, the arrangements I need to make and whether I can make them today, before I finally finish my sentence.

'... then I think I will leave you to it, Andrew.'

He frowns. 'Meaning?'

'I'm moving into the Old Surgery. You'll get along so much better without me under your feet.'

And as his jaw hangs open, I lock myself in the en suite so he can't see how much my decision scares me.

In the shower, I plan the details of my departure, refusing to allow myself to think about the why of what I'm about to do, and concentrating instead on the how.

In my head, I've chosen the suitcases – the big floral one that Andrew would be too embarrassed ever to use, plus a little weekender rollercase for my shoes and toiletries. As I use each product – shampoo, conditioner, shower gel – I add it to my mental going-away list. Moisturiser, foundation, lipstick, eyeliner. Deodorant, toothbrush, toothpaste, dental floss. And, of course, everything I've collected to do with my father.

As I brush my teeth, I think about how I'm going to tell Sasha. Matter-of-fact is the only way, with a detailed explanation of arrangements. I need a couple of days to get the Old Surgery ready for her to live with me. It's not perfect, of course, but it's only temporary, after all, till I get my head together. If I can persuade Andrew to look after her at the weekend, then I'll have a chance to think. At last. I know my mother-in-law will be only too keen to come to the rescue after her precious son's desertion by flaky old Lucy. I bet Andrew's on the phone to her already.

But when I come out, he's still sitting on the bed. 'Are you really leaving?'

'It's not *leaving*,' I say, softly. 'Not for good. But you're right, I'm confused about a lot of things and there's no time here to think. No room.'

Even as I say it, I wonder why I'm bothering, if it's just a gesture, like a one-day strike by some group of government officials whose absence will barely be noted.

'And there is no one else?'

'No.' Because there isn't. Not really. My crush on Seb is just that. But my crush on what he represents – a different life – that's the biggest threat to all the things we've taken for granted for so long.

He nods. 'And what about Sasha?'

'I'm going to talk to her now. I think your mum should be able to pick her up and give her tea till you're home tomorrow and Tuesday, which is when she's got Brownies, so I can fetch her and then she'll stay with me for the rest of the week.'

'So you're planning to be gone a week?' He looks hopeful.

'I mean, after a week we should review things.'

'Right. I see. You've got it all planned, haven't you?'

I stare at him. If only he knew. I have never felt more like I'm jumping out of a plane without a parachute. 'I know it's going to be tough, Andrew. And I know you don't understand this. But can we try to keep things stable for her? I'll definitely be able to take her to Brownies.'

I'm already wondering how I will explain this to Terri, when I can't explain it to myself.

He walks out of the room without looking at me, and goes into his study. I wonder if he's crying, or just wants to check his email. Andrew doesn't do high emotion.

I dress in the jeans and T-shirt I always wear on Sundays, then knock on Sasha's door. When I push it open, she has her back to me and her headphones on, playing her new Harry Potter game on the PlayStation. But I know she's only pretending things are normal. By this time on a Sunday she should be stuck into asking about buy-to-let and stealing my toast.

I touch her on the shoulder. 'Sweet-pea ... I need to talk to you.'

When she faces me, the muscle in her cheek is twitching and her Quentin eyes are unblinking. 'Mum, I was in the middle of the game.'

Can I do this to her? None of this is her fault. But then, perhaps a few days away will be all it takes to get Mummy back to normal. They might even *miss* me. 'Sasha, I'm sorry to interrupt. But I'm going to Granny's house for a little while.'

The nerve stops twitching. 'Oh, OK. I can stay here with Daddy now, can't I? I've got to finish this level.'

I try again. 'Well, yes, but the thing is that I'm not just going for the day. There's still so much to sort out so it'll be much easier if I live there, tidy in the evenings. So Grandma Collins will pick you up from school tomorrow, but then from Tuesday you can stay with me, and then come home to Daddy at the weekend. It's only temporary.'

'For how long?' The twitch is back.

'It depends how I'm getting on, sweet-pea. Granny had so much *stuff* – you saw that for yourself. It's like a jumble sale.'

She looks at the computer screen, where Harry is frozen in mid-air on his misbehaving broomstick. 'You're not *leaving* Daddy, are you, Mummy?' Her voice sounds normal, but hearing her use the word *Mummy* makes me want to cuddle her, reassure her. But how can I?

'No, no. Just spending a little time in my mummy's house, Sasha. You know, I haven't been feeling all that happy lately, a little bit sad about Granny dying so I think it'll cheer me up.'

'Do I make you sad, Mummy?' The nerve is twitching faster and I pull her close to me, getting tangled in the headphones.

'No, Sasha, my baby never makes me sad. But I don't want to make you sad either so that's why I'm going. It'll be like a holiday for you for a couple of days. No one to nag you about doing your homework!'

She stares at me for a little too long, then nods. When I finally trust myself to speak again, I say, 'I'll get a big bedroom ready for you and when you stay, we can have a picnic. Or you can bring your sleeping bag. It'll be like camping.'

I reach out for a cuddle, and she goes along with it for a few seconds, then wriggles out of my grasp and puts her headphones back on, dismissing me from her room. When I close the door behind me, I feel too guilty to cry.

My bags are packed, but there's no big send-off. Andrew's already made himself scarce in his study, playing Bryan Adams' 'Everything I Do' at top volume through his computer speakers. I'm relieved that there'll be no doorstep goodbye. Perhaps if I was really walking out, it would be different; I'd want a bigger moment for my personal history book.

I drag my cases down the stairs and find my car keys before nipping to fetch some Nurofen from the kitchen drawer. Maybe it's the hangover kicking in, or maybe it's a tension headache, but my brain feels too big for my skull.

Miaow.

Buster snakes around my ankles. The suitcase is a trigger for giving me the full guilt treatment as he does when we're off on holiday. Though the neighbour's over-generosity with Whiskas and cuddles means the cat's generally more annoyed when we get home.

But I can hardly ask the neighbour to cat-sit while my husband is still living here. Buster meows again and I weigh up his chances. Andrew never wanted a cat anyway, and as two territorial males sharing the house they've never bonded. And though we got a pet for Sasha's sake, to teach her all those life lessons about nurturing and responsibility, she lost interest long before Buster lost his testicles in the neutering operation at six months. Neither Andrew nor Sasha would notice if his food grew mould or his water ran dry.

I carry my bags to the car. I know what I have to do. Sighing, I find the cat basket under the stairs and open its hatch very quietly, so as not to alert Buster to my plans. He hates being left alone, but not as much as he hates being taken anywhere in his carrier. Then in a single, practised movement, I scoop him up from the kitchen floor – bloody hell, he's heavy – and plunge him feet first into the basket, closing the grille before he can lash out with his claws.

'It's for your own good, Buster,' I say as I carry him and a huge bag of dry cat food outside. I close the front door behind me and start the car, turning the music tape up loud so I can't hear his pathetic cries.

It's *La Traviata*, of course. This tape's been on my stereo for weeks.

As I reverse out of the drive, I look up. Sasha's headphoned silhouette looms at her bedroom window but she doesn't wave. I think I can see Andrew, too, at the study window, but I can't be sure.

I put my foot down and Buster stops whimpering. 'Right, then, mate. To infinity and beyond ...'

Somewhat short of infinity – in fact, a mile round Andrew's precious ring road, the pinnacle of his career – we arrive at our destination. I sit in the car and look at the Old Surgery as if I'm seeing it for the first time. And before my eyes, it changes from a prison to a refuge.

The metal window frames always reminded me of bars, but now the fretwork seems reassuringly strong, supporting the multiple squares of glass to stop anyone seeing inside. The ivy's more vigorous than ever, covering the brickwork in jungly green strands and forming an overgrown, friendly canopy over the front door. Sunlight on the gravel drive dazzles me, leaving purple and orange imprints on my eyes.

As I let myself in, the old smells – damp and beeswax – welcome me inside. Even the way the house blocks out so much light seems to be nurturing, protecting me from the outside world.

I carry Buster's basket into the kitchen and shut the door. Damn, I need a litter tray for him, as if I let him out now he'll probably try to go home and I don't fancy his chances along the ring road. I undo the catch on the basket grille and he emerges tentatively, looking around him before making a dash for the darkness of the larder. Cats always do that when they're scared, head for the smallest space they can hide themselves until the danger's passed. I wish I'd been born a cat.

I fill a bowl with water, another one with *Fishy Bite* biscuits, and then open the cupboard where Mum kept newspapers for recycling. Bingo! As I remove a small pile and place them in a corner of the larder, hoping Buster will take the hint, I notice the top one is dated the week before Mum died. The headline reads: *Troughton Traffic Crisis Predicted by 2020*, and I know Andrew will be quoted in the article. I smile at the idea of Buster peeing all over his words, then cringe at my own pettiness and close the larder door to stop the cat escaping.

The next decision is where I'll sleep. I carry my cases upstairs and, on a whim, open the door to my grandparents' room. Anywhere I choose here involves sleeping in dead people's beds, unless I go back to my old bedroom – and I can't face that.

My grandparents' room overlooks the garden. I find bedding in the linen cupboard – old-fashioned sheets and blankets, laundered and starched a thousand times – and make the bed, with hospital corners and perfectly straight lines, the way Mum taught me.

As soon as I've made it, I long to climb in, though it's still only eleven o'clock in the morning. I ought to unpack, then go to buy enough groceries to tide me over, plus some bloody cat litter. And then I ought to call Terri, to let her know what I've done.

But then I realize. There's no one here to tell me what I ought to do. *Ought* is the word that's ruled my life for so long. And it's about time it was put back in its place.

I peel off my T-shirt, step out of my jeans and climb between the sheets, catching the faintest scent of the lavender water my mother used in her iron ... it makes me smile. I lie under the bedclothes, my head poking out, looking at the soothing shimmer of the leaves on the tallest oak tree in the garden.

It's only now that it occurs to me why I feel so differently about the Old Surgery today. Why it's no longer a prison.

It's because for the first time in my life, I have chosen to be here. And it feels like home.

Chapter Twenty-four

Waste of time is the worst of waste. We can never get those moments back again and it is very nearly impossible to buy time, however much money you have.

I'm out of practice when it comes to pleasing myself, but in the two days since I decamped to the Old Surgery, I've been catching up.

What I can't get over is how much time I have, without the constant tasks involved in running a husband and a daughter and a home. On Sunday, I slept for three hours before waking up in the middle of the afternoon and having a long bath. True, the immersion took an hour to heat the water, which then gushed out of the old pipes rust-coloured, but at home I only ever have time for a shower and even then, someone's usually banging on the door asking me how long I'm going to be or where their shoes or sandwiches are.

After my bath I went round the corner to buy fish and chips, and ate them in front of *Songs of Praise*. The pious singing reminded me to call Terri.

When she answered her mobile, she sounded distant. 'Hi, Lucy. Look, I'm sorry for racing off like that yesterday. It was rude. Did you have a nice time?'

Yesterday seemed like years ago. 'Yes, fine thanks. We got through some more wine and had pizza and had a catch-up.' I decided not to mention the cannabis. 'And are you OK?'

She hesitated before answering. 'I've been better, to be honest. I don't want to go into detail, but Colin and I aren't together any more.'

'Shit. But surely you hadn't sorted him out yet?' I realized this didn't sound quite right, but the news was so unexpected. Usually we talk for months about the best time to despatch her latest protégé out into the cruel world. 'I mean, mostly you send them off all *finished*.'

She laughed at the other end of the phone. I could hear the hymns playing on my TV set echoed on hers. 'Yes, well, maybe Colin wasn't quite as ready to be made over as the others so the project had to be terminated unexpectedly. Anyway, like I said, I don't want to talk about it.'

I wondered if Colin could have finished with *her*. It didn't seem possible, yet she sounded so fragile. 'It must be something in the air.'

'What do you mean?'

'I've left Andrew. Well, Saxon Close, anyway.'

'WHAT? Where on earth are you? I'm coming over.' I heard her switch the TV set off.

'No, don't. That sounded more dramatic than it is. I haven't left him, exactly, not for good. I just needed a bit of a break, so I've come to stay at Mum's.'

'Golly, things must be bad for you to go there.'

'Actually, it's almost comforting being in the old place.'

'But it's been empty for two months. And it's hardly your favourite address.'

I looked around the living room. It was certainly dusty and shabby, and I hadn't attempted yet to restore order. 'I can cope … So long as Sasha's room is tidy, it'll be fine and I don't suppose it's going to be for long. I just needed some space to think.'

'About what?' Now I could hear a kettle boiling, no doubt for tea to help her get over the shock of my departure.

'You know I haven't been happy for a while, Terri. Nor has Andrew.'

'He seemed content enough last time I saw him with his feet up on the sofa.'

'Yes. Well, I think if he wasn't constantly knackered, he'd

spot the fact that we're not happy. This morning he asked me if I was having an affair.'

'Bloody hell. I mean, apart from anything else, when would you have time? In your lunch hour?'

I wanted to tell her about Sunny and Seb but I remembered her warning against going after my father. And now seemed the wrong moment, one saga too many for Sunday teatime. 'I was in quite late from Chris's last night. And it's always what men think, isn't it? They can't imagine that you might actually just be tired of them – there has to be someone else.' *Tired of him? Is that what I am?*

'Oh, Lucy. Nothing's been right since your mum went, has it? Nothing. What about Sasha?'

'I told her I needed to do some work here in the house, get it ready to go on the market.'

'Do you think she believed you?'

'I don't know. I don't suppose it matters, so long as I get my head straight soon. She's coming over on Tuesday anyway, for Brownies, and then she'll stay for a bit and then I'm bound to go back and Andrew will be a bit more grateful and then we'll live happier ever after, won't we?' But as I said it, I didn't believe it, and guilt coursed through me as I imagined Sasha like the children in those abuse adverts, in a darkened room, anorexic or shooting up, and telling the camera it all began when her mother abandoned her.

'Seriously, would you like me to come over? It's no trouble.'

But I put her off. There was no point in going in search of time to think, if you immediately found another person to distract you. And sharing my guilt wouldn't reduce it. I knew, somehow, that I wouldn't be going home yet. I hadn't made my grand gesture to slope back at the first sign of trouble. I had to be strong.

I called home and after a monosyllabic conversation during which Andrew confirmed he was OK, and I informed him I was OK and so was Buster (no one had noticed that the cat was absent without leave until I mentioned it), he put me on to Sasha.

'What have you done today, Sasha?'

She sounded surprised. 'Well, it's been quite nice. Daddy took me to Frankie and Benny's in town and I had a chocolate banoffee sundae and then he told me everything's going to be fine with you and him once you come to your sensibles.'

'Sensibles? Or senses?'

'I don't remember, Mummy. But he says mummies quite often have strange moods and that it's part of being a woman.'

'He does, does he? And are you all right, Sasha?'

'I think so, Mummy. I'm a bit worried that he won't know he has to cut the crusts off my sandwiches.'

I felt choked. What else wouldn't he remember? I reminded myself that no child ever died of having to eat a few crusts. 'Well, make sure you tell him. And Sasha, I'll pick you up from your Grandma Collins's house on Tuesday and then we'll have tea together here and I'll take you to Brownies. That'll be nice, won't it? You, me and Buster.'

'Hmmm,' she said. 'I need to go now, Mummy. Daddy's bought the DVD of *The Incredibles* for us to watch with tea.'

After I put the phone down, I went straight to the larder for Mum's cooking sherry, and discovered that Buster had ignored the newspapers and instead sprayed wee up the walls to mark his territory. As I donned the rubber gloves and searched for disinfectant, there was something oddly comforting about having this menial task. And, I thought, if I could pee up the walls, I'd probably do it too. Just for the sake of it.

On Monday morning, after a dreamless night's sleep, the shock of waking up on my own – well, except for Buster, who'd cuddled up to me in this ghost-filled house – lasted a good few seconds. Then I remembered. I checked my watch: six thirty. With no school run, no lunch preparations, and no drive to work, I could have a lie-in for another hour.

The novelty wore off after about fifteen minutes, so I put on my slippers and went to see how bad a state the house was really in. I checked all five bedrooms, both bathrooms, and poked my head up into the loft. The early morning light left no doubt that the Old Surgery was showing its age. I'd never really *looked* before. Mum only really used five rooms – her bedroom, the bathroom, the kitchen and the living room, plus the study, where chaos and a slight scent of decomposition had always gone with the territory. She claimed her limited occupation was to save on heating, but judging from what I saw on Monday, my ultra-capable Brown Owl mother was as paralysed by the scale of the task as I was.

In my grandparents' old bedroom, the 1960s built-in wardrobes were full of clothes in muted colours, plus flesh-coloured supports and implements that maintained my grandmother in her last years, so intimate I blushed to touch them. My teenage bedroom was packed with books and cutesy ornaments and batwing jumpers: stuff I never bothered to pick up when I left home.

But the scale of this task wasn't only about the clothes mountain or the impossibly chunky and ugly furniture. The condition of the building itself was woeful. Pools of water gathered below rusted radiators. Paint peeled off the window frames and polka dot circles of mould were growing on skirting boards. When I walked into the old guest room, which couldn't have been used in ten years or more, a flight of dull-brown moths escaped into the rest of the house, and as I knelt down to touch the carpet, I realized they'd eaten it threadbare.

I got dressed and then walked to the Cozee Café for breakfast, armed with a copy of the *Mail* to hide behind so no one could ask me any awkward questions. There was no need for the girls in the shop to know what was going on. After all, I was bound to come to my sensibles before too long.

After work on Monday – unremarkable except for a bossy woman with a broken purple stiletto threatening to sue us for the loss of a potential relationship after the heel collapsed during a first date – I went to the supermarket to fetch exactly what I liked for dinner. This consisted of taramasalata, Italian breadsticks, and a bottle of Cava. I also shopped for Sasha: fairy cakes, fizzy drinks, crisps, plus a few pink accessories and a new duvet set to transform my old room into hers.

Andrew and I hadn't even split up and I was already planning to buy her loyalty with E numbers.

I watched TV in my pyjamas, letting Buster lick the fishy

pink dip from my fingers with his scouring tongue. I tried to call Sasha earlier but she was at ju-jitsu so I left an 'oh so light' message in reply to my own voice on the home answerphone.

So all I had to do until I went to bed was get drunk and feel guilty. No wonder the producers of *Kramer vs. Kramer* didn't bother to show what the evil mother got up to when she left her son behind. There's no drama in snacking.

What the hell was I going to do? I still couldn't quite believe I'd done something so extreme, so un-Lucy, without asking someone's permission. The first time I'd spent more than two nights apart from Andrew since we married – and that was always him away at some conference while I kept the home fires burning. And I'd never been away from Sasha. Any minute now the police were going to knock on my door and ask me for a certificate countersigned by an adult to prove I was allowed to be home alone.

Or, worse, the ghost of my mother would appear to harangue me, to demand that I bucked up, and returned to my posting on the frontline of domesticity.

I fell asleep after three glasses of wine and woke up when the carriage clock sounded midnight. In my grandmother's bed, I dreamed of family photographs with my face blanked out.

'Lucy, come on in. Goodness, you're looking well.' Andrew's mother opens the door wearing a pink apron and a brave smile. She gushes constantly, an oil well of compliments. As a result, I never believe a word she says. That's one of the differences between me and my husband: he's never doubted for a second that her high opinion of him is shared by the rest of the world.

'Thanks, Glenda.' I catch a whiff of lavender perfume as I step into her immaculate house, wondering what she really thinks of my life, or her own. If you gave her the Truth Drug, would a lifetime's worth of bitterness be unleashed? Or maybe she is as perfect as she seems.

Sasha's sitting at the whitewashed wooden kitchen table, writing in an exercise book. It could, almost, be a normal Tuesday, as Glenda always looks after her on the days when there's no after-school club.

'Hi Mum,' my daughter says guardedly, waiting for me to approach and reach out first. I want to hug her properly, but I worry that I might cry and then any notion that this is just a 'holiday' will fall apart. So I kiss her on the cheek and make a big show of looking over her shoulder.

'Doing your homework?' I turn to Glenda. 'I don't know how you always manage to get her to do it.'

'Sasha always behaves herself for me,' she says. 'Will you have a drink?'

'No, sorry. I'd love to but we have to have tea before I drop Sasha at Brownies.'

Glenda frowns and her blue eyes disappear behind her heavy lids, the way Andrew's always do when he's tired. 'Well, I fed her as soon as she came round here. She was hungrier than usual.' She sounds reproachful, as though Sasha had been close to starvation rather than peckish. And she's outsmarted my plan to use confectionery to get on the right side of my daughter.

'Oh. Maybe Daddy needs some packed lunch lessons,' I say and Glenda's eyes flicker at the criticism of her darling boy. 'We'd still better get going. But thanks so much for stepping in while I get everything straight at the house.'

'You know I'll help as long as it takes,' she replies with a knowing look. 'When Ted ... you know ... went ... I didn't know if I was coming or going. But I set up new routines, made sure I never had a moment to think. It took a while to adjust but it's true about time healing. And the best way to encourage it is to keep busy.'

As if I ever have any other option.

Sasha and I lift her little suitcase into the car – I hope it was packed by Glenda, because if Andrew did it, something vital will have been forgotten. As we're backing out of the drive, Sasha suddenly shouts STOP and I wince in anticipation of the bitter outburst I deserve. But instead she tells me in a small voice that she's forgotten Mac – the raincoat-wearing rabbit comforter she's ignored for the last two years. She returns to the car cradling the bunny, its left leg swinging, wellington-less

219

since Buster ripped off the plastic boot. I clutch the steering wheel until my knuckles are bloodless white.

Sasha's very quiet on the journey to the Old Surgery. I'm not used to this: normally it's me trying to get a word in edgeways. Finally I decide to ask her outright. 'Are you upset with me? Sasha? Because that's OK if you are.'

'I won't be when you come home,' she says simply, still staring out of the window.

Buster greets her when she walks through the door. 'It smells of wee in here,' she pronounces. 'Is that you, Buster? Are you making puddles? That's what you always do when you're not happy, isn't it?'

I bustle forward into the kitchen, 'And you're definitely not hungry? I've got cake.'

Sasha eyes me suspiciously. 'Not really. I'd like to get changed now. I don't want to be late. We're starting our Science Investigator badge tonight.'

'Gosh. We didn't have that when I was a Brownie. Right, let's get you up to your bedroom. I hope you like it.'

We take the suitcase upstairs and she looks around the bedroom silently; at the new swirly duvet cover and the bedside light with a daisy-shaped shade. I pull out carefully folded clothes, but there's no yellow sweatshirt, no brown shorts. Oh shit. Glenda hasn't packed it. Sasha stares into the case and then accusingly at me. Irresponsible Runaway Mother Mistake Number One. It's my fault. 'Sweet-pea, I'm sorry. I don't have your uniform here,' I look at my watch, 'and I don't think we've got time to go back home through the traffic to fetch it.' This last statement is debatable: if I'm honest, I'd rather ramraid the local Brownie uniform stockist than go home and risk bumping into Andrew.

'But Mum, I can't go like this.' She waves her hand angrily at her school uniform.

'Your Auntie Terri won't mind.'

'I will. I don't want to be *different*.' Her bottom lip is trembling.

'You can't help but be different, Sasha Collins, because you're *fantastic*. You're brilliant. You're clever and you're pretty and you're my girl.'

'So why don't you want to live with me and Daddy any more?'

'Oh no, no, that's not it,' I say, rushing forward to hold her. 'It isn't you. It's me being silly.'

She lets me hold her but then when I step back, she says, 'Does that mean we're going home?'

I open my mouth to say yes, because it's the easy thing to do, and then ... I find I can't. 'Sasha. Come and sit down next to me.'

She scowls openly now but does as I say, drawing up one of the old dining chairs to the table where I used to do *my* homework, where I used to watch my mother eating or knitting or doing the crossword, and wondered how on earth we could be related.

'You know how horrible it felt when Granny died?'

'Mmm.' She closes her eyes for a few seconds, then opens them again. 'I'd forgotten how sad I felt. Knowing we'd never see her again. I feel horrible that I'd forgotten that as well. But then, she was very sad herself, wasn't she, Mummy? Very poorly.'

I smile at her. 'You're right and you know what? Granny would have been so annoyed if she'd thought you'd stayed sad for very long.'

Sasha nods. 'She'd have been cross with you, then, wouldn't she?'

I laugh out loud. 'Oh, yes, she'd have been cross with me all right.'

What would Mum have said to me now? I picture her in the parlour – the place she reserved for lectures and pronouncements – sitting in the carving chair. Maybe she'd be saying, 'You've made your bed; it's no other bugger's fault you're uncomfortable, so now lie in it.'

But then I'm less sure. Sunny hasn't told me much but it's enough to make me wonder if she was always as staid and set in her ways. The way he talked about her in the car when he took me home – I was too drunk to remember the words he used, but I do know he talked about her as a woman people loved and lusted after.

Is there a chance this new *Judy* might understand me running away? *Oh, so you're sticking up for yourself now then, are you? About time, too. Shame you have to get my granddaughter caught in the crossfire, but then Quentin women will always survive, whatever happens, regardless of men. She will survive, you know, Lucy.*

'Mummy?'

The image of Judy, the sound of her voice, was so strong that now I'm astonished to find only Sasha and I are at the kitchen table.

'You were saying about Granny and how she'd be cross at us for being glum because she's not here.'

'I was, yes. The thing is, Sasha, I'm still feeling glum. I know Granny seemed really very old indeed to you but when you're bigger yourself, you'll realize that actually she had a long life still to live and her dying has made me think about my own life. Well, all our lives. Mine and yours and Daddy's.'

She looks uncomfortable now and I think I've gone too far. My daughter is bright but isn't the trick with children to drip-feed the information, get them used to Fact One, Mummy's going through a tricky time but she still loves you, with a suitable interval before Fact Two, Mummy's tricky time is actually more about Daddy being a bully, a pig, a different person from the one she thought she'd married, but she still loves you. And then another gap before the clincher Fact Three, Mummy and Daddy are breaking up.

I don't know if that is where we're headed, me and Andrew. It's surreal to imagine a world where that might happen, where Lucy the Good Girl might leave for good.

'I want you to know one thing, Sasha. I am your mummy, I will always be your mummy and this topsy-turvy living won't go on for long. It's just that I have to work out what I want and to do that, I need a little bit of time on my own.'

'Will you and Daddy get divorced?' She's put her hand over the part of her cheek where it twitches. I haven't seen this gesture before and I bet the muscle's twitching underneath.

'I don't know, Sasha. I don't think so, but I don't want to make a promise that one day I might have to break.' She nods and I wonder whether I'm being too honest. People lie to their kids all the time. 'I hope not.'

'I hope not as well.' She stands up suddenly. 'Perhaps we don't have to go to Brownies tonight, Mummy? Perhaps we could have the picnic in Granny's garden?'

Through the kitchen window, I can see the sun's setting, bathing the lawn in bronze evening light. Terri and I used to sneak out there after school, with the sweets Terri's parents bought and my mother banned. We felt the ticklish warmth of the moist grass on the backs of our legs and necks as we lay looking up at the sky.

'Sweet-pea, that's the best idea I've heard in ages. There, what did I tell you? You're the cleverest girl in Troughton.'

Chapter Twenty-five

God would like every Brownie as a real
friend. You may tell him about things that
frighten you and the things you are sorry
you have done.

Terri helped herself to porridge from the catering-size cauldron, then looked around the refectory. As she'd only arrived last night when everyone was asleep, she didn't yet know the unspoken rules of the retreat. Was it bad form to sit close to someone who might be in deepest contemplation, or bad form *not* to sit close to someone because you'd look aloof? At least it was still early and there were few diners in the room, each one eating with eyes cast downwards.

She chose the second bench, which was empty, and slid her sturdy bum across the shiny wood until it reached the third indentation along. How many random bottoms would it have taken to create each dip? And why were they here? When the lecturer at college had suggested that some 'time out' might help Terri find her faith again, he'd handed over a folder full of leaflets. Clark House was the last one and she chose it because a) it wasn't named after some infinitely holier-than-thou saint, b) the philosophy seemed to be to leave visitors to their own devices and c) it was set up in 1969, the year of her birth. That seemed to be the nearest to A Sign she was getting from anywhere at the moment.

Apart from her lecturer, she'd told no one. But then, as she'd worked out on the endless train journey from Manchester to Glasgow, followed by a slow stopping service to the coast, there wasn't really anyone who'd notice her absence for four days. She called her parents only once a fortnight, and poor Lucy was preoccupied with her own crisis. Terri had dropped in on her the night Sasha didn't turn up at Brownies and, failing to get an answer at the Old Surgery, she'd let herself in through the stiff side gate to the garden. She'd found the two of them lying asleep next to each other on a rug, surrounded by bottles of limeade and empty chocolate and biscuit wrappers. Lucy had looked barely older than Sasha, sleep smoothing away the frown lines so the resemblance between mother and daughter and, yes, Judith too, was striking. Usually Sasha never stood still long enough to make the comparison.

Terri had sneaked back through the gate to avoid frightening them. But the image stayed with her. Whatever Lucy chose to do, whether the separation from Andrew became permanent or not, she would never be truly alone. The knowledge taunted Terri. Judith gone, Colin gone, and her parents never really there for her in the first place. Now God seemed to have disappeared as well, like a conman offering a spiritual savings plan 'for a rainy day' and then disappearing without a trace when the monsoon arrived.

'Would you mind if I sit here?' The man was probably a couple of years older than her, well-built, thin and oddly grey, from his curly hair to his pale skin and mercury eyes.

She nodded. 'That's fine.' Her voice sounded odd to her in the echoey hall. She didn't want company but neither did she want to be rude.

'Thanks. I'm Howard,' he said, stretching a bony hand across the table.

An old-fashioned name. Perhaps he was a ghost. Perhaps she was too. This was purgatory but no one had bothered to tell her. 'I'm Teresa. Terri. I arrived last night.'

'I thought I hadn't seen you. And I would have remembered,' he said, smiling. If it hadn't been for the setting – and the total implausibility of anyone being interested in her – she'd have thought he was being flirtatious. 'First timer?'

'Yes. I mean, not the first time to a retreat, but I've never been here before.'

'Me neither. But I've been here since the beginning of the week. I can show you the ropes.' His voice was soft, not quite Scottish, but not quite English either. His colouring suggested he was a stranger to sunshine. 'For example, the porridge is completely inedible unless you add a lot more sugar.'

'Hmmm.' She tasted a spoonful. 'You're right. I thought it would be spiritually purer somehow to eat it au naturel.'

'Me too. I'm sure they do it on purpose, to save on the sugar bill.' He stood up and went to the counter to pick up the sugar bowl, then came back to scatter three teaspoons onto the congealing oats.

'Thanks,' she said, wondering how soon she could warn him off for good by mentioning her status as a vicar-in-training. 'So what are you in for?'

He grinned at her. 'Oh, just a bit of topping up of the spiritual batteries. I'm an RE teacher, so my faith is under pretty constant assault from the godless. I like to spend a bit of time away at half-term.'

She smiled, and began to wonder if there was more to it than that, feeling that telltale itch to know more, to help top up those batteries. But then she frowned, despising herself for thinking she could help anybody else when she couldn't help herself. 'Right.' She focused on her breakfast, trying to close off the conversation.

Terri felt Howard's eyes staring, challenging her to look up. 'I was going to ask you what you were in for, but I get the sense you'd rather I didn't,' he said.

She relented and looked just past the side of his ear, avoiding direct eye contact. 'Oh, that's fine. I'm preparing for ordination and my lecturer said this was a good place to come.'

'Ah. A woman vicar! You know, I've been looking for one to come to talk to my kids, but all the ones I've found have been really old and, well, rotund and not exactly a role model. More a roly poly model. Maybe you're the answer to my prayers: a foxy young female vicar.'

'Have you had your eyesight checked lately?' she said, blushing. Perhaps he was making a joke about her fox-red hair. Before he had the chance to challenge her, she added, 'And I haven't actually been ordained yet. You never know quite how it'll turn out. Where's your school?' Oh flip, she thought. Now I've shown an interest, he'll never leave me alone.

'Berwick. As far north as you can go in England. Lots of old walls and bridges. Definitely worth a visit if you like old walls.'

Terri looked down at her bowl and realized, with some relief, that she'd finished her porridge. 'Unfortunately, I live in Manchester so it's a bit far. I must go. Silent contemplation to be done; you know how it is.'

'I do indeed. See you at lunchtime, then. Though I warn you the food doesn't get any better.'

'I'll bear it in mind.' She moved towards the serving hatch reserved for dirty dishes, aware he was watching her. She felt as though she'd forgotten how to walk normally, what to do with the hand that wasn't carrying her bowl. Then as she reached the door, she turned her head slightly. He was still watching her. Why, she couldn't imagine. Without make-up, her hair unwashed, wearing her drabbest, loosest clothes, she was hardly an attractive proposition. He had to be some sort of weirdo.

Perhaps she'd be better off taking all her meals in her room for the next two days.

Chris sat in her office, listening as the coffee maker spat into life. It would be an hour before anyone else arrived, but today she needed time to settle herself before the news came in.

It wasn't looking promising. One of the retail journals had published a piece yesterday saying the two biggest corporate shareholders had already indicated that they'd accepted the Eros offer. In which case it was all over.

She poured a coffee and took it into the open-plan office. Everything in here had been chosen to fit the brand identity and working style she'd wanted Love Bites to embody. The furniture, the laptops, the photographs on the walls. They would still exist without her, but the changes in culture would be inescapable. Geoff said Eros would almost certainly offer her a role, with a massive package to match, but she didn't want to know. They were well known for their aggressive attitude to business, which left little room for innovation and creativity. They'd take her brand and turn it tacky and she wanted no part of it.

Chris felt a draught as the heavy door opened. She turned to see Kian there. Mornings weren't his strong point – he regularly complained that work meant he had to go to bed by three a.m. on weeknights – so she was surprised he was in so early.

'I knew you'd be in at the crack, so I thought I'd make the effort,' he said, scratching his hair and sniffing. 'Picked up some muffins on the way in. Had a feeling you'd need carbs.'

Chris smiled at him, then sat down on the big leather sofa in the brainstorm area. 'That is above the call of duty, K, but I appreciate it. I only hope Eros recognize your talents, too.'

'Hey, we don't know anything for sure, pet,' he said, peeling the greasy paper bags off the muffins and presenting her with the choice of a chocolate one, an orange one or one with indeterminate red fruits. She went for chocolate. 'And you're looking *good*.'

She nodded. Today she was in full armour: her favourite deep green suit, which brought out the conker colours of her hair. And stilettos. 'I need to be prepared for the worst.'

His eyes opened wide: he had the longest eyelashes she'd ever seen on a man and when he looked surprised, he reminded her of Bambi. 'The worst, as in you get a few hundred thou for your shares *and* you're free to go and start an even more success-ful business, with everything you've learned setting this place up?'

'I know when you put it like that it doesn't sound so bad, but … you know me, K. You know how important this place is. If they take it away from me, why will I get up in the morning? I wouldn't have the energy to do it all over again.'

'In which case, you could go and get your groove back on a luxury cruise or whatever it is you women of a certain age get up to.'

'Cheeky!' She pretended to hit him. 'Just because you're only just out of puberty.'

They ate their muffins in silence and then Kian said, 'What-ever you do next, Chris, you know I'd love to stay working for you.'

'Oh, so that's why you bought the muffins.'

'No, don't be daft. I'm serious. You're the best boss I've ever had.'

'I'm the *only* boss you've ever had, smart-arse,' she said, hoping he couldn't tell how touched she was. 'Don't think I'm so senile I'd forget I hired you straight from school.'

'Ah, but I did have a paper round before that. Compared to that newsagent, you definitely win Boss of the Year.'

'K, don't. You'll have me weeping tears of gratitude.'

Kian gathered up the wrappings and the crumbs and put them in the bin. 'You can say what you like, but I won't stay long if you're not here. Working for Geoff the Gorilla wouldn't be the same.' He pulled a face.

'Geoff? I can't see Geoff staying here if I leave,' Chris said. It had never occurred to her that he might. 'We're a team.'

'Really?' Kian looked surprised. 'Maybe it's just me, but I'd never trust a man with that much chest hair. Has he never heard of waxing? Right, must go and spike my fringe. Greater love have I never shown than to come into work with limp hair for you, Chris.'

He disappeared into the loo with his tub of Fudge Hair Putty. Chris felt the stodgy muffin in her stomach and hoped it was that, rather than Kian's last comments, that was making her feel so sick. At least the waiting was nearly over.

It was while she was climbing into the bath – always a high risk occupation – that Paula noticed the change for the first time. But she disregarded it and began the arduous process of washing all the parts of her body that chafed. This wasn't something that could be hurried, because if she missed a bit, she'd suffer later on, especially now that walking had turned into a daily routine.

She still didn't quite believe it, but the pedometer seemed to have almost superhuman powers. On the day after her first walk, she'd felt so exhilarated that she'd even worked out how to programme it to go off every day, like an alarm clock, and she found it impossible to ignore. So now it beeped bossily every morning at 8.45 – just after the kids went to school. She didn't want them to know her secret because they were bound to laugh.

The beeping would continue until she launched herself into the kitchen, where she'd hidden the pedometer in the breadbin the previous night. It nestled next to the sliced loaf, to remind her she was allowed four whole pieces as a reward after she returned from her five thousand steps. It was only half the recommended number in the instructions, but she had to be realistic. It was a hell of a lot better than none.

Before toast, though, came bath. Paula finished the soaping operation, then grabbed the side of the bath to push herself out. The secret was to leave enough water in the tub to keep her buoyant, like an oversized ocean liner in dock. If she pulled out the plug too early, it was almost impossible to get out.

'Phew.'

There it was again. She grasped the bath towel around her and scurried to the bedroom where she forced herself into an old bra and pulled a large T-shirt over her upper body before she allowed herself to look in the mirror.

It was true. She did a slow twirl, still unable to trust her own eyes, but there was no doubt at all. At the side of her calf – both legs in fact – she could see an indentation. She pointed her toes like a ballerina and it became more pronounced.

For the first time in twenty years, Paula could see a muscle in her leg.

And for the first time in six months, she wished she could call Neil, because he'd be the only other person in the world who could understand why it meant so much.

So that was that.

Chris held her mobile in her hands and turned round to face them, her facial muscles already aching. How come it never hurt to smile when you did it naturally? 'Well, we tried, folks. And in a funny way, it's a compliment that we had such an insistent suitor for Love Bites.'

They waited. She stared at the message from her account-ant. SORRY CHRIS. ALLIED & CONNELLY HOLDINGS BOTH TKN OFFER. GOT 2 THM 2 L8. EROS HV

CONTRL. A decade's worth of blood, sweat and tears, destroyed by a message in juvenile text-speak. 'The two biggest corporate shareholders have accepted the Eros offer. They always held the balance of power. If it's any consolation, I know the majority of private shareholders believed in us, in what we were trying to do … but to the big guys, it's all about quick returns.'

She turned away, walked towards the fridge. Shit, it was tough being a good loser. All she wanted to do was slam the door to her office, burst into tears and call Matt. But then Matt wasn't on her speed dial any more. Hadn't been since that night in the penthouse.

One by one, she took out the six bottles of champagne she'd brought with her this morning. Although it'd been almost certain they'd be toasting a new owner, she'd been determined to say thank you. As Kian had said, she would now be a very rich woman.

'Cheers, my friends.' Her fingers were trembling as she tried to unwrap the foil around the champagne cork. Both Kian and Geoff moved forward to help her. Geoff got there first. He smiled at her and she wondered whether his smile was genuine. Was it possible that he'd betrayed her, collaborated with Eros, in return for a promise of a top job when the sale was completed? No, she was being stupid. Kian was such a little bastard, putting ideas into her head. There was no point in getting paranoid at this point in the game. Though wasn't it Game Over now?

'Time to wet the new baby's head,' she said, wrestling the icy bottle back from Geoff and popping the cork to tumble pink bubbles into a dozen glasses. 'Here's to Eros. And to us. Every one of us at Love Bites and especially to Kian for being my right-hand boy. To Jan for the breathtaking product designs that made us such hot property. And to Geoff for battling with me to save us from Cupid's sodding arrow.'

They cheered and she tried to freeze-frame the moment, because she knew it would be the last time she was part of the team.

'And now, I think we should all get excessively drunk. That is my last order.'

Terri sat on a rock and tried to think about God. It was a struggle. The daylight was tickling her skin – she was bound to burn, even here under a wan Scottish sun – and it was hard to stay focused. Every time she tried to concentrate on what God was, or did, or meant, memories of Judith kept drifting into her mind.

Perhaps if I talk to Him, Terri thought. *Not praying, but asking, as though it was a normal conversation.* She looked around her. She'd walked a good two miles from the retreat after breakfast and there was no one else around.

'The thing is, God,' she began, feeling self-conscious, 'I wonder if me believing in you has ever been a rational process. The reason I always think of Judith whenever I try to think about You, is because I think I only started the whole religion thing because *she* was religious and so it represented everything my parents weren't. Permanence. Certainty. That's a joke now, eh?'

She laughed but the faint coastal breeze carried the sound away. 'And now I wonder whether Judith believed, or whether she was just going through the motions. Because You hardly gave her good reasons to believe, did You? You really did have it in for the Quentin family.'

Terri was surprised at how bitter her voice sounded, but also at how good it felt to speak these forbidden thoughts. Cathartic. It was frustratingly one-sided, though.

'It's just not working out between us, is it, Lord? I'm sure it's me, not You. I need a bit more from a relationship. I'm not shallow, You know that, though a little physical contact would be nice.' She giggled. 'But I can see that's non-negotiable. It's the lack of feedback that I find hardest. I know there are other girls out there who are less demanding, who don't need that constant reassurance, but all I need is one little sign, something to show You care.'

Nothing happened, of course. She hadn't really expected it to, had she? Perhaps a shaft of sunlight might have been nice. Or a change in direction of the wind, a hint of rainbow, or even a squawk from one of the dozens of seagulls. There were so many bloody options open to Him.

'Playing hard to get, eh?'

She stood up and pondered on what He would say, if he spoke. At college, they were doing a module on Pastoral Care, which involved role-playing various scenarios. At first it had been agonizingly embarrassing to pretend to be a frustrated housewife looking for guidance on resisting an affair, but before long, they were hamming it up like am dram veterans.

'Just what would it take to convince you, Teresa?' she said. The voice wasn't bad, infused with gravel and gravitas. And God would inevitably use her full name.

'I do want to believe in You again. I do believe there's *something*, there has to be, to make sense of all this ...' She looked out to sea and sensed the power of the waves, the vastness of the unknown world under the water and beyond the sky. 'But I feel so lost without Judith. It was almost as though she was the closest I could get to having You guide me to do the right thing, not just the convenient thing.'

She closed her eyes as she thought up God's reply. 'But Teresa,' she said to herself, 'don't you think that Judith's wisdom is still there, if you want to call on it?'

'It's not the SAME.' Terri had to admit that she was sounding like a sulky teenager whose parents didn't understand her. 'I miss her.'

'It's painful, but at least missing someone proves how much they meant to you. Do you want to live the rest of your life completely alone? Imagine being in a world where you never missed anyone, where you never allowed yourself to get close enough to anyone to risk missing them.'

'It'd be safer than this world.' But as she said it, she knew how pathetic that sounded.

'So is that the answer, Teresa? Cutting yourself off from life so you don't get hurt?'

'No, but ...' She shook her head. This was getting silly. Grown women didn't stand on cliffs pretending to be God. It was time to head back before she began having delusions that she was Marie Antoinette or Elvis Presley.

But as she walked along the coastal path, that question kept playing over and over in her head. *Do you want to live the rest of your life completely alone?*

However hard she tried, it was the one question she couldn't avoid.

Paula sat with the plate on her lap, waiting for the computer to come to life. Contacting Neil was out of the question, so trying SheriffJack was the – admittedly poor – second choice. It wasn't that Jack wasn't funny and kind and clever. He seemed all of those things. It was simply that she couldn't be honest with him about anything. To admit her excitement about seeing a muscle in her leg would destroy his image of Cuteycrimefighter.

As she logged on, she popped one of her postage-stamp-sized squares of toast in her mouth. Another TV top tip from the mad guru. *Divide all your food into the smallest portions you can and savour each one: it takes twenty minutes of eating for the brain to send a message to the stomach that it's full.* She managed to turn each slice into a dozen squares and tried hard to make each last a good minute.

There he was … whoops. In her excitement she swallowed a piece without the required chewing.

Paula clicked onto his name to start talking.

CUTEYCRIMEFIGHTER: Hey Jack. What's happening in the good old US of A?

She waited. He was definitely there – the computer said so – but she managed to finish the rest of her toast without any reply.

CUTEYCRIMEFIGHTER: Woo hoo … is there anybody there?

Still nothing. Not even the pop-up telling her 'SheriffJack is typing a new message'. Perhaps he was making a cup of coffee or making the kind of vital decision an IT company executive had to make at – she did her sums – two a.m. Seattle time.

The door bell rang so loudly that she dropped the plate and it smashed into three chunks. 'Shit.'

'Bloody hell,' the postman said as she opened the door. 'I've been working this round for ten years and I've never seen who lives here. I need a signature from you.'

Paula scowled at him, initialled on his clipboard and took the letter inside. The last signed-for letter had been Judith's. Perhaps it was her cheque. God knows, she needed the money.

She sat back down by the computer, kicking away the broken plate with her slippered feet, and tearing open the envelope.

'Oh, double shit.'

She looked up at the screen and saw that Jack had finally replied.

SHERIFFJACK: Hey, Cutey. I'm here. I'm good. And how's it hanging with you?

Paula stared at the letter, unable to believe it had come to this.

CUTEYCRIMEFIGHTER: It's hanging. Just contemplating a little house move.
SHERIFFJACK: Really? The penthouse apartment cramping your style?
CUTEYCRIMEFIGHTER: Something like that … you know, sometimes you feel like a change of scenery.

And sometimes, Paula thought, it didn't matter what you felt. You had no choice.

SHERIFFJACK: Will you be going far?

Fuck knows, she thought. The options for a woman and two teenagers about to be evicted were pretty limited. The amount the housing association thought she owed was more than she could ever raise, even if she sold everything in the flat.

Her parents' sofa looked the most likely destination right now. Perhaps Sadie and Charlie would be reunited with their father rather sooner than they'd expected.

CUTEYCRIMEFIGHTER: No, not far.

She typed the words before the screen blurred through tears

of frustration and self-pity. How had she made such a mess of everything? She was a fat, hopeless failure, a dead loss as a wife and a mother and a person.

SHERIFFJACK: Cutey?
CUTEYCRIMEFIGHTER: Yes?
SHERIFFJACK: I know it sounds dumb, but I have this strange feeling things aren't right for you.

She stared at the screen, tears now rolling down her face, wondering how he knew. But she couldn't coordinate her fingers to type a reply.

SHERIFFJACK: And I just wanted you to know that if there's anything an ageing, slightly balding computer nerd in Seattle can do to help ... well, you know where I am.

Paula gulped, trying to swallow enough tears to see the keyboard. It was laughable, that her only friend on the entire bloody planet was thousands of miles away in a place she'd never visit. But the fact that he existed at all was oddly comforting. Though, of course, the computer would have to be sold and with it, her one friend.

CUTEYCRIMEFIGHTER: Thank you, Jack. I will remember that xxx.

She clicked out of the chatroom and shut down the computer. She needed to work out how the hell she was going to tell the kids.

'And another thing,' Chris said, aware but not caring that the people at the next table were staring at her, 'I know you lot want to be loyal to me, but you have to think of yourselves first. You all have mortgages to pay. Well, except you, Kian, but you've got a cocaine habit to support so you need a regular income too.'

Kian shrugged and sniffed simultaneously, and Chris felt a

wave of sadness at this familiar gesture. There was so much she wanted to say to her team, but after four hours of sustained drinking, her ability to express herself was fading fast. Immediately after the announcement, she'd sent a statement out via their PR company, regretting the shareholders' decision, but wishing Eros the best of luck. And then they all headed for the Cock O' Manchester gastro-pub.

She reached out to top up her champagne, but the bottle was empty again. Geoff winked at her and clicked his fingers for the waitress to bring them another, on Chris's Amex, of course. The table was crowded with bottles, and plates of food ordered too late to soak up the booze. Already the youngest copywriter, Tish, had gone home in a flood of drunken tears, accompanied by randy Jan the Dutch product designer, who obviously saw an opportunity to comfort her.

Chris knew she'd have to head home herself soon, or she might collapse in front of everyone. She couldn't face going yet, though. The idea of returning to her empty flat, with no reason to leave it ever again, wasn't appealing. So she sat tight, a wired Kian on her left jabbering on about nothing in particular, and an attentive Geoff to her right, keeping her glass full and the questions about his loyalty at bay. If he was *really* double-crossing her, then surely he'd have made his excuses and headed off for a victory celebration with the wankers at Eros?

'I'm going to resign,' Kian said. 'Are you sure you don't need a personal assistant to run your new life as a lady of leisure? I can book your hair appointments, coordinate your personal training sessions and manicures. You'll be in demand as an after-dinner speaker as well, and I bet I can get you the top rates.'

His pupils were enormous, dominating his young, unlined face, and she humoured him. 'I'll think about it, but I wouldn't resign just yet, Kian. Someone like you, with all the knowledge of how things work, will be worth your weight in gold to the new company, so keep your options open.'

Geoff touched her on the elbow. 'But, Chris, you'd be worth more than your weight in gold, too. I mean, I understand why you think you'd prefer not to work for Eros, but they'd pay you bloody well.'

She frowned. 'Are you recruiting for them or something?'

'Me?' He looked hurt. 'I know where my loyalties lie, don't worry. But together, we could clean up. Look at it from their point of view. No other bastard knows more about Love Bites than us two.'

Chris ran her finger round the inside of her champagne glass, trying to wipe away smears of the lipstick she'd so carefully applied this morning. 'I couldn't do it, Geoff. What's the point in responsibility without power?'

'Oh, I've never been one for responsibility. But power ... now you're talking. Power has always given me the horn.' He smiled at her. Actually, it was more than a smile. It was a no-holds-barred leer.

'That's good,' she said. 'Because I hate a man who is intimidated by a woman with more balls than he has.'

And as she saw his pupils grow wider even than Kian's, she felt relieved as she realized that, this afternoon at least, she wouldn't have to go home alone.

The first person Terri saw when she returned to the retreat was Howard. If it didn't seem so implausible, she would have sworn he'd been lying in wait.

'Ah, the delightfully saintly Teresa. Are you going to lunch?'

She would have said no, but she was ravenously hungry. Talking to God did that to a person. 'Yep.'

He stepped in alongside her, pushing open the door to the dining hall. 'At a guess, it'll be overcooked vegetables on a bed of slightly dried-out brown rice, only just this side of edible. People who run retreats seem to believe that spiritual thought is only possible with a rumbling stomach.'

'Are you an expert on retreats, then?' she asked, before cursing herself. A question could only be construed as encouragement.

'Retreats, I've had a few ...' he sang, 'but then again, too few to mention.'

She couldn't help giggling. 'Don't tell me. You did them your way.'

He rewarded her with a big grin, revealing wolfish teeth. 'The success of a retreat is, I find, directly correlated to the people you meet along the way.' He handed her a tray and then took one for himself. 'I know that might seem strange, given that the point of a retreat is to retreat. But I've tried the silent ones, and I get bored with my own thoughts pretty quickly so it's the snatched conversations with other people that often prove the most illuminating. Ah! What did I tell you?'

Terri watched as a mean spoonful of greyish rice was tipped onto a plate by the woman behind the serving hatch, topped by an even sparer portion of rust-coloured stew. 'But that's chilli,' she said.

'I don't think that the addition of a few prehistoric kidney beans will qualify this sorry dish as chilli, I'm afraid,' he whispered. 'Though if you stick with me, kid, I might be able to help.'

He led the way towards the corner of the refectory and watched as she tasted the first forkful. 'Yes, I do see what you mean,' she admitted. 'Still, I suppose at least no animals were killed in the making of this lunch.'

He put a finger to his lips while he rummaged inside his jacket pocket and pulled out a tiny hip flask. 'This should perk things up.'

She shook her head. No wonder he was so pale, if he couldn't even manage a retreat without a drink. 'I won't, thanks. I came here for the *Holy* spirit, not that kind.'

'Take a sniff.'

Reluctantly she took the flask, turning her body so that her shoulder shielded the flask from the view of everyone else in the room, and resenting Howard for involving her in his seedy secret. Terri sniffed. Then sneezed.

'Pepper? What is it, then, some kind of pepper vodka?'

He grinned sheepishly. 'It's chilli oil. My secret weapon for surviving retreat food. You thought I was an old drunkard, didn't you?'

She blushed. 'Well, you can't blame me. And I'm not sure I approve of *any* kind of stimulant on a religious retreat.' But she was smiling at him and he smiled back.

'The offer's there,' he said, shaking the amber oil onto his food.

Terri took a forkful of her own meal and nearly spat it out.

'Oh golly. That is staggeringly tasteless. How can anyone cook something with that little flavour?' The ticklish scent of chilli rose from Howard's plate and she felt her mouth water.

He held out the flask and she nodded. He poured oil over her plate, turning the rice mottled orange. 'Is that enough?'

She tasted the rice. 'Yes, that's much better. Thank you.'

'My pleasure,' he said, screwing the lid on tight and stashing the flask away. 'To our little secret.' He clinked his water glass with hers.

'Yes,' Terri said, wondering why she felt so certain that this wasn't the end of sharing secrets with Howard. And why that made her feel so nervous. And excited.

Geoff went in for the kill as soon as he stepped into the lift with Chris. He kissed the same way he did business: forcefully and with absolute confidence. When the doors opened at the penthouse level, they both stumbled into her flat, the champagne making them unsteady on their feet, but united in purpose.

'Nice pad,' Geoff said, clocking the view of the city and then steering her towards the sofa.

This, Chris thought vaguely, as Geoff unbuttoned her DKNY shirt, was love in the afternoon. She'd never had time for it before. Even at university, afternoons were for working, nights were for booze and sex. Everyone else was at it 24/7 of course, but Chris was preoccupied with studying and plotting her future. Anything but go home to Troughton.

But now – he was unhooking her bra, taking a ragged breath as he cupped her left breast in his hand – she would have nothing to fill her days but sex and shopping. And watching the rest of the world from her window. God, it would drive her mad to be an observer, like her mother.

He kissed her again and she felt sweet and needed and pleased that he was here. He ran his fingers down her back to hook his thumbs under her pants. He tugged so they moved down beyond her hips and then let go so they fell to the floor. As she stepped out of them, still in her stilettos, he smiled.

Strange that she'd never fancied him before, but then they'd been so focused this last month, desperate to protect the company. Now was time to give in, to let someone else take control. Maybe she could get used to love in the afternoon.

She pulled at his belt but he shook his head and unbuckled it himself, before stepping out of his trousers and his boxers in one movement. His penis was large and she felt a twinge of anticipation as he removed his shirt to show a hairy, slightly rounded belly to match the hairy *Baywatch* chest. He slipped off his socks – thank God he wasn't one of those men who kept them on, as if they were planning to make a dash for it afterwards – and lay on the couch beside her, nuzzling her breasts. He didn't seem in any hurry, though when she reached down to touch his penis, he looked less detached and his eyes closed as she ran both hands up and down the shaft, in a slick movement straight off a Love Bites 'educational' video. Well, she might as well put her expertise to good use. The booze was making her feel less inhibited than usual. She knew that for someone who made their living through sex, she could be surprisingly uptight the first time she slept with someone.

She smiled. *Slept with someone.* There'd be no sleeping this afternoon. Well, not unless the champagne made one of them nod off before they'd finished.

This was going to be fucking, pure and simple. In Chris's view, the only *truly* safe sex: sex without love getting in the way. Muddling things. Destroying lives.

He reached out to her, parted her legs with his hands, and they began the awkward to-ing and fro-ing involved when strangers try to bring each other off. Like patting your head and rubbing your tummy at the same time, few people could manage it, yet almost all felt obliged to try, out of politeness, causing awkward knots of limbs.

She was ready, anyway. He must have realised *that.*

'Condoms,' she said, climbing over him to fetch a packet from her bedroom. As she prepared to walk back into the living room, she wished the blinds were drawn, that the Manchester daylight wasn't so harsh. She knew there was scarcely an ounce of fat on her, thanks to three sessions a week with her personal sadist, sorry, personal *trainer*. But she still felt gawky and vulnerable when she was naked.

As she approached the sofa, he turned over. If anything, his erection was bigger than before. Chris handed him the condom, and averted her eyes while he fumbled a little. She wondered where, when and with whom he'd last had sex. He wasn't *that* much older than her, just the other side of forty, but in good physical condition, with impressively muscly legs and arms. She imagined that he was the kind of bloke who owned and actually used a Bullworker and had installed a bar in his bedroom door frame for nightly chin-ups, to keep the vodka calories at bay.

He touched her cheek gently and guided her across his body. Oh good. She liked being on top, despite the fact that it wasn't the most flattering position, stomach-wise. Judging from his expression as she lowered herself onto him, he wasn't about to complain about her imaginary spare tyre.

Chris concentrated to begin with, finding the rhythm that worked for him by watching his face, before, sooner than she expected, the sensations started to overwhelm her and she closed her eyes. The booze had made her more relaxed and she felt the tremors begin inside her and spread outwards, more and more powerful until all her muscles felt like they were about to explode from the tension and then the feeling of him underneath her tipped her over the edge and she cried out—

'Matt!'

The movement stopped but the orgasm didn't and it was few seconds before she opened her eyes and saw the irritation that had replaced ecstasy on Geoff's face. Now *where* had Matt's name come from?

'Oh, shit,' she said, catching her breath. 'Sorry ... my last boyfriend ... it's been a while.'

'I dunno. If I'm going to make you come so bloody quickly, the least you can do is remember my name.' But he was half-smiling while he said it, knowing he was definitely still owed an orgasm of his own.

She smiled back and dismounted. 'You're right, Geoff. I'm so *rude*.' As she turned his body so he was sitting upright, and then parted his legs so she could kneel between them, he perked up considerably.

'*How* rude, exactly?' he stuttered.

'Extremely,' she said, post-orgasm mellowness making her bold. 'People have said this is my *second* greatest talent, after having a head for business. And you're going to be in the very best position to make a judgement for yourself.'

'I'll let you know,' he managed to gasp before his powers of speech deserted him entirely.

After their initial bonding over chilli oil, Terri and Howard's new friendship was cemented by Benson and Hedges.

'I never quite trust someone who doesn't have at least one vice,' Howard said, taking a puff of Terri's cigarette. 'I'm meant to have given up, but it doesn't count so long as you never buy any of your own.'

'Isn't that just replacing one vice for two more?' Terri said. They'd scrambled up the rocks behind the retreat to a sun-warmed spot where they could see for miles around, and more importantly, no one would see them. 'Addiction, replaced by meanness and self-delusion?'

'Call it bartering, supply and demand. You needed chilli oil, I need a little hit of nicotine after a good meal in good company,' he said. 'Lovely, but I couldn't smoke a whole one. That would put me back on the slippery slope.'

Their fingers touched as he handed back the cigarette, and Terri looked away, feeling embarrassed. She hoped he wasn't getting the wrong idea. But then she blushed deeper. She knew it was preposterous to imagine that he might find Big Bird attractive.

Her initial assessment of him as a bloodless creep was wrong; his sense of humour made him shine and, in the soft-edged coastal light, his face seemed to glow with energy. In contrast, she could feel freckles forming across her face, merging together like a big brown ink blot. And the sun always made her ginger hair look like a ragged coil of copper wire. No wonder no one ever wanted to run their fingers through it.

'So, Miss Vicar-to-be, are you finding this place an aid to spiritual enrichment?'

Terri picked a sprig of heather from the bush alongside them, and tore the spiky buds away one by one as she thought about it. 'Yes and no. It's a lovely setting. Very peaceful. But I had …

a loss, recently. And it made me think about things I'd taken for granted. Not least God. I think that getting my *effortless* belief back will probably take more than a few days away in a big old house.'

He stared out to sea, then took her cigarette from her. 'Do you want to talk about your loss?'

'She was someone I'd been close to for a long time. Almost like a mother to me. My own is still alive and well and sometimes I wish it was her—' Terri stopped. Having those thoughts was bad enough, without admitting them to a stranger.

'And this other person. She died?'

'Yes. I mean, it's been a while now. I should be feeling better. I've always been the strongest person, out of all my friends, my colleagues and everyone, but now I know I'm not. I'm weak. My faith couldn't even stand up to one death.'

Howard took a deep drag on the cigarette. 'At the risk of sounding like a fortune cookie, weakness can be strength. If you're not flawed in some way, if you haven't been hurt and challenged, then how will you be able to empathize with your flock?'

Terri thought about it. 'What doesn't kill us makes us stronger, eh? I suppose it would make sense, if I wasn't so unsure about my reasons for wanting a *flock* at all. Thinking you can help people is the worst variety of egomania. I expect Stalin or Hitler started out thinking they could help people.'

He looked at her. 'Do you make a habit of being this hard on yourself?'

'To be fair, I'm just as hard on everyone else. Just ask any of my ex-boyfriends.'

'Ah ... you know, I've been curious about that. Why you're single. Doesn't every vicar need a spouse? To administer tea and scones and sympathy?'

Terri blushed again. She couldn't believe she'd been stupid enough to mention boyfriends. It was asking for trouble. 'Yes, well. I've always had strange taste in men. I've gone for good causes, blokes who need a bit of bossing about, then they pull themselves together and that's it, my job's done.'

'It all sounds very logical,' he said. 'Were you in love with any of them?'

'Ha!' She clasped her hand to her lips. 'Sorry. It's not funny, is it? I realized when my last relationship ended that I was fond of him, the way you're fond of a slightly dopey pet, like a ...' She was about to say stick insect, but it sounded too harsh. 'A guinea pig or something. But no, I don't think I've ever been in love.'

'Bloody hell, Teresa. You deserve more than a pet. Though I can see why a man might be intimidated by you. You are, as my randy old uncle would probably say, "a feisty wench".'

Now she laughed openly. 'A wench? More of a confirmed spinster. Less Bette Midler, more Ann Widdecombe.'

He carried on looking out to sea. 'No, that's definitely not true. I don't fancy Ann Widdecombe.'

'Ah ...' Terri blushed again and tried to work out how to respond, how to let him down gently. She turned towards him and noticed he was blushing too, and as she opened her mouth to explain, he must have misinterpreted because one minute he was there, on the opposite side of the rock and the next minute he was kissing her, tentatively at first, his lips barely making contact, and then as she responded, he crossed to her side of the rock and it felt so unexpected, yet so unexpectedly familiar and then ...

She pulled away. It was too much, too soon, too dangerous, too ... nice? Passion just wasn't her style. 'Howard. I'm really flattered—'

'Flattered?' He let go, dropped his arms to his sides. 'No, you've every right to feel thoroughly pissed off. Here you are seeking spiritual enlightenment and I cross the line. I'm sorry.'

'It's fine. In other circumstances ...' She couldn't finish the sentence. In other circumstances, she still couldn't imagine being with someone like Howard. He was too likely to walk away when he discovered what she was really like. And anyway, it wouldn't work: something told her that Howard didn't need fixing.

She stood up, then brushed off her skirt with her hands, fussing to remove a speck of dust, anything to avoid looking at him again. 'I don't think the retreat is helping. I'm going to head home.'

'Don't leave. I'll go, if you like. It's my fault.'

Terri shook her head. 'No, I think I'd have left early anyway. Coming here was running away, something I've never done, and I'm not about to begin now.'

He smiled wryly. 'Really?'

She ignored his implication. 'I hope you find what you're looking for here. And at least with me gone, you won't run out of chilli oil.'

She nodded, then walked away, telling herself over and over, don't look back don't look back don't . . .

Only when she'd reached the main building did she turn round to see him, smaller now than her hand, still in the same position on the rock.

Do you want to live the rest of your life alone?

Now she knew the answer was yes, at least she could get on with living that life.

Chapter Twenty-six

*Dreamers, idlers and lazy folk must
expect to be left behind in the race.*

Essential ingredients for Friday night in Saxon Close:
Prawn Pad Thai for me, Chicken Black Bean for Andrew,
delivered by motorbike. A tip of two pounds to the teenage son
of the bloke who runs the Chinese. He skips red lights to get
it to us hot.

A DVD from the local video shop. Semi-naked scene with
Brad Pitt desirable, but not essential.

Two bottles of red, three-quarters of which will be consumed
by the man of the house, inducing amorous intentions that will
prove hopelessly unachievable, nine times out of ten.

Essential ingredients for my first Friday night at the Old
Surgery:

Whatever the hell I like.

There's something terrifying about having no rituals. Humans
need them. It's why as soon as I go on holiday I frantically search
for things to anchor our days: what we will eat for breakfast,
who showers first, what time we go to the beach, when we're
allowed a beer to celebrate handling another stress-free day.

But I'm trying hard to resist rituals here. I have this theory
that the less I plan, the freer my mind will be to work out what I
really want and to decide whether it's really worth putting Sasha
and Buster and me and, yes, even Andrew, through this pain.
He's got Sasha this weekend, so tonight my plans are limited
to a vague intention of getting mildly drunk, and enjoying my
brand new habit of singing at the top of my voice to one of my
Grampa's opera recordings. It's my daily treat, the only ritual I

have adopted, and the biggest pleasure involved in living in a huge sheltered house with dungeon-thick walls. On Wednesday I dropped Sasha off at ju-jitsu and I sang *Madame Butterfly* while she learned Eastern martial arts. And last night while she was at swimming practice, I romped through *HMS Pinafore*.

It's like this: I pick one of the greats from Grampa's heavy boxed sets and play it from overture to epilogue – or at least till my mobile beeps, telling me it's time to pick Sasha up – following the words with my finger along the cramped lettering of the libretto booklet, and joining in during soprano solos and exuberant chorus set-pieces. Grampa's old-fashioned stereo – as big as a sideboard, with built-in speakers and a nifty lever that flips over the record and plays the other side – lacks subtlety in the gentler duets but when the orchestra is in full throttle, it's as powerful and thunderous as Grieg's trolls. The music follows me through the house; even Buster seems to be warming to the grand composers.

When my mobile rings, it's only six thirty and, taking advantage of my Sasha-free status, I'm already in my pyjamas, wavering between my old favourite, *La Traviata*, and the less familiar *Cavalleria Rusticana*. I'm tempted not to answer it, but then there's always the fear that something might be wrong with Sasha. When I retrieve the phone from my handbag, it's Terri.

'Hey, Luce. What are you up to tonight?'

I look at the pile of records. 'Nothing much.'

'Do you fancy some company?'

It's not like her to want to face Andrew's blessed bypass to join the millions commuting home on a Friday night, so something must be up. I say yes, though it'll curtail my singing. When she arrives, just after eight, she's red in the face.

'You been sunbathing?'

'Ha ha, Luce. Have you bothered to get up today? I hope you're not turning into some kind of layabout.'

I didn't see the point in changing back into my day clothes. Besides, apart from my shop uniform, I'm running out of things to wear, putting off the evil moment when I have to head back to Saxon Close for more.

She comes in and sniffs. 'It stinks of Buster in here.'

'Yes, he's still protesting against the move occasionally.'

'I'm not surprised, Luce. I'd forgotten how neglected this place is. Aren't you finding it a bit depressing?'

I show her into the living room, which is at least tidy. 'Not as depressing as being with Andrew.'

She walks over to the pile of LPs. 'Wow. These are out of the ark.'

'I've been doing some singing.' But I decide it's unfair to impose opera on a woman whose idea of classical music is a rousing Salvation Army carol concert, so I find one of my mum's old Bee Gees albums to play instead.

Terri sits down on the sofa and slips her shoes off as the Gibbses' falsetto voices squeak through the speakers. Buster stalks towards her and, recognizing a familiar scent, begins to writhe over one of her scuffed black loafers, as though it's a particularly foxy young tortoiseshell cat. 'Nice to be popular,' she says.

'And how have you been? Heard anything from Colin at all?' I ask, choosing a crystal flute from the sideboard, wiping it with my pyjama sleeve and filling it with white wine.

She takes it. 'These must be antique, you know. You ought to get them valued. No, nothing from Colin. But there've been ... other developments.'

'Really? Sounds more interesting than anything that's happened to me this week.'

'I went on a retreat. Someone at college recommended it, said it might help me feel better about everything that's been going on with Colin and your mum.'

I feel annoyed that she didn't tell me. I pour my heart out to Terri, yet she's as closed as a Gideon Bible in a Las Vegas hotel room. 'When was this?'

'I should still be there now. But something happened. Well, a man happened.'

'A *man*. You little raver. Colin's only been gone five minutes.' I tuck my legs underneath me on the sofa, feeling all the anticipation of a teenager begging for details of her best friend's first kiss.

'Don't get over-excited. It was nothing. I was meant to be

finding God again but instead this guy was there, flirting like crazy, and it made me uncomfortable so I came home.'

'And it was only flirting?'

'Well, he kissed me, but—'

'I knew it! I knew you looked different.'

'What, like some Sleeping Beauty awoken from a coma? Don't be bloody ridiculous, Lucy.'

I'm shocked. Terri *never* swears. 'He kissed you. And did you kiss him back?'

'I did, but then I didn't. Look, it was a kiss. I know I'm terminally virginal but I have kissed a bloke before.'

'So how did it compare with the ones before?' I can't remember how it feels to kiss anyone but Andrew.

Terri blushes. 'OK, OK. It was probably the best kiss I've ever had.'

'Phew ... but you ran away from him.'

'It was hardly the right thing to be doing on a religious retreat.'

'Was he a vicar then? It's just like *The Thorn Birds*.' I had a Richard Chamberlain fixation when I was twelve.

'No, he's an RE teacher.'

'And does he have a name?'

'You sounded just like your mum then. His name is Howard, he comes from somewhere near Scotland that I can't remember the name of, and he likes chillies. And that is all I know about him and all I'll ever know about him. Now, can we talk about something else?'

This seems a bit rich when, presumably, the only reason she's driven over here is to talk about it. 'One more question?'

She sighs. 'OK then, if you must.'

'Why did you run away from the best kisser you've ever met?'

She bites her thumb. 'Because ... I'm no good at relationships, Lucy. I'm a cold fish. What good would it do to swap phone numbers with some poor bloke who lives half a day away and who has nothing in common with me, no idea how difficult I can be? You can be sure when he finds out, he'll be running for the hills.'

'But you've always been the one who does the dumping, Terri. You're the only woman I know who has never been dumped.'

'Ah, well, that's where you're wrong,' she says, so quietly that I wonder if I've misheard her.

'*Colin* dumped *you*?' She nods. 'The cheeky bastard.'

'I don't think I blame him, Luce. I can't imagine anything worse than being someone's project.'

I think it over and I suddenly know how Colin feels. It's humiliating if you never ever come up to scratch, if you're always the weak link. I had it for thirty-odd years with my mother, so I should know. Mind you, since I've been set free from that feeling of failing, look at what I've done: fail even more spectacularly than I did before.

She nods. 'See? You can't deny it.'

'Maybe it's a sign that you should stop going out with men who need reforming, and go out with the kind who've got a bit of va-va-voom to begin with.'

'Maybe,' she says, but she sounds dubious. 'Anyway, enough of my non-existent dating dilemmas. What about you? I half-expected you'd have gone home by now.'

'So did I.'

'So why haven't you?'

'It's not that I haven't thought about it. I've been waiting for that homing instinct to kick in, but it hasn't. I feel like shit for dragging Sasha between two houses and I know it's upsetting for her, but then again I almost feel we're getting closer … like the other night, when she should have been at Brownies, we had the nicest time we've had together since before she started school.'

'I know,' Terri says. 'I saw you. I was worried when you didn't show up so I came round the back and the two of you were fast asleep on a picnic rug.'

'I didn't know you came round. You should have woken us up.'

'You looked too peaceful. It would have made a lovely picture.'

'Hmm … I woke up when the sun went in, and Sasha was lying there, her hair all spread out against the tartan wool and I could see myself in her, and I thought, you know, I have to do the best for *both* of us. I can't be a proper mum to her until I work stuff out. I haven't been myself in such a very long time.'

'And who is yourself, Luce?'

'Well, that might take a little longer to sort. I know I can't stay away for ever without telling Andrew what I'm going to do. But I'm getting there. That's kind of what Saturday was about. You see, I wasn't totally honest about why I was so late in. I was pretty drunk at Chris's but then … you know I told you I was going to try to talk to people who knew my father?'

'Ye-es?' She purses her lips in disapproval.

'Well, I did it. Traced a man he trained with. A surgeon, Sunny Bandele. I went straight from Chris's to have dinner with him.' I wait for her to tell me off.

'Oh my God, Luce. Why didn't you talk to me? I mean, I know you're not happy with Andrew, but this Sunny must be old enough to be your father – sorry, that came out wrong, but still …'

'Not like *that*. His wife was there. And his son.' Now, I sense, is not the time to mention the fact that his son could be a male model. 'I want to find out more about Dad's family. About the other half of my genes. It might help me make sense of things.'

'I can see that,' Terri says, 'although genes aren't the answer to everything. Look at my parents. How come the two laziest hippies in Cheshire created me and my obsessive work ethic? So dare I ask what you've found out so far?'

'Nothing dramatic,' I say, struggling to remember what Sunny said to me on the way home. And then remembering the photo of Daddy as Prince Charming. 'Except music. I'm really wondering whether music is part of me that needs to find an outlet.'

'You always had a talent, Luce.'

'I know. I wasted it. I think …' I pause, trying to work out if what I'm about to say will sound arrogant. 'I think I'd like to find out whether it's still there, Terri.'

'And would your *new friends* in Manchester—'

Is it my imagination, or does Terri sound jealous?

'—be able to help you find that out?'

I think about it. 'Well, yes, actually. Sunny's lad plays clarinet for the Philharmonic. I suppose he might know someone who could tell me if I have a chance.' Even as I speak, I realize how laughable this is. A chance of what? And why would Seb want to help me?

'You're really thinking that this might be a *job*? At your age?'

'I didn't until now,' I say, surprised at how annoyed I feel that she's writing me off at thirty-five. 'But actually ... well, now this house is mine, a job isn't as important. It's worth more than I'll earn in a lifetime in the shop. And you know, just maybe it's not too late to try following my dreams. God, I sound like a self-help guru.'

'Self-help is the only kind that works. And after a lifetime of leading horses to water, and patently failing to make them drink, I ought to know.'

'I know it's a pipe dream, Terri, but you've changed career once. I think it's about time I gave it a bash. Pick myself up, dust myself off and—'

'Start all over again? You know who you sound like again?'

As she says it, I understand. 'My mother. Bloody hell. Well, maybe I'll make her proud one of these days.' Though looking around this room, remembering the number of times I saw that disappointed expression when I failed some other hidden test, I doubt it. 'In the meantime, I'm starving. Do you fancy a Chinese?'

'Yep. All this soul-searching gives you a hell of an appetite.'

I fetch a menu from the kitchen drawer, then turn back. 'No! I *always* have Chinese on Friday. How do you fancy a Mexican instead?'

'Whatever you fancy, Luce. Incidentally, talking of blasts from the past, you'll never guess who I heard from yesterday.'

I think of the most unlikely person possible. 'Simonetta?'

'Not quite that weird. But nearly. No, it was Bethany, or more accurately Bethany's agent, replying to the letter I sent him two months ago. It seems he finally got round to passing it on to the celebrated Miss Kendall and she'd just *love* to meet up with the other Pixies. So much so, she's invited us all down to London for tea.'

'Blimey.'

'That's what I thought. But never look a gift daytrip in the mouth, eh? And I feel bad about how I behaved at Chris's place, so this might cheer us all up.'

I'm not sure a tête-à-tête with Bethany would cheer anyone up, but don't want to upset Terri. 'I wonder what she's like?'

She shrugs. 'Awful, I expect. But it could be fun to have a good nose at our most famous Brownie.'

'I'll drink to that,' I say, topping up our glasses. And then I do.

July 1979: A trip to the Big Smoke

Judith smelled London before she saw it.

'Mummy, open your eyes: we're here!' Lucy tugged at her sleeve, but Judith had already recognized the smoky perfume of oil and dirt. It made her ache with loss, even now.

Cities did this to her, which was why she avoided them. Troughton smelled of natural things, blossom or manure, depending on the time of year. Neither reminded her of Jim. The constant emotional ambushes in the weeks after his death, triggered by a blast of diesel outside the hospital, or a drift of gingery rotisserie chicken as she walked through Manchester's Chinatown, had helped convince her she had to move back home. Home held no dangerous memories.

She wouldn't have come to London now if it hadn't been for Bethany's stupid father. While other ten-year-olds were lucky to get a birthday party in the Macclesfield branch of McDonald's, Trevor Kendal had decided to treat all the Pixies to a trip to London to celebrate his little angel hitting double figures. His blatant attempt to buy Bethany's affection made Judith feel queasy, but she couldn't deprive Lucy of the day out.

They'd left Crewe at six. Trevor had booked seats together for everyone else, but reserved his own in first-class, claiming he had some business to attend to, 'and anyway, my Bethany will feel so grown-up travelling without her dad to keep an eye on her'. More like, her dad was palming his daughter off on the women because he hadn't got a clue what to say to her. She *looked* grown-up – too grown-up, Judith thought, in a pair of trendy Calvin Kleins that hugged her ten-year-old body. And she seemed to be wearing lipstick, though her lips were naturally a prettier shade of pink.

Every Brownie was accompanied by a parent. Chris was with dour Dina, who seemed to be having a mid-life crisis; she'd smothered her sallow skin with thick foundation, and had adopted a ludicrous giggle that was even more irritating than her usual glum demeanour. Meanwhile, Chris was impossibly surly.

Terri's mother Lorna had broken the habit of a lifetime and got up before noon, though she looked as though she'd been dragged through an entire Cornish hedgerow backwards. She wore an outdated saffron-coloured cheesecloth ensemble, and was burbling on about 'going down Carnaby Street to buy some threads'. Patsy wore a polka-dot dress several inches too short for a woman of thirty-seven, but at least she was keeping an eye on the girls, especially Paula, who kept tearing up and down the train until the conductor threatened to throw her off at Milton Keynes.

Which left Bruno, the only person worth talking to. But Judith had seen the way other women clustered round him and she wasn't about to act like them. Occasionally, when she half-opened her eyes during the long journey, she caught him looking at her; when he realized she was awake he raised his eyebrows at the others, an expression of amused solidarity that made her feel a little less alone.

Only Bethany and Simonetta had ever visited London before, and on the train they tried to outdo each other with Tube station names and double-decker bus etiquette. But once they got to Euston station, all the girls shrank back, overwhelmed by the rush-hour crowds. Judith grasped her daughter's sticky hand, as the other parents reached out to their daughters. Only Bethany was left unanchored in the sea of people, her complexion no longer peaches and cream, but sickly London white. Her mouth hung open as she scanned the stream of passengers in search of her father's face.

Judith felt herself being pulled forward by Lucy, dragging her towards Bethany. She linked arms with her Sixer. 'I hope you're going to show us all the sights,' Lucy said, and Bethany's face changed from worried to smug.

'Oh yes. You see so much more with someone who knows the city,' she boasted.

'Right, all present and correct?' Trevor appeared, clutching a W.H. Smith bag. He must have gone to buy a paper before checking his daughter was OK.

'Shall we get going, rather than hanging around in all this chaos?' Judith snapped.

'Quite right, yes. Well, first stop Hamley's toyshop!' he declared, reaching into his briefcase and taking out a Tube map. 'Oxford Circus is the nearest station, so if you take the Northern Line southbound and then the Central Line westbound, we can all meet up near the Star Wars figures in,' he looked at his watch, 'about forty-five minutes.'

He turned to go but Judith caught his shoulder. 'Hang on a second. So how are you two getting there?'

'Black cab. It is her *birthday*,' Trevor said, patting Bethany on the head as you'd pat a golden retriever.

Patsy looked nervous. 'What, we've got to go on our own? In the Underground? But what if we miss our stop and end up in the East End?'

'Well . . .' Trevor looked at Bruno for support. 'The Tube's *very* simple. And with Bruno to navigate, you'll be perfectly safe.'

Judith stared after him as he disappeared into the scrum of suits with his daughter. 'Unbelievable,' she muttered, to no one in particular.

'A stupid man,' Bruno whispered. 'But we will have more fun on the Tube than in a boring taxi. Won't we, girls?' he said more loudly, and Judith wasn't sure if he was addressing the Pixies, or their mothers.

Then he opened his arms wide, like Jesus in an illustrated children's Bible, and they followed him towards the red and navy Underground sign. Terri and Lucy raced ahead to walk alongside him, and Judith felt a twinge of guilt as she wondered how much her daughter missed her father. They never talked about it – least said, soonest mended, was the Quentin strategy, but even so . . . sometimes she felt that if Lucy had to grow up with one parent, Jim would have been better.

She gritted her teeth. *Stop it.* Jim had been a failure as a father, though Judith saw it as her duty to make sure Lucy never knew.

Patsy followed nervously, clutching her tiny handbag to her stomach in case of daylight robbery, while Lorna floated languidly through the crowd and Dina skipped to the front, pathetically eager. Perhaps the poor woman had some menopausal crush on Bruno, like that stupid Wendy Craig in *Butterflies*. Judith had met Dina's husband – already retired, as brittle as autumn leaves – so it wasn't surprising that Bruno made an impression. But she felt embarrassed on Dina's behalf at her loss of dignity.

Judith hung back with Paula and Netta. Somehow she sensed there'd be time later to compare notes with Bruno, to laugh at the silliness of the other women. Patience was a virtue.

Judith's virtue was rewarded immediately after lunch. The girls were exhausted, after a frenzied morning of non-stop gawping. London, Lucy had whispered to her during the Tube ride to the Tower, was so full of things to look at that it made her eyes sting.

They'd queued for toys in Hamley's, for the Crown Jewels at the Tower, for the loos pretty much everywhere, and now they were in Soho, in a backstreet coffee bar Bruno suggested. Judith had expected Trevor to insist on some awful steakhouse, or an ice-cream parlour that would make the girls sick on the train home. But instead he looked relieved, and passed Bruno a brown envelope before disappearing.

'Cheese and ham toasties all round, Giuseppe,' Bruno said, as they swept into the tiny café.

'Just cheese for me,' Lorna said. 'I'm vegetarian. At least people understand that down here in the Smoke!'

The skinny man behind the counter unleashed a stream of sulky-sounding Italian before Bruno passed over the contents of the envelope – Judith counted three ten-pound notes. Then Giuseppe perked up, his nicotine-stained hands starting work on the sandwiches.

She marshalled the girls and their mothers into two tiny booths, then took refuge in a third, glad to be alone for a moment. The orange melamine was patterned with rings of indeterminate brown liquid, but the smell as Giuseppe ground the coffee was irresistible. Bruno brought her the first tiny cup, and squeezed in next to her.

'Without you and me, this day would have been a disaster, no? The others –' he whispered conspiratorially, gesturing behind him to the booth where Patsy, Dina and Lorna were debating banana versus strawberry milkshake, '– are worse than the children. Chattering, fussing. You're a city slicker, like me, aren't you?'

'I was once.' She sipped her coffee, so hot it burned her tongue and so strong that the caffeine instantly made her skin tingle and the colours of the café blaze. 'But that was a different time in my life. When my husband was alive.'

Bruno was so close that she could smell Juicy Fruit chewing gum on his breath. He reached across and covered her hand with his. It was huge, the fingers honey brown, thatched with black hairs, the nails Snopake white. She felt dwarfed. To her surprise, it was a nice feeling.

'You are very brave, to be independent. But some time, you will want to love again. And your strength … it is one of the most desirable qualities a woman can possess.'

Judith was lost for words, another unfamiliar experience. 'Right. Well, that's nice.' He seemed in no hurry to remove his hand and hers was beginning to sweat.

At last, Giuseppe appeared, holding two chipped plates, each bearing a perfectly square toastie. He glared at Bruno before returning behind the counter, and only then did Judith get her hand back.

An hour later, when Trevor still wasn't back, the girls were getting restless.

'Is there a park somewhere near here?' Judith asked Bruno.

'Soho Square. We can go, and Giuseppe will tell Trevor where to find us.'

Judith counted the children and their shopping, checking they had the right number of carrier bags emblazoned with toy soldiers: Bethany had three, containing a hundred pounds-worth of stuff: a Japanese gadget that let you play games on your TV, a *Wonder Woman* costume, a Princess Leia doll, a Paddington

Bear so enormous that its wellingtons would fit Lucy, and an array of pony-related trinkets.

The others had borrowed against future pocket money, so their bags were smaller: a Frisbee for Paula, a Holly Hobby jotter and pen set for Chris, a mock-coral bracelet for Netta, and a tiny musical organ for Lucy: it was as small as a matchbox, and played *Yesterday* in tinny tones when you turned the handle.

Dina scuttled – there was no other word for it – up to the counter and leaned in to speak to Bruno, who laughed as though she'd said something incredibly funny. Which was not at all likely.

Judith approached them. 'What's the joke?'

'Oh, nothing.' Dina giggled, an unpleasant sound. 'I was just thanking Bruno for lunch.'

Bruno opened out his broad hands in a gesture that suggested modesty, generosity and good grace rolled into one. As Dina scuttled away again to 'powder her nose', he whispered to Judith, 'I didn't want to embarrass Trevor by explaining about the money.'

The girls reverted to type in Soho Square. Terri and Lucy peered through the windows of the little mock Tudor house, until Bethany sulked and told them that, as it was her birthday, they should join her sunbathing on the grass, though Terri's Celtic skin went pink within seconds. Chris refused to speak to anyone: instead she toured the square, scowling up at the buildings, and making little sketches in her new jotter. Netta and Paula chased each other until they collapsed in a laughing, panting heap, to regain enough energy to do it all over again.

This was different from Manchester, Judith thought, as she leaned against an ancient tree, listening to the rustling of the leaves above her. Greener. More genteel. Perhaps one day, when Lucy was grown up, she'd return to the city. If Bruno was right, she might even return with a man.

'*Allocco*? Brown Owl?' Bruno was next to her, with such an intense look on his face, she thought for a moment he might be about to kiss her. How ridiculous.

'It's beautiful here, isn't it?'

'Yes.' He seemed agitated, kicking against the exposed roots of the tree. 'I am confused, Judith. Trevor ... his wife, do you know what she looks like?'

She tried to remember from the few Brownie events Eileen Kendal attended before she disappeared with her lover to Notting Hill or wherever it was she was living in sin. 'She didn't look like an Eileen at all, when I met her. Blonde, like Bethany. Painfully thin.' She followed Bruno's gaze to the far side of the square and there, on a bench shielded by bushes, were Trevor and a skeletal blonde woman, in floods of tears.

'Like that?' Bruno said.

Judith nodded. Together they watched the silent drama. The blonde shook her head repeatedly and then stood up as though she was going to run towards the girls. Trevor caught her arm, shouting and holding onto her. Finally Eileen ran in the other direction, faster than a woman in wedge heels should, out of the square and into the road, so that a taxi was forced to swerve and sound its air horn. The notes ricocheted off the buildings.

'What do you think that was about?' Judith asked eventually, as they watched Trevor sit back down on the bench, his head in his hands.

'I try not to spend too much time thinking about other people's lives, Judith. Too complicated for a simple man.'

Trevor stood up, shook his head and ran his fingers through his hair to tidy it. Then he picked up a bouquet of roses from the ground before walking towards Soho and the café. Bruno ambled in the same direction, deliberately crossing his path, but making it look accidental, with a comedy double-take. Judith watched as Trevor approached Bethany, his arms behind his back, and handed the flowers to his daughter with a flourish and a kiss.

She walked up in time to hear him say, 'To the number one woman in my life.'

As they raced out of the park to catch their train, Judith noticed Trevor drop something. She just stopped herself calling out to him, but instead picked it up. It was a tiny card, decorated with Cupids and embossed with the address of a Covent Garden florist on one side. She turned it over and read:

To my Eileen, my love. I need you. Your daughter needs you. Come home. Your loving husband, Trevor.

Judith felt sick. Clearly Eileen wasn't coming home. And, reading between the lines, the price she would have to pay was her daughter. Men never understood.

She ripped the card in two and threw it into a waste bin. Then she caught up with Lucy and, to both their surprise, kissed her daughter quickly on the forehead.

On the train home they were delayed just outside Watford, and Bruno bought drinks from the buffet car; Babychams for Dina and Patsy, Cinzano and lemonade for Lorna, Heineken for himself and Trevor, who'd joined them in second-class. Judith and the girls drank Vimto and ate Salt 'n' Shake crisps – someone had to stay sober. Chris refused to eat or drink anything, rudely turning away when Bruno tried to pass her a can of pop.

Judith decided she'd have a word with her about manners at the next Pack meeting.

As the delay dragged on, the girls fell asleep in their seats, and Trevor got in another three rounds. Judith watched the so-called adults as Patsy snored, Lorna chain-smoked, Trevor blew his nose a lot, and Dina fawned over poor Bruno.

That woman really had no shame.

Hostess

1. Show the tester letters you have written:
   a) inviting a friend to tea
   b) saying thank you for a visit
   c) accepting an invitation.

2. Welcome and look after a guest or guests either in your own home or at a party, or at a Brownie event. Prepare at least some of the refreshments yourself, and make a flower arrangement to place on the table or tray.

Chapter Twenty-seven

A Guide is a friend to all, and a sister
to every other Guide, no matter to what
social class the other belongs. A Guide is
never a SNOB.

'Are you *sure* this is it?' Terri looks as surprised as I do as we
draw up outside a postcard-pretty hotel building, complete
with grey-uniformed doorman. 'It's a bit swanky.'

The cabbie has all the celebrity gossip. 'Yep. Symphony
Hotel, Covent Garden. This is where all the movie stars stay
when they're in town. Scarlett, J-Lo, Harrison … And Lourdes
had a birthday party here.'

I'm tempted to ask whether he's had any of them in the back
of his cab, but as I lean through the window to pay the fare, I
see he has *Heat* in the front.

I climb out first, then help Paula out of the taxi. She's
definitely looking trimmer, though she seems subdued. On the
train down she only had one small doughnut, while the rest of
us tucked into toasted breakfast ciabattas.

'Bit of a step up from last time we all came to London,' Terri
says, peering at the international flags hanging above the hotel
reception. The building looks like a wedding cake, tier after tier
of ornate white plasterwork.

'I'd still rather go to Hamley's,' Chris says. She's another one
who looks as miserable as sin. I think the only reason she's here
is because she's got nothing else to do since losing the business.
'It was all so inspiring.'

'Terrifying, more like,' I say, as we emerge through the majestic revolving doors into reception. 'All those sales assistants juggling glow-in-the-dark balls. And those remote-controlled pink pigs snuffling around at our feet. I had nightmares for weeks.'

That trip to London put the wind up everyone. The freedom made the grown-ups behave out of character. Actually, that's not true: they were more like themselves than ever, their personalities magnified by traffic fumes or whatever it is that drives city-dwellers crazy. Lorna bought joss sticks and a rainbow headscarf that she insisted on wearing, though the hippies she remembered from Carnaby Street had been replaced by punks with striped hair and safety pins, who prowled along the beige and orange rubberized pavement, their radios blasting out 'Hit Me With Your Rhythm Stick' and 'Are "Friends" Electric?'. Mum got bossier, and irritated with Dina, who wouldn't leave Bruno alone. Patsy – I still remember her ludicrous pink spotted dress, with matching handbag – pouted and panicked at every new experience, from the Tube to tipping.

Bethany was unbearable that day too. I knew why, of course; we all did. However embarrassing our mothers were, we wanted them with us on our birthdays, yet there she was, being led around town by a dad who didn't seem to be sure what age she was, never mind what she might want for a present.

Now I remember something else from that day. While I was exploring the funny little half-timbered house in the middle of the square, I'd *seen* Bethany's mother. She was *so* beautiful, so different from anyone else's mum, slim and blonde, like a wispy fairy who might float away at any moment.

She was sitting next to Bethany's father, and I darted behind one of the walls of the house so they wouldn't see me. Then I joined Bethany making daisy-chains and I felt bubbly excitement, knowing she was about to get what was surely her biggest birthday wish. Her mother must, finally, have been coming home to Troughton. I knew how much it would mean to me to see Daddy again, but I also knew it was impossible, so a reunion of Bethany and her mother would be the next best thing.

Only Bethany's mother didn't come back. When her dad

came over, he was silent and his eyes were pink, like a rabbit's: it reminded me of the way my eyes looked after I cried, but I knew men didn't cry so it must have been hayfever. I kept thinking Mrs Kendal would reappear, but by the time we were on the train back to Crewe, I realized it wasn't going to happen and I burst into tears myself. Mum just assumed it was the excitement of the day. She was kind to me that night, letting me try on Daddy's suede jacket, a treat normally reserved only for birthdays.

'Terri! Lucy!'

Bethany is sitting in a low armchair, and as she pushes herself up from its elegantly distressed tan leather arms, she is as poised as Audrey Hepburn. Her sandals are *beautiful*, made from the narrowest straps of creamy white suede, which surround her slim feet and then snake their way up her ludicrously smooth brown ankles.

It's true what they say about TV putting ten pounds on you, because that time on *Coronation Street*, Bethany looked like a size twelve. Now, in an elegant cream wrap dress, it's clear that she's a size eight. And unlike Chris's slenderness – the result of her training her natural curves into submission – Bethany is gazelle-slim, naturally long and lean. Yet she doesn't have that pinched look of the usual anorexic celebrity. All in all, it's hardly surprising she's on TV.

'Girls, it's *wonderful* to see you.' Her voice is surprisingly posh and hearty, like a boarding school headmistress.

She's standing now, and reaches out a delicate hand to Terri first – 'Big Bird! My faithful deputy!' – then to me. If this scene was in one of her TV dramas, she'd be clasping us to her (is that silicone-enhanced?) bosom instead of keeping us at arm's length.

'Oh Lucy, look at you: you're still all angelic and cuddly and gorgeous,' she says, scrutinizing my face and concluding, I assume, that I'm no threat to her role as Queen of the Pixies. I know I'm being bitchy. Making up for lost time, perhaps: for so many years, I idolized her and even once I saw her for the gorgeous charming *bully* she was, I still forgave her everything, because of her mother.

Shit. Could I be turning Sasha into the new Bethany?

'No, *you're* gorgeous, Bethany. You've done so well for your-self.'

She tosses her head in a familiar gesture. 'Oh, nonsense. And Chris ...' She stares at her. 'You're so muscly! Gosh, that must take so much work.'

'Well, we can't all be natural beauties,' Chris says, evenly.

'And ...' Bethany peers at Paula with open fascination. 'Golly. Paula. You look ... *well.*'

'Don't you mean fat?' Paula asks, shifting from foot to foot. She shouldn't do that, really; it draws attention to her horrible scuffed trainers.

'Oh, I know how hard it is to shift those stubborn pounds,' Bethany says. 'Or stubborn stones ... anyway, calorie-counting is on hold this afternoon because the Symphony's afternoon tea is a legend.'

She sways gently as she walks towards the lift and I gaze around the lobby. It looks like English country houses ought to look, but never do, because the aristocracy tends to prefer the shabby end of chic. Here, though, all the colours comple-ment each other: duck-egg blues and egg-yolk yellows. Even the shade of the flames in the open fire – unnecessary in June, but I guess Japanese tourists expect it – mirror the interior décor precisely.

There's a man to operate the lift, pulling the concertina gates across with a clatter as we step inside. We travel the four floors in silence, and I wonder yet again what's prompted Bethany to organize this reunion. Actually, according to Terri, it's been her agent who's organized it all because our old 'mate' has been far too busy doing whatever it is showbiz types do. In the train on the way down, Chris and Paula were cynical, wondering if she was playing Lady Bountiful so she could gawp at ordinary people and feel superior.

'Here we are, madam,' the liftman says.

'*Marvellous* job,' she says and I'm sure she winks at him, though he must be sixty. Then she tips him deftly, pressing a coin into his hand. How rich must she be, to pay someone for pushing two buttons?

She takes the second of the two doors to the left of the lift, marked Vivien Leigh Suite, and when we walk inside, the sunshine's dazzling.

'Bloody useless chambermaids,' she says, rushing over to the windows to fiddle with the blinds, like a vampire whose very existence is threatened by daylight. I join her, trying to lower them, but they're being uncooperative. Standing alongside her, I notice her face is more lined than I expected, a fan of tiny creases around her eyes where she's squinting against the outside world. Her skin looks puffy, but her forehead is utterly smooth, except for two little pink marks between her brows. I've read enough women's magazines to know what that is: Botox. Nice of her to make the effort.

But there's a bigger shock to come. As I reach across her to fiddle with the cord, I catch an unmistakable whiff of alcohol on her breath. And not white wine spritzer, but whisky.

Our eyes meet and she looks away.

Chris joins us and instantly manages to lower the calico blinds, which shield the fiercest rays, diffusing the light to a gentler glow. The suite is massive, furnished in the same understated pastels as the lobby downstairs, with an enormous bouquet of lilies and roses in a clear glass vase on the marble mantelpiece. There are glossy magazines – *Conde Nast Traveller*, *Vanity Fair*, *Elle* – laid out on the coffee table. Through a connecting door, there's a huge four-poster bed, so high off the floor you'd need a ladder to climb in. The pale blue carpet is so thick that I long to take off my shoes and sink my feet into it. But what would my mother think?

Paula's less inhibited. She flops into a huge chair and kicks off her trainers leaving threadbare socks to cover her feet. 'So ... you said there was food?'

For a fraction of a second, Bethany's expression is of pure disgust, but then she composes herself and says, 'This hotel is going downhill. The tea was meant to be here when we arrived.'

I'm listening now for slurring, but I can't hear any behind her fake accent. She's lost all hint of Cheshire vowels.

'Do you live here then?' I ask, as she marches over to the desk.

'I ...' She hesitates, then picks up the phone. Is it my imagination or is her hand shaking? 'Hello, this is Bethany Kendal in the Leigh Suite. We're expecting afternoon tea and I'd like to know why we're waiting. Three thirty, you say? I don't know who told you that. I'd like it here *now*!' She slams down the phone. 'Complete incompetents.'

She picks up an enormous bowl of fruit and plucks a single black grape before offering the bowl to us. 'There'll be cake soon, don't worry,' she says to Paula, who scowls in response and takes a banana.

'Lucy was asking whether you lived here,' Terri says, perching awkwardly on the edge of a lemon silk-upholstered chaise longue.

She waves her hand dismissively. 'Oh no. Only when I'm staying up in town.'

'So where's home then?' I persist.

'I'd actually rather not say. It's nothing personal, but I guard my private life very closely.' And she taps the side of her nose.

'Eh?' Paula says. 'What, you think one of us might turn into a stalker?'

Bethany pouts. 'I've had several. You can't be too careful.'

Chris, who has been staring out of the window at the *Mary Poppins* London skyline, comes out of her daydream. 'I've had a stalker, too. I thought it was quite funny. Poor sod. He was totally unthreatening, just the odd smutty letter. But imagine being sad enough to want to stalk *me*.'

'Mine is now an in-patient at a psychiatric hospital. On *drugs*,' boasts Bethany, proving that Chris's stalker was a pale imitation of the real thing.

'I'm surprised you're famous enough,' Paula says. 'I mean, what have you done? A fortnight on *Coronation Street* and a few mentions in the *News of the World* when you got divorced.'

Bethany sighs. 'Oh, Paula. Don't you watch TV? And I had you down as a bit of a couch potato. You obviously missed me in *Doctors*, *Holby City* and the entire *Headache Relief* campaign. And then of course, there was *Miss Marple*.'

'I'm sure I saw you in that,' I lie. 'What are you filming at the moment, then?'

'Oh, lots in the pipeline. I'm giving the soaps a wide berth, looking for something a little more challenging. I might do some theatre, if the right project comes along.'

Paula gives her a fake smile. 'But you've nothing on at the moment, then, duck? So you're *resting*.'

Bethany shakes her head slowly. 'Well, I wouldn't expect you to understand the importance of planning your career. My agent says that the difference between a mediocre actress and a good one is being choosy enough to—' There's a knock at the door. 'That'll be afternoon tea,' she says, and opens it.

But it isn't room service. A scruffy man in his forties is standing outside, carrying a khaki holdall. Behind him there's a young girl with a huge vanity case. 'Hi, Bethany, I'm Len. You're expecting me, right?'

She looks flustered. 'Excuse me a moment, girls,' she says, before stepping out into the corridor.

'Who do you think that is?' I ask.

'I know him,' Chris says, looking puzzled. 'He's a photographer. Can't remember his surname, but I did a shoot with him a couple of months ago. He was a lecherous bastard, too. God knows what he's doing here.'

Terri stands up. 'I wonder ...'

'Maybe this is what life's like for her now. Always being pursued by ... what do they call them ... the Pavarotti?' Paula says.

'Paparazzi,' Chris corrects her.

But Terri holds up her hand. 'No. I wondered why her agent got in touch, rather than Bethany herself. I think we've been set up, girls. This isn't a cosy catch-up. It's a *photo opportunity*. She's taking us for a ride and I for one am not going to hang around to be a pawn—'

The door opens again but instead of Bethany – whose angry muttering we can hear outside – in comes a woman dressed in a black uniform, pushing a trolley. 'I'll put these over here, shall I?' she says, and before we can answer, she's laying out supplies. Half a dozen three-tiered cake stands, each laden with tiny triangles of sandwiches, raisin scones, miniature blueberry muffins, sticky nut and cherry Florentines, chocolate éclairs, fondant fancies, and heart-shaped jam tarts no bigger than a two-pound coin. Two full cafetières, two porcelain teapots with steam coming out of the spouts. Pots of yellow-crusted clotted cream and fresh strawberries. An enormous pale orange cake decorated with tiny marzipan carrots, and a huge meringue nest filled with raspberries and redcurrants and sprigs of mint.

And three bottles of champagne.

'On the other hand,' Paula says, 'it seems a shame to let all that food go to waste.'

'There's something else,' I say, as soon as the waitress leaves. 'I think that Bethany might be drunk.'

Terri looks at her watch. 'But it's not even two o'clock yet.'

Chris leans down beside the sofa and picks up Bethany's pale pink leather tote. Now I think about it, it is a huge bag for such an understated and elegant woman.

'Chris, you can't!' I protest, but she's already unzipped the bag and begun to rummage.

'Come here!' she says, and we gather round, peering inside. In the zipped central compartment, she's found a half-litre bottle of supermarket whisky. 'Looks like she's had most of it already. If she's got to be a daytime drinker, she could at least go for a single malt.'

'How did you know?' Paula asks me.

'I could smell it on her breath. What should we do? If she's drinking during the day, well … maybe Bethany's not as perfect as she wants us to think. I don't think we can walk out on her. '

We exchange glances, knowing that although our Pixie bond is twenty-five years out of date, we won't break it. We're waiting for Terri, though: with our Sixer under the influence, the Seconder takes control. Eventually she sighs. 'OK. Lucy's right. We can't draw attention to her *problem* while the photographer is here, but as soon as he leaves, so do we. She might be in trouble, but it's no excuse for lying to us.'

'Girls!' Bethany bounces back into the room. 'What are you all gossiping about? Listen, there's been a bit of a misunderstanding. I don't have a clue how it happened, but my agent seems to have mixed up the dates and guess what! There's a photographer here who was meant to be doing a shoot for a magazine and he wondered ... well, as we're having tea anyway, he had this great idea. What I'm trying to say is, would you mind having your picture taken?' Her face is flushed, her eyes are shining, and although her story is ridiculous in the extreme, I can see how much this matters.

'Bethany ...' Terri says. 'You don't have to pretend any more. We'll go along with this, for you, but credit us with a little intelligence, please.'

Bethany blinks several times, digesting the information. 'Oh, I don't know what you're talking about, Terri. My agent's hopeless like this.' But she sounds less certain.

'Tell you what,' Paula says. 'Give us twenty minutes to dig into the tea, and then we'll pose for the pictures.'

'But the whole point of the pictures is that we're all eating ...' She tails off, realizing what she's said, then nods and disappears into the corridor.

'Good work, Paula,' Terri says. 'A few cucumber sandwiches might sober her up.'

'Bugger that,' Paula says. 'I'm just hungry.'

'Let's hide the champagne while she's gone,' I suggest and we grab the bottles, stashing them under the duvet in the four-poster bed. The chambermaid's going to get a little bonus.

'I'm sorry for getting you all into this,' Terri says.

'Do you see me complaining?' Paula says, as she takes her first bite of scone. Her upper lip is coated in cream. 'It's bloody weird, though. Hasn't she got any showbiz friends she could have her picture taken with?'

I look over my shoulder to see her trying to charm the photographer. 'I bet it's lonely, being on TV. You probably never know if someone wants to get to know you for you, or for what you can get them.'

The door slams and Bethany moves towards the trolley. 'He's going for a walk around the block. It's all so stressful.'

'What about a nice cup of tea to calm you down?' I say. Despite it all, I feel sorry for her. Her face is no longer flushed and she looks older than any of us, somehow.

'I'd prefer something stronger. They were supposed to bring champagne. Where is it?' She walks around the suite, searching, then stops abruptly. 'I'm exhausted. While you eat, I might have to have a little lie down.' When she picks up her bag before disappearing into the bedroom, Terri raises her eyebrows at me.

'We can't leave her to drink even more,' she says, sounding resigned. 'Come on, Lucy. I think it's time to remind Bethany about Brownie values.'

Bethany is lying on the bed with her shoes on, and she opens one eye as we approach.

'This looks suspiciously like a deputation,' she says wearily.

'It'd be great if you could join us,' I say, trying to force some chirpiness into my voice. 'We'd love to hear what happens behind the scenes on *Coronation Street*.'

Bethany pushes herself up and sits blinking like Sleeping Beauty, just woken from a century of slumber. As she stretches, her arm hits a lump under the bedclothes. 'Ouch.' She puts her hands under the duvet and pulls out a bottle of champagne. 'What is that doing there? Five-star hotels have some very strange ideas these days,' she says, sounding bemused and much drunker than before. On the bedside table, there's a tumbler full of pale brown liquid.

'Yes, come on, Bethany. Buck your ideas up. We've come a long way to see you; it's not really on to fall asleep.' Terri tries to look stern.

Bethany sighs. 'I'm just so tired. I want to look my best in the photographs.'

'Well, let's hope the make-up girl is a miracle worker.' Terri turns to me. 'Lucy. Can you fetch a cup of coffee? Better still, the entire pot.'

'But caffeine's terrible for my system,' Bethany protests.

'Not as bad as whisky,' Terri says.

I bring through the coffee. Terri's rearranging the pillows in best matronly manner, propping them up behind her patient. She holds up a cup and waits while Bethany drinks it, her eyes screwing up in disgust.

'Good. You can have another one in a minute.'

'Anything if you'll leave me alone.'

Terri looks hurt. 'I just don't get it, Bethany. I know you've only asked us here as a publicity stunt, but aren't you just slightly curious about us? Or are you so self-centred that no one else registers?'

Bethany sighs. 'It's not that. The thing is . . . It *was* my agent's idea. I really didn't want to go along with it.'

'Because you didn't want to mislead us?' I ask.

'Kind of . . . Look, stardom isn't all sweetness and light, you know. Sometimes I even wonder if I should have stayed in Troughton. I mean, let me guess. You're probably married, two kids, a boy and a girl. Nice house. Nice husband. Nice life. Am I right?'

Terri and I look at each other. 'I've only got one daughter. But apart from that, you're not far off.'

'Then there's Chris. I read about her company being taken over in the paper. So she's rich, but she's rich on her own merits. Unlike me. I get paid because my face fits. Or used to fit. Thirty-six years old and over the hill.'

Terri pours another cup of coffee and forces Bethany to drink it. 'It's the booze that's making you feel sorry for yourself. You've got a great life. Luxury hotels, photo shoots. The works.'

But even Terri doesn't sound convinced. Because if Bethany's life is a dream come true, why is she drunk at lunchtime?

'You don't have to live your life like this, Bethany,' I say. 'You could come home to Cheshire. You could still meet someone. Train to do something different . . .' I tail off.

She looks at me pityingly. 'Like what? None of us have changed, Lucy. Chris was always a dreamer. Terri, you were always a doer. I've always been like this. Using people. Even you, Lucy. Trying to make me feel better, though all I ever did was take advantage. We can't change.'

'I'm changing,' I say, hoping rather than knowing it to be true. I've always been a sucker for hope, even after successive Christmases where neither my father nor a Sindy white-and-gold bedroom set (complete with miniature hangers) materialized. *Dear Santa*, perhaps I will write this year, *I'd like lashings of gumption and my ration of backbone, which seems to have been allocated to someone else.*

Terri gives me a thoughtful look and nods. 'Actually, I think perhaps you are.' She turns around and sits on the upholstered bench at the end of the bed, her arms folded across her chest. 'As for you, Bethany, you *have* changed. You were never the kind to feel sorry for yourself. Which is not going to do anybody any good, frankly – least of all you.'

'But—'

'No buts, Bethany Kendal. Because if there's one thing I bet hasn't changed about you, it's the fact that you *love* an audience. And this afternoon, you need to put in a stellar performance as a woman having the time of her life.'

The next three hours are surreal. I don't know whether it's the caffeine or the camera, but Bethany's switched on full-beam nice.

'Isn't this delicious?' Bethany asks Paula, who is struggling to contain herself as the photographer tries to keep some food back for his pictures. 'I'm so pleased that you came all this way to be with me today. After all these years ... we have so much to catch up on.'

Paula raises her eyebrows at me and I shrug. Then she glances at the photographer and nods as if to say, *Ah, I get it. She's putting it on for him.*

Bethany pours tea and asks endless polite questions, every inch the perfect hostess, though her words are spoken with laboured precision, so they don't slur. Only occasionally does she let the mask slip, and her expression reminds me of the times when poor Sasha gets constipated.

Sasha. Each time I look at Bethany I wonder if this is the way Sasha's going to end up, all because of my selfish behaviour.

'And your daughter's a Brownie now, too, is she, Lucy?' Bethany's saying, her head cocked quizzically to one side. 'I hope she's a Pixie.'

'Yep, she's flying the flag all right,' I say, just as the flash goes off yet again.

'That's me done,' he says, and turns to pack up his things. 'The reporter'll give you a ring in the next couple of days to do the interview.'

Now, I think, we'll see the real Bethany again. But I wonder

... is there a chance she might have enjoyed this? Might want to spend a little time with her old chums?

Paula's waiting too and as the snapper closes the door behind him, she says, 'Right, duck, shall we get out of your hair then? I'm sure you've got a manicure lined up. Or a male model.'

'No!' she says, panic in her voice. 'Please don't go. I know when you first arrived I was a bit ... odd.'

'Drunk, more like,' Paula whispers.

'What about going somewhere else? It's so stuffy in there. I could do with some air. I could show you the sights.'

Paula's jaw drops and Chris jolts out of wherever she is in her head.

Terri answers for us all. 'I think that would be nice. Where would you recommend?'

'Well, there's the Natural History Museum, the Victoria and Albert, or the Tower of London. Um ... or shopping. Harrods is nice, or Selfridges.' When none of us reacts, she continues. 'OK, well I suppose it is a bit hot for the shops. It's too late for a matinee. Shit, the best city in the world and I can't think ... hang on a minute, though. I've got an idea.'

Twenty minutes later and we're there. It was inevitable, I suppose.

Soho Square.

It looks almost the same as I remember, but it seems smaller. I suppose I am bigger, so that makes sense. It's slightly tatty: the benches are grey with age and the grass is bleached out in places. I head for the Tudor house and its arches are so low that they touch the top of my head.

'What do you think that is?' Bethany says behind me. She's been to one of the coffee shops across the square to buy an enormous tray of hot drinks, and a big bag of cakes in case anyone gets hungry again. 'Go on, have a guess.'

I try to peer through the windows but they're too grimy. 'An Elizabethan ice-cream kiosk?'

'Hmm ... not a bad effort. But wrong. No, it's a Victorian garden shed. I love that about London. It's full of surprises. I used to come here when I first moved down, learning my lines and people-watching. I couldn't really believe I was allowed to be here.'

'That's silly. You were always going places.'

'Yeah.' She grins. 'What happened, eh, Lucy?'

We sit down together on the grass. 'Well, you got famous.'

'I know,' she says. 'Just look at me having to fend off the autograph hunters.'

I stare at her before realizing it's a joke. It's the first time I've ever heard Bethany take the piss out of herself. Maybe there is some hope for her. 'Is it really as bad as you said? They'd write you off because you're over thirty-five?'

'Sort of. I haven't done myself any favours lately. It's a bit of a shock when people have indulged you all your life, and then they stop.' She smiles ruefully, as though I should know what she's talking about. 'Don't you want to know if the stories are true?'

'I don't really read the papers.'

'Oh, so you won't have seen the one about me storming off set because the stylist used the wrong hairspray? Or refusing to get in an ordinary black cab to the studios for an early call because they'd promised to send a limousine.' She's still smiling, but I can hear the bitterness in her voice.

'No. Were they true, then?'

'The first one wasn't, and the second one, well, let's just say it was during the toughest time of my divorce. London's the best city in the world, but it can be lonely.'

I look around the square. A procession of orange-robed shaven-haired men passes by, chanting 'Hare Krishna'. The few tourists and lazing office workers duck out of their path or avoid looking at them, so they won't be targeted for mid-afternoon redemption. 'You could always get religion.'

She giggles. 'Orange just *isn't* my colour, Lucy.'

We sip our coffees, and I notice that I'm sitting exactly where I saw Bethany's mum and dad sitting twenty-five years ago. 'Now you're in London, do you, um, see your mother?'

Her face loses its colour. 'I don't. No. I decided a long time ago. If she couldn't be bothered to get in touch with me for all those years ... well, why should I be bothered now?'

'But how do you know she didn't want to? She might have

been scared of how you'd react.' I watch her face, trying to work out how far I can go. But she looks steely.

'She was brave enough to run off with her lover and leave her only child behind.' Coffee slops onto the cracked pavement; she's crushed the paper cup in her hands. 'I'm sorry. I just don't talk about it. But sometimes, I catch a glimpse of a woman on the Tube, you know – the Central Line passes through Notting Hill. And the District Line. And I think it might be her.'

'And have you ever approached the woman?'

She shakes her head. 'I always get off. Change carriages. There's nothing there for me, for either of us. No going back.'

I consider saying something else, but then Terri comes over. 'It's been lovely, Bethany. But I think maybe we ought to be heading off now, before rush hour, if you wouldn't mind pointing us in the direction of the nearest Tube.'

We walk back onto Oxford Street in silence, Bethany and I, while the others gawp at the glamorous transvestite who is tottering a few steps ahead of us, six foot two in his stiletto heels. At Tottenham Court Road, we exchange air kisses, ignoring the tuts of people trying to pass.

'We must do it again,' Bethany says and I can't tell if she's acting or if she means it. I can tell from Terri's expression that she thinks it's yet another performance.

'Yes,' I say and then on an instinct, I find an old envelope in my bag and write my mobile number on it. 'You know ... if London gets lonely again, you can always come home.'

'Oh Lucy, I don't believe in going back. But thank you,' she says, taking the number and putting it away in her purse.

As I step onto the down escalator – sleek metal now, not the wooden slats that made my eyes go funny – I peer at all the faces sliding past in the other direction. I can't shake the image of a blonde woman travelling by Tube, looking for her daughter, and that daughter changing carriages to avoid her.

Whatever happens, that won't be Sasha and me.

On the train home, we raid the buffet car for drinks to wipe out the dirt and noise of London, just as our mothers did.

'Poor cow,' Paula says. 'Do you think she's drunk all the time?'

Chris peers out of the window, her eyes flicking forward and back, forward and back, in time with the sounds of the train. 'I know why she does it. It's the days, stretching ahead of you.'

'Mmm,' Paula says. 'Now that's something we've all got in common.'

Beyond the grimy glass, we're speeding past thousands of houses a minute, thousands of blurred Saxon Closes, where millions of people are merely existing, their days stretching ahead of them.

Tomorrow I'm calling Seb.

Chapter Twenty-eight

A Guide goes about with a smile and singing.
It cheers her and it cheers other people,
especially in time of danger, for she keeps it
up then all the same.

I'm a regular city girl these days. London one week, Manchester the next. All I need is a twenty-a-day habit, a wine rack full of Chardonnay and I'll be like Bridget Jones with stretch marks.

Except that Bridget loved the city whereas I get scared whenever I buy a day return to anywhere with a population over twenty thousand. Muggings, rapes, robberies, taking a wrong turn and being kidnapped by a drug-crazed gang.

As always, shoes are my talisman. I'm wearing morale-boosting, but stable, chunky heels, navy blue with a narrow white trim. Very Jackie O. With them, I'm wearing my pale pink suit, styled like a classic Chanel design, in a bobbly woollen fabric. I'm surprised at how tight it is around the hips until I remember: the suit is *ten* years old, bought for a school friend's register office wedding. It's older than my marriage, and certainly in better shape. Ah well. According to my magazine, vintage is *in*.

'Off shopping, love? I'll carry your bags on the way back if you buy me a drink.' The young ticket collector is *flirting* with me. Terrifying.

In Manchester, I do a final check in the station loo. Not bad. I still look like a shoe shop manageress hitting the summer sales on her day off, but there's something else. I *have* made an effort, blow-drying my hair and excavating the mascara, lip liner and foundation from the powdery depths of my make-up bag. It's more than that, though. Beneath the slap, there's colour in my cheeks and a brightness in my eyes suggesting that at least this shoe shop manageress has a life. Or a hope of getting one back.

I check my side view, breathe in and stride out onto the concourse with half-closed eyes, not wanting to seem too keen.

'Lucy!'

His voice carries above the hubbub and I follow it to see him by the coffee shop, completely still and with feet slightly apart like a statue honouring the working man. Last time, I'd forgotten how beautiful he was. This time, the shock is his size. He makes the people buzzing around him look trivial and tiny.

'Seb ...' My voice is feeble, not a good sign for later. 'Hope you've not been waiting for ages?'

He shrugs. 'I like stations. Do you want a drink, or shall we get straight to business?'

I'm not moving, but my insides have their own momentum, swaying gently as if I'm still on the train. 'Um. Well, let's get going. No time like the present.'

'We can walk it,' he says and as I follow him, my solid heels feel as precarious as rollerblades.

He moves quickly, his legs pumping back and forth. They're so muscular that the denim of his baggy jeans curves and stretches across their contours. When I wear tight trousers, the fabric moulds around the undulations of my cellulite.

'Now I need to warn you that Victor's an awkward bugger. His bark and his bite are savage, but he also has the best ear I know. They call him Vic the Voice Doc at college and people wait weeks for the chance to see him.'

'How ... did you get an appointment so quickly?' I'm trying hard not to puff as I keep up with Seb's strides. When I called him the day after my trip to London, his helpfulness surprised me and I don't know whether to be grateful or suspicious.

'Well, as well as being an animal, Vic was my flatmate when

we were studying music. So I know enough about his bad habits to blackmail him into anything.' He stops walking. 'You OK? You look a bit hot.'

'Fine,' I stammer. He probably thinks I'm menopausal.

'It's me, isn't it? Going too fast. Always doing it; drove my last girlfriend crazy but she lost half a stone without going to the gym while we were together.' He grins, without a trace of modesty. 'Mind you, wasn't *just* down to the walking.'

It's a good job my face is already deepest beetroot from being out of breath, because otherwise I'd be blushing to my roots. 'Right.'

'Sorry, shouldn't talk like that,' he says, but he doesn't look sorry. He slows down, keeps glancing at me. 'It's just the way things are at work. Non-stop innuendo. You know, it's funny, but sometimes I can't believe that there's only a couple of years between us. Our lives are so different. You're all grown-up, with a kid and a husband – I bet you've even got a hatchback, haven't you? Or a four by four?'

'You got it right the first time,' I admit.

'And then there's me, such a slacker that I moved back in with my parents when I ran out of cash. The eternal teenager.'

We walk past a shop window and in my ridiculous suit, I look like his mother. 'I definitely feel older than you. By about a hundred years.'

'Nah, but that's the thing. You don't *look* older. In fact, you look better than the last time I saw you. For a housewife, you're a bit of a babe, Lucy.' He smiles.

'Don't be daft.'

We're definitely in studentland now. All the people passing me by are young and purposeful, like the cast of a post-millennium *Kids from Fame*. And everyone's wearing jeans. I can feel sweat soaking through the fabric of my shirt and I wish I could take my jacket off and dump it in the nearest bin. But then Seb would see my bingo wings.

'I mean it. There's something different about you ... a bit of a glow.' He puts his finger to his lips as if he's trying to solve a puzzle. 'Now what could it be? Pregnant?'

'God, no.'

'Well, that's a relief. It'd be a shame to spoil that foxy figure ... hey, have you got a secret lover back in Cheshire?'

'No!'

He stops outside the full-height glass entrance hall to the Royal Northern College of Music. I never dreamed I'd come here. Though it'll probably be the first and last time.

'So what is your secret then, Little Miss Glow-worm?'

'The only thing that's changed since you saw me last, is that I've moved out. I'm sort of ... separated, from my husband.' I feel instantly embarrassed, as though I'm signalling that I'm available. As if he'd be interested! As if I am ... 'But it'll blow over. And I don't want to talk about it, if that's OK. I don't exactly feel like I'm glowing, put it that way.'

'I feel a right tit now.' He throws a geeky, little boy expression. 'Owe you a stiff one, once Vic's done his worst. A drink, that is.'

'Oh. Well. If you insist.'

'I do. And I have a feeling you might need it.'

Vic the Voice Doc has his lair on the third floor of the college, a cell-like white-painted room dominated by a big piano with a small metronome on top, the sign of a true musical pedant. I can't see how the piano was ever squeezed in here, unless it was lowered in by crane before they added the roof. There's not much room for anything else, so a small grey filing cabinet seems to serve as a desk, with a pen pot, an anglepoise lamp and a laptop all jostling for space on top.

Seb knocks and walks straight in. 'Hey, Vic the Prick!'

A smile cracks Vic's trimmed George Michael-style beard, then disappears again. I can't tell if he looks at me, because he has such puffy eyes that you can hardly see the pupils underneath. 'You still have a filthy tongue as well as a filthy mind then, Sebastian.' His voice is arid, scoured of colour.

'I don't think you're in a position to lecture me about filth, Vic, given that you were scarcely housetrained when we moved in together. Anyway, this is my friend Lucy.' He pushes me forward gently, a tiny movement on the small of my back. It's crazy but I can feel the warmth of his hand there long after he takes it away again.

'Hi,' he says, scanning me for a millisecond, then looking back at Seb. 'A little older than your usual. Very *Educating Rita*.'

'Ignore him, Lucy. And Vic, a) she's not old and b) she's a family friend and c) she's married. I don't know why you always think I'm motivated by sex.'

'*Don't* you?' He squeezes through the tiny gap between the end of his piano and the wall. 'Shall we get this over with, Linda—'

'Lucy,' I say, embarrassed at having to correct him.

'Whatever, dear. A couple of questions. What's your range?'

'Um … soprano.'

'Dear Lord, one day will you bring me an alto, just for variety?' he says, staring at the ceiling. 'Training?'

'I haven't really had any since school. But I sing in the church choir at home in Troughton.' I daren't admit I haven't been since Sasha fulfilled her Brownie ambitions, and I put mine on hold.

'Age?'

'Thirty-five.'

Vic sighs. 'Right. Do you have some music with you?'

I'm so nervous I can barely speak, so how am I going to sing? I hand him the sheet music for my favourite aria, from *La Traviata*. He raises a dismissive eyebrow.

'Hmm. Nul points for originality. We'll start with a warm-up; you can stay where you are for that, and only come round next to me when we do your audition piece. I hate anyone looking over my shoulder. Do you need water?'

I cough slightly, to clear my throat. 'That'd be great.'

He frowns at me. 'You shouldn't cough like that. It damages your voice. Mind you, that's assuming there's a voice there to be damaged. Seb, make yourself useful for once in your life and fetch your lady friend some water from the cooler down the corridor.'

I'm facing Vic now across the piano, and I can just see the pitted remains of acne scars at the top of his cheeks. Maybe he grew the beard to cover up more scars. I catch a glimpse of his eyes, which are pond green.

'A word of advice. Don't bother thinking you'll change Seb, Linda-Lucy-whoever you are. In three years, I never saw a single one of his women manage to get past his monstrous ego to any feelings underneath. Though judging from the sounds that emanated from his bedroom, he's not a bad bet for sexual gratification, if that floats your boat.'

'That's not what it's about,' I snap back. 'It's a very long story.'

'I don't want to know. But don't say I didn't warn you.'

Seb returns with the water and I'm grateful for the ridges in the plastic cup, because without them to grasp, the bloody thing would drop out of my trembling hand.

Focus, Lucy. Have you ever failed an audition in your life? No. But then the only auditions I've ever had – at school, or the choir – were in Troughton, where I was a big fish in the smallest pond. Whereas I am now in a *Pop Idol* sized ocean of brilliance, with no prizes for guessing who is playing Mr Nasty Simon Cowell.

'Ready?'

I look around for somewhere to put my empty plastic cup and rest it on the top of the piano.

'Oh, for fuck's sake, do you want to stain the wood?' Vic says, snatching the cup and tossing it into a bin behind him.

'Sorry.' I sneak a quick look over my shoulder at Seb, who gives a thumbs-up. 'Ready.'

'Scales first, then,' he says and he sets the metronome going. Does he think I'm such an amateur I won't even be able to sing scales to his exacting rhythmic standards? As his fingers touch the keys, the piano is almost overwhelmingly loud; each note bounces around the walls, but I can still hear the metronome above the chords, like a workaholic woodpecker. 'I want you to sing Aaaaahhhh.'

I open my mouth and the first note emerges. Wavery to begin with, so I close my eyes and focus on the sound, on matching the tone of the piano as exactly as I can, on merging with the note until there's nothing here except the sound and just as I've managed that, the chord changes and I imagine myself *becoming* the next note and then ...

'Right,' says Vic, closing the piano lid. 'Time for a coffee.'

I blink and look at the clock on the wall. Twenty minutes has passed and I can't remember a thing.

As we step into the corridor and Vic locks the door behind him, Seb leans down to whisper into my ear. 'That was great, Lucy. Really. The girl done good.'

But he would say that. The only person whose verdict really matters is Vic, and when I try to catch sight of him as we walk towards the college coffee bar, his face gives nothing away. Perhaps he's only taking me to a public place to avoid a scene, the tactic used the world over by people dumping their partners.

'Double espresso,' he says to the fat girl behind the counter.

Ah well, in a moment I will find out for good. I try to consider the alternative hobbies and dreams open to me once he's delivered his verdict, but it only makes me more depressed. Somehow no one would think crochet was worth leaving your husband for.

'So ...' he says, finally, when we've got our drinks and I've behaved like a proper housewife by clearing a table cluttered with lipstick-stained cups left by slovenly music students. 'Why does singing matter so much to you?'

I'm taken aback. It's like someone asking me why I like breathing.

'I suppose I've always been a singer. You know that ABBA song where the woman's started singing before she could talk? I used to hum along with my daddy when he played the guitar ...' I tail off. Vic doesn't want to hear this. 'Then when I was a little girl, I had some lessons and the teacher said I could do something with my voice.'

'And this is ... *thirty* years ago?' he says.

I flush, but I also feel angry. He's deliberately keeping me hanging on, refusing to give his opinion, like the spider and the fly. 'Twenty-eight, actually.'

'I'm not a mathematician, Linda. I'm a musician.'

That anger is back, the same ice-cold, red-hot, churning feeling that made me slap Terri, made me walk out on Andrew, makes me *dangerous*. 'Look. It might sound daft to you, but things have happened recently that got me thinking about lost chances. And last chances. That's all. I just want to know whether there's something I could still do with my voice.'

My heart is racing, and it's not surprising. I *have* just done something unprecedented: stood up to a bullying stranger.

Victor doesn't appreciate the significance of this moment, because he raises his eyebrows and says, '*Do*?'

Seb turns on his friend. 'Oh for fuck's sake, Vic. Stop being such an arsehole. What do you think she means? Enter the bloody national gargling competition?'

Vic downs his double espresso in one. 'Good news or bad news first?'

'Good,' I say. 'I've got enough bad in my life already.'

'You can sing.'

It's only when I hear myself sigh very deeply that I realize how long I've been holding my breath. 'Right.'

'You're in tune, and you'd be surprised how many people I hear who aren't and don't even know. For someone who hasn't had lessons as an adult, you have a nice tonal quality. The breath control's shot, but then we could do something about that.'

I try not to dwell on the *we* but I do register that means he's not ruling me out as a potential student.

'I could leave it there, if you like,' he says. 'It's better than what I tell most people. You can head off back to Toytown or wherever it is you live, tell everyone else in the choir. In fact, that might be the best plan all round.' He stands up, his chair squeaking on the lino.

'That's not why I came. I know I can sing.' Not that I would have said it as confidently before he gave his verdict, but now I'm furious. 'You can't give me half an answer.'

'OK. Three things. One, singing in that choir of yours or in the bath or whatever might have damaged your voice; I could hear something forced in your lower register that I'm not happy with. Two, you don't sight-read properly, do you? That's going to make life difficult, like playing the clarinet with one hand tied behind your back.' He sneers at Seb. 'Mind you, that's how Sebastian sounds most of the time.'

'And the third?' I mumble, wondering if even the way I speak is doing irreparable damage to my vocal chords.

'Look. I'll be honest. I don't see the point. If you'd come ten years ago, I might have taken a different view, but now you're probably too old to build a career. If your voice isn't knackered from bad habits, trying to get you to professional standard, or semi-professional, will take months, maybe years of work. Three months to even begin to unlearn the terrible breathing and amateur phrasing. And then what?'

I wait, and then when I realize it isn't a rhetorical question, I speak up. 'I'd like to take a chance at going for professional choral roles, festivals, that kind of thing.'

'Paying you less, hour for hour, than you'd earn in Tesco?'

When I finally feel I can speak again, my voice is low and controlled. 'Listen, Victor. I know you think I'm the woman from *Educating Rita*, but this is my life and I've done bugger all to live it so far and if I don't do it now, at thirty-five, I never will. The money's not important. So don't mock me for having that dream, eh? Just because you're too cynical to believe in dreams, it doesn't make you superior.'

'Well played,' Seb says. 'Game set and match to Miss Glow-worm, I think. So what does the loser have to say for himself?'

Victor's eyes are closed again and I can't see whether he's angry or just bored. 'So the country bumpkin has spirit. How astonishing. I'd like another coffee and a word with my friend Sebastian, please, Lucy. Get one for me? And yourself, if you like.' He produces a five-pound note from his pristine wallet and waves it at me.

I know I ought to throw it back in his face, but suddenly I'm exhausted. I do as I'm told, and as I sprinkle chocolate onto my cappuccino – well, he's paying – I understand how ill-equipped I am to enter this world. So my voice has promise? So what? I peer around the canteen at the competition. They're so bloody young, so passionate, so *tall*. There must be something in the water that's making them giants.

And even if there are roles for frumpy, short women who can't sight-read properly, how am I going to get them? I'm Lucy-wouldn't-say-boo-to-a-goose, after all. The girl who was born without any pluck. Why on earth would anyone cast me to appear in public when I have so little presence that even my husband and daughter barely notice I exist?

Ah, but there's the problem. The alternative means going backwards, back to Saxon Close to pretend that my life is full and satisfying, that I have everything I ever wanted. And I'll have lost my chance and I'll never know if I could have done more.

'Sure you've got enough there?' I hear Seb's voice close to me, and then I look down at my cup and see I've managed to coat the top of my drink – and most of the tray – in a layer of cocoa powder.

'I can't seem to get much right today, can I?'

'It's nothing to do with you. I told you he was a prize shit, didn't I? But we've got an idea.' He takes the tray from me and I follow meekly back to the table.

Vic looks at the mess on the tray but doesn't comment. Instead he clears his throat – well, I suppose he has such a horrible voice that he can't ruin it – and then says, 'Seb thinks I've gone too far. It's a habit of mine. So if I offended you, I apologize. I don't apologize for being realistic, though. If you want to try to sing professionally, you're going to have an uphill struggle with no guarantee of a pot of gold at the end of the rainbow.'

Seb chuckles. 'Shit, mate. You're terrible at being humble.'

Vic continues. 'I don't have time to gamble. But if you want to find yourself another teacher, work with them on the basics for a month, say, see how far you get, then I'll see you again. Oh, and have a specialist check out your vocal folds. If you've managed to ditch the basket-case breathing, and you can reassure me that your voice can stand up to the rigours of real training, then I will consider taking you on privately.' He takes the second double-espresso from the tray and swallows it. 'By the way, you're not a true soprano. You're more of a mezzo, I'd say. If you were a soprano you'd definitely be too ancient to have a hope. So. What do you say?'

It's only now that reality bites. There's the cost of lessons. The hopelessness of trying to get in and out of Manchester two or three times a week. The sheer impracticality of trying to be a singer and a shoe shop manageress and a mother. Not to mention a wife, if that's what I still am. It doesn't add up. I've been living in cloud cuckoo land.

So no one is more surprised than me when I put down my sickly cappuccino and say, 'I think that sounds a very good idea.'

I feel I can be more honest with Seb. 'I can't do it, of course,' I say, when we sit down in a sandwich bar near the station. 'I only said I could because I couldn't face another lecture from Vic.'

'Don't be so defeatist,' he says, picking up the menu. 'You did so well back there. I've seen him reduce people to tears, but he liked you.'

'If that's his way of showing he likes someone, then God help his enemies. And thank you. I'm just sorry that you've gone to all this trouble for nothing.'

'You can be quite annoying, can't you, Miss Glow-worm?' He's smiling as he says it. The teenage waitress approaches our table and as soon as she clocks Seb, she straightens up and licks her lips involuntarily. 'We'd like a big pot of tea for two and two cheese baguettes and two beers. OK with you, Lucy?'

It's exactly what I would have ordered for myself. 'Um. Yes. Great.'

The waitress leans over unnecessarily low to pick up a napkin on the floor, giving us both a prime view of her bottom. Seb gives me a conspiratorial wink. 'Is she after me or after you, do you think?'

'You. Definitely.'

'Too young for me. Ugh. Girls that age have nothing between their ears. And not a clue what's going on between their legs. Now, where were we? I was about to tell you how we're going to make you a star, wasn't I?'

'Look, Seb, I appreciate what you're trying to do, and I wish I could make it work, but I don't see how I can. And I'm still getting over the shock of finding out I'm a mezzo.'

He nods. 'I can see that'd be a bit of a surprise. OK then, Miss G. What's stopping you?'

'I don't see what good … All right. Well, cash for a start. I mean, lessons would cost a fortune, wouldn't they?'

'Not necessarily. Thirty quid an hour, maybe forty for some-one shit hot. But you'd only need one a week. Plus plenty of practice.'

'Well, that's the other problem. Time. I mean, it's all right for you, you're single. Your time's your own. I don't have a spare moment to myself as it is.' But as I speak, two things occur to me: that I sound thirty years older than I am, and that what I'm saying isn't even true. I'm currently living the most self-ish existence possible. 'I mean, I do at the moment, since I left my husband, but when that's resolved, I'll be back on the school run and the Brownie run and the running Andrew home from the pub run. As well as working full-time. I just don't see—'

Seb holds up his hand. 'Miss G. Listen. First, the money. Your mum left you some, didn't she?'

'Yes, it's all tied up in the house really, but it will be a fair amount.'

'There you are then. You deserve to spend some of it on yourself. When can you get your hands on it?'

'Not till I sell the house. And I haven't put it on the market yet.' Is *that* what interests him about me? My cash?

'Look, it needn't be an issue, that's all I'm saying. And the second thing ... can I be really, really cheeky?'

'You're going to be anyway, aren't you?'

'You've walked out on your husband. Isn't that about the biggest hint you've ever given yourself that your life isn't exactly one hundred per cent? That you need to do something?'

I suppose it's the stress of the day and the strangeness of someone paying me so much attention, but I feel a lump in my throat and then, in broad daylight in the centre of Manchester, the tears roll down my face. I thought I'd cracked being a stupid cry-baby.

'Oh, Miss Glow-worm, I'm sorry,' he says, taking a wad of napkins from the stainless steel dispenser on the table. I hold out my hand to take them, but instead of handing them over, he reaches across and dabs the tissue against my cheek, like a mother comforting a child.

'No, I'm always doing this. I'm like a leaky tap. Things'll get better; it's just a phase I'm going through.'

The waitress is hovering with beer and baguettes. Seb takes them and waves her away. 'I have a proposal for you, Miss G. What if *I* taught you?'

'You?'

'Don't sound so surprised. I'm insulted.' He pulls a hurt face. 'Used to sing myself. We had to do two instruments at college and that was my other one. There's lots about me you don't know; that's how I ended up sharing a flat with Vic the Prick. We were in the same group.'

'Victor was a singer, then?'

'Hard to believe he ever made a sound you'd want to listen to, isn't it? That's why he's such a bitter old bastard. Had a stunning voice, the kind of bass you'd never expect to come from a skinny teenager. People used to do a double take when he began singing, but that was the trouble; it wasn't sustainable. He was forcing his voice and by the end of the first year, the damage was showing and by the end of the second, he sounded like he does now. Poor sod. Can you imagine?'

'No.' The thought of Victor spending twelve months listening to his own voice disintegrating makes me cry harder.

'Oh, don't cry for Victor. He always had a better ear anyway. Makes a great teacher, despite his despotic tendencies, and you can't let the chance of learning from him slip away. I know how he works, how he thinks. If we met up just once a week, we'd make a difference.'

'Seb, why are you doing this?'

'Well, Dad wanted me to keep an eye on you,' he says.

'You're doing this as a favour to your dad?' I feel so stupid. Why else would a man like him take an interest in a woman like me?

'No! It was a joke! But I hadn't realized how little you thought of yourself. Truth is, Miss G, you intrigue me.'

'I can't see why anyone would find me intriguing.'

'Which is exactly what's so intriguing about you.' He passes me my beer. 'And you also asked me for help. After thirty years as a selfish bastard, that has novelty value. I'm always craving new experiences! So what do you say? You in?'

'I don't know.' I clink bottles with his. 'Victor warned me about you, you know.'

Seb opens his eyes wide. 'Good old Vic. What about if I promise not to misbehave?'

I blush. 'I didn't mean ... I'm sure you wouldn't ... oh, God.' I look at his supermodel face and I see the challenge in his eyes but also a vulnerability I hadn't noticed before. *He actually wants me to say yes.* And, of course, I've always done what other people want. 'All right. Yes, why not. What's a month?'

'Cheers,' he says, swigging beer straight from the bottle. I do the same. 'Oh and Miss G?'

'Yes?'

His face is stern. 'That'll be your last beer for the next four weeks. Alcohol and singing don't mix. OK?'

I stare at him. 'Are you serious?'

'Dead serious. Do you have a problem with that?'

I have a feeling this is going to be more demanding than I thought. But it won't do me any harm to stay off the booze for a month. 'No, boss. No problem at all.'

Chapter Twenty-nine

Are you a W.W.? Just occasionally you may
find that all the other Brownies in the Pack
want to do a Venture which does not appeal to
you. If you are really trying to be a Brownie,
you will know there is only one thing to do
– to join in. In other words be a Willing
Worker or W.W.

The kids knew something was up. Though they only exchanged monosyllables with Paula, they had a superhuman
instinct for trouble. They'd been skulking around the house for
a fortnight, trying to avoid her, but on Saturday she finally
cornered them.

'You know things haven't been easy since your dad left,' Paula
began.

'Since you went mental and chucked him out, you mean,'
Sadie snapped back. She was sprawled on the sofa next to
her brother, both with their arms crossed and their legs
stretched out in that *go ahead, make my day* position teenagers loved. They were surprisingly good-looking kids, despite
their sour faces. They'd inherited Paula's height and fair hair,
but had somehow escaped the spots she'd suffered at their
age.

Paula sighed. 'Since we agreed to a trial separation.'

'Whatever. Is this going to take long?' Sadie whined.

'It will if you keep interrupting. Charlie, are you actually
awake?'

He opened one eye. How did he *do* that? 'Yeah.' Then he shut it again.

Paula started again. 'Things haven't been easy for any of us. Your dad's paying as much as he can afford, but it's not enough. Not for all the bills, food and everything.'

'You *could* try eating less,' Sadie said.

'Well, in case you hadn't noticed, I have been,' Paula said sharply. It was true. For the first time in her life, her clothes felt baggy. If she had the money, it'd have been time to buy smaller sizes, but instead she was using one of Neil's old belts to hold her trousers up. 'But it's more serious than that.'

Charlie opened both eyes this time. 'Don't say you're going to cut our allowance.'

'Aw, Mum,' Sadie chipped in, 'I already get less than my mates. I can hardly afford a bra since my boobs have got bigger.'

'Yuck, too much information,' Charlie said.

'Oh for God's sake. This isn't about allowances or buying own-brands or cancelling the internet,' Paula said, knowing that coming off the web was the biggest sacrifice she could think of. 'We're in the shit. Deep shit. We're five months behind on the rent and I don't have the money to pay it.'

The kids sat silently for a moment, taking it in. Charlie sat up and said: 'What happens if you can't pay the rent?'

Paula couldn't look at him. 'You get evicted. If you can't find the arrears or provide them with proof that you can pay it off within six months, then that's it. They've given us notice to quit.'

Sadie's expression lost all the bravado and she looked like a little girl again. 'We're going to have to leave? But … when? Where will we go?'

'I've spoken to your father and his parents are happy about you moving in there. Only temporarily, till we work out what happens next.'

Charlie looked puzzled. 'But Granny and Granddad only have two bedrooms. How's that going to work?'

'Well, just for now, you and your dad and Granddad will share the big room, and Sadie'll be in the smaller bedroom with Granny.'

'What, share with an eighty-year-old woman?' Sadie sounded hysterical.

'She's only just turned sixty. Look, I know it's not ideal, but—'

'Hang on, though,' Charlie interrupted her. 'Where are you going to go?'

'Back with my parents,' Paula said, trying not to think about it. 'I can't move back in with your dad, can I? Not with everything that's happened.'

Sadie was silent for a second, then flew up from the sofa and launched herself at her mother. Paula held her hands up to her face to protect herself as little sulky slaps came at her from all angles, before Charlie put himself between them, grabbing his sister's wrists. 'Stop it, Sadie! Bloody stop it. This is bloody stupid.'

'No, *she's* the bloody stupid one,' Sadie shrieked, her wrists jerking as she tried to break free of his grip. 'She lost Dad, she's losing us and she can't even hang onto our bloody flat. No wonder Dad's found someone else.'

'Leave it, Sadie,' Charlie hissed, but it was too late.

'What do you mean?' Paula said, suddenly feeling as if the breath had been squeezed from her lungs.

'We don't know anything for sure, Mum,' Charlie said, letting go of his sister. They all sensed she'd just done far more harm with her words than she could with her fists.

'Well, what do you know?' she said, putting all her effort into trying to sound calm.

Sadie smiled nastily. 'He's been singing. Humming to himself. And Granny said the only time she's ever seen him do that before is when he was *in love*.' She giggled, as if the idea of her father in love was the most ludicrous thing she could imagine.

'It could be that he's feeling a bit better,' Charlie said, weakly.

Paula stood up. 'Well, do you know what? I don't blame him. I can't expect him to stay single for good.' Though, strangely, the thought of him finding someone else hadn't occurred to her, and now it made her feel faint with rejection. 'And maybe she'll be a better mother to you both than I have.'

'Mum, don't ...' Charlie said.

Sadie stared at her mother, judging her. 'I can't imagine anyone being worse. I'm going out.' And she grabbed her silver clutch bag and left the flat, slamming the door.

'She doesn't really mean it,' Charlie said. 'It's her hormones.'

Despite everything, Paula smiled. 'You've always been old beyond your years, Charlie. I make a big fat mess of everything, but you know I've never done it on purpose, don't you?' She inched forward and he let her hug him for a second before shuffling free.

'Yeah, I know, Mum. Is there anything we can do?'

Paula's shoulders slumped. 'Not much, love. Not unless we win the Lottery.'

'I'll buy a scratchcard. We deserve a bit of luck,' Charlie said, putting on his denim jacket. 'See ya later.'

Paula watched him from the window as he trudged across the quadrangle towards the park and, when he was nearly out of sight, broke into a joyful run. He'd survive. So would Sadie. And so, by the sounds of things, would Neil.

The only casualty from this mess would be herself.

Terri was drinking her sixth coffee of the day in the halls of residence kitchen when the communal payphone rang. This was unusual, now everyone owned a mobile. When she'd done her hospital training back in the eighties, the payphone in the draughty hall of the nurses' home was red hot, as dates were made and engagements broken, fuelled by a stream of 2p pieces. And when it wasn't suitors, it was Reg the heavy-breather, calling in the early hours to ask what colour knickers they were wearing.

Perverts seemed to have less interest in the underwear of theology students, but otherwise there were more similarities between Terri's life then, and her life now, than she liked to admit. The same permanently sour smell in the shared fridge. The same labelling and marking of milk and cheese and pasta that failed to deter phantom food stealers. And the same Saturday afternoon isolation, when the other students headed into town to meet friends or do part-time jobs or spend time with their families, and she stayed put, alone in the building.

She was meant to be revising, so she ignored the phone at first. It rang twenty times before the caller gave up. Exams had never worried her before: she always prepared a careful revision timetable, in forty-five-minute blocks for different subjects, and she always did fine. Not brilliantly: she was never outstandingly bright, like Chris, or eternally lucky, like Bethany, who only revised a tiny section of the syllabus but still pulled off straight As.

This time, Terri had made the usual thorough plans but they weren't working. She was restless and fidgety, constantly craving one more coffee or cigarette to help her focus. The unthinkable was suddenly possible: Teresa Rowbotham might be about to fail her exams ... and maybe kiss goodbye to ordination.

The phone rang again. Sighing, she walked into the living room. 'Sycamore Hall?'

'At bloody last. Is that Teresa?' It was the grumpy old porter. 'I knew you'd be there if anyone was. It's for you.'

She heard a couple of electronic tones as he worked out how to put the call through. She felt afraid: it could only be bad news if someone was calling her on this number. A hospital or the police or—

'Hello?' A man's voice, uncertain, with the sound of traffic in the background. 'Terri?'

'Howard?'

'Yes!' She sensed the excitement in his voice at being recognized. 'Now ... I am sorry to contact you out of the blue like this, but I felt that things ... well, um, when we were at the retreat together there was a ...' Terri heard a rustling noise near the receiver.

'Howard, are you reading this out?'

There was a pause and then he laughed nervously. 'Um. Yes. I wanted to get it right. It's so easy to get it wrong.'

'Get what wrong?'

'Like I was trying to say, I know this sounds a bit loopy, but I felt this *connection* when we met before, at Clark House. It was like, everything changed when you were there, and everything went black when you went, and I wanted ... well, I wanted to see you again.'

Terri's mind flashed back to the rocks above the sea and the sounds and the sunshine on her skin and his lips on her lips and for a moment, she felt like her legs might give way. But then she forced herself back to the present. 'That's very nice. Very flattering, Howard. I'm sure I can't understand why you'd feel that way but it's good to know I made an impression. The thing is, it's not practical to meet up, really, is it? With me in Manchester and you nearly in Scotland—'

'I'm here.'

'What?' Now she thought about it, the sounds of cars and buses and people in the background were far too urban for the one-horse town he'd described.

'I'm in Manchester. That's why I've written it all down. I didn't want you to think I was some kind of loon. Though I must admit I have never done anything this crazy before.'

Terri felt utterly confused: excited, yet cornered. She could hardly refuse to see him as he'd come all this way, yet she wasn't prepared for what she supposed was a *date*. 'Where are you?'

'Across the road from you, in the phone box next to the grocer's.' When she said nothing in reply, he added: 'I know, I know. I bet you've definitely got me marked down as a stalker now, even if you didn't before. I'm not, though. Cross my heart. Just an old romantic, like in—'

She cut in. 'Can you see Droitwich Street from where you are? It should be in front of you.'

'Yes.'

'If you turn down there, walk a hundred yards or so, on the left there's a little park. Tiny place, next to the community centre. I'll meet you there in . . .' she did some calculations, 'half an hour or so. OK?'

'That'll be smashing,' he said, sounding a bit too excited.

'This doesn't mean anything, Howard. It's only because you've come all this way. If you'd told me this was what you were planning, I wouldn't have agreed to meet you at all.'

'I know,' he said, more quietly. 'That's why I did it this way.'

'I'll see you in half an hour then.' Terri replaced the receiver and ran back to her room, trying to stop her hands shaking.

Chris took the train, rather than a taxi, to Troughton for two reasons.

One, there was no longer anything coming into her bank account. OK, so her bank balance was mid-six figures, but she couldn't ever imagine starting over. So it was as well to avoid extravagance, as her retirement was set to last fifty years.

Two, she needed to be out among *people*. For the last week, the furthest she'd gone from her flat was the newsagent's on the corner, and even then she'd deliberately gone mid-morning, when there'd be no one else in the shop as she bought milk and the *Financial Times*.

But it was time to pull herself together before her mind trapped her inside the penthouse for ever, like a twenty-first-century Rapunzel, endlessly brushing her tangled hair.

The train journey added to her sense of isolation. On Saturday afternoon, all the traffic was the other way, as Troughton folk went shopping in Manchester. When Chris boarded the train at Piccadilly, it was empty, but messy, the bins overflowing with a colourful lava of rubbish. She picked her way through the debris like an archaeologist. A bottle of Ribena surrounded by a dried moat of pink liquid, next to copy of *Chat*: maybe left by a mother and two little girls, off to buy sparkly things at the Arndale Centre.

On the next table, last week's *Private Eye*, with a photograph of Tony Blair appearing to snarl at George Bush on the cover. A dark-brown bottle with a dribble of yeasty-smelling lager at the bottom. A Pepperami wrapper. And an empty triangular carton that once held a Marks and Spencer avocado sandwich (Troughton's mayor had recently performed the grand opening of a brand new M&S Simply Food convenience store). Definitely a man, Chris thought, heading for a beery session in a sports bar with the lads.

She chose the cleanest table she could find – sixteen screwed-up Orbit foils, maybe left by a hungry teenager scared of getting fat – and sat facing backwards, so she could see Manchester for as long as possible.

Chris woke up feeling disorientated, and cross with herself.

She had no idea how long the train had been in Troughton, and no idea why she'd nodded off when she was already sleeping at least sixteen hours a day. She felt dizzy and stretched her legs out in the aisle, because her knees had locked. She'd *never* felt her age before, but this last week she'd noticed the grey hairs on the crown of her head, and the blotchy patches on her cheeks that, when she peered at them closely, turned out to be tiny networks of broken red veins. Logically, she knew they couldn't all have appeared since Eros bought the business, but the signs of physical decay seemed to match her mood. A dried-up, washed-up husk.

She crossed the footbridge over the railway track. There was the bus shelter where she'd touched a penis for the first time, and on the corner, the off-licence that had supplied the first cider she ever drank, the cause of her first ever hangover.

Being back didn't give her an indulgent tinge of nostalgia for times gone by. It made her feel ridiculous. She might as well have stayed in Troughton, taken the retail management job in Marks that ought to have been her destiny, before getting on with the real business of procreation, like Lucy.

Sex. Screwed if you did, screwed if you didn't. It was almost funny, really. Her mum's life screwed up by mistaking lust for love, and now her own screwed up by making sex her living. At least if she'd had a baby, there'd be someone to remember her when she was gone.

The curtains in the front windows of her parents' semi were closed, to shield its occupants from the fierce mid-afternoon sunlight. Home sweet home. Her sister's husband's people-carrier was in the drive. He was an actuary, calculating the odds against people living long enough to collect their pensions.

At least there'd be no shortage of conversation, although she feared it would all be about how premature deaths were making him rich.

Paula didn't really want to talk to Jack – she'd gone online to play *Lawless* because it was the only thing apart from toast that would take her mind off being in the biggest hole of her life.

But when his name flashed up, inviting her to join a conversation, it would have been rude to ignore him.

> CUTEYCRIMEFIGHTER: Hey Jack.
> SHERIFFJACK: Hey Cutes. What's the headline in your life story right now?

She normally found his eccentric turns of phrase amusing, but today she wasn't in the mood.

> CUTEYCRIMEFIGHTER: How about same shit, different day?
> SHERIFFJACK: That's not like you.

She laughed bitterly to herself. He didn't know her at all.

> CUTEYCRIMEFIGHTER: Sometimes we're not what we seem.
> SHERIFFJACK: Ooh, very mysterious. I suppose you're going to tell me you're a plump, middle-aged housewife who never budges from her computer!

For the first time in their conversations, he added a smiley ;) to show he was joking. But Paula wasn't smiling. She froze in her seat, staring at the words. What the hell was going on? Had he found some secret way of watching her over the internet?

> SHERIFFJACK: Cutey? You there?

She forced her hands across the keyboard and managed to type:

> CUTEYCRIMEFIGHTER: Yes. Sorry, got distracted.
> SHERIFFJACK: What I mean is, things could always be worse.
> CUTEYCRIMEFIGHTER: Really?
> SHERIFFJACK: Gee whiz, you do need cheering up, don't ya? Well, I got news.

Paula told herself in advance not to get jealous when he announced some million-dollar business deal, or a new woman. A real one. If even Neil could find one then Jack would have no trouble at all.

> CUTEYCRIMEFIGHTER: What news?
> SHERIFFJACK: I'm ...

She waited.

> SHERIFFJACK: Coming to England! To Manchester. So we're gonna be able to meet at long last!

Paula stared at the screen in horror. The room seemed to shrink, as though her walls were moving together on hidden runners, until they crushed all the furniture and the computer and then her.

> SHERIFFJACK: Cutey?
> CUTEYCRIMEFIGHTER: I'm here.

The walls had stopped moving now, but she could hear her blood rushing around her head, a sound like a waterfall in her ears.

> CUTEYCRIMEFIGHTER: I was just thinking ... when is this?
> SHERIFFJACK: Well, that's what I wanted to ask you. My trip dates are kinda flexible, depending on when you're gonna be free. How are you fixed up in two weeks' time?

Paula covered her eyes with her hands, then massaged her temples, as though it would somehow stimulate her brain into action.

> CUTEYCRIMEFIGHTER: Would you believe it? I don't have my diary here.
> SHERIFFJACK: OK. Maybe you can let me know soon. I have to book it all.

CUTEYCRIMEFIGHTER: Of course. But, you know, things are really busy for me lately.

She typed the last bit with her eyes half-closed, oddly convinced that this, of all the lies she'd told this poor man over the months, would be the one he'd be able to see through.

SHERIFFJACK: I'd like to meet with you, Cutes. Nothing has to happen, if that's what's bothering you.

Paula smiled bitterly at the misunderstanding. Nothing would happen anyway, if he got one look at her grotesque body. However much walking she did, she was never going to be Elle MacPherson.

CUTEYCRIMEFIGHTER: It's not that. It'll be fine. I'll come back to you with a date as soon as I can. It's lovely that you want to meet up.
SHERIFFJACK: I can't wait.
CUTEYCRIMEFIGHTER: Nor me. Listen, I have to go now.
SHERIFFJACK: Have a great day.

Have a nice life, Paula thought. She clicked out of the chatroom and took one final tour around *Lawless*, already feeling nostalgic for its virtual alleyways and invented felons. She went to the control panel, clicked on the 3D model of Cuteycrimefighter and gave her one last twirl. Then she pressed the big red button marked Liquidate.

A pop-up appeared. *Do you REALLY want to permanently delete character #101871, Cuteycrimefighter? This action cannot be undone.*

She clicked on yes and watched the screen as Cutey's blonde curls and catsuited body exploded, leaving behind a message reading *Rest in Peace*.

When SheriffJack logged in tomorrow, it would be as if Cutey had never existed. Which was, of course, true. Cruel to be kind, thought Paula: better leave him with a wistful memory than allow him to face the appalling truth.

Time to log off, and start facing up to reality.

'So how much did you make, exactly?'

Chris knew it was hopeless trying to avoid the question. Jill's husband Justin was like a terrier, licking his narrow lips as he scented money. Next to him, Jill, Mum and Dad sat around the table in the new shady conservatory. What was the point in a conservatory in a north-facing garden?

'It's a bit early to say.'

'Hasn't stopped the newspapers speculating though, eh?' he said, raising his eyebrows with a broad, bared-teeth grin. 'Go on, you can tell family.'

They were all waiting now. Jill's moustache was particularly prominent as she pulled her lips together. Mum and Dad were peering into their sherry glasses, as though this talk of money was *too* vulgar, but Chris knew they were every bit as fascinated.

'I think in the end it could be around the seven hundred mark.'

They looked disappointed. 'That's excluding your assets, though?' Jill said.

'Yes and no. The penthouse in Manchester's mine, but the Covent Garden flat was owned by the company, and then leased back to me for business use. They've given me till the end of the month to decide if I want to buy it from them.'

'Oh, you'll be wanting to keep a base down in the Smoke, surely,' Justin said. 'When the next offer comes, it's bound to be London-based.'

The next offer. Chris thought about it. 'I don't think there'll be a next offer.'

'Don't be ridiculous,' Jill said, sounding as shocked as if Chris had suggested she was planning to join a convent. 'No use crying over spilled milk. We're not quitters in this family, are we, Dad? Mum?'

Dad mumbled his agreement, and Mum looked out of the window, chewing noisily on a Shrewsbury biscuit.

'That's only because we never actually bother *thinking* about what we're doing,' Chris said quietly.

'Well, now you're being silly,' Jill snapped. 'Just because you've always been Dolly Daydreams doesn't mean we're all sheep, Chris. We just get on with things.'

Chris sighed. She didn't have the energy for this, but what else could she do? 'Oh yes. That's the Love way of doing things, isn't it? Always preserve the status quo, whatever the cost, eh, Mum?'

Her mother sighed. 'Not now, dear.'

Chris wanted to shake her, to make her admit to ever feeling anything except *fine*, *hunky-dory* or, very occasionally, *a touch under the weather*.

Her father groaned. 'Why does it always have to be a ruddy drama with you, Chris? Drawing attention to yourself. Your mother learned her lesson; why can't you?'

Justin was out of his seat, heading for the door. 'Work call to make.'

'You see?' Chris said. 'It seems normal to you but even Justin can't be in the same room when you get going.'

'There's no need for this,' Jill said. 'Mum and Dad are happy the way they are.'

'You think so?' Chris knew she couldn't win, but she'd watched them for twenty-five years and there was no way she could ever describe her parents as happy. 'Mum, are you happy?'

'I ... I'm not *unhappy*.'

'Despite the fact that Dad's devoted his life to undermining you?'

Her father's eyes narrowed and in the gloom of the room, the sharp angles of his nose and cheekbones cast long shadows across his face. 'Don't you dare blame me for the way things are, Christine. If you knew how it felt to be humiliated, to be—'

Chris shook her head. 'Oh, we all bloody know that, Dad. I heard it, what, four times a week *minimum* for nine years. And Mum's heard it for twenty-five years. For one mistake.'

'Chris ...' Her mother's hands were shaking, her voice even fainter than usual. 'I don't need anyone to fight my battles for me.'

'You heard her,' Jill said. 'You've been having a difficult time, we know that, Chris, but you're getting confused about who's to blame. Don't take it out on Dad when it's Eros you're really angry with.'

Chris opened her mouth to protest, then shut it again. God, she hated it when her sister was right. Her father was an arrogant bastard, her mother was a spineless victim, but it wasn't their fault she was feeling this way. Not directly, anyhow.

'I think I'll go now,' she said, and no one protested. She kissed her mother stiffly, avoided her father's eye, and nodded at her sister. On the way out, she found Justin standing by the double garage, smoking.

'You know those things increase the risk of dying young?'

He smiled lamely. 'I could tell you by how many percentage points.'

'No thanks. But I think it's safe to go back inside now. A few funny stories from the coalface of being an actuary could be just the thing to lighten the mood.'

By the time she boarded the train back to Manchester, Chris had remembered that there were worse fates than living alone.

Terri caught her breath when she saw him. He was leaning against the brightly painted wall of the community centre, a tall, pale figure in the midst of the primary colours of the Brazilian rainforest mural. Was he attractive? Her mind tried to make an independent assessment – he really was far too thin by any objective standard, not to mention thinning on top.

But her body told a different story. This was lust.

She stood still, hoping he wouldn't notice her across the square, so she could watch him a little longer. In any case, her legs felt weak, as though she'd just run a marathon.

This was definitely lust. And she had definitely never felt it before, not really. It had been worth waiting for.

He took a drag on his cigarette, and then looked up in her direction, but he didn't seem to see her. She could remember his mercury eyes, as reflective as a pair of skier's sunglasses. As she watched him, her whole body seemed to be softening, melting like butter left out in the sunshine.

While her limbs still felt solid enough to carry her, Terri walked across the square. He noticed her now, and smiled.

By the time she'd reached him – thirty steps, maybe less – she knew that this would be the afternoon she lost her virginity.

July 1979: A barbecue at Bruno's

The humming heat of the sun behind her curtains woke Terri up.

'Oh, fudge!'

Her parents laughed at her pseudo-swearwords, but then they laughed at most things she said and did. Not in a nasty way, Terri had to admit. Nastiness would take energy that Dave and Lorna Rowbotham simply didn't have. Alcohol did that to grown-ups: sapped their strength so that even getting up seemed a massive effort, because everything was funnier vertical. Terri wasn't laughing.

She climbed out of bed and went to the window. As she moved the curtain aside, the light made her eyes water. Sunshine was always the enemy. Her ginger gene came from her father's Scottish roots, and Terri knew enough about the world to realize that if she'd inherited her mother's light brown hair and tannable skin, life would be much easier.

There was an inevitability about the weather. Things always went Bruno's way. Terri had noticed that he seemed to attract women and luck, but she felt uncomfortable. Could anyone really stay fortunate all their life?

The level of excitement about what was believed to be Troughton's first ever barbecue had caused near-anarchy at last week's Brownie meeting. Actually, things hadn't been right in the Drill Hall for weeks, but the speculation about Bruno's party – where, it was rumoured, a whole pig would be roasted and grass skirts and bikinis were the dress code – added to the tension.

Terri's skills as Seconder were being tested to the limit. She'd only just grasped the fact that the success of the Pixies as a Six had relied entirely on Bethany reigning supreme. Since the balance of power had been disturbed by the arrival of Simonetta, the group was fracturing and it seemed there was nothing Terri could do to prevent it. Bethany and Netta – one blondely beautiful, the other as dark as she was mysterious – spent each session eyeing each other like fencers waiting to inflict a killer blow. Paula watched with open-mouthed curiosity and even Chris was feeling the strain. Meanwhile, Terri and Lucy tried in vain to smooth ruffled feathers.

On Tuesday, it'd been worse than ever. Bruno had sent embossed invitations to the families of each Pixie, presenting Bethany with an impossible dilemma. If she stuck to her contemptuous refusal to acknowledge Netta's existence, she'd miss out on pretty much the most exciting social occasion to hit Troughton in her lifetime.

Finally, after sulking for the entire meeting, she waited until Netta disappeared to the toilet, then gathered the other Pixies together in a pow-wow ring. 'I've decided that although none of us would ever go to that girl's common little party out of choice, it would seem rude not to turn up,' she pronounced, as though they'd been waiting for her official statement. 'But unless an adult is present, I don't expect any of you to talk to her. If you do . . .' she shook her head, 'well, I don't think I need to spell it out.'

'What, send her to Coventry?' Lucy gasped. 'That's cruel, Bethany.'

Bethany's blue eyes narrowed so that all they could see was the jet-black of her pupils. 'And don't you think it's more cruel that the only reason she's invited Paula and Paula's mum and dad is to show off?'

'Hang on—' Paula began, but Bethany held up her hand.

'Oh, don't say you hadn't got it, Paula? She's only friends with you because no one else wants to know her. And because it makes her feel superior because you have no money. Anyone with half a brain cell can see that.'

Paula's brow furrowed as she considered this, and when Netta returned from the toilet and whispered something in her ear, she shrugged her off.

That was all bad enough, Terri thought. She opened her rickety wardrobe, already knowing there was nothing in it she wanted to wear. But there was another reason she was dreading the barbecue.

Her parents were going, too

At ten past three – a good hour later than the invitation had specified – the Rowbotham family arrived outside the Castigliano residence. They'd walked 'because it's such a lovely sunny day', Lorna had said. They all knew that their white Cortina hadn't started since May, but she still felt the need to pretend. And at least it meant Terri didn't have to worry about her father drink-driving them all home.

She had plenty else to worry about. First, there was Bethany's likely response to her horrible outfit. The only thing in her wardrobe that actually seemed to suit her was, strangely, her Brownie uniform: at least brown didn't clash with her stupid hair. But she couldn't wear *that* so she'd tried to find something that would cover her knees – the most likely part of her to get sunburned. Hardly anything in the house was washed, and everything was second-hand and hippie-style and smelled of damp or incense or animals. There weren't even any pets in the house – Lorna objected to them on the principle that no living thing should be owned, and Dave had enough sense to know that he was barely able to look after himself, never mind a furry creature.

In the end Terri chose a cotton dress, so at least she could sprinkle it with water and hang it out on the washing line to air. But it was still highly embarrassing: a pinafore dress from Clothkits, a mail order company that specialized in brightly coloured, overly patterned frocks that mums loved and kids loathed with equal passion. Its unique selling point – apart from the garishness of its designs – was the fact that each item came in kit form, printed on a single sheet of right-on unbleached cotton, ready to be 'hand made' by seventies earth mothers.

But Terri's yellow-and-blue pinafore dress was more embarrassing. It was *second-hand*. Someone else's mother had sewn it badly and someone else's daughter had disliked it enough to stand up for herself and insist on its disposal in a charity shop. Where Lorna, attracted perhaps by the familiar musty smell that reminded her of home, had picked it up and decided it was roughly the right size for Terri. And it was, if you ignored the way the fabric under her arms was so tight that it rubbed her skin raw.

'I can't believe he's rented this place,' Lorna said, taking the invitation out of her tie-dye handbag. Although her clothes were at least ten years out of date, she did look beautiful, Terri thought: a flowing kaftan the colour of lemon Spangles that emphasized her sleek, tanned legs. Plus huge Sophia Loren sunglasses holding back the waves of fine fair hair. 'The Terrace. Yep, this is definitely it.'

Dave whistled. 'Hey, now that's what I call an entrance.' He'd made a special effort, too: trimmed his moustache (though it still glowed red in the sun) and teamed his one decent pair of brown cords with a toffee-coloured lumberjack shirt.

Bruno's house had huge black wrought-iron gates, set into high walls made from angry orange brick. Through the metal curls, Terri could only see thorny rosebushes. But she could hear Blondie's 'Sunday Girl' in the distance.

Dave fiddled with the gates but they wouldn't budge. He looked helplessly at his wife, the expression he adopted at least once a day, whenever something was beyond his comprehension. Then, just when Terri was hoping the gates would stay shut and they could all head home, there was a squeak as two metal pins rose from the ground as if by magic, allowing the gates to swing gently backwards.

'Blimey,' Dave said, shaking his head. 'And I never even said Open Sesame.'

They followed the path past the rosebushes, then along a gravel driveway that curved up towards the house, a three-storey building as sharp-edged as the bricks from which it was made. Next to the neighbouring houses, with their worn-away faces, it looked like an impostor from a child's Lego kit: too garish to belong in Troughton, but definitely designed to impress.

'I think it's ugly,' Lorna said. 'Whoever built it was a big, fat show-off.' Then she giggled and Terri blushed. She loathed it when her mum acted like a little girl.

She closed her eyes briefly, wishing she could be anywhere but here, but the sounds and smells of The Terrace were too intriguing to allow her to stay miserable for long. There was splashing from a paddling pool, and squealing and chatter, and a smell of burning that wasn't unpleasant. Actually, it was making her mouth water. She opened her eyes again and followed her nose around to the side of the house.

'Ter-ezza!' Bruno's voice carried above the hubbub, his unique pronunciation of her name making her feel momentarily like an exotic creature. He was standing behind two stacks of more orange bricks, which were bridged by a metal grille topped with indistinguishable slabs of meat. 'And Lorna and Da-veed ... welcome to our house!'

Terri couldn't help staring at Bruno – he was so different from the other men: the blue and white striped butcher's apron he wore over a plain white T-shirt with fresh sweat marks under the arms; the tiny bottle of beer he held in one hand; and the tongs he wielded so expertly with the other.

She deliberately moved away: there was more to see in the garden.

For a start, the splashing hadn't come from a paddling pool, but from a *swimming* pool. A proper, sunken-into-the-ground affair lined in turquoise plastic, with a silver step-ladder at either end, it was currently full of Brownies. True, it was so small that it only took Bethany, Paula, Lucy and Chris to fill it, but even so ... *no one* in Troughton had a pool, not even Bethany, though she was looking gracious under the circumstances, sitting on the step slightly above the others to show off her stringy yellow bikini, sipping Coca-Cola from a real glass bottle through a bendy straw.

Around the pool, parents were clustered together, trying desperately to look as if this was the way they spent every Saturday afternoon. Chris's dad – legs white and studded with blue knotty veins below his brown hiking shorts – was in conversation with Bethany's father, who didn't attempt to hide his boredom, kicking against the tiles with his sandaled foot. Paula's parents were sitting together on the edge of a sun lounger, holding hands and shooting each other nervous smiles, as though they were afraid someone would notice they were too common to be there, and throw them out.

Chris's mother stood next to Lucy's, both downwind of Bruno. Their eyes were pink from the smoke and they looked like two stoical British wives posted to Africa, Judith in her practical khaki shorts and faded yellow T-shirt, Dina in a pink tea-dress. But despite the smoke, they both gazed in the same direction, at Bruno. The king of all he surveyed.

'Hey, come over. I will give you burgers and beer!'

They trotted towards him, the charcoal catching in the back of their throats as they approached the grill. Judith waved at Terri through the fug.

'So this is a barbecue then?' Dave asked, after a pause.

'Yes. I am making hamburger in the best American style. Well, my wife, she prepared it for me. But the barbecuing, you know, Dav-eed, it is the man's job. Like cavemen.'

Lorna frowned at the meat patties. 'I'm vegetarian. And so's Dave.'

'Yes,' Dave mumbled sadly. 'Well, I'm doing a trial run. For my health. What are the green bits?'

'Ah, they have also a little Italian in them, these burgers. Fresh basil leaves. We have grown them ourselves.'

Lorna still looked sceptical. 'I need a drink.'

And off she went, with the drunk's innate ability to locate alcohol at a hundred paces, towards a trestle table loaded with wine – unrecognizable bottles with dusty labels and Italian names (all unopened) alongside empty brown ones that once held Black Tower – plus Vimto, Tizer, Carling and Strongbow. On the floor was a keg with its own little tap, dribbling a thin stream of beer that ran off into the pool.

Lorna picked up a plastic cup, filled it with lemonade and then looked around her before sneaking a tiny bottle out of her bag. Vodka. Terri sighed.

'You OK, Ter-ezza? You not a vegetarian?' Bruno poked at a burger with his tongs. It was ragged round the edges and among the browned meat she could see shiny slivers of onion. Her mouth was watering uncontrollably now.

'No, not me,' she said, and he tucked his beer bottle under his armpit while he reached across for a crusty roll, split it with the tongs and then flipped the burger into it. He passed it over and as Terri bit into it, her gums burned but the flavour was worth it. Lorna's idea of home cooking was beans on toast and she managed to serve *them* below room temperature.

'And for you, Dav-eed, I have something special.' Bruno stooped down below the barbecue. He reappeared with another small bottle of beer, which he dashed against the bricks, sending the bottle-top shooting into the air. 'Peroni beer. I have it flown over from Italy. I save it for my friends who appreciate the good things in life.' He winked at Dave, who licked his lips.

Terri concentrated on her burger. God knows, her father needed no encouragement to drink beer. Once he'd even bought a reduced-price home bitter kit from Boots. When it exploded all over the kitchen, he'd actually mopped it up and poured it into bottles ready to drink. 'No use crying over spilled beer,' he'd said, proud of his joke.

'Terri!' Lucy was calling from the pool and, relieved to have an excuse to get away from the grown-ups, Terri walked towards the pool-bound Pixies.

'I didn't bring a bikini,' Terri said. Actually she didn't have one, only a black school one-piece that always smelled of chlorine and damp and would have been quite wrong for a day in the sun. And anyway, she'd never have let people – well, Bethany – see how her freckles covered her body like a rusty rash.

'Did your mother make that dress?' Bethany asked, her voice conveying her disapproval.

Terri winced. She hated lying, but the alternative – to admit that *someone else's* had made it – was worse. 'Mmm.' There, that wasn't quite a lie.

'I love the colour,' Lucy said. She was wearing a pink gingham swimsuit and a matching hair band. 'Like sunshine.'

'Thanks.' Terri smiled gratefully, then looked around. 'Where's Simonetta?'

Paula frowned. 'In the kitchen. Her mum's upset about something.' She kicked the water sulkily.

'She thinks she's too good to spend time with us, you mean,' Bethany said. 'Just because she's got a swimming pool. Well, it's not really a swimming pool. You couldn't even manage doggy paddle in here.'

'I think it's nice,' Chris said dreamily, looking up from the patterns she was making with her feet in the water.

'Oh, there's Netta.' Lucy pointed towards the house.

She was carrying two large Pyrex bowls, one full of salad, the other full of what looked like brown trifle. She wore a fitted black cotton dress that made her look older, and a scowl that did the same. Her carbon-copy little sister trailed behind her, clutching a long loaf of bread firmly to her chest, as though it was a teddy bear. When she put it down on the table, a ghost of flour clung to her clothes.

'I'm going to say hello,' Terri said, desperate now to get away from the pool.

Paula pushed herself out of the water by her skinny arms, revealing that she was wearing a vest and gym knickers. 'I'm coming too.'

'I bet Bethany had something to say about *your* outfit,' Terri whispered, as Paula dried her legs off with a towel.

'I don't care.' Paula shrugged. 'Mum's really cross with me for growing so quickly. She only bought me a new costume five months ago.'

Terri nodded. 'You know, I don't think Bethany's right about Netta being a snob. What she said about showing off to you because you don't have much money. I don't think that's true.' Terri wasn't sure if she'd spoken out of turn, but of all her qualities, her determination to see justice done was the strongest.

Paula looked at her as she pulled on her shorts, the water from her knickers instantly soaking through. 'Bethany's the snobby one. Netta's the nicest person, Terri, when you get to know her. Maybe she seems a bit unfriendly to begin with, but she's really funny. She showed me her tropical fish today and said I could have some guppies next time they have babies. She's not like anyone else I've ever met.'

She forced her feet into a pair of flip-flops a size too small, then flip-flopped across the tiles with Terri. They reached Netta just as her mother emerged from the house: she was English, bony where Bruno was well padded, pale where he was dark. But now her face was mottled with emotion as she hissed something in her husband's ear. He attempted to put his arm around her waist, but she jumped away as though she'd been burned. She said something else to him, and this time Bruno raised his eyebrows at Dave, handed him the tongs with a regretful look, and followed his wife into the house. Netta stared after her parents, apparently trying to work out whether to follow them.

'Is your mum not feeling very well?' Paula asked, touching her friend lightly on the arm.

Netta turned sharply. 'They are like this all the time. I don't think they have ever loved each other.'

Terri looked at her feet, embarrassed. She'd never considered whether her parents loved each other: it was something she'd always assumed was true, because otherwise why would they have married in the first place?

Paula said: 'Everyone's parents fall out sometimes, Netta. It doesn't mean they're going to get divorced or anything.'

'Oh, they'll never get divorced,' Netta said. 'They need each other. Carlotta, come here!'

Her sister was walking around the side of the house. Netta followed her, and so did Terri and Paula, unsure what to say next, but both somehow not wanting to leave her alone. As they approached the back door, they heard Bruno's voice.

'You're jumping to conclusions, like you always bloody do.'

It was weird, because his accent sounded different – more Cockney than Italian now – but then Terri thought perhaps it was just because he was angry. She felt embarrassed to hear their argument, and turned to go. Carlotta was dodging away from Netta, running around so that her sister couldn't catch hold of her.

'Oh, that's right, Brian.' It sounded like Brian to Terri, anyway, though she must have misheard. 'Deny it often enough and I'll believe you, is that it? You forget. They believe you because they don't know what you're like … but I do. That's the bloody crucial difference between me and every other woman here.'

'I think we should leave,' Terri whispered to Paula, who was frozen to the spot.

'No, the difference between you and every other woman, Maggie, is that you're a fucking bitch.'

Carlotta stopped running and Netta grabbed her, pushing her away from the house. When Terri dared to look at her face, Netta's eyes were black with rage. She was starting to understand more than she wanted to about the life of the newest Pixie.

Avoiding Bruno was hard work. Over the last two hours, he seemed to be everywhere Terri looked: laughing with Bethany's dad, topping up Lorna and Dave's drinks (as if they really needed it), flirting with Dina, turning up the radio when 'We Are Family' came on, and chasing the kids around. He even cornered Judith for ten whole minutes.

Terri didn't know why she hadn't seen it before. He was a creep. Anyone who was nice as pie to near strangers, but could speak to his own wife like that, was obviously a bit crazy. And no wonder Netta was so distant sometimes, if she had to listen to carrying on like that. Lorna and Dave weren't perfect but they never raised their voices.

Netta's mum hadn't come back out of the house, but the grown-ups seemed too drunk to notice. Lorna was still upright, but Terri could already see the slight droop in her mother's eyelids, and navy kohl around her eyes was beginning to travel down her cheeks.

'Penny for your thoughts?' Judith sat down next to Terri on the sun lounger. She wasn't glamorous like Lorna, but she looked more like a proper mummy, with only a hint of rose-pink lipstick, and she smelled like a mummy too, with peppermints instead of alcohol on her breath.

'Nothing, really,' Terri lied. She wondered how long she'd been sitting there on her own.

Judith frowned at her. 'I'm not sure I believe you, Teresa. You look very glum. Are you sure nothing's wrong?'

Terri traced the chocolate-brown flowery fabric on the lounger cushion with her finger. Should she tell her about Bruno and what she'd heard? Maybe Judith would be able to warn the other adults that something wasn't right. Yet what she'd heard seemed so insubstantial compared to the other evidence: Bruno's smiles and generosity and wealth.

'Do you like Bruno?' Terri said eventually.

'Like him?' Judith spoke slowly. 'What on earth do you mean?'

'Well, do you think he's nice? A nice person?' Terri shouldn't have asked, she realized now, but she couldn't go back.

'Nice is one of those words, Teresa, that doesn't say anything about anyone except the person who says it. I think Bruno is …' she peered at him, on the other side of the pool, talking animatedly to Paula's parents, 'an entertainer. Someone who has, I don't know, a passion for life that's rare. Especially in Troughton. He's not sensible like you and me, but that makes him interesting. I've only ever met one or two people like that before, and that makes him good to be around.'

'Oh.' Terri couldn't think of anything else to say.

Judith smiled. 'And you don't like him, do you?'

'I …' She felt silly now and there was nothing to do but tell the truth. 'I don't know. I did like him, but then I saw him be cross with Netta's mum and I think that's bad.'

Judith looked away. 'Cross isn't good, that's true. But one of the things about being a grown-up is realizing that what you see is only a tiny fraction of what's *really* happening. And you become less keen on judging people.'

'But …' Terri felt like telling Judith that he wasn't just cross, he was cruel. But she sensed already that it was pointless; no one was going to listen. 'I suppose there are things I won't understand till I'm older,' she said contritely, thinking, *like the fact that Bruno seems as rich as Freddie Laker, though he doesn't seem to do anything for a living and Simonetta has to wear a second-hand uniform.*

Judith smiled at her, but seemed distracted. 'You're already pretty mature for a nine-year-old, Teresa. But men stay a mystery to most of us, even when we're grown women. You know for all their bra-burning, the women's libbers are wrong when they say we're the same as men.'

Terri blushed, terrified that Judith was about to give her a talk about the birds and the bees.

'Oh, it's not the physical stuff you need to worry about. It's their minds. They call us the weaker sex, you know, Teresa, but it's a smokescreen. Women have the endurance ... you know what that means?' Her voice sounded very serious now, very urgent.

'Like men climbing mountains or surviving for days when they fall down cliffs.'

Judith nodded. 'Well, yes, that's part of it. But think what you need to survive. Up here!' And she tapped the side of her head. 'Gumption. Strength. Men think they have it, Teresa. But very few of them do. It's as well to know that now, rather than be disappointed later.'

Terri looked at the ground. It wasn't making much sense to her.

Then, suddenly, Judith laughed. 'Oh dear me, what am I on about? Take no notice of your silly Brown Owl, Teresa. Too much sun. Just don't be in a hurry to grow up, eh? It gets complicated soon enough. Shall we go and find out what they're up to?' She gestured over to where Bruno was now chinking his beer aggressively against Patsy's and Nigel's glasses, like a comedy German in a beer tent.

'What are you celebrating?' Judith asked as Bruno gave Patsy a big kiss on the lips, and tried to do the same to Nigel, who ducked away just in time.

'The most wonderful possible news!' Bruno grinned so broadly that all the lines on his face joined up. And his voice was pure passionate Italian again. 'Just as the Pixies are together, we parents will be together.'

The other adults were circling now: Terri heard Chris's father whisper to her own, 'Oh Lord, you don't suppose he means wife-swapping, do you? Even if the spirit was willing, my back's too weak.'

But Bruno, knowing he now had their full attention, put them right: 'Myself and the wonderful Nigel and the beautiful Patsy ... we are to be a team. They are joining me in my latest business venture.' He paused to allow the news to sink in. Bethany's father had a puzzled smile on his face, while Chris's mum was frowning. And Chris's dad looked relieved.

'Well, I never,' said Judith, breaking the silence. 'Who'd have thought it?'

'Definitely not me,' Dina said sourly. 'I'm surprised he didn't say anything.'

'In the habit of talking business to our local Italian stallion then, are you, Dina?' Trevor Kendal asked, smiling as her skin turned pink. Terri thought that for a moment, she almost looked young. Then the blush faded and she looked as wrinkly as ever. It must be awful for Chris to have past-it parents.

Bruno seemed irritated by the lack of spontaneous celebration of his announcement. He put down his little bottle of beer, and opened up his arms. 'But this calls for more than beer. This calls for ...'

He sprinted back towards the house. Dave leaned over towards Trevor. 'What line of business is he in, exactly?'

Trevor grinned again: it was easy to see where Bethany got her smug smile from. 'This and that, was what he told me when he was trying to persuade me to invest.'

'He wanted you to come in with him too?' Dave said.

'Yup.'

'And?'

'Not a chance. I would never invest in "this and that". I think, from what he was saying, it's some kind of timeshare operation.'

Dave looked puzzled. 'Timeshare? What's that?'

Trevor laughed. 'It's for mugs. You sort of buy property on the continent, but you don't really buy it at all. You're only entitled to a couple of weeks' holiday there, which sounds like all you need, but then they end up being in bloody January when it's as cold as it is here.'

Dave shook his head. 'Makes my brain hurt. But I suppose Nigel knows what he's doing ...'

Trevor cackled like a witch. 'You think so? Invest in Italy? Even if the flats exist, they're probably next door to some Mafia boss. Hasn't Nigel seen *The Godfather*?'

Dave shrugged. 'Well, Bruno seems to be doing OK out of it. Talk of the devil.'

Bruno had reappeared, his hands behind his back. 'Oh yes. Time for celebrations. And the only way to celebrate, you know, is with a little ...' He brought his arms round the front of his body to show he was carrying two bottles in each hand. 'Feez!'

'Blimey,' Dave said. 'Champagne. Now that's better.'

Trevor sniffed. 'Pomagne, actually. I suppose it's the thought that counts. But I'm sticking with bitter.'

He turned suddenly and his eyes met Terri's. 'You all right, Freckles?'

'Yes. Fine thank you, Mr Kendal. Just thinking how clever Simonetta's daddy must be.'

They both looked across at Bruno at the same moment, then back at each other. Trevor winked at her. 'Not much gets past you, does it, Freckles?'

And then he walked past her to fetch another drink, leaving Terri feeling that there was at least one grown-up in the world who wasn't fooled by the Italian stallion.

Chapter Thirty

Singing strengthens the lungs, helps us to
march, and cheers us. It should not be loud.
Low, soft singing is the pleasantest, with the
time well marked by the tambourines.

I don't know how he talked me into it.

Well, actually, he didn't. It was more of a fait accompli. I
suspect it's always like that with Seb.

'I've borrowed an electronic organ from a mate, as you don't
have a piano,' Seb said when he phoned me the day after the
audition. I was actually holding my mobile, steeling myself to
call and tell him I'd changed my mind. 'When's your day off
next week?'

'It's Friday ... but, the thing is—'

'Excellent, I can drop it off and we can have our first singing
lesson at the same time.'

'Seb, I don't think—'

'Rubbish, Miss Glow-worm, it's no trouble. Did I tell you
I'd bought a motorbike? It was that or put down a deposit on
some poky flat, so there was no contest. And you'll never get
the organ back on the train, so all I have to do is strap it to the
back of the bike and Bob's your bloody uncle.'

'I ...' But I knew there was nothing I could say. 'The house
is a bit of a tip,' I said, finally.

'Do I strike you as the kind of guy who gets uptight over
dust? How does ten thirty sound?'

For the last seven days I have been wondering precisely what kind of guy he is. The kind Vic the Prick thinks he is: a walking libido, with a secret perverted fondness for shy housewives? A conman after a share of my mother's money and coming to see me to case the joint? Or a male tart with a heart?

None of the explanations add up, but then nothing in my life does these days.

When he finally rings the door bell, I feel a week's worth of tension in my body as I make the short journey from kitchen table to front door. He's so tall he has to stoop under the porch: behind him, heavy rain is blurring the world, bringing his features into sharper focus.

'Hey, Miss Glow-worm. What a house!' He bends again to enter the hall, almost too tall for the Victorian doorway. 'And what do you think of my organ? Impressive, eh?' He's holding it close to his body, the motorcycle helmet jammed onto the end. He winks at me and I actually flinch.

'It's ... a whopper,' I say, meaning it as a joke, but there's an awkward pause.

'So where are we going to do this then?' he says, rescuing me from my embarrassment. I wait while he unpeels the wet, skin-hugging waterproofs – I have to look away because it feels too intimate to watch – and lead him into the living room.

'I thought we could prop the organ on the sofa and I could stand by the mantelpiece and then you could be here, but if it's no good then—'

He holds up his hand, the skin on his palm a surprisingly pale pink. 'Slow down. You seem more nervous than you did with Vic the Prick. I reckon we should start with some breathing.'

He puts the organ and helmet down, then touches my elbow lightly, to move me into position opposite him. The clothes I'd chosen today to make me feel relaxed – a fleece and a T-shirt and stretchy leggings – now seem unnecessarily slouchy, disrespectful almost. His jeans are baggy but I can tell it's the latest kind of bagginess, just as the shirt he's wearing is this season's green and his trainers have been painstakingly scuffed in all the right places.

Seb begins an exaggerated form of breathing. 'Try to keep

pace with me; I've got bigger lung capacity so you might find it tricky at first, though I noticed early on that you've got a good pair of lungs, Lucy.' Then once we're in sync he reaches out to take my hand and places it just below his ribcage. 'I know you think you know all about the diaphragmatic technique, but it's always as well to be reminded. You have to train it every day. Every breath you take. Make it second nature ... can you feel the expansion and contraction as I breathe?'

'Hmm.' I have an urge to giggle, as I stand with my hand on a strange man's belly, in the living room where my Grampa Quentin's idea of outrageous was watching Pan's People. I can feel the movement of Seb's ribs, but more than that I can feel the warmth through the cotton shirt and even the slight breeze from his breath through my fringe.

He steps back, suddenly. 'Right, time to get singing I think.' He sets the organ up, plugging it into the old-fashioned socket in the wall: Mum had planned to get the house rewired this year. He plays simple scales, writing down the note combinations for me so I can repeat them later, on my own, and I work hard, concentrating on the sound, but my voice seems tense and forced.

He sits down on the sofa, closes his eyes for a moment. I'm convinced he's about to tell me he's changed his mind, that my performance in front of Victor was a fluke.

'What music do you love, Miss Glow-worm?'

I think about it, wondering if it's a trick question. 'Well, Mozart, obviously. Verdi. Bizet. If I'm in the right mood, I'll even enjoy Wagner, not to sing but to listen—'

'I don't mean classics. What do you love to sing for fun? Who do you listen to to relax?'

I'm flustered. 'I don't know. I rarely get any time alone so when I do it's always opera.'

'Need a change from your husband's middle-of-the-road tastes, I guess.'

I stare at him. Why is it always OK for you to slag off your nearest and dearest – but the moment someone else does, it infuriates you?

'Sorry. Below the belt,' he says. 'But there must be someone, a singer whose voice you love, whatever they're singing?'

'Dusty Springfield?' I say, as if I'm asking permission.

'Yes, OK. She's got a hell of a range.' He bounces across to the stereo, and begins rifling through the racks of LPs. 'So what's the betting there's one here ... blimey, Nana Mouskouri *and* Maria Callas ... and Leo Sayer. Eclectic doesn't cover it.'

'The Leo Sayer is mine,' I admit. 'I'm allowed youthful mistakes, surely?'

'It's the adult mistakes you need to worry about,' he says. His back's to me but he sounds surprisingly serious. 'Aha! I knew it.'

He takes out an album, sliding the record out of its sleeve. Then he runs the back of his hand across the vinyl to remove any dust before slipping it onto the turntable, moving the needle across to the first track. Everything he does seems effortless yet purposeful.

Through the speakers, Dusty's voice emerges: effortless yet purposeful, expressing so much in every note and word ... 'The Look of Love' ... I'd forgotten how good she was.

Seb turns down the volume. 'You know the words, don't you? Sing like she does.'

I hesitate, waiting for the refrain again. I remember seeing a documentary about Dusty, all the losses and denials of who she really was, just because she happened to love women more than men. I open my mouth and try to express sorrow and self-control.

The song finishes and I look up at Seb. He's moved a little closer to me now and says, softly, 'The next one – sing it as if you mean it.'

'But what if I don't remember the words?' I say, then the opening chords whisper through the speakers and I nod. *You don't have to say you love me ...*

This song never fails to make me cry as she offers her dignity in return for love.

I felt like that, once, for Andrew. But did I *really* love him? As I sing the words, I struggle to remember. I was that woman, that helpless creature, unable to insist on anything for fear of upsetting people. And now, as I sing the lyrics, I feel a new strength behind the words.

And then behind me, Seb places his hands gently around my sides. 'You're like the hunchback of Notre Dame; those shoulders are up around your neck. Lower them. Good, good ... but don't forget the breathing now.' As he says it, I'm fighting momentarily to catch my breath and he loosens his hands so that it takes deeper breaths for me to feel them on my ribs again. The song's crucial key change happens and my voice follows it, resilient and flexible, singing words of weakness but knowing I've moved beyond that.

I whisper the last phrase, the music fades and Seb moves away slowly, removing the needle from the record and switching off the stereo; there is a light thud through the speakers as the power shuts down.

'How did that feel?' he asks.

'Wonderful,' I say. 'Almost like letting go. I can't explain it.' I realize with a jolt that I'm crying again but these are different tears from the ones I'm used to. Tears of release.

'Oh, Miss Glow-worm,' he says, pacing back towards me. 'I'm making a habit of upsetting you, but you know, sometimes when you find your real voice, it can be emotional.'

My real voice. 'I know. But bloody hell it feels good.'

He smiles at me, a confident grin that makes me feel shy in its full beam. 'Atta girl, Glow-worm. We'll show Vic the Prick, eh?'

The tears are gone as quickly as they arrived and we get down to proper work. For the rest of the hour I swear I can still feel tingling where his fingers rested on my ribs.

House Orderly

Help at home in the following ways and be ready to show or tell the tester what you have done or can do. The tester will ask you to do two things at the test.

1. Clean two of the following:
    Window; basin; cupboard; brass; silver.

2. Tidy and dust your bedroom.

3. Wash your socks.

4. Make your own bed for a week.

5. Lay the table for dinner and wash up the dishes and cooking utensils.

6. Be able to do one of the following:
    a) use a vacuum cleaner
    b) defrost a refrigerator
    c) use a washing machine
    d) use an electric iron.

Chapter Thirty-one

*Every Guide is as much a 'hussif' as she is a
girl. She is sure to have to keep house some
day and whatever house she finds herself in,
it is certain that that place is the better for
her being there.*

Flaming July and it's still raining.

It's three hours since Seb revved off into the clouds, leaving me the organ and a list of daily exercises. I feel restless, itching to get out, but the rain's too heavy. Through the window, I see people and traffic moving more slowly.

Normally I like the rain. The smell, the coolness, the way it washes away the dirt. But tonight I'm meant to be having the Pixies round for supper on the lawn, and as the garden is more like a swamp, that's out of the question.

When I rang them to suggest it last weekend, the sunshine felt like it would last for ever. Then the weather broke last night and downpours have been blanketing Cheshire ever since.

I call Terri. 'I think I should cancel; there's no way we can eat outside in this. And indoors isn't an option either – you've seen the state the place is in.'

'It'll be fine, Luce.' she says. 'Chill out.'

I nearly drop my mobile. I've never heard Terri say 'chill out' before. And she is sounding very chipper. 'Are you up to something?'

'No,' she says, but now her voice is bubbling with unfamiliar lightness. For a fraction of a second, I feel almost irritated on Mum's behalf: is Terri *over* it by now? Surely it should take longer than that. 'Listen, why don't we help out? Many hands make light work. And we all passed our house orderly badges.'

'It's a big job, Terri. Probably beyond the four of us.'

'Rubbish. If you keep us fuelled with wine, we'll make a huge dent in the mess. And I'm staying over anyway so I can keep going all night! Can't wait to see you; there's so much to catch up on.'

As I hang up, unsure what exactly Terri might have to catch up on, I wonder how the others will feel about being roped into an evening of desperate housework. I check the wine situation – four bottles should be enough for all of us, especially as I'm not drinking. And it's a relief to think that someone other than me is going to be able to assess this stuff independently, as it's the only way the house is ever going to be cleared.

I still don't know whether to sell the Old Surgery. It's been my sanctuary for a whole month now – even though I only intended to stay a week – and somehow we're all managing to ignore the fact that the longer I stay away from home, the harder it becomes to imagine life ever being the same. Andrew and I spoke this morning as part of our regular catch up and it went something like this:

Me: How are you?

Andrew: Fine.

Me: Sasha's looking forward to seeing you. Glenda's still OK to pick her up from school tonight then? And you'll drop her off again on Sunday evening?

Andrew: Yes. That's fine.

Long pause.

Me: I promise I'm going to have my head sorted soon. I know I'm being crap.

Another pause and for a moment I thought I'd been cut off.

Andrew: I'll see you on Sunday then. (Hangs up.)

It'd be easier if he'd rant and rave, but there's nothing in his voice at all; he's managed to remove any hint of anger or hurt or whatever else he might be feeling.

Sasha seems to be taking the whole thing brilliantly well, setting us an example with her maturity. She hasn't cried once, not in front of me, anyway, and she maintains a cool silence whenever I explain the arrangements. I never drive her to Saxon Close. Perhaps it's because I fear that once I go back, I might never be able to pluck up the courage to leave again.

I think, oddly enough, that the Brownies might be helping Sasha. They're certainly a lot more touchy-feely these days. Last week she showed me her glittery work-books, and told me that her Sixer Daniella had talked to her about how she was feeling, because Brown Owl had said Sasha might need someone to talk to.

'And Daniella said this exercise was normally for older Brownies but that as I am very grown-up for a seven-year-old, I could try it out,' Sasha said, passing over the book.

I looked at the exercise, which was called 'How do I feel?' and had little face-shaped circles labelled Monday to Sunday, where Sasha was supposed to draw smiles or frowns depending on how she felt each day. Then she should discuss what made her happy or sad with a leader, and think about how to cheer herself up. The spaces were blank. 'You haven't done it yet,' I said, feeling almost relieved. I don't know what I'd have done if she'd drawn tears down each cartoon face.

'Oh, *I* don't want to do it, Mummy,' she replied, slightly impatient. 'But I remembered what you'd said about being miserable since Granny died and I thought it might help you be happier.'

She allowed me to hug her for a full five seconds after that.

Yes, I really would think that she was coping if it wasn't for the way she was with Buster. At home, she hardly registered his presence unless he was sleeping on a chair when she wanted to sit down, or occasionally when he chased shadows or phantoms we couldn't see, leaping into the air and making her giggle.

Now he's her best friend. When she's here at the Old Surgery, she stalks him into a corner and forces him to submit to cuddles and whispered confidences. I try to hear what she's saying, but if I approach, she goes quiet. And every time that happens, the guilt multiplies. None of this is her fault. It's no one's fault but mine.

I've set myself a deadline now, otherwise my procrastination will last for ever – my audition with Vic will be a few days before Sasha's end of term. If I haven't worked out what to do with my life by then, I *will* go home. Two weeks and four days to find an answer, or I'll accept my lot. I know it's not a bad one. I have more than most people and should be grateful. And yet …

And yet then there's Seb and what he has, what I might have had, being something more than a mother and a wife. If I hadn't gone looking for my father, then I'd still be in Saxon Close, with a vague restless twinge that cropped up now and again, too weak to threaten the status quo. There *must* be a reason for this.

I walk upstairs to my mother's bedroom for a better view of the clouds. The door's been shut since I moved back into the Old Surgery so when I step into the room, it smells musty. The sash window squeals and rattles as I open it and rain splashes onto my face. On her bedside table, I see a bottle of her favourite perfume. *Rive Gauche*. Its striped blue, black and silver packaging always looked so sophisticated to me. Mum had explained how it was named after the trendy Left Bank in Paris, and the scent had always seemed too potent, too decadent for the mum I knew, with her small-town Brown Owl respectability.

Only now, with Sunny's hints about 'Judy's *joie de vivre*', does it make sense. I press down on the nozzle, which sticks at first, because it hasn't been used in months, and then perfume gushes out, liquid dripping down my wrists and, milliseconds later, particles of *that smell* surge through my nostrils to the bit of my brain that is programmed to respond. Images of my mother heading out to church each week in hat and gloves and perfume, or, less frequently, to a church social or fundraiser, a surprising slick of colour highlighting her lips and making her look beautiful to my little girl eyes.

But the images are followed rapidly by emotions: sadness, regret, yes, but anger too. Anger because my mother left before my questions could be answered. Or, to be more accurate, before I even knew I had any questions to ask.

'You *shouldn't* have gone,' I shout. 'I wasn't ready.' I walk across to her enormous dark oak wardrobe.

I rifle through the clothes before I find it. My father's jacket.

Worn toffee-coloured suede that feels velvety against my face. It smells of dry-cleaning fluid. In the pocket, I find a receipt. It was cleaned in March, just a month before she died. She was trying to put her house in order. But she forgot the important stuff: telling me the loose ends of her own story . . .

How did *she* feel, trading the city lights and city life for Troughton? Judith the Brown Owl belonged here, of course, bustling round suburbia with a sense of purpose and a 'stiff upper lip' in the face of grief. But what about *Judy*, the Cinderella from that photograph who lost her Prince Charming before the Happy Ever After? Judy, the urban party girl who fell for the Peter Pan of the children's ward, and who was left behind, like Wendy, when my father embarked on the adventure of dying, with only a daughter and a suede jacket to remind her? Judy who tried so hard to give her daughter wider horizons, only to see her take refuge from life and risk, in the safest of marriages.

For the first time, I can actually believe that Mum might have understood why I've left Andrew.

'Oh, God.' I wait for the tears, but to my surprise, they don't come. Instead I feel different. Lighter.

I can't let my own daughter be in the dark about who *her* mother is. And to be able to tell her, I suppose I need to find out myself first.

I'm upstairs, filling a bin bag with Mum's clothes when I hear banging at the door.

'Bloody hell, duck,' Paula says, huffing her way into the dark lobby. 'I've been knocking for ages.'

'Sorry, I've been working upstairs.' I feel irritated that she's arrived so early, interrupting me, but I say nothing. I lead her into the kitchen and in the early evening light, I see how much weight she's lost. You couldn't describe her as slim, but her face has lost several chins and though she still has a couple going spare, she almost looks *gaunt*. The shadows under her eyes are blue-black and I can't pretend she looks any better for the weight loss. 'You look so different.'

She shrugs. 'Maybe. Not in a good way, though, eh?'

I blush. 'No, you look great. Really.'

'I've gone down three dress sizes already but I can't bloody afford to buy new clothes.' She walks over to the kitchen table, where I've lined up wine and peanuts and garlic bread. 'I couldn't afford to bring any wine either.'

I want to ask her if things are really that bad, but it's not as though I can do anything to help. 'Maybe when Mum's inheritance arrives ...'

She snorts. 'Huh. A thousand pounds is neither here nor there in the scheme of things.' Then she frowns. 'Sorry, that sounded bloody ungracious. Everything'll be fine.'

'Right. Well, the wine's my treat, anyway. Shame about the rain.' I fiddle with the foil at the top of the wine bottle and to my surprise it comes away in one satisfying tear. Then I look at my hands and spot why: for the first time in decades I've grown fingernails.

'So what time's bossy-boots turning up then?' Paula asks as the wine glugs into her glass. I'm sticking to water.

I peer up at the kitchen clock. 'Oh!' It's quarter past seven, a good hour later than I thought it was. I've found a new ruthlessness that's enabled me to fill five bags full of Mum's clothes, without the slightest regret. They're not *her*. All I've allowed myself to keep is her jewellery, neatly arranged in a velvet-lined wooden casket, and the shoes she wore on her wedding day: a pale pink pair, so unpractical and so unlike my mother. On the right shoe, there's a spot of mildew on the delicate muslin that swathes the toe. I wonder how long ago she last looked at her wedding shoes, how often that disciplined mind had permitted itself to think of the past.

'Lucy?'

'God, sorry – I'm worse than Chris these days, head permanently in the clouds. Not like Terri to be late, is it?'

'Hmm.' Paula looks around her, sipping the wine. 'So when are you going to sell this place, then? You'd make a fortune from some yuppie who likes Victorian gloom.'

'Soon.' As I say it, an image enters my mind, as clear as a photograph, of a family in this house, children's voices echoing up and down the staircase, windows open, the smell of damp and sickness replaced by fresh air and fresh scones, my bad memories gradually edged out by someone else's good ones. And in that instant, I know that whatever my future holds, this place is my past. I need to sell it, to move on.

'So what will you do with the money?'

'I really don't know,' I say, more sharply than I intended. I do wish Paula would stop going on about it. 'Money's not really the big thing in my life at the moment.'

'Lucky you.' Then she looks up at me. 'I'm being a jealous cow, aren't I? Let's talk about something else.'

'Good idea.' But my mind empties of topics of conversation. Finally Buster saves the day, slinking in from the garden. I'm always relieved to see him, because I keep expecting him to sneak home to Saxon Close: my attempts to apply butter to his paws were violently resisted and my endeavours at keeping him in were defied with the ingenuity of a prisoner in Colditz. In the end I've had to trust that Buster has enough common sense to realize what side his bread – if not his paw – is buttered. That if he went home, he'd never be fed again.

Paula stares at him. 'Oh God, what's he got in his mouth?'

I recognize the rictus smile that indicates Buster has had a successful hunting trip. As I get closer I can see a tiny green leg kicking out between his teeth. 'It's another bloody frog. He's always bringing them in.'

'Has he killed it?' Her voice is horrified, yet excited.

'No, he's delicate when he brings me presents. It'd spoil the fun.' I crouch alongside my cat and reach out carefully to stroke his back, a long sweeping movement that triggers a purr as loud as a Geiger counter at Sellafield. He's eyeballing me, knows what I'm up to … yet within a few seconds, the waxy white third eyelids appear, as he surrenders and my other hand is poised to rescue the victimized amphibian as Buster's jaw relaxes when—

RAT-AT-TAT-TAT.

Buster jumps at the sound of the front door being thumped. For a moment, Paula and I wait for frog blood – will it be red, or maybe slime green? – to emerge from his mouth, but instead the cat performs a feline shrug (*Who, me? Scared of a knock at the door? That must have been some other cat.*) and then spits out his captive, before slinking off into the pantry. The frog follows the light and hops out of the kitchen door, apparently unharmed.

'I'm always finding dried-up frogs under the sofa, back at home,' I say to Paula as I head for the door. *Home*. Will Saxon Close ever be that again?

'You're late,' I scold Terri as she comes into the house, Chris behind her.

'For once in my life!'

When they join Paula in the kitchen, I notice the difference in Terri first. Her face is flushed, as though she's run all the way from Manchester, and her eyes are wide open, challenging me. Her clothes are different too: a red T-shirt that dips a little at the front, revealing more of her freckly chest than I've ever seen in public before, and her chinos are so low on her hips that there's even a hint of belly button.

Paula's noticed too. 'Hey, goody-two-shoes, since when did you start buying clothes from Top Shop?'

'I'm allowed a change of image once every thirty years, aren't I? I decided the Brownie look was maybe just that bit too young for me.'

'So you've decided to dress like a teenager now?' Paula says, smiling.

'Sticks and stones may break my bones, but words will never hurt me,' Terri says piously. At least she hasn't changed completely.

'How are you, Chris?' I hand her a glass of wine.

'Bored to death. The only thing I have to do these days is eat, drink and watch daytime TV. My clothes are getting tight but, you know, I can't be arsed to go to the gym.'

In fact, she looks almost shrunken. Those legendary boobs are braless and low-slung, and all the high-maintenance touches have disappeared: her nails are unvarnished, her eyebrows no longer perfectly arced and her hair is frizzy, with the odd grey hair at right angles to her head.

'That's because the gym's pointless,' Paula says. 'Walking, that's the way forward.'

'Yeah, but why would I bother to walk? I'm not *going* anywhere.'

Terri and I exchange glances and her face changes, back into Brown Owl jollity. 'Right, girls, we need something to take our minds off the rain. And as luck would have it, Lucy needs help with the house.' She stares pointedly around the kitchen. 'Not that we haven't all noticed.'

'If you think this is bad, wait till you see the rest of it,' I say.

Paula pouts a little, but she knows there's no arguing with Terri.

We begin in the parlour, the room I haven't touched since I moved in. This was strictly for visitors or big pronouncements. Everything that has shaped the Quentin family was heralded here. It was where my father must have asked for my mother's hand in marriage, and where Andrew asked Grampa Quentin for mine. It was also where my mother, with her firm ideas of etiquette, summoned Andrew and me to tell us that she'd been diagnosed with cancer and that she would be dead within six months. She hadn't even told me she was having tests.

'Let's get some light in here.' Terri sweeps back the heavy green damask curtains and the room is unrecognizable. Mum never allowed sunshine in the parlour. It would have been as inappropriate as swearing.

'What a state.' Paula runs her finger along the mahogany bureau and a dust bundle as big as a ping-pong ball forms. 'Even the dust is dusty. Yuk.'

It's a museum piece, this room, pre-dating *Changing Rooms* and designers with frilly sleeves and silly ideas. Everything here was chosen originally to convey status and seriousness of purpose, from the dark furniture to the dour wallpaper, with its nightmarish pattern of black-red roses and spiky thorns.

Yet again I have this sense, as amber evening light fills the room, of a new life and new colours for this space: a teenager at a beech IKEA table, doing homework with headphones on, and a younger brother on a PlayStation, steering his way through a Grand Prix circuit, a plateful of toast going cold at his elbow.

'First things first,' Terri says. 'We need bin bags.'

'And more wine,' Paula adds. 'A lot more wine.'

Terri divides the room into thirds: she, Chris and Paula each take one section and a roll of bags, while I will float between the 'zones', deciding what to keep and what to throw out. 'But,' Terri warns me, 'you're only allowed to keep one bag of stuff. The rest is going in three piles: for the tip, for the charity shop and for sale.' She also produces a pile of Post-it notes from her handbag and explains that we can use these to label the furniture the same way: KEEP, SELL or GIVE AWAY.

Before now, this would have made me feel anxious, but now I'm excited. Wearing the rubber gloves Terri brought with her, the girls pick things up and I give the verdict on each item. We're as industrious as oompah-loompahs on speed.

'These?' Chris says, holding up a stack of purple raffia place-mats, the height of cool circa 1972.

'Bin.'

'They're quite retro now. Maybe Oxfam could sell them as vintage.'

'OK, charity shop then.' I look over at Paula, who is waving a horrible Chinese vase. 'That can go too.'

'It might be worth something,' she says, looking at the bottom as though she might find a price label.

'Um ... yes, I suppose so.' I blush. 'Listen, I meant to say, if anything takes your fancy, any of you, feel free to take it. Mum would have wanted things to go to good homes.'

Terri puts down the clock she's been dusting, and picks up her wine glass. 'To your mum.'

We clink glasses and for a moment, I know we're all thinking about Judith and the Brownies. Perhaps Chris is remembering how Mum let her daydream ... Paula recalling the tomboy games she used to play before it all went wrong ... Terri thinking of her surrogate mum, who shaped her life more powerfully than her own hopeless parents.

'I've lost my virginity.'

There's a loud crash: Paula has dropped the vase. 'Shit. Sorry.'

'Did you just say what I think you said?' I manage and then see from the smile on Terri's face that I heard her right. 'When? Where? And who the hell with?'

'Shouldn't we clear up the vase?' Terri says.

'Bugger the vase,' I say. 'I hated it anyway. We need the details, Teresa Rowbotham. Now.' I sit down at the table, and the others do the same, Terri in the same seat my mother always took. Yet again, the parlour is the site of breaking news. Perhaps we should rename it CNN.

'OK. It was two weeks ago. With the guy I met at the religious retreat.'

'You told me nothing happened!'

'Calm down, Lucy. Nothing did happen then. Except it confused me completely. I really liked the bloke. It was so different from how I'd felt about any other man before, that's why I did a runner from the retreat.'

Paula shakes her head. 'See what happens when you get religious types together? Dog collars on heat, the lot of them.'

Terri gives her a dirty look. 'Do you want me to tell you what happened or not?'

'Yes, miss,' Paula says.

'I was really depressed after the retreat. Well, I've been feeling low ever since Judith died, but this ... it felt like a missed opportunity. Maybe my last chance. I know that sounds overdramatic but ...' She stops herself. 'I'd been thinking about all sorts. Giving up the whole idea of ordination. I mean, what did I have to tell anybody about how they lived their lives, when I've never actually dared to have one of my own?'

'Don't be silly, Terri,' I say, but she holds up her hand.

'It's OK now.' She allows herself a little smile. 'Howard came to see me out of the blue. He called me from a phone box across the road from the college. He'd tracked me down to Manchester. It was like – how do I put this without sounding like a bodice-ripper – a thunderbolt, when I saw him. I just knew.'

'Blimey!' Paula says. 'So did you shag him straight away?'

Now Terri blushes. 'We ... went back to my room, and yes. We made love. I was terrified; I was actually shaking and he kept asking me if I wanted him to stop, but I didn't.'

'And was it ... what you expected?' Chris says.

Terri's eyes are half-closed, as if she's reliving it. I almost blush myself as she opens her eyes again and a broader smile transforms her face. 'Oh yes. After twenty years of imagining how it would be, I thought it was bound to be awful: uncomfortable, maybe painful. But it wasn't. It was like, we were meant to be together. We just kind of fit.' She giggles. 'Does that sound cheesy?'

'Yes, duck,' Paula says, 'but we'll let you off, just this once. So what happened afterwards?'

'I was scared that he'd disappear into the night. So I drank coffee to stay awake; I must have had six cups, all double strength. Then I lay there and watched him breathing.'

I'm astonished, yet pleased with my perceptiveness. It's more than new clothes. I look at her face as she remembers her self-induced insomnia, and I see something different: tenderness. Tenderness has transformed Terri from a Brown Owl into a fully-rounded human being.

Chris says: 'So you stayed awake all night?'

'No. I woke up at six-ish, quite panicky, realized and then I felt all tingly, you know. Down there. Which reminded me what had happened. But all there was of Howard was a dent in the pillow.'

'Oh God,' I say.

'I felt so foolish. But even then I didn't regret it, you know. And then when he reappeared, carrying a cup of tea, I knew I'd been right to trust my instincts.'

'Thank Christ for that,' Paula says.

'Well, I'd like to think the entire Holy Trinity played their parts,' Terri says, and winks at me. I think Big Bird might just have traded her virginity for a sense of humour.

After Terri's bombshell, productivity slows down considerably, until she finally loses patience and despatches us each to a different area of the house, with her acting as camp commandant, checking up on our progress. Paula's staying in the parlour, which is looking stunningly minimalist compared to an hour ago. Chris is in my mum's bedroom – Terri thought that she looked peaky and so it seemed sensible to put her somewhere she could have a lie down if she needed it.

I'm in the bathroom, which I thought was relatively clean, but Terri has higher standards. And I actually like cleaning bathrooms – there's no other place in a house where you can make such a fundamental change with a few sprays of citrus-scented toxins. The downside is getting up close and personal with the toilet, but any woman who has had a baby knows there are far worse things than limescale in your loo.

I'm scrubbing at the wonderful hotel-sized bath taps, when Terri comes in to inspect my work so far.

'I think Paula might be taking home half the contents of the parlour to flog off,' she says. 'Did you know she's about to get thrown out of her flat?'

I look up from the taps. 'God, no. Poor woman. What's she going to do?'

'The kids are going back to live with her husband's folks, and she's moving back in with hers.' Terri pushes open the frosted glass window. 'Can I smoke?'

'Yes, of course. What a nightmare for Paula.' I peel off the rubber gloves, rinsing my hands under water to get rid of the sweat. 'Do you think I ought to invite her to come and stay here?'

Terri takes a first drag as she thinks it over. 'Well, I'm all for Christian generosity and everything, but having ten-ton Tessie as a sitting tenant might not be a selling point.'

'Ouch. That's not very nice. Anyway, she's lost weight.'

'Eight-and-a-half-ton Tessie, then. Look, if I thought it'd help her, I'd say yes, take her in. But there's no point in becoming a hostel for waifs and strays unless it's going to make a differ-ence, and I don't think it will to Paula. I know what you're like: you'd be bringing her buttered toast in bed and running her hot baths. Whereas moving back home with Patsy the Bimbo and Nigel will definitely have her reconsidering her future.'

I smile. 'I always felt more sorry for Patsy than Paula. She thought she was going to be Troughton's answer to Joan Collins. Living in a house like Bethany's dad's, with her husband the biggest property tycoon in Cheshire.'

'Well, in the words of Mick Jagger, *you can't always get what you want*.'

'No.' I sit on the loo seat. 'Though in your case, it's more like Rod Stewart. *If you think I'm sexy* ... I can't believe you didn't tell me.'

'Sorry. I've been rubbish, but I didn't feel like talking to anyone until I knew how I felt. It's like Howard has shaken everything up inside ... don't laugh, I don't mean *inside* literally. I mean that he's has thrown everything I expect out of life into the air. And I didn't know how I was going to feel until it all sort of landed again.'

'And has it landed?'

She brings the cigarette to her lips again and then raises an eyebrow and it takes me a moment to realize she's checking herself out in the mirror. Then she manages to blow a perfect smoke ring. 'Hey! I can't tell you how long I've wanted to do that for. I wish we had a camera!' She turns to me again. 'Yes, it has landed. I feel like a different person. I mean, I can look at my reflection now and not hate the way I look, not feel ashamed.'

'Is that really how you used to feel?'

She stares at me. 'Oh yes. Ashamed. Sickened. And so blooming guilty about it too, because I know this is the only face I'm ever going to have, and the only body, and they work fine, and I'm lucky to have them, but I hated it all. And now I don't.'

I'm shocked that I knew so little about how bad my best friend felt about herself. 'And what about God?'

'Ah. Well, I've given this a lot of thought. I mean, I should be feeling guilty, you know? What I did went against what I've always believed: that sex is sacred and the marriage bed is the only place for it. So I waited for that familiar feeling of self-loathing ...'

'And?'

'And the guilt never came.' She takes one final, triumphant drag, then tosses the butt in the toilet. There's a slight fizz as the burning end is extinguished. 'I think it's because I believe Howard is the One. I feel that even if we never marry, he was the one I was meant to be with. I mean, sex is the most joyous joint activity I've found since the Brownies,' she raises her eyebrow again, practising the new look, 'but if we're no longer together, I can't imagine ever doing it with anyone else.'

'What about you becoming a vicar? How does he feel about that?'

'He thinks it's funny. I've decided to keep going, Lucy, because I think this is going to make me a better vicar than ever. I mean, would you trust a vicar who'd never been in love?'

I'm about to answer when Chris appears in the doorway. Her face is still pale but there are scarlet patches on her cheeks, so bright they look as though they've been painted on, like a wooden doll.

'Are you OK, Chris?'

'No I am not fucking OK.' And then I notice that she's holding a handful of letters.

'What . . . ?' I begin but then she throws the letters at me, and as I bend down to pick them up, I notice one begins 'Beautiful Judith . . .' I feel a flash of anger: what the hell is she doing going through my father's love letters to my mother? And then a moment of excitement: this could be what I'm looking for, the missing piece in the jigsaw that will help me understand my parents. And myself.

'I've had twenty-five bloody years of feeling like a second-class citizen because my mum was the biggest slut in town, and guess what?'

My eyes skim across the opening lines of the letter . . . *BEAUTIFUL Judith* . . .

If you are the owl, I am the eagle. I have never soared like I did tonight . . . How can one meeting of lips, brief as it was, feel like the meeting of two souls?

'Saintly fucking Judith, our great Brown Owl, was at it too. Shagging Bruno.'

I grasp the radiator to stop myself falling. It can't be true. My mother was there for me. She gave up so much. She would never have put our family life at risk.

'That's enough,' Terri says quietly. In the brief silence we hear Paula's heavy tread as she rushes up to the bathroom.

'What's going on?' she says, breathless.

I open my mouth but nothing happens. Chris frowns and I notice that the heat has disappeared from her cheeks, replaced by a green tinge as though she's about to be sick. 'Ask Lucy,' she says, and walks out of the room. The window rattles when she slams the front door behind her.

Judith, my allocco, my brown owl,

I made my decision today, at the barbecue. I had to tell you. What I have to say may be surprising, shocking, but I profoundly hope and wish that it will be none of those things ... that when you read on, you will know this is the secret you have been keeping from your own heart.

Judith, I am in love. With you. I thought I had been in love before but it is not so. I realize I was fooled. THIS is how it feels.

When I see you, it is like someone has given me a drug to speed up my heartbeat until it is not possible for it to go any faster without it exploding. When I hear your voice, I want to lie down and only listen.

Is this mad? In Italian madness is pazzo — it sounds a little like passion, no? I do not wish to frighten you, allocco, but I must tell you. And now I have told you, I must wait ...

Your own
Bruno

Chapter Thirty-two

Never rattle your friend's skeleton's
bones. The girl who gets on well is one who
has tact enough not to say the very thing
that will cause the skeleton in her friend's
closet to rattle.

After Chris leaves, Terri and Paula offer to stay with me, but
I need some time alone with the letters. It's eleven o'clock
now and I've read and re-read them fifty times. The image of
Mum as an upstanding Brown Owl, living a useful life unsullied
by anything as squalid as feelings for any man except my father,
has been obliterated: I have no idea what to put in its place.

The letters span just a few weeks – but with only one side of
the correspondence to go on, I've had to guess at my mother's
responses. Bruno's personality vaults off every sheet of Basildon
Bond blue writing paper: a racy choice of colour, no doubt, for
1979. His handwriting is as loopy and florid as the words.

Two days after his confession of love, Bruno writes a second
letter, stepping back a little from his Italian stallion gallop: *I
have frightened you. It was always a risk but for a man who feels
as I do, less of a risk than never to tell the truth. To spend a lifetime
not knowing, but wondering: what if I had told my Judith? Would
she be mine now?*

Instead of intense passion, this time he uses flattery: *Your
strength to me is your most beautiful quality. To me you are St Joan,
Mrs Thatcher, Boudicea. A woman for me must be my match. You
have endured so much, uncomplaining. You are my inspiration.*

Despite the shock, his compliments make me smile: I can't imagine any woman except my mother being seduced by a comparison with the Iron Lady. But, judging from his third letter, she fell for it, because just a week after the barbecue, they've shared a kiss. *If you are the brown owl, I am the eagle, the aquila. I have never soared like I did tonight. I am sitting in the kitchen, my girls asleep upstairs, and I know I should not, but I feel wonder, along with guilt. How can one meeting of lips, brief as it was, feel like the meeting of two souls?*

How did my mother feel? Was she wracked by guilt, or alive with excitement? I try to remember her that summer, but I can't distinguish her behaviour in 1979 from any other year. Capable, bossy, no-nonsense. Cold …

How *could* she risk it all, for a creep like Bruno? But even as I condemn her, there's a tiny part of me that feels the warmth of his words. *The gentleness of your lips was like nothing I'd ever felt and made me want to protect you and keep you, my allocco, in our nest together.*

I wonder if Mum read the letters sitting here at this table, shivering in the north-facing kitchen despite the heat of the summer, and wondering if it might be her turn for a time in the sun? *Before it seemed almost a game, Judith. A wonderful pastime, a summer of love after the winter of discontent. But now, this is serious. Sealed with a kiss, as our mothers and fathers wrote in wartime.*

I am soaring. Soar with me, Judith. Tonight, nothing feels impossible.

But I shake my head. Like me, my mother was a grown-up, with responsibilities. A pragmatist. She could no more put me at risk than I could endanger Sasha.

Another week passes before the fourth letter: Mum's obviously given Bruno his marching orders, but he's not ready to give up yet. *A week ago, I was an eagle. Now I am bound to the earth, my wings clipped by your silence. An owl is wise and a man is foolish. I know this may seem to you the ramblings of one who cannot accept fate, who raises his fists against the inevitable until his knuckles are raw. Maybe so. But sometimes just when you are about to admit defeat, fate will show a little compassion and offer a glimpse of hope.*

Bruno, the master manipulator. This letter I read and re-read, tying myself in knots, wondering whether there is genuine pain there, behind the poetry. For the first time, this pantomime villain of my childhood, the baddy who scandalized Troughton, is coming into focus. Was this real? Or yet another one of his cons? Try as I might, I can't see what he hoped to gain from my mother, except her love.

I know you are afraid. Me also. I am afraid of what such feelings make me do and want and need. And of how all the colour is drained from my life if I cannot see you, allocco. All the warmth.

He tries to justify himself, trotting out a typically florid version of that old chestnut, 'my wife doesn't understand me', claiming that he's decided to leave his family anyway. *I am, in my heart, a good man. A flawed man, but a good one. Not as good as you and so maybe I do not deserve you, but with you, I could be better and you could be happier. I have never begged anyone anything in my life ... but now I will beg you.*

Clever Bruno. He must have realized that my mum, just like Terri, couldn't resist the needy. His fifth letter, nine days later, suggests his approach paid dividends. *I have been home for three minutes, but already I miss you, need to be with you again. And because I cannot be with you in reality, I must be with you in my words. Except what are words but collections of letters?*

I cringe over the next bit, but I have to read on. *They are inadequate to convey what happened to us this very night. I am shaking from the power of it: this was not about parts of our bodies but about the whole of our souls. The softness of your breasts, the gentleness of your breath in my ear and your body under mine: yes, they hint at what we are to each other, but no more than that.*

I wonder where it happened? In the Drill Hall, among the pennants and first aid kits, close enough perhaps for Bruno to admire his reflection in the Wishing Pond?

And then he goes for the jugular. *We can build our life else-where. I hate to leave my family, yet I know I must. My daughters are beautiful to me, but I am a failure to them. They need their mother, not their imperfect father. I also have reasons to leave that I am not proud of. I have dragged my family around and around, like suitcases, searching for something. I believed it was money I* needed – for money, despite how my life seems, does not come easily to me. But it wasn't money that was leading me to Troughton.

It was you.

Again I imagine my mother, sitting in the dark, considering her options. Did she seriously consider leaving Troughton? *And what about ME?*

His last letter, eight days later, certainly suggests she didn't rule out following him.

We can do this. Do not lose faith. You must not lead half a life. You will not be responsible for another's unhappiness, if you leave. Children are resilient. They forget. Mine will be better to forget me. It is only with you I become a man worthy of being their father.

Every time I read this one, it makes me feel sick. Was she really planning to abandon me, leave me with my grandparents?

You are a wise owl, and without you I am the dodo. Extinct.

There is, I know, the usignolo to think of. I know this is what stands in your way, but it need not. It can be taken care of. I know that this is the hardest decision you will ever make. All I can promise is that if you embrace this life, I will devote mine to you. Together we will be the people we were meant to be.

Your own

Bruno

The usignolo ... is this code for divorce? It sounds like signature. Perhaps, as an Italian, he was Catholic and so they needed permission—

RATT-TATT-TATT.

It's too late for a knock at the front door, and the sound makes me jump. I leave the letters on Mum's bed and creep to the other side of the hallway to peer out of the window at the drive.

Andrew's car.

Oh my God! Sasha!

I run down the stairs two at a time, tripping down the last three and only just managing to stop myself falling face first on the tiled floor. My hands are shaking as I fumble with the door chain, before I finally open it and try to read Andrew's face for clues in the darkness. 'It's Sasha, isn't it? What's happened? What's wrong? Oh God, Andrew, where is she?'

He holds up his hand to shut me up. 'Bloody hell, Lulu. Stop panicking. She's fine. She's tucked up in bed. I asked my mum to babysit while I nipped out.'

'But why ... what?' My heart is beating at double speed as he walks into the hall. 'I thought something had happened. I thought ...'

I step back as he comes inside, and when he moves left, I go right, as though we're waltzing hands-free.

'Yes, sorry. I probably should have called but it was a bit of a spur of the moment thing.' He shrugs, slightly embarrassed. Spur of the moment things are not Andrew's style. 'I was also worried you might not let me come if I rang to ask.'

I don't know how to answer. 'Well, you're here now. I'll get you a drink.'

I'm trying to work out whether he's come for a kitchen conversation, or a parlour pronouncement. God knows I've had enough revelations in the past few hours, without more from him.

He follows me meekly into the kitchen where Buster is asleep on a chair. The cat opens one eye lazily and doesn't bother to acknowledge Andrew, though they haven't seen each other for weeks. Then again, I haven't seen Andrew for weeks either.

I look at him properly. He's still matinee-idol handsome. But his suit is creased, his blue eyes are ringed with red, and the square shoulders are sloping. I can't imagine his father ever looked this dishevelled, but then Andrew's mother wouldn't have allowed it. Collins men depend on their women.

'Wine?' There are four empty bottles on the table. 'The girls came round earlier.'

'And there was me thinking you'd turned to drink because you were missing me,' he says, waving away the open bottle.

'So what triggered the spur of the moment thing, then?'

'Coming round here was spur of the moment,' he says, correcting me, 'but I've been thinking about what I want to say for a long time.'

'Right.' I wait.

'I know I'm not the most ... right-on of men,' he begins.

'To be fair, you never pretended to be,' I say.

'I'm a logical person, Lulu. My parents' marriage seemed to work, seemed to keep them happy, and so it made sense to copy that. It's what you wanted, too, once.'

He pauses. I think he's waiting for me to say I still do. But I don't know if that's true.

'I know something as momentous as your mother's death is bound to change you, and I see now that I've been pretty unsympathetic in not taking that on board. I'm sorry.'

It's only when he says those words that I realize I can't remember Andrew ever apologizing before. He always makes jokes instead, shrugs his shoulders to ask for forgiveness, but he refuses to say sorry. 'It's OK,' I say, wanting to make him feel better.

'But you see, I don't think it is. I've had time to consider how I can put things right, a lot of time. I want us to be a family again, Lulu. It's what makes me happiest, being a provider, knowing I can take care of my girls. That they'll always have the best of things.'

His eyes look brighter now. Could those be tears? I gulp, hard, because I won't be able to stand it if he cries.

'I know.'

'I've been selfish. I always knew you wanted a house full of children, all the noise and excitement that you missed here.' His voice echoes around the empty kitchen. 'But I put myself first, my ambitions and my career. Now I see I was wrong.'

I brace myself for what I am sure is coming next.

'Lulu, what about it? Another baby? You and me and Sasha and a new baby – maybe a little boy, for Sasha to boss around. Or a girl. I don't mind. It's what I want and I know it's what you want.' He reaches out across the table for my hand and I let him take it, hoping he won't feel that my body has gone cold.

'I don't know, Andrew.'

'I know it's a surprise; maybe you'll find it hard to believe me right away. But I mean it, Lucy. I want us to be the way we used to be. Better than that.'

His face is open, pleading for reassurance. He definitely believes this is what he wants. Maybe it's what we need. A baby would break the curse of Quentin only children. Take my mind off the past, fill it with activity and hope and excitement and possibility . . . but then I think of my mother again: torn between passion and duty, between my needs and her own. Even more now, I think she might have understood. Another baby means another eighteen years of putting someone else first. Maybe I am more selfish than my mother, but right now I don't know if I can do it.

'I can't rush into anything, Andrew. I know it sounds easy, but we've forgotten, both of us, how hard it is. The sleepless nights, the money, the mess—'

'The dirty nappies, yes, I know all that. I really want it now, though, Lucy. I'll be much more hands-on this time. Baby wipes in my holster, bottles in my briefcase. All that. Like a proper New Man. It'll change everything.'

I squeeze his hand back, very gently, then withdraw it. 'It's a . . . surprise. I'm not saying no but I need to think about it. You do understand?'

He blinks, then smiles, like Mummy's brave little soldier. 'Yes . . . yes, I mean, it's taken me a while to get used to the idea.' He claps his hands together, back into business mode. 'Right. Great. Well, thanks for letting me in. Sorry I gave you a shock. I just wanted to let you know my latest thinking straight away.'

'Mmm. Thanks. I'll let you know, too. Soon. I promise, Andrew.'

We walk into the entrance hall. There's a pause as we try to work out whether we should embrace, shake hands, kiss. Eventually I lean forward, towards his shoulder, and our bodies meet for a split second in an awkward hug. His shirt smells of sweat and Eau Sauvage, the same aftershave he wore when we first met. The memory makes my eyes sting.

He marches out of the door, his shoulders at stiff right angles again, and I keep the door ajar until he's switched the engine and the lights on, and reversed out of the drive.

I have no idea what to do next. So I disregard Seb's no-alcohol rule, find some old port in the larder, and sit in the kitchen, imagining a little boy with Andrew's eyes and my hair. Watching the candle burn down and waiting for the sun to rise.

But things are no clearer in daylight.

Chapter Thirty-three

Stick to it, the thrush sings. One of our worst diseases nowadays is that people don't seem to have the energy to stick to what they do; they try a change. This is a fatal mistake. Whatever you take up, do it with all your might, and stick to it.

Today I will be seeing three men I've kept secret from my husband.

First of all I'm seeing Seb: who will circle my waist with his huge hands, checking my diaphragmatic breathing as I try not to hyperventilate.

Then Vic the Prick, who will almost certainly take pleasure in skewering my dream of becoming a singer, but will at least put me out of my misery.

And then Sunny, who will finally tell me the truth about my father. Though I thought he already had.

I wonder, driving through the backstreets of Manchester looking for the hotel Sunny has booked for me, whether I might have had more than enough truth lately. It's a fortnight since Chris literally threw the reality of my mother's deceit in my face, and since Andrew made the offer he felt I couldn't refuse. I still don't know if I can refuse it. I'd forgotten that craving for another baby, the neediness I felt the first time Sasha ducked out of my embrace, but now he's made the offer, I'm sure I can smell that intoxicating toasty-infant scent every time I pass a pram in the street.

It could make me complete ...

I finally spot the hotel sign and steer the car down the side street, and decide there must be some mistake. When Sunny called to say he needed to talk to me, he offered to book me into 'a little place I know just over the bridge in Salford, so we can have a civilized dinner and a drink without you worrying about getting home'. I'd only agreed because Salford summoned up an image of an unassuming B & B.

But this is no guesthouse. This is a great big swanky white hotel, moored like a luxury cruise liner on the edge of the canal. I stop the Fiesta and, to his credit, the porter manages not to giggle as he takes my keys to valet-park it for me.

The surreal nature of my arrival increases when I walk into the lobby, which has a turquoise iceberg in place of a reception desk, and an impressive glass staircase. Behind the iceberg, a coiffed woman finds my booking instantly and summons a uniformed lad who picks up my frayed overnight bag and leads me to my third-floor room. I fumble around in my pocket for a tip, and only find a dry-cleaning ticket, but instead of snarling, he gives a comedy shrug like Laurel and Hardy and then winks as he exits.

Inside, I feel like a different woman, the kind who stays in stunning minimalist hotels with waterfall-cool Egyptian cotton sheets on a bed the size of my bathroom. The kind of woman who might sit at the dark oak desk and write little notes on headed paper to opera fans, before ordering a light, fruit-based room service breakfast to be delivered the morning after her virtuoso performance.

I laugh at myself in the mirror. The sunlight from the window stretching the full length of the room gives me a Ready Brek glow but simultaneously highlights the lines on my face. Who am I kidding? Maybe I should go back to Fancy Footwork and accept that Troughton is the limit of my ambitions. I'll never want for money again; my mum's will has seen to that. And the baby ... It's what I've wanted for so long. A house full of noise and love.

And yet ... Bruno's letters prove that anyone is open to temptation if their life is unfulfilled.

I wonder how close my mother came to abandoning me, whether she ever replied to that last letter. When did she realize Chris's mother was Bruno's other bird in the hand? The fact that she kept the letters, that she didn't stop him writing, must suggest she was tempted.

I sit on the banquette at the end of the bed. The TV is tuned into the hotel's own channel, 'welcoming Mrs Lucy Collins to the Lowry for the night of the 23 of July', inviting me to sample the spa or cocktail bar, and instructing me to enjoy my stay.

23 July. School breaks up on Monday. I have four more days before my self-imposed deadline expires, and I know one thing: my mother might have considered abandoning me, but I won't do that to Sasha.

As for the rest ... it's in the lap of Vic the Prick.

I could do with a shower to clear my head, but don't have time: I'm meeting Seb at the college for a last practice before I endure Trial by Victor. I fill the marble basin with water, splash my face, then grab my sheet music and reluctantly leave the sanctuary of my room.

I was intending to walk to the college, but I don't know how long it would take and besides, a guest at a hotel like this surely never walks anywhere. I ask reception and the taxi is there in seconds, so I arrive early for my appointment.

I stride through the campus with more confidence now: I've been back three times and have even noticed the odd student over the age of twenty-two. Seb always manages to get us a little rehearsal room with a piano, although he hasn't studied there for ten years. That charm is worth millions – the staff all give him indulgent smiles as he pushes his luck time after time. They never seem to mind. Then they look at me and I can tell they don't see how it adds up: a God-like musician helping a dowdy old housewife.

I mentioned it in our second lesson.

'You're not dowdy. Or old. But if you really fancy fitting in more, we could go shopping for jeans.'

I'm wearing my 'student outfit' now: thank God he didn't take me to some vintage clothes store or skateboard outlet. We went to a place called Diesel and instead of going for the first pair I saw on the sale rack, he asked me my size (I didn't dare lie) and stacked three pairs in my arms.

'They're all the same,' I said.

He raised his eyebrows. 'No. The fabric's all the same because it's the latest reverse thread and colour. But the fits are all different. Come out with each pair on and I'll tell you which one suits you the best.'

The first pair was reassuringly baggy, but he shook his head impatiently. The second looked like the kind my mum would have worn, straight legged and straight laced.

But the third ...

'Hey, Miss Glow-worm. Like your style! J-Lo's got competition.'

As I climb the stairs now, I can feel the way the fabric curves around my bottom, giving it an instant lift, and then tapers away to make my legs look slimmer than they really are. Seb picked two fitted T-shirts for me too: an orange one emblazoned with names and numbers from an American baseball team, and the other, my favourite, two angels printed against a khaki background, with glitter sprinkled across their faces like fairy dust. It's the kind of top I might have picked for Sasha – though there's something distinctly tarty about the angels – but never for me. Yet now I love it almost more than shoes.

'Miss GW,' he says as I step into the room. 'You're looking fabulous. Are you feeling fabulous?'

I always blush when he says something like that, though I know he doesn't mean it – it's his way of trying to boost my confidence. 'I'm feeling nervous.'

'Nervous is good. Anything that gets the blood pumping always improves my performance, I find.' He does his raised eyebrow thing, which makes me blush more. It's incredible that I've achieved anything at all in the sessions with him, but as he plays the first scales and I begin to warm up my voice, I can hear a difference. The sound is purer somehow, and stronger, and I feel less tension in my throat and more power coming from deep inside me. The breathing tricks he's shown me felt unnatural at first, like relearning how to walk, but now they're becoming second nature and I feel the difference.

We move onto the piece I'll be singing to convince Vic that I'm worthy. Carmen. Singing the habanera.

> *L'amour est enfant de Bohême,*
> *Il n'a jamais, jamais connu de loi,*
> *Si tu ne m'aime pas, je t'aime,*
> *Si je t'aime, prend garde à toi!*

This change from soprano – all sweetness and light, light melodies – to mezzo – full of brooding emotion and dark sexuality – has been easier than I expected. Maybe because I'm finally singing the music my voice was intended for: *love is a gipsy child ... if you don't love me ... take care ...* The unfamiliar passions it stirs are exciting, rather than frightening.

'Miss Glow-worm, that was knockout,' Seb says. 'If Vic doesn't want you after this, I'll wring his stupid, scrawny neck.'

Before I know what's happening he's leaning forward and for a fraction of a second I am sure he's going to kiss my lips and before I've worked out how to respond, the direction of his head changes and instead he moves my fringe to one side with his fingers and kisses my forehead, once, twice, three times. 'For luck,' he whispers.

It's such a tender gesture, and it reminds me so much of the way my mother used to calm Sasha's crying when she was a baby, that I feel light-headed and have to grip the piano to steady myself.

'Thank you,' I mouth back.

'Time to go,' he says and I follow him out of the room. Only the sound of my feet making contact with the floor reassures me that I'm not floating.

Vic looks up from his laptop – balanced precariously on the top of his low filing cabinet – as we enter his office. He gives the tiniest of nods to acknowledge our presence.

'You didn't give up then.' His Guy Fawkes beard hides his expression, so I can't tell whether he's pleased or annoyed. 'Who did you find to teach you?'

Maybe I should play the game, pretend it's some musical guru, but I can't be bothered. 'Seb has been helping me.'

This time I do catch a flicker of a smile on his lips. 'I'll tell you what, shall we skip the audition? There's no way Seb will have achieved anything like the improvement I'm looking for, and he's only been doing it to get into your knickers. Has he managed it, by the way? Purely academic interest on my part.'

I'm trying to think how to respond when Seb turns on him. 'Vic, what is your fucking problem? Are you ever going to stop acting like a cunt, or shall we just leave now?'

'Goodness, Linda, isn't he coarse?'

I stare at him. 'It's Lucy. And as I've made the effort to come back, I think you could at least do me the courtesy of listening.'

'Oh, *very* mezzo,' he says. 'Isn't it funny what finding your voice can do to a person? OK, let's get on with it then.'

Seb stands behind me, as if he's protecting me, but Vic waves him off. 'Do bugger off, Sebastian; I really don't need to be looking at your ugly mug while the lady and I make beautiful music together, do I?'

Seb winks at me and leaves, telling me to meet him in the refectory when it's over. When he closes the door, Vic scrutinizes me for just a fraction too long, which unsettles me still more.

Like last time, he sets the metronome going on top of the piano, but unlike last time, its relentless rhythm soothes me. I start to sing and the room dissolves again and I am Carmen the gypsy, outside the factory, smelling the chocolate scent of steamy tobacco, feeling the sunshine on my skin and singing for life and love itself.

When I've finished, he gestures to the chair next to his filing cabinet and sighs. I wait for him to patronize me with his brush-off, but a little of Carmen's defiance remains, because I know I've just given the best performance of my life.

He rolls his own stool round from the piano and sits opposite me. 'Seb's told you, hasn't he? About what happened to my voice?'

I nod, tolerating his cat-and-mouse game because I pity him.

'He's a blabbermouth.' He reaches across to open the top filing cabinet drawer and retrieves a packet of herbal cigarettes and rolls himself back towards the window to open it. 'It's like a fairy story, I sometimes think. A witch's curse. '"*You, Victor, will have your voice taken from you, yet you will have to watch other, better singers build their careers, because music is the only thing that gives your life meaning*."' He laughs bitterly and lights his cigarette.

'It's a cruel thing to happen.' I can't think of anything else to say.

'If it's a fairy story, then there must be a spell to release me from my curse, mustn't there? For years I've looked for it in my students. Didn't work.' He looks sad. 'I even slept with a couple of them in case I was missing the point. Not strictly allowed, but I always made sure *they* left *me*, so that there were no heart-broken girls causing a stink with the authorities. I didn't have to try too hard; women tend to tire of self-pity before too long.'

I don't nod this time, though I can imagine how impossible it would be to spend much time with Victor.

'My point is, music as a career promises so much but it rarely delivers. I want you to know that, Lucy.' It's the first time he's got my name right.

'I do know that. I'm never going to be Kiri Te Kanawa or Maria Callas. The reward for singing, for me, is singing. I just don't want to squander what little ability I've been given.'

He turns away from me and smokes out of the window. I realize the metronome is still ticking, the needle moving from side to side, and I follow it with my eyes, counting one minute, two minutes, before he turns back.

'If you want to be my student, I'll be your teacher.'

I shake my head slightly, unsure I've heard him correctly. 'Really?'

'Really. If you want to be taught by a misanthropic depressive with issues. I am bloody good, though.' And for the first time, he smiles like a real human being. 'And I promise I won't try to sleep with you. You look shocked.'

'I . . . I suppose I wasn't expecting that.'

'Neither was I.' He smiles again. 'You know, Seb's done a

pretty good job. You're breathing better, and you've lost the habit of forcing the low notes through your larynx like a parcel too big for your letterbox. You've got potential. So what do you say?'

'I'm very grateful.' I want to tell him yes, straight away, but I know I can't. 'I have to think it over. Not whether I'd like you to teach me, because I would. But whether I can be committed enough to do this.'

'If you don't do it now ... well, time is not on your side, as they say.'

I can tell he's pissed off that I'm not falling to my knees and hugging his legs with raw gratitude, but there's no point pretending. 'Can you give me a week?'

He nods. 'Ring me when you decide.'

As I walk to the refectory, I feel deflated. I've done something that only six months ago would have seemed an impossible fantasy. All it's achieved is to confuse me more. My music, or my marriage? A new baby, or the tiniest chance of becoming a new me.

Pushing open the swing doors to the refectory I see Seb at a table by the window, tapping his foot nervously on the lino floor. I realize something else. Now that Vic's offered to make my dream come true, there's no reason to see Seb again.

Chapter Thirty-four

Fish are not like fatalists who sit down under misfortune instead of battling against it.

Terri looked at her watch. Decision time.

When Colin called up originally to ask to meet, she'd said no. When he insisted, 'I really do think it would be beneficial to you,' it had annoyed her so much that she'd said yes to get him off the phone and then decided to stand him up.

But she knew she couldn't go through with it. However infuriating a person was — very, in Colin's case — she hated to think of him waiting there for her at the new Trinity Bridge, doggedly certain that she was simply running late, smiling bravely at passers-by, until it got cold and dark and he had to admit she wasn't coming.

She'd been feeling out of sorts since Howard left. School broke up early in Northumberland and he'd spent a whole week in Manchester, booked into a hotel where she stayed each night, revelling in the pleasure of waking up next to someone you wanted to be with.

But he'd had to go back yesterday, to visit his mother, and Terri felt panicked by his absence, as though life had frozen over again. Love was spectacularly good, it was true, but it made her afraid, an emotion she couldn't remember feeling with such intensity before. Did he think less of her, because they'd slept together? Could she really love someone who seemed so strong, when he was bound to disappoint her, just as Judith had warned? She still felt this terrible fear that he was taking her for a ride, was tricking her into love, before leaving for good.

It would do her good to see Colin, to remind her how far

she'd come: better to have loved and lost, even if Howard did turn out to be a commitment conman. *That's not a very nice way to think about Colin*, she told herself, but somehow just by picturing him and then picturing Howard, she felt better.

She headed for the bathroom on her floor to get ready, wondering if she'd be able to resist telling Colin she'd finally lost her virginity.

Chris walked out of her dressing room, disgusted at how horrible she looked in the mirror, and decided to roll a joint. It was the first decision she'd made all day.

She took the Rizlas and the grass from the cocoa tin, and began work. The familiarity of the process was soothing: she'd always been good with her hands. Five o'clock already and what had she done? Drunk endless coffee (probably what was making her so edgy), stared out of the window, read a pile of magazines without taking in a single word, and debated whether she could face her big night out.

Kian had organized it, rounded up all the old faces. 'Can't believe we haven't seen you for so long, pet. Time to get shaking that ass again, don't you think?'

And yet all she could think as he spoke was, *you're still there. You promised me you'd leave.*

She'd rejected his original choice of venue – some subterranean gay bar where she'd have felt like the oldest fag hag in town – and he'd compromised on the bar at the Lowry Hotel, which was at least grown-up and served reliable cocktails. The plan was to meet at seven and then see what everyone fancied doing: maybe something to eat, maybe clubbing. Chris had played along, but knew she wouldn't stay long. She was appalling company these days. And Geoff was meant to be there too. They hadn't been in touch since their brief encounter on her sofa, to her relief, but she was hurt to hear he'd been taken on by Eros. His job title was the same, as far as she knew, but Kian had let slip that he'd moved into her office and she dwelled constantly on the question of whether he'd fucked her over before fucking her.

She'd always thought of herself as a strong person, someone

who could weather the storms. She'd learned to escape her parents' unhappiness through her daydreams, and then used the imagination she'd developed out of necessity, to claw her way out of Troughton for good. But her mind was playing tricks now, endlessly speculating on the events of summer 1979. The Troughton love triangle. Though she supposed that strictly speaking it was a love rectangle, with Bruno, his wife, her mother and Brown Owl behaving like characters in a West End farce.

Chris was ashamed of her own behaviour at Lucy's, but the irrational anger was still there. The taint of her mother Dina's adultery – mentioned in hushed tones whenever anyone spoke of Bruno Castigliano – had destroyed her parents' lives. Yet all the time the pillar of the bloody community had been as guilty as Dina. OK, so Judith was widowed, but her whole attitude proclaimed that she was more upstanding, more righteous, holier than thou.

And if it hadn't been for Chris's ludicrous curiosity, she'd never have known. She'd been cleaning Judith's old room, throwing herself into the mundane tasks because they stopped her thinking. While she was dusting under the bed – something no one had done for several decades judging from the mess – she'd noticed that one of the boards was loose, almost as though the sides had been shaved away. Intrigued, she'd pressed her finger around the sides and realized it *was* deliberate, and she began imagining some ancient hiding place to store jewels or perhaps birth certificates revealing the true parentage of a nineteenth-century servant. As she fantasized, the floorboard suddenly popped up and there were the letters, tied together with a piece of crepe bandage, the kind they used in Brownies to practise slings.

Chris finished the joint but still felt edgy. She walked back into the dressing room and picked the first black trousers and black top she could find. They reflected her mood only too well.

There was just one bonus to going out with the team. After seeing her mood tonight, she was sure they'd never invite her out again.

Paula balanced on the end of Sadie's bed and pointed the bubblegum-pink hairdryer at her damp head. She couldn't remember the last time she'd tried to style her hair and it felt unnatural stretching her arm round to dry the awkward bits. She'd attacked her overgrown fringe with nail scissors, and tried to put the parting so that the grey hairs were hidden behind the mousier ones. She checked in the mirror, but while the front view was passable, the back of her head still looked like a pan scourer.

'Oh sod it!' she said out loud, throwing the dryer onto the bed. It was the least of her worries. More pressing was the fact that SheriffJack was expecting a gorgeous slim blonde for dinner in Manchester tonight. And though her weight loss had accelerated in the last month – she'd been too worried about the eviction to eat, and walking for miles along the canal was the only way to tire herself out enough to sleep – she was still a hefty size sixteen.

There was a lesson there. If you were going to lie to someone on the internet and then try to disappear without a trace, it was best not to hook up online with an international web entrepreneur. One week after she logged off *Lawless* for good – how painful that had been, worse than giving up toast – she checked her email and found one in her junk folder from Jack.

In it he explained how he'd been worried about her since her unexplained departure from *Lawless* so he'd got a colleague to trace her via her IP address (she hadn't known she had one) and through that he'd found her details. *If you're giving me the brush-off, I understand,* the email said, *but at least please mail back to let me know you're OK, otherwise I wonder if I should go to the police or something. Or call in on you when I come to the UK.*

She'd had no choice to mail him back, an apology and an excuse, something pathetic about being so busy at work that she had no time any more to go online. His response was immediate: an invitation to dinner on the following Friday, when he'd be in Manchester. 7 p.m., the Lowry Hotel. He would be carrying flowers. She'd emailed him again, making more excuses, but the message bounced back immediately, an out-of-office autoreply saying he'd left on business in Europe and would respond on his return.

She tried to put it out of her mind, telling herself that it wasn't her fault the man was too thick-skinned to take no for an answer. But an image of this man, the only person who seemed to care whether she lived or died, sitting in a hotel lobby with a bunch of wilting carnations, was too much.

And she was curious, too, about whether Jack might really have been the man of her dreams. In the end, she decided to pose as her own 'assistant' and deliver a note in person. It was still dishonest, of course, but it seemed like the kindest thing to do. This way, he would keep his image of the gorgeous, glamorous woman he'd played with online. And she would have a glimpse of a life she could have had, without seeing the crushing regret in his face if she told him the truth. Wasn't her life already full of disappointment? She felt proud of herself for coming up with a workable solution.

As she stood up, Paula tripped over a purple handbag. There was no way all of Sadie's stuff was going to fit in Neil's parents house, but she hadn't yet been able to face telling her daughter that the eviction date had finally been confirmed. In three weeks, the kids would be back with their dad and Paula would be back with her parents.

She'd never felt so alone.

Chapter Thirty-five

Some parents may have faults for which
they should be pitied. Children should be
the first to forgive any failings and to help
their parents to be honoured by other people.
Would you not wish your children to stand
up for you?

My hair stinks of smoke, my lipstick won't go on straight and my brain is messed up. Seb took me for a congratulatory drink, which turned into three, just enough to make everything fuzzy. Now I'm trying to sober up before I meet Sunny, or he'll definitely think I'm an alcoholic.

A shower helps, and just swapping my pseudo-student clothes for my grown-up black suede skirt and flowery top makes me feel a little steadier on my feet. Lucky we're meeting in the restaurant so the opportunities for me to fall over are limited to the journeys between my room, the lift and the table Sunny's booked.

I feel so flat now Seb and I have said goodbye. He was all smiles and excitement that he's helped me get the chance I wanted, but that seems to be it. So long, farewell, etc. Another conquest completed. Of course. What the hell else did I think it was about?

I squeeze my feet into shoestring-pink suede sandals and take a few tentative steps, watching myself in the enormous mirror. That's not too bad; you could almost imagine my slight wobble is the deliberate sway of a sexy woman. I just hope poor Sunny doesn't think I'm trying to seduce him.

The lift is so quiet and so fast that I feel dizzy when it deposits me on the restaurant floor. He's waiting there, wearing what resembles a safari suit, yards of creamy creased linen stretched across his frame. He looks more like a black Christopher Biggins than a great jungle explorer but despite the clothes, he has presence. Years of being treated like God by nurses and patients, I suppose.

'Lucy! My dear!' He strides towards me, gives me a bear hug, but when we separate, there's a wariness in his eyes and he looks away quickly. I shiver, knowing that whatever he's going to tell me is going to throw me into more confusion.

'Hello, Sunny.' This time I hold his gaze, granting him permission to hurt me with his words.

'Shall we have a drink before we eat?' He reaches out to take my arm, locking it under his elbow in a gesture that makes me feel protected. We pass Friday-night drinkers: a group of young office workers dominated by a boy with blond highlights who looks too young to be served alcohol, a man virtually hidden by the enormous bunch of white roses he's clutching in front of him. I love that about hotels: the sense that stories are constantly beginning and ending in the lobby or the bar or the bedroom.

And as Sunny and I take a leather banquette in the quietest part of the bar, shielded from everyone else by full-length bamboo screens, I know that my father's story will end here tonight.

Once we've ordered – a Scotch for Sunny and a mineral water for me – we both clear our throats at the same time, then laugh nervously. 'Do you like my choice of hotel, then, Lucy?' he says.

'Yes. Not what I'd ever have chosen for myself.'

'Sometimes we don't give ourselves what we deserve. And I think you've had a tough few months.'

I nod, as the waitress returns with our drinks and a dish of roasted nuts.

'Lucy, I can understand why you think that knowing everything there is to know about your father is going to help, but it may not be what you're expecting.'

'You don't have to protect me.'

He shakes his head. 'Sorry, I don't mean to be patronizing. You're a grown woman. But you're also an orphan and I know that's tough whatever age you are.'

Orphan. I think back to the funeral, to the tears I thought would never stop. I can't believe it's only four months ago. Mum's death was the trigger for all of this: the singing, the search for my father, my 'break' from Andrew. I have to close the circle. 'It is tough. But then, you know, Sunny, I am beginning to think I might be quite tough too.'

He laughs softly. 'Of course you are. You always were.'

I stare at him, astonished. 'Was I?'

'Definitely. As a toddler, you were constantly tripping up, trying to run before you could walk, and you never cried.'

I close my eyes for a moment, struggling to picture this fearless version of myself. 'But I thought ... I mean, I've always been the cry-baby.'

'Oh, Lucy.' He throws back his head and laughs, a generous rumble that goes on and on. 'You were a little girl. Of course you cried. That's the thing about little girls: they feel things deeply and it's a habit too many of them lose when they become all *grown-up*. Bottling up your feelings leads to all sorts of trouble. And as a heart surgeon I've seen what happens.'

The waitress returns to usher us to our table and I'm sure that as I walk across the bar, I'm a tiny bit taller. Proud, brave Lucy.

Our table is the last on the long balcony that overlooks the canal and its quirky white-metal bridge, which glows in the evening light. 'This is lovely. Very Mediterranean,' I say, as he gestures for me to take the seat with the best view.

'Not really my cup of tea. Not gritty enough. But I asked the boys at work where they'd take their girlfriends for a treat. Somewhere with good food, champagne, but enough privacy to talk properly.'

We order from the fancy menu, take bread from the basket, are served a crisp white wine by the sommelier and toast the summer and then ... we're alone. Even though it's hot enough to go without my cardigan, I shiver. 'So. My father.'

'I think I've made it worse by putting this off, Lucy, but it's hard to know where to begin.'

'At the end?'

'Quite so. At the end.' He puts his glass down and folds his hands together. 'Your father died of an overdose, Lucy.'

I stare at his hands for a long time. Surgeon's hands. I notice his nails – they're almost perfectly square, with tips so white he looks like he's had a French manicure, and beautifully shaped half moons waning above each cuticle.

'Lucy?'

'Not a heart attack, then?' My voice sounds as though it's coming from somewhere a long way away.

'Well, he would have arrested, in that the drug would have suppressed his breathing, and then his heart would have stopped. That's what went on the death certificate, but it wasn't quite the whole story.'

I look up. 'What did he overdose on?'

I see a slight crease in his eyes, a flicker of concern, before he delivers the blow. 'Diamorphine.'

'Which is ... *heroin*, isn't it?' I've watched too many medical dramas for my own good.

He nods. 'I'm sorry, Lucy.'

The image of my father, the bright, handsome, fiercely committed children's doctor who called me Looby-Lou, is fading as fast as the memory of a wonderful dream you try to hang onto on waking but can't quite recapture once you're back in the real world. And in its place, there's an image of a man with my father's face, jabbing a syringe into his arm, the eyes rolling back in his head as he understands what he's done and—

'Had he done it before? I mean, was he addicted to heroin? Was he alone?' The questions come as fast as thoughts. 'Was it, I mean, could it have been deliberate?'

Sunny holds my gaze. 'Since you first called, I've been wondering how to answer that question. I mean, the powers-that-be convinced the coroner it was a freak accident, which kept the press at bay.'

'But?'

'But I don't think we'll ever know, Lucy. He was alone, yes.

He had taken drugs before, to be honest; a lot of the doctors did. Uppers, downers – but rarely diamorph. It was seen as a step too far, by most of us. And the risk of discovery was incredibly high. So I like to think not. The toxicology report was confidential, but if, as I suspect, he was taking other drugs … it could just have proved too much for him.'

'Wouldn't he have known that?' I'm surprised at how these rational questions keep popping into my head. I feel like I'm hovering above myself, watching as I sit calmly in a glamorous restaurant, hands folded neatly on the starched tablecloth. You would never guess my world had been knocked off its axis.

'He might have done. It's something I've debated in my own mind for the last thirty years. Jim was a mercurial character. Brilliant company sometimes, but appalling to be with at other times. With someone as extreme as him …' Sunny looks over my shoulder, lost in memories that make his eyes dance, before he refocuses on me. 'I truly don't think it was deliberate, Lucy. He adored you; he loved Judy with all the intensity that made him who he was. He had a need to escape, too, and that made him experiment, but I don't believe he wanted to leave behind what mattered most.'

'Right.' I try to smile at him, to thank him, but nothing happens. 'I appreciate you being honest with me.'

The waitress delivers our starters – gazpacho soup for me, ham and melon for Sunny – before he can reply. 'I think you've been in the dark for long enough. Though maybe this isn't the best place to find out. I just didn't know how to tell you.' He reaches out to touch my hands. 'You're frozen, Lucy. Would you like me to see if we can move inside? Or you could go back to your room if you like.'

'No, I'm not cold, just …' I try to think. 'Numb, I suppose.'

He's still touching my arm lightly across the table, as we each eat awkwardly with one hand. But I don't want him to let go.

The soup tastes of summer. The air smells of barbecues and traffic. Everything is clearer, sharper, in focus. There are no more secrets.

On the shimmering bridge, a man is looking at his watch. It's truth o'clock.

Chapter Thirty-six

Don't let any man make love to you unless he wants to marry you and you are willing to do so. Moral courage is one thing that all Guides keep a stock of.

Terri saw Colin before he saw her. He was standing next to the enormous pylon that thrust up into the air from the centre of the Trinity Bridge. Trust him to position himself next to the phallic symbol.

She approached stealthily, determined to catch him unawares, to regain a little control over the situation he'd engineered. He was staring into the River Irwell, a grey figure against the white metal curves and cleverness of the bridge. Neat in his tweed jacket, thinning hair newly cut. A small man in every sense of the word.

She hoped he wasn't going to ask her to come back to him.

'Hello Colin,' she said, when she was only a few steps away. He turned slowly, as if he'd always known she was there.

'Teresa.' His use of her full name made her feel uncomfortable, somehow. He didn't smile, but looked her up and down as though he was appraising a second-hand car. She felt suddenly conscious of her clingy denim skirt, and clingier T-shirt. 'Thank you for coming.'

His formality made her impatient. 'Well, I was curious to know what you thought was so important you had to tell me in person.'

'Some things aren't appropriate on the phone.' He pointed over at a curvy metal bench on the Salford side of the bridge.

'Shall we sit down?'

'You look well,' Terri told him as they walked across. It was a lie. He looked exactly as tired and uninspired as he always did, and she'd only said it to force him to say the same about her. She knew she did look different. Love or sex or both had got her hormones pumping so her hair and her skin shone. Even the tutors had noticed.

'Do I? You look rather under-dressed,' he said. His voice sounded more self-righteous than before. Perhaps he'd brought her here to boast about something, though she struggled to imagine what. Maybe he'd finally finished that bloody screenplay.

They sat down one bench away from a group of three teenage girls, who were taking photos of each other with their mobile phones, then laughing loudly as they debated who to send each picture to.

'A lot has changed since we broke up,' Colin said abruptly, not looking at Terri.

'Hmm,' she said, wondering if she was going to be able to keep her temper and not gloat about Howard.

'I have found Jesus.'

She stared at him. 'You? But ... how? I mean, you were never remotely interested when we were seeing each other.' She felt irritated. If anyone was going to convert Colin, surely it should have been her.

'God moves in mysterious ways,' he said, without irony. 'I had more time to think with you gone and I began to wonder what the point was. Of existence. And then I found it.' And he touched a badge on his lapel, shaped like a fish.

'Well, um, good for you. Congratulations.' She smiled at him. 'Can I go now?'

He shook his head. 'I didn't call you here just to tell you that,' he said, as the girls at the bench began to giggle, hoiking up their skirts and pulling down their tops to pose for another snap. He frowned his disapproval. 'They can't be older than fifteen. Our society is sick to the core.'

Terri suppressed a laugh as she remembered Colin's vast collection of *Loaded* and *Maxim* magazines. 'I think they're harmless enough. They're just kids.'

'Now, you see, that's directly connected to why I wanted to talk to you. There is no easy way to say this, Teresa, but I think you're crossing the line in your behaviour and if you're committed to the church, you should look at yourself.'

'Eh?' Terri felt dizzy: the landscape was familiar, but black was white and white was suddenly black. 'What are you talking about, Colin?'

He blushed. 'Sex,' he whispered. 'I'm not going to spell it out, but frankly the way you used to behave was *not Christian*. The things you were willing to do, they go beyond what anyone who believes should be doing outside marriage, never mind someone who intends to go into the clergy.'

She blinked hard, but when she opened her eyes, he was still there, wearing that sanctimonious expression. 'The things I was willing to do? You mean, the things *you* more or less blackmailed me into doing?'

He squirmed slightly. 'I didn't understand the importance, the sanctity of the sexual act, at that stage. But you did. And yet you still ... touched. And allowed yourself to be touched. I don't believe in dwelling on the past but I want to warn you that it's not appropriate behaviour.'

'Oh yeah? And what are you going to do about it?' Terri realized she was shouting: the teenagers stopped what they were doing to look up at them and nudge each other.

'Really,' he blustered. 'I don't know exactly, I just wanted to make it clear to you and ... well, I don't suppose the authorities at the college would be all that happy to know what one of their students has—'

'So let me get this straight.' she interrupted him. 'You'd actually tell tales ... I don't know, repeat *pillow talk* out of some sort of misguided moral crusade. I've heard it all now. And what would be the point of that?'

He put his fingers to his lips to shush her, as the girls were now watching them closely. 'There's no need ...' He blushed again. 'I suppose the truth is that, well, I also wondered ... now we understand each other, and have so much in common, I thought you might like to consider getting back together.'

'Oh my Lord.' Terri didn't know whether to laugh in his

face or slap it. 'You've got one hell of a nerve. You are quite, quite insane.' She stood up, determined to leave before she said something she regretted.

'Now there's no need for that.'

'There's every need, Colin. And actually, I've got some news for you, too.' She paused, to make sure the girls were still looking, then said in her loudest voice, 'I've lost my virginity! After all that time with you feeling dead from the waist down, I finally met a man who could make me feel like a woman. And do you know what? It was flipping well worth waiting thirty-five years for. I am only glad that I didn't waste the experience on a lily-livered moron like you.'

Colin's mouth hung open and she allowed herself a good look at him before turning to go. Whatever happened now with Howard, right and wrong were no longer about rules, but about gut instinct.

As she walked past the teenagers, one of them called out, 'Go, girlfriend!' and Terri grinned back.

She was glad she'd made the effort to come out after all.

Chapter Thirty-seven

Let us be able to look back at our lives as if
they were a string of pearls. We can do good
in many little ways and each good act is a
beautiful pearl, which any of us can put
onto the string of our life.

It's colder now that the sun has set, but a waiter has been
weaving his way between the tables, switching on gas burners
that, together with the candles on each table, offer enough soft
lighting to see my main course – and my dining companion.

'Eating al fresco in Manchester,' Sunny says, those huge
brown eyes twinkling at me. 'Whatever next?'

'I wonder what my father would have made of it.'

'Oh, Jim was more the type for smoky basement bars, someone singing a little jazz, a bottle of red or three.'

Perhaps it's the wine, or perhaps it's just Sunny's matter-of-
factness, but I want to talk about my father. The shock of his
awful exit from this world is softened by the way his best friend
remembers him as someone who made life livelier, brighter,
more spectacular. Someone who burned brightly before he
burned out.

'And what was Mum doing while he was propping up the
bar?'

'Ah, Judy. She'd be up on the dance floor. Lovely mover, your
mother.'

I shake my head in disbelief. 'I can't picture it at all. But
then again, I never imagined she'd have been the type to have
an affair.'

Now it's Sunny's turn to look shocked. 'What do you mean?'

'Oh, I can see why now. It makes more sense now I know the kind of person my father was.' It's true. Suddenly I don't feel angry with her for being tempted by Bruno. But I do feel hurt by how close she came to giving up on me.

'Neither of us meant it to happen,' Sunny says, and his eyes are wet. It takes me a few moments to understand what he means.

'You ... and Mum?'

'Yes,' he whispers. 'I wasn't going to tell you – I couldn't see what purpose it would serve. But you guessed.'

'No, I didn't mean ...' And then I tail off as the tears run down his face.

'It only ... happened twice. Your mother needed someone, Lucy. She was so alone, looking after you and after your father too, who was sometimes harder than a child to deal with. But it shouldn't have happened at all. And I can't help wondering, well, if your father knew.'

'Could he have known?'

'We were very careful and we put a stop to it almost as soon as it began, so I don't think he suspected. But I can never know for sure.'

'And your wife? Did she know?'

He nods. 'After Jim died, I confessed. I couldn't bear there to be more lies.'

The final detail, and it all makes sense. My mother's refusal to talk about my father. Turning her back on the life I know she must have loved, and the people who could have helped her. Sunny's wife's reaction to me. But there's one more thing ...

'It's OK,' I say, reaching out for Sunny's hand, comforting him this time. 'I didn't guess, you know. The affair. This was later. She was carrying on with the father of one of the girls I was in the Brownies with, in Troughton. We found letters.'

'No. Not Judy. Not after what happened.' He's shaking his head. 'The guilt she felt ... she wouldn't do it again.'

'They're love letters,' I say. 'Saying things that only a lover would say. He wanted her to run away with him, to leave me behind. And it looks like she considered it.' I can hear the hurt and betrayal in my own voice, a child's sulky refusal to acknowledge that a parent could have any other identity.

'I cannot believe it.'

I reach into my bag. 'Read this.'

'Are you sure you want me to?' He takes the letter when he sees the look on my face. He reads it slowly and then nods. 'Life as a widow must have been even lonelier than I thought. But this *usignolo*. What does he mean?'

I shrug. 'It sounds like signature, something legal, official. I thought perhaps he was forbidden to get divorced. Being a Catholic. Maybe that's why she wouldn't leave — because she could never marry him.'

'Maybe.' Sunny reaches into his briefcase, takes out a hand-held computer. 'I'm such a gadget addict.' He clicks on the screen a few times, then peers at the letter. 'What if *usignolo* is you, Lucy?'

I sigh. 'Yeah, right.'

He passes me the computer. '*Usignolo* isn't signature, Lucy. Or divorce. It means nightingale.'

I stare at the screen, where a webpage shows a picture of a drab brown bird with its mouth open. Alongside it the caption reads: *L'Usignolo*: (*Luscinia megarhynchos*) *Dal canto molto ricco e melodioso*. 'But …'

'You must speak a little Italian, from your love of opera,' he says.

'Well, yes. *Canto* is song, *molto* is very … rich and melodious. I don't see—'

'Lucy, he was the *aquila*, the eagle. And your mother *allocco*, the brown owl. It's like a code. People become birds. So the nightingale — with the beautiful voice … he's talking about you.'

And now I read the letter again: '*There is, I know, the usignolo to think of. I know this is what stands in your way, but it need not. It can be taken care of. I know that this is the hardest decision you will ever make.*'

'She chose you, Lucy.'

'She chose me.' My voice is low.

'She had the choice between staying with you, or leaving with Bruno. She made the only choice she could,' Sunny says, more calmly.

'Yes.' Unlike me, Mum didn't run away.

'She was a strong woman, Lucy. Under exceptional pressure.'

For the first time, tonight, I understand exactly how strong. My mother – younger than I am now – back in the small town she'd fought so hard to escape, saddled with a needy little girl and an enormous grief and a terrible secret she wanted to keep hidden. Who could blame her for succumbing to a charming newcomer with the gift of the gab? And yet despite my shortcomings as a daughter, she chose me.

As Sunny wipes away the last of his tears, he smiles and in the candlelight, he looks so much like his son that I blush.

'I know she was.' I line up my knife and fork on the plate, take a slug of wine. 'Stronger than me.'

'Don't be so hard on yourself, Lucy. This is so much to take in in one night. I think you're handling this phenomenally well.' He tops up my drink. 'You need support now. Will you tell your husband?'

'I've left my husband.'

'Ah.'

He waits for me to tell him why. 'Everything's changed since Mum died and I haven't known where I am. But I've been so selfish. Poor Sasha's been left not knowing if she's coming or going.'

'Children are more resilient than we give them credit for. What about you?'

'Oh, I never know if I'm coming or going.'

The waitress takes our plates, and leaves in their place a dessert menu, which I scan although I'm full, to give me an excuse to stay here with Sunny, because he seems to help everything make sense.

'I suppose,' he says, when we've both ordered the chocolate fondant that the menu says takes twenty minutes to arrive, 'the most fundamental question is whether you actually love your husband.'

Oh God ...

I look at Sunny. If I can make anyone understand, it will be him. 'He's ... just always been there.' I falter, but Sunny smiles back, encouraging me to carry on.

'He's a good father. A good provider, loyal. I care about what happens to him. He's been part of my life for so long that I find it hard to imagine life without him. I'm used to him. I know his limitations and I understand why he is the way he is. Is that love?'

He holds his big hands up as if to say, who knows?

'He's talking about having another baby. A new start.'

'Ah,' he says. He has an ability to say so much in a syllable.

'I'd love another baby. A family. I really would. It could be what we need.'

'Babies are wonderful things,' he says. 'But they don't often save marriages. They complicate things. What do you *really* want, Lucy?'

'Isn't that irrelevant? It's not right to throw all our lives up in the air for the sake of ... a pipe dream.'

Sunny smiles again. Then, he whispers, 'Tell me about your pipe dreams, Lucy.'

Chapter Thirty-eight

Our plan ought to be to help others by:
thinking only the best of them, speaking only
well of them, doing well by them.

Paula walked into reception and the receptionist shot her a
look that said: *you* don't belong here.

Before the woman could challenge her, Paula spotted the
sign for the Ladies' and dashed inside, locking herself in the
first cubicle. She sat on the closed toilet lid and wondered yet
again whether she could go through with it. Jack would realize
immediately that something was wrong, because 'Cutey' would
never employ a personal assistant who looked like an escapee
from the Women's Institute Fat Camp. Yet her curiosity had
propelled her this far.

She left the cubicle and blinked at herself in the full-length
mirror. She hadn't seen herself this clearly for years, probably
not since she squeezed herself into her wedding dress under
the nervous eyes of the seamstress, her body straining against
the unforgiving satin. It was a testament to the dressmaker's
thoroughness that there'd been no splits or accidents during her
Big Day.

This was different. The cloakroom was bigger than her living
room, and had twenty tiny lights embedded in the ceiling, which
cast a flattering glow. The multiple mirrors reflected an infinite
line of Paulas. But these women were not what she'd expected.
Sure, she knew she'd lost weight, but this was a shock.

Peering back at her was a *normal*-shaped woman. Not skinny,
nor glamorous, but normal, the kind who could walk into a

normal clothes shop without automatically being shown the door and directed to a store with an outsize range. Not that she could afford new clothes. Today the only thing she could find that didn't swamp her new size-sixteen figure was a faded flowery dress from the back of the wardrobe, more suited to the seventeen-year-old she was when she'd last fitted into it.

Surprised, she found her lipstick in her handbag, and put more on, drawing back slightly see the effect. Her skin was better since she'd begun walking, too: her spots and the bags under her eyes had gone. It was hard to know what would happen when she moved back in with her parents, though. The endless reminders of their family's failures would have her gorging on toast again before you could say Chivers Marmalade. She shook her head, feeling her resolve fading by the second.

Come on, Paula, she told herself. *You haven't travelled all this way to leave without even seeing this man.* She straightened up, pulled out the handwritten note that she planned to hand to Jack (or if she lost her nerve again, to give to a waiter to pass on) and walked out of the toilets.

Straight into an enormous bunch of white roses.

'Will you watch where you're—?' Then she stopped, speechless. Because behind the roses was her husband.

'Looking for someone?' Neil said, guardedly.

'It's none of your business,' she snapped. Was he meeting his fancy piece here? Could it really be a coincidence or was this some sort of sick joke?

'Paula, Jack's not coming.'

'What do you mean?' Paula mumbled.

He looked embarrassed now. 'Jack ... doesn't exist.'

'But ...' Paula felt almost faint with confusion.

'I'm Jack,' he said and he opened out the hand that wasn't clutching the roses, in a gesture of apology. 'I arranged it all. The messages. The game. This meeting.'

'I don't understand. Jack is American. From Boston. Or was it Seattle?' She stopped. Which was it? Hadn't he mentioned both? 'He knows all about baseball. And thinks brownies are made of chocolate ...'

Neil looked on the verge of tears. 'I had to try to get you

back, Paulie. The computer was what drove us apart in the first place so I thought it was the only thing that could bring us together again. I didn't want to lie, but I couldn't give up on us.'

Paula managed to stumble across to the enormous red sofa in the lobby. She had to sit down. 'So you joined *Lawless* and you found me and ...' She stopped. 'But you don't have a computer.'

He looked sheepish. 'No, but there's one at the library. I did a course and everything; some of the kids played for me until I got good at it. The librarian chucked me out in the end, so I used the computer at the Job Club instead. I've got so good at it, they've even offered me a job teaching the other fogies how to use the internet.'

But Paula wasn't listening. She was trying to remember all the things she'd said on the computer: most of it was lies, of course, because otherwise she'd been so sure Jack would be disgusted by the reality of her life. Yet she'd always felt Jack understood her better than anyone else ... and now she knew why. 'You deceived me for *months*.'

'It was the only way I could think of to get you back.' He slumped next to her on the sofa, placing the roses in the gap between them.

'You strung me along.'

'Yes.' He shrugged. 'I hoped it would work. You and the kids are all that matter to me. It was worth a try.'

'That stuff about me being slim and beautiful. You let me make a fool of myself.'

'You are beautiful, Paulie. You've always been beautiful to me. And now you're slim as well. You look amazing.'

The concierge, dressed in a designer black suit, hovered nearby and eventually Paula looked up. 'Is there anything I can help you with, madam? Directions? A taxi?'

She shook her head. 'Don't worry, we won't be cluttering up your lobby much longer.'

As the concierge moved away, Neil grasped her hand. 'Please can we try again, Paula? We could make it work. With my new job, we might be able to talk the housing association into letting us stay in the flat. The kids want it, and I want it and I know it's cheeky of me, but I can't help thinking you might want it too. Deep down.'

She left her hand in his as she thought about it. He had lied but he'd done it for the right reasons. It was romantic, in the strangest way. He was a decent person, but she wasn't: she was worthless, the reason their marriage broke up, because she destroyed people. Nothing could change that.

Paula let go of his hand, too embarrassed to look up at his face. And then she saw the blood covering her palm and his. 'What have you done?'

'Oh,' he said, withdrawing his hand quickly and putting it in his pocket. 'I cut myself on the thorns. It's nothing.'

That was when it ambushed her, this overwhelming rush of compassion that she hadn't felt in so long, the protective instinct she experienced, despite herself, whenever Charlie or Sadie had tripped over or been stung by a wasp. 'Oh, Neil. God, I am such a bitch. Why would you want to be with someone like me? Give me one good reason.'

He looked at her then and she felt a strange recognition, as she finally accepted that this was SheriffJack, the one person in the world who seemed to understand her. She was being offered another chance. 'Because I know you're not a bitch, Paulie. You're human. And you can't see what's special about you. But I can. And there's no one else I want but you.'

'But what about the woman the kids keep talking about?'

He blushed. 'Oh. You mean the size-six supermodel with the successful business in Manchester and the highest score in *Lawless* this side of the Pennines? It was always you.'

'I don't know, duck. There's so much we couldn't work out before, so many complications.' But as she said it, she realized how much she wanted him to argue back.

The concierge was openly staring at them now. Neil shook his head. 'There's nothing we can't solve if we put our minds to it. Listen, why don't we carry on this conversation somewhere else? Somewhere that's a bit more *us*. I passed this brilliant-looking Chinese on the way here. Quiet enough for us to talk. It's on me.'

She nodded. 'All right. I'm not saying yes to getting back together.'

He grinned. 'But you're not saying no either, Paulie. And I can't explain how that makes me feel.'

Chapter Thirty-nine

Girls can even be brave enough to shoot
tigers, if they can keep cool.

By the time the chocolate fondant arrives, raised from the plate on toffee struts, like a beach hut, I've told Sunny what might just make me happy. To begin with, it doesn't amount to much: an image of myself waiting in the wings, the feel and smell of greasepaint on my skin, before I step into the limelight.

'What do you think you're about to sing?' Sunny says when I apologize for the vagueness of my vision.

'Oh, God knows.' I laugh, though actually I know exactly what it is. Carmen's 'Habanera'.

He raises his eyebrows. 'I'm sure you can do better than that.'

So I tell him – and then prompted by his questions, I focus first on my costume, the tightness of my curly Latin wig. Then I imagine the wonderful intensity of the feeling as I prepare to perform. Then I try to summon up the audience. Sasha is there, of course, and Terri, Chris and Paula.

'And what about Andrew?'

I close my eyes, concentrating. Is he smiling to encourage me, or trying not to cry as I sing my first solo role, or leading the standing ovation? I can't see him doing any of those things. There's an empty seat in the front row.

I push my spoon into the fondant, and a pool of hot liquid chocolate escapes onto the plate, melting the minty green island of ice-cream next to it. I raise the spoon to my lips, but can't swallow because my eyes have filled with tears. 'I can't see him.'

'Oh, Lucy,' Sunny says. 'It's just a silly exercise. It doesn't mean anything.'

But I think he's wrong. If I can't see my husband in the future I dream of, then what business do we have being together? I shut my eyes, trying not to see the empty seat, but instead someone sits down. It's not Andrew.

It's Seb.

I feel sick. How stupid am I? A sad middle-aged woman, with a crush on the first decent-looking man to be nice to her in years.

Sunny expertly changes the subject, begins to quiz me on what I need to do to get a break in music. I sheepishly admit that Seb has been helping me, but he just smiles. 'I knew he was up to something. I can always tell. And he's quite a talent-spotter, my boy is, so you've obviously got something going for you.'

'The thing is ... I know you said this doesn't have to be a pipe dream, but if I do what I want, it will break up my family. Family was what I always wanted.'

Sunny thinks it over as he licks the spoon clean of the last of the chocolate sauce. 'The question you need to ask yourself is whether *not* doing what you want will save your family.'

I look at my plate for a long time as the ice-cream melts and the whole pudding disintegrates. He's right. 'I think that—'

But then we hear raised voices from the bar, a drunken woman's, then a man's, then a whole screaming match that seems to stop, then start again three times before an uncompromising manager shouts them down. There's a final scuffle as we hear them being ejected.

'You were saying, Lucy?'

I feel very tired, suddenly. The thought of that enormous bed, and the prospect of forgetting all I've learned and done and agonized over today, is too tempting. And the longer I look at Sunny, the harder it is not to think of his son. 'Do you mind if we skip coffee, Sunny? I'm exhausted.'

'No, not at all,' he says. 'On condition, of course, that we do this again very soon. If you'll forgive me.'

'Forgive you?' I say. 'Oh yes. And thank you for telling me.

I still don't know where I'm going, but at least I know where I came from. And you wouldn't believe what a difference that makes.'

Chapter Forty

Remember that drink never yet cured a single
trouble; it only makes troubles grow worse
and worse the more you go on with it.

Chris would swear later that her feet didn't touch the ground
as the bouncer escorted her, Kian and Geoff out of the
Lowry Hotel. It was little details like that – throwing people out
without them feeling a thing – that earned a venue five stars.

Once her feet were back on the ground, albeit a ground that
felt far from steady, she wasn't sure what to do. The argument
with Geoff that had seemed so important in the bar, surrounded
by her former colleagues, suddenly lost its sting and she felt
embarrassed.

'Are you two going to play nicely now, or am I going to have
to bang your heads together?' Kian stood with his hands on his
hips. 'Do you know, that's the first time *in my life* I have ever
been chucked out of anywhere? Though the concierge was very
gentle, I must say. Lovely hands.'

'Do you ever give it a rest?' Geoff grunted.

'Now don't start on Kian,' Chris said, feeling her hackles rise
again.

'With all due respect, love, it wasn't me or Kian who had us
ejected from the sodding premises.'

There were just enough brain cells left unsaturated by alcohol
for Chris to recognize Geoff was trying to wind her up, but she
couldn't figure out why. She'd arrived late and stoned and drunk
and, thanks to the cocktails her former colleagues had insisted on
buying her, got progressively drunker as the evening progressed.

She kept thinking of questions she wanted to ask them – about Kian's plans to buy a studio flat, about Jan the Product Designer's engagement to Tish – but somehow they didn't come out right. Instead she sat wedged into the central seat of the circular banquette, feeling oddly paralysed and shy among the people she'd thought were her friends. As they gossiped about the new management and the brainstorming awayday they'd all gone on in Amsterdam's red light district, she realized they weren't friends, just ex-colleagues. Worse than that. Ex-employees, once paid to be nice to her. They were only here now, supplying her with booze and pretending to be interested in her frankly tedious life, for the same reason they'd take flowers to an ageing maiden aunt. Pity. They were probably counting the minutes until they could make their excuses and leave.

In the end, she'd saved them the trouble. A stray, no more than averagely superior comment by Geoff – she couldn't quite remember what he'd said now, some boast about a long boozy lunch he'd shared with the MD of Eros – had been enough. All the rage and hurt and betrayal she'd been bottling up came out in a torrent of slurred abuse. She accused him of being a traitor and a Judas, of plotting against her to stitch her up and steal her company from under her nose, and other things that made her blush to recall.

'Fair point,' she said as the three of them stood, aimless, outside the hotel.

Geoff said: 'So are we going somewhere else? Like … your place.' There was a definite leer in his expression and she had a momentary flashback to the sex they'd had. It was only six weeks ago, yet the image of herself that night seemed like it belonged to a different person: a confident, sexy woman with a life.

'No thanks. I'm sure there must be a lap-dancing club around here that'll give you what you want. A man of your … standing shouldn't really be spending his nights out with an unemployed old soak and a gay secretary, should he?'

Geoff stared at her for a moment, as if he was deciding whether to say something else. Eventually he smiled at her. 'Word of advice, Chris. Get back to work – doesn't matter what you do – before you go mad. People like us aren't meant to sit around on our arses watching the world go by. We're meant to be in the middle of things, shaking them up.'

Then he trudged off across the bridge, leaving Kian shaking his head. 'I wish he'd shake it up somewhere else. He is such a twat, Chris. I can't tell you how much we miss you.'

Suddenly she felt tears in her eyes. 'Miss me? A silly old drunk.'

'What is it with the "old" all of a sudden, madam?' He put an arm around her and steered her across the bridge. 'You're a woman in her prime. At your sexual peak, isn't that true?'

'What's the point in being at your sexual peak if no one wants to mount it? I think I'm going to go home, Kian.'

He peered at the time on his retro digital watch. 'No, don't go yet. Listen, why don't we sit down here for a bit, shoot the breeze. I've got an E if you fancy one.'

The bridge ahead of her was blurry through tears and she wasn't sure she could make it across without tripping up, so she joined him on the steps. 'No thanks. I feel so old, though, Kian. Past it. And what have I got to show for it?'

'Shedloads of cash for a start. You sure about the E?' he said, taking out a tiny envelope and offering her a pill. When she shook her head, he tucked it away again and found his cigarettes instead. She took one because she thought smoking might stop her crying.

'But what's money if you can't do anything with it? Except buy friends.'

'I'll ignore that, cheeky mare. Do you think I'm here because I'm after your cash, Chris?'

'No, but—'

'You're bloody brilliant. Best boss I ever—'

'I know, I know; you said that before.'

'So why do I bloody keep saying it, Chris? Because we need you.'

Chris frowned. 'I don't think I'm ever going to win an OBE for services to the sex industry, Kian.'

He sighed theatrically. 'Oh bloody hell, boss. How much do you want me to spell it out? We miss you.'

In the darkness, Chris felt a flicker of excitement. Maybe she *was* needed. Maybe this didn't have to be the end. The idea of being back with people, creating new products or marketing new ideas, made her skin tingle more than sex ever did. Then she thought of her flat and her parents and absent friends and felt empty all over again. 'You remember when the girl I knew from the old days came into the office. Terri?'

'Oh yeah. The vicar.'

'Since then, we've met up a few times, you know, the others from the Brownies. And they've all got something that matters to them in their lives. Two of them have got kids and even Terri's got God. I don't have anything that matters.'

'Anything, or anyone?'

'OK. Anyone.'

'Whatever happened to Matt? I liked him. Cute bum.'

She closed her eyes. 'We were wrong for each other. Well, I was wrong for him. Not nice enough.'

'I don't think that's true.'

She sighed. 'I must be really pissed, Kian, because you sounded just like—'

Then she felt a hand on the nape of her neck, in exactly the place guaranteed to make her purr with pleasure.

'Like me?' asked Matt. Chris opened her eyes and turned around.

'Yes. Like you. But how ... ?'

Kian grinned. 'Just call me Cupid, boys and girls. I invited Matt here along to your drinks. But the silly bugger had to be late, didn't he? We might have avoided that scene if you'd bothered to get here on time!'

Chris looked at Matt and the relief she felt at seeing the person who understood her best was reduced by her unbreakable rule reverberating in her mind. *Never mix sex and love.* 'Well done, Kian. Maybe it's time for Cupid to fly off somewhere else?'

Kian looked at them and nodded. 'Oh yes, you lovebirds will have some *talking* to do, won't you? Just don't forget what I said about work, Chris.' He turned back towards the hotel. 'I think they might let me back in. That concierge gave me a definite wink on the way out.'

'So ...' Chris said, when Kian had gone.

'So ...' Matt said. He'd made an effort: perfectly gelled hair, a spicy, musky scent wafting from his freshly shaved face, and new black glasses. 'You look different.'

'I feel different.' The streetlights made him still more attractive, but even here, at his handsome best, she knew there was a reason why they'd never worked, and why they never would. 'Unemployment gives you time to think.'

'Kian said you were going through a rough time. I wish you'd called.'

'I didn't want to *use* you to offload my troubles on.'

'I'd never feel used, Chris. We're friends. That's what friends do.' His face told her how hurt he was, how much he missed her.

Chris sighed. 'But that's the thing. I knew you wanted more and I knew I couldn't give you that. And I still can't.'

His face didn't change. 'You don't buy friendship with blow-jobs, Chris.'

She looked at him. 'No, but it's not fair to play with someone's emotions.'

'You never promised me anything. I've been doing some thinking too. I'd rather be in your life as a friend, than outside it.'

'But is that fair to you? I mean, I don't think we ought to fuck any more. It complicates things.'

He pulls a mock-horrified face. 'What about kissing?'

'I think we ought to avoid that too.'

'Understood,' he said, but the corners of his mouth were already turning up into a smile. 'Although ... well, I just wondered whether we could begin the platonic thing officially tomorrow? And whether, just for old times' sake, we might at least have a bit of a snog.'

Chris laughed properly for the first time in months. She nodded just enough to give him permission and as he moved in and their lips met, she felt a wave of happiness and familiarity. Yes, she was weak. But there were worse things in life than being weak.

Maybe, just maybe, things were going to be OK after all.

Chapter Forty-one

I often think that when the sun goes down
the world is hidden by a big blanket from the
light of heaven, but the stars are little holes
pierced in that blanket by doing good deeds
in this world.

Through the vast plate windows of my room, I see Manchester sparkling against the midnight blue. The city of opportunity. I wonder whether my father ever saw it like this, whether it would have changed the way he felt about the world.

I feel less shocked by Sunny's news than I should. Maybe I always knew there had to be something shameful about Jim Gill's death, because otherwise we'd have talked about him, been proud of his life, instead of embarrassed by his memory.

Knowing my mother had not one, but two affairs, isn't so hard to accept either. We all need kindness. Who am I to resent her for taking it where she could find it? Of all people, I should know that marriage and children aren't an antidote to loneliness.

I think ... no, I know, that I am going to sing. I have to. And, thanks to Mum, I have the money to follow my dream. I'd like to think *it's what she would have wanted*, but I'm not sure that's true. She would see singing as a trivial, flighty thing, but maybe she'd have more respect for me making a difficult decision, rather than doing what I have always done – fit in with what everybody else wants.

And the baby that Andrew and I could have, my chance to lift the Quentin curse? Though I can almost feel its feathery baby hair, smell its new baby skin, I know Sunny was right. Babies don't save marriages. I've been blessed with Sasha. That should be enough.

I fill the little travel kettle with water from the tap. In the bathroom mirror, my pupils are wide with excitement, and the Quentin streaks of orange and gold are brighter than ever. Coffee probably isn't a good idea. But the tiredness I felt earlier has disappeared, and this night feels too momentous for something as mundane as sleep.

I switch on the TV and surf the hotel's pay-for-view channels including an insipid comedy with Eddie Murphy, a thriller involving some teenagers trapped in a house after a power cut, and some porn. I watch with curiosity – I've never seen any before, Andrew and I aren't into that sort of thing – and when a message appears on the screen telling me I will be charged if I carry on watching, I press the 'yes' button to confirm that it will appear on my bill (the message reassures me that it won't specify the title of the movie, *Dirty Girls Get Wet*). It's a night for being reckless.

For a while, it's intriguing and, surprisingly, slightly arousing. The knock at the door comes when I'm tiring of the fake boobs and faked ecstasy.

Ten past twelve. I wonder if it's a drunken guest trying to get into the wrong room. Then there's another knock and even before I hear the voice calling 'Luuu-cy,' I think I know it's Seb. The man who fills the empty seat.

'Is it OK if I come in?' he asks, more tentative than I've ever heard him before. I open the door and he walks in hesitantly, waiting for me to lead the way.

'How did you know? I mean ...'

'Dad mentioned a few days ago that he was having dinner with you. I didn't think I'd say anything but then I came home after the audition and I hated the thought that it might be, well, the last time ...' He looks embarrassed, his hands waving in the air as he tries to explain himself.

'Why did you want to see me?' I say, registering, as he does, what's on the TV screen and fumbling around on the bed for the remote to switch it off.

'You don't know?'

He looks different now: none of the swagger I'm used to. There's only one reason I can think of that he's here, but it seems ridiculous to believe that he could want *me*.

Slowly, so that there is no doubt about what he's going to do and there's plenty of time for me to move out of the way if I want to, he takes three tiny steps forward and then leans down – his height shocks me again, though we've been this close many times before when he's corrected my breathing – and in that millisecond before he kisses me, I feel afraid and alive and I know nothing else will ever be the same again.

August 1979: The Pack holiday
ends unexpectedly early

'Psssst ... Lucy. Terri. Are you awake?'

For a moment, Lucy didn't know where she was. The greenhouse heat, the plasticky smell, the sweat wherever one part of her body met another. Then she opened her eyes.

Camp.

At least it was the last day.

Beside her, Terri was still snoring gently, her lips quivering with each breath. Lucy had never slept next to anyone else before and the noises and strange movements were frightening at first. But after three nights, she thought she'd miss her best friend's solid presence.

The zip at the end of the tent was being pulled down, and with it a triangle of bright light grew before Lucy's eyes adjusted to the sun. Paula's pointy face appeared through the gap.

'I can't find Netta. She's gone.'

'She's probably gone to breakfast,' Lucy said, congratulating herself on her good sense. That was the kind of thing Terri would say.

'It's only six o'clock in the morning. And all her stuff is gone. Except her sleeping bag, and she'd stuffed that with her pillow to make me think she was still there.'

'Oh.' Lucy felt silly now. She reached out to touch Terri's shoulder. 'Terri,' she said softly, 'wake up. Something's happened.'

Within seconds, Terri was bolt upright, frowning as Paula explained that she remembered Netta behaving oddly last night. 'She kept saying that she'd never had as good a friend as me.'

'And what did you say?' Lucy asked, feeling quite tearful.

Terri had never said anything like that to her, even though everyone knew they were Official Best Friends.

'I kicked her. It was soppy. Do you think she's run away?'

Terri manoeuvred herself out of the sleeping bag, put on her lace-ups, and wiggled through the tent entrance, her substantial Snoopy-clad bottom only just squeezing through. Lucy followed her.

It was a morning out of a glossy magazine: the sky seemed to be turning a deeper blue before Lucy's eyes, and the dew had washed the fields emerald. She could feel goosebumps on her legs as her bare feet touched the damp grass, but after the clammy tent, it felt delicious.

'Do put some shoes on, Luce,' Terri ordered. 'We've already got a missing Brownie. The last thing we need is a Brownie with pneumonia into the bargain.'

The Pixies were pitched in the furthest corner of Bethany's father's grounds, in recognition of the fact that they were now the most senior Brownies. This would be the last summer as Pixies for everyone but Chris and the Pack holiday had a fairy tale quality about it: long, perfect days, late evenings eating damper scones and roasted bananas straight from the campfire, and whispered confidences between tents into the night. Even Netta and Bethany seemed to have declared a truce. And then, when it was dark, everyone wanted Lucy to sing 'Kookaburra' and 'Three Little Angels'.

Despite her long-term loathing of the whole regime, Lucy already knew somehow that these memories would be imprinted in their minds, the first thing they'd think of as adults if anyone mentioned the Brownies.

The camping made it special, too, though Lucy missed her own bed. It made a change from the youth hostel-style dorms they'd stayed in before. Brownies weren't allowed proper 'canvas' camps like Guides but after Bethany's dad allowed them the use of the grounds, Judith had applied for special permission from HQ to set up a camp. As Brown Owl, she ran it with her usual efficiency, establishing potato-peeling production lines and water-fetching rotas. Yet even the chores seemed fun, away from home.

Terri opened the flap into the biggest tent, which was being shared by Paula, Netta and Chris. Bethany had her own, in Barbie pink, and she wore fluffy earmuffs 'to block out the birds. I hate being woken up early.'

They all peered inside Paula's tent: without the strict tidiness rules Terri had imposed on Lucy, it looked like a bomb had gone off at a Blue Peter bring and buy sale. On the left, Chris was propped up on her elbows, surrounded by T-shirts and socks and comics. 'I heard her leave the tent,' she said, 'but I thought she was just going to have a wee in the bushes.'

'And you didn't think it was strange when she didn't come back?'

'I fell asleep,' she said. 'Sorry.'

Terri sighed. 'Right, well, the fact she took her stuff with her probably means she hasn't been kidnapped. We should go and talk to Brown Owl right now.'

Paula shook her head. 'No! We'd have to go home early.'

'I don't think that's a very sensible—' Terri began, but she was interrupted by Bethany, who'd emerged, sleepy but still more elegant than Olga Korbut, from her tent.

'What are you playing at, waking me up?'

When Terri told her, Bethany shrugged. 'About time. She didn't fit in, did she? Can I go back to sleep now?'

'But we need to tell the grown-ups,' Terri insisted.

'Who exactly is in charge here, Terri?'

'You are, but …' Terri's voice trailed away. In the competition between duty and loyalty, loyalty would always win. Terri would never dream of pulling rank.

Bethany smiled. 'We don't say anything. If anyone asks where she is, we tell them she's not well and wanted to sleep undisturbed. Then once they find out, we can say we didn't notice because of the way she packed her sleeping bag. At least she's done us a favour by covering it up.'

Lucy felt sick. It wasn't right. What if something *had* happened to Netta? As Bethany padded back across the field in her feather-trimmed slippers, Terri turned to the others. 'I think we should search the tent for evidence.'

Paula groaned. 'We'd never find an elephant in there.'

Chris poked her head out of the tent. 'No, what we need to do is a fingertip search. I read it in a book. We divide the area into inch-wide squares and each take one, until we find it.'

'Find what, though?' Paula was unconvinced.

'Well, if we knew that, we wouldn't be looking in the first place, would we?' Terri said.

An hour later, and they'd found nothing unexpected, though they'd scoffed an entire packet of hairy Rolos that had somehow ended up in Chris's sleeping bag. But Lucy felt even sicker.

It was only when they began to get dressed, preparing for breakfast with the fatalism of a condemned man, that Paula discovered something tucked into her sock. A note. Although it was addressed to her, she handed it straight over to Terri, who unfolded it and read the contents out loud:

'To Paula. I am sorry. I wish I could have told you we were going, but I couldn't. It's always secrets. That's how my family is. I hate leaving you behind, because I have been happiest here. And I hope we might meet up when we're grown-ups and when I can decide where I will live. I hope you will have forgiven me by then. Your friend, always. Simonetta. PS: will you have my tropical fish? They should still be at the house and I worry they'll die unless someone rescues them. I named the baby guppies after the Pixies. Bethany is the most stupid one. Lucy hides in the greenery. And Paula is the fastest.'

'Well, really!' Bethany said.

Paula took the note back, stared at it for a long time, then said: 'Why would I have to forgive her for anything?'

They passed the note between themselves for a few minutes, waiting for something to occur to them, but it didn't. Finally, Terri said, 'At least we know she's OK. And I think we should stick to what Bethany says. If Netta's family have really disappeared, our parents will realize themselves soon enough.'

That realization came at breakfast. As they queued along the trestle tables, spooning out what remained of the Corn Flakes and Coco Pops from enormous tin dishes (the notoriously clumsy Gnomes had been on early food duty so most of the cereal was in the grass), Lucy tried to stop her hand shaking.

The others kept their heads down, though they'd already worked out it was Terri who was going to lie if Brown Owl asked where Netta was. Terri never lied so would automatically be trusted.

Once they sat down, Lucy focused on the other girls' shoes, to stop the shaking. A pair of scuffed dirt-brown T-bars – attached to a pair of equally battle-scarred legs – were kicking against the air, propelled by frustration. Paula.

Navy-blue lace-ups with white knee socks. Terri's feet must have been *boiling* but they were motionless, a couple of inches from the grass. Red slip-ons and odd socks – one blue, one brown – could only belong to Chris. There was far too much going on in her daydreams to bother making things match. Even now her right and left feet were at angles to each other, as if arguing or trying to head off in different directions. Lucy looked down at her own shoes, the yellowy sandals with pink leather flower buckles already beginning to blur in the latest deluge of tears.

And missing from the gathering: black pumps from Woolworths, right foot crossed over left ankle, like a grown-up. The bump of Netta's toes always showed through the fabric at the rounded end of each shoe because they were too small for her, and the rubber was coming away. Yet she'd taken those with her too.

'Paula?' Chris said, after a few moments. 'Isn't that your parents?'

They all peered up now, even Bethany. Patsy and Nigel were standing next to Lucy's mum. Patsy's face was as pink as her dress; her blonde hair hung limply without its carefully constructed wave, while her little hands were clasped together, as if she was worried what they'd do if she let them free. Nigel's shirt buttons were done up wrong. He pointed over at the Pixies and they began to walk over.

'Oh God, what now?' said Bethany. 'Don't forget your story, Terri. Lucy's mum never believes what I say anyway.'

Lucy thought her mother looked strange as she approached. Her face was deliberately smiley, as it was when Lucy had a dentist's appointment. 'Hello, girls. Now then. Where's Netta got to? Not like her to be late for breakfast.' She turned to

Paula's parents, who were not smiling at all. 'Appetite like a horse, that one. Mind you, so's your Paula and I don't know where she puts it all.'

The girls sat in silence, watching Terri. 'I . . .' she said. 'I don't know but I think perhaps—'

'Bruno's gone,' Nigel said sharply. 'He hasn't called me back for a week, not since he paid our bankers' draft in for the time-share. We were meant to be flying out to Italy. He was booking the flights and arranging our passports and everything.'

Judith frowned. 'Perhaps he's got held up in London. These things take time.'

'No! I rang the airlines. No one even flies from Britain to the airport he said we'd be going to. And then I went to the house. The gates were locked and I couldn't get an answer and I couldn't see his car in the drive.'

'I'm sure they've just gone away,' Judith said cheerily. 'While Netta's been here, perhaps they wanted a break by the coast. It's such wonderful weather.' But Lucy noticed her mother's eyes were darting around the field, trying to spot Netta.

Nigel's voice was getting higher and higher. 'I called the letting agent and they said . . .' he cast a nervous glance at his wife, 'they said he was in arrears. Months of arrears.'

Patsy moaned.

'It wasn't like he could have been short of money,' Nigel continued, 'because he'd just paid twelve . . . thousand . . . pounds . . . of our money into his bank account.'

'Golly! That is a lot of money,' Judith said.

'We remortgaged our house,' Nigel whispered. 'And there's something else odd. Bruno gave us strict instructions to get the bank to make out the draft to B. Castigliano. And when I called them, they had no record of a Bruno. Only a Brian.'

'Brian?' Lucy's mother's voice was sharp. 'Brian,' she repeated, as though it was a strange, foreign word, instead of the name of the snail in *The Magic Roundabout*. 'But . . . I'm sure there's some simple explanation. I mean, they wouldn't have gone far without Simonetta.'

Lucy closed her eyes. After what seemed like for ever, Terri said: 'Netta's gone too. She's taken her shoes.'

'*Stupid*,' Bethany said under her breath.

'Ugh.' Patsy made a strange noise and then her legs began to give way: her husband only just rescued her from falling head first into the Coco Pops.

'Girls! Let's lie Mrs Tucker down so that the blood returns to her head. Terri, hot sweet tea. Lucy, go and wet a flannel for her forehead. I'll be back in a moment.' Judith turned back towards the house, breaking into a run.

For the next hour the adults took centre-stage while the Brownies watched them, feeling a strange excitement at this drama they couldn't quite understand. Bethany's father appeared from the house and muttered something to Nigel, which made him clench his fists and then punch a tree.

Patsy sat for a long time with her head between her knees, and had drunk four cups of tea, but she still looked like she'd seen a ghost. Tawny Owl was despatched to call the other parents and then Brown Owl gathered the girls together.

'Brownies, it's been a wonderful few days – one of the most outstanding Pack holidays ever, and one we will always remember. But unfortunately we're having to cut it a little short, so I'd like you all to head back to your tents and gather your things together ready for when your parents arrive to pick you up. In uniform, please.'

Lucy noticed her mother hadn't mentioned Netta's disappearance.

Back in the tent with Terri, they worked without speaking, bent over as they placed underwear and grass-stained T-shirts into the canvas bags they'd brought with them. Eventually Lucy said: 'Where could they have gone? I don't understand it.'

Terri glanced at her. 'I think Bruno has run away.'

Lucy giggled, more from nerves than amusement. 'Don't be silly. Adults don't run away.' But then she thought of Bethany's mother. And then, for no reason, she thought of her own father. But he'd died. So why did it feel like he'd run away? Because just like Netta, he'd never been able to say goodbye.

'Lucy . . . are you OK? Don't cry. It'll be all right.' Terri patted her arm, though for some reason it made things feel worse. 'It really will be all right.'

They finished their packing and walked up towards the house with Chris. Paula had stayed with her mum after she came round, the two of them munching their way through a packet of Jammy Dodgers, their jaws moving rapidly like a machine. At least it had stopped Patsy howling. Bethany sat down on the lawn, watching this drama on her doorstep. A swarm of brown uniforms was congregating and beyond them, the first cars were arriving: a yellow Chevette and a big beige estate and . . .

'Isn't that a police car?' Terri said, pointing at a white car that was progressing along the sycamore-lined driveway (they'd done a full nature trail of Bethany's dad's grounds the day before and learned to identify twelve species of tree).

Lucy felt too weak to climb the short bank towards the house. Police cars were about death and bad news. But she couldn't go back, so she followed mutely, glad that she could always depend on strong Terri and brave Mummy.

They sneaked around the side of the house, towards the drive. Mummy was standing quite still as the police car pulled up, and a very tall rosy-cheeked policeman climbed out. He nodded as Mummy spoke to him, taking out his little notebook and beginning to write.

'It's my dad's car!' Chris hauled herself up the bank by clutching at bracken. Lucy and Terri followed, and as Dina and her husband got out, Mummy went over to them too, whispering and then turning just in time to see the children as Dina cried out, like a wounded dog, 'No, no, not Bruno. No, he can't have. He was going to wait . . . he told me he was going to wait. I can't believe—'

The girls watched as, almost in slow motion, Judith's hand shot up from her side and slapped Dina across the face. 'You have to CALM DOWN,' she said. 'The children can see you.'

But within seconds, the howling resumed again as Dina clutched the car door and her husband stared, a look of complete confusion on his face. Then it changed to one of anger.

'*Whore!*' he whispered.

'Girls. Girls, come with me, right away. Christine, your

mother is a little overwrought due to the heat. We shall give her some air.' With that command, Judith began to bustle everyone else, including the policeman, towards the house.

It was impossible, of course, but as she drew alongside Brown Owl and clutched her hand, relieved at its firm certainty, Lucy actually thought she could see tears in her mother's eyes. Cross her heart and hope to die.

But Mummy never cried. Looking at the other Pixie mums and their tantrums, Lucy thought it was one of the best things about her.

Musician Badge

1. a) Sing one verse of 'God Save the Queen' or of your own favourite hymn, or a religious song of your own choice.
    b) Sing two songs you have chosen because you enjoy them. One of these must be a folk song of the British Isles. The tester will be interested to know why you enjoy these songs.

2. Satisfy the tester that you can read music by doing a simple piece of sight reading.

3. Take a piece of music to the test and tell the tester what story you can hear in it.

The Inaugural Troughton Guides and Scouts Thinking Day Gang Show

22 February, 2006

In aid of the Judith Gill Memorial Trust

My face is hot and heavy with make-up, the scent and sensation like Plasticine applied directly to my skin. I'm sure it'll warp when I sing.

The Scout band is tuning up and if I open the curtain just a millimetre I'll be able to see the front row. But for a moment, I'd rather just imagine it.

Stage left, Chris and Kian. No Matt tonight. He's already flown out ahead of them to Rio, the first stage of their journey. Chris has had a new idea and plans to relaunch herself as the sex industry's answer to Anita Roddick: Fairtrade dildos and rainforest-sourced aphrodisiacs. So she's about to take her two right-hand men on a sexual Grand Tour. *Around the World in 69 Days*. She's even planning to write a book about it, got an agent and a publisher and everything. Kian has insisted he's going to return with piercings in places that make me want to cross my legs and never open them again.

To their right is Victor, scowling, no doubt, at being brought to the sticks. But he loves it, really. He's a gem, as well as a misanthrope.

Next to him, Paula, Neil and the kids. Everything seems to have stabilized in Paula's life, including her weight. I never did find out what happened to get them back together, but Neil's managing to pay off their arrears by working all hours in the Job Club and I've promised that once the house sale is through,

I'll give her a loan to help her set up her own 'slim 'n' walk' club. They've sold the computer, though: apparently *Lawless* has lost its appeal.

The sale. Yes, in ten days' time, the Old Surgery will finally leave the Quentin family after ninety years. The new inhabitants are the Hobleys: two teenagers and a last-chance-before-the-Change toddler; a dog and two cats; and a husband and wife who can't believe their luck at landing what they told the estate agent 'is the house of our dreams. A home where our grandchildren will play. And theirs too.'

Bethany's not here, but she sent me a huge bunch of pink gerberas and a note instructing me to 'break a leg, darling'. She also sent me a copy of the article featuring 'our' photoshoot, which has apparently led to a spurt of new auditions for her. I think the magazine must have airbrushed on our smiles, because despite the agonies that day, we all look like we're having the time of our lives in that hotel room. And now, eight months on, we actually are.

I wonder what Bethany's doing tonight. Some glamorous movie premiere or B-list party? I can't help hoping that one day she will bump into her mum on the Central Line.

And I wonder too, where Simonetta is. The one Brownie we couldn't find. Paula told me in confidence that she's put Neil and his new-found computer skills on the case, searching internet message boards and directories, leaving messages to let her know that the Pixies of Troughton would love to hear from her.

Look out, we're the jolly Pixies, helping others when in fixes.

The rest of us, even Bethany, are less in a fix now than we were before, so perhaps we can help Simonetta, too. Maybe Mum had planned this all along, when she sat down to write those letters before she died.

I hope she'd have approved of the concert. It was Terri's idea but as soon as I heard it, I was desperate to sing, just as I'd wanted to at her funeral. But I won't only be thinking of Mum when I perform; I'll also be remembering Dad. Whenever I find myself dwelling on their deaths, I remember Sunny's photograph of them in *Cinderella*. I owe it to Jim and Judy to be happy, to make the most of my life. Perhaps it's fanciful, but I like to imagine they'll be watching tonight, somehow.

Howard and Terri will have been the first to arrive and I bet they're snogging already, in full view of everyone. It's a bit undignified at her age, but then she has a lot of catching up to do. I don't know how it'll go down in her first parish, but by then she and Howard will be married, anyway. I'm maid of honour.

I'm not cynical about marriage. Saddened and disappointed at my own failure to make it work, certainly, especially as Andrew was never a bad person. Just not the right person for me.

And next to Terri ... Seb. Is *he* the right person? I still don't know if he's the love of my life, but that's OK. He's charming and sexy, but he's also selfish. The first time I watched him play the clarinet – at the Phil, me sitting in the second row – he was so lost in the music that I wondered whether he'd ever feel the same way about me as he did about his instrument. And sometimes I look at him asleep and I think he's too beautiful for me. I'm ordinary. Even my singing so far – a string of paid solos at Christmas, a tiny part in the Alderley Edge Spring Opera in the Park – is just an adjunct of extraordinariness in my Lucy-like life. But it makes me feel special.

Andrew doesn't get it at all. He's found a new girlfriend himself (she's a feisty environmental campaigner he met at a congestion-charging seminar), but he's still convinced I must have been seeing Seb when I first left Saxon Close. But I didn't leave my marriage for Seb.

I left it for myself.

Now I can't resist. I move the curtain aside to try to catch a glimpse of my daughter. She's had some adjusting to do, and I feel guilty at least once a day when I catch her looking wistful or confiding in Buster. But we're closer now than we've ever been, and she's the best thing in my life, something I was too uptight to recognize before. To think I used to blame Sasha for keeping me in my place. *A seven-year-old.* There was only one person to blame for keeping Lucy in her place, and she's the thirty-six-year-old in the Carmen wig and huge earrings about to belt it out to the collected Guides and Scouts of Troughton (poor things). It just took me a while to realize it.

Love is a gipsy child ...

There she is, sitting in the centre of the front row, wearing her Brownie uniform. Her eyes blaze even in the dark, her legs are crossed and she's holding the velour arms of the stalls seat like a queen on her throne. She reminds me of my mum: confident, the tiniest bit imperious, but her most important qualities are those that have been passed down the generations: bravery and loyalty and the need to love, in her own way. A Quentin through and through.

Just like her mother.